Content Warning

Please be advised this book contains instances of graphic violence and infertility.

SHATTERED SECRETS

LILIAN HARRIS

Editing/Interior Formatting: CPR Editing

Proofreader: Judy's Proofreading

Cover Design: Bitter Sage Designs

This book is for my dog, Gatorade. We had you and loved you for almost twelve years. You were there through the start of our life, through three kids, through all the ups and downs. And we still miss you terribly. Putting you into this story was my way of keeping you alive forever.

Thanks for loving us.

We will always love you.

Part One

ONE LAST GOODBYE

One

HUDSON
NINETEEN YEARS AGO
AGE SIXTEEN

"Grab his legs, Benjamin!" I whisper-shout to my brother, who picks up the baseball bat from the floor and throws it into the fireplace.

The wood crackles, the evidence and blood consumed by flames.

"Coming." He rushes over a short distance, taking the man's legs and helping me carry him out toward the exit.

"Are you sure this is a good idea?" he huffs, practically out of breath, while the weight of the body causes my shoulders to burn.

But Benjamin and I are pretty strong. Working out all the time has its advantages.

"We have to bury them deep in the woods. It's the only way. Then we can report them missing. Not like they haven't left us for weeks before, and the cops know it."

But when the cops are their friends, no one cares what happens to us.

"Yeah." Benjamin nods, though his face is tight with nerves.

Not that I blame him. Killing two people is a big fucking deal, and if anyone finds out, we're both screwed for the rest of our lives.

We continue to carry the body out to the pitch-black driveway. There are no homes for miles. No cameras anywhere in sight. No one ever goes into the woods either, except us. There is a small muddy area we can dig up and pile both bodies into, then bury them deep where no one will find them.

The back of their minivan is already opened, and we lift him up some more and throw him on top of his dead wife.

Her brown eyes stare at us, as though still screaming our names, cursing us to hell for spilling milk on the floor. But she can't beat us anymore. Neither of them can.

They're dead now. And we're free.

"Fuck, he's heavy." Benjamin rubs his bicep, flexing it a little.

I slide the door closed, glad I'll never have to see them again.

"Who's gonna drive?" Benjamin asks.

But neither of us can. Our adoptive parents never bothered to teach us a thing. Too busy starving us or beating us to worry about that.

"I'll do it. You sit back there with the bodies and stay down in case we run into anyone."

I fix my simple black baseball cap, the one my adoptive father always wore. If anyone catches us at this late hour and sees his hat, they're bound to think it's him.

Once they're buried, we'll clean the van and I'll drive it to the next town over and leave it at Sal's Autobody Shop. He's never around and leaves the gate unlocked half the time.

"Get in while I lock up the house," I say to him.

Fetching the keys from my pocket, I rush back to the hell that has been our home since we were both ten.

Giving the foyer a lingering look, I close the door and leave it all behind…hoping it never catches up with us.

Two

HUDSON
PRESENT DAY

Everyone has secrets. Some are bigger than others. Mine are unforgivable.

I often wonder what would happen if my wife, Hadleigh, discovered all the things I've fought like hell to hide. Would she still love me? Would she forgive me for keeping her in the dark about the kind of man I truly am?

I often fear the answer.

The thought of losing her haunts my dreams until I wake up with sweat coating my forehead, staring at her side of the bed just to make sure she's still there.

Hadleigh has been the best thing to happen in my life, because she is that life. The blood in my veins that keeps my heart beating.

But how long can a person run before their past crashes into their present? The things I've done—the things I *do* as an attorney—are far too ugly for someone like Hadleigh.

She doesn't know that I'm not just a criminal attorney working for his own firm, but the go-to lawyer for the underworld. I not only handle their criminal cases, but everything and anything they need.

Not all of it is legal. Many times, it's violent and cruel. I know how to hide my fingerprints from it all. I've perfected that over the years.

Being with Hadleigh has made me want to become a better person. But I'm too ingrained in this life to ever be that man.

With her, though, I *am* him. It's the only place I can be. I love my wife with everything I have, and I will love her until the day I die.

Even if one day, she may stop loving me.

Before I met her, I was just a shell of a man who did everything to survive the brutal life he was born into. She doesn't know any of it. Not the foster care. Not the fact that when I was seventeen, Patrick Quinn became my guardian.

He saved me. He gave me a home. He funded my education. It's thanks to him I became a lawyer, and a damn good one.

Patrick is the head of the Irish Mob, a man who, when I was almost seventeen, scared me, but I was also in awe of him. Because I wanted to be him. To be someone people feared instead of being the one afraid.

The first time I met him, it was while I was in prison, after I saved the life of another inmate: his nephew. A boy like me who was about to be killed, until I stepped in.

"Hey, new kid." Griffin shoves Ryan in the shoulder.

But he doesn't say anything, staring into his plate full of the nastiest spaghetti you'll ever eat. Ryan never talks to anyone. He prefers to stay to himself.

"Are you deaf?" Griffin laughs, his two friends chuckling in unison. "Guys, I think the pussy is deaf," he taunts, slamming a fist into the back of Ryan's head.

But he doesn't even flinch. Instead, he grinds his teeth, nostrils flaring. He's a big kid, but not muscular. Tall and lanky, and maybe that's why they pick on him. Been like this for the past week. Every time he's in the cafeteria, they start with him, and he never says a word.

Sitting beside him, I don't say a word either. Surviving juvie means staying quiet. Taking your sentence without trouble and getting the fuck out of here is the goal.

When I got caught stealing a bunch of food from a convenience store and stuffing it in my backpack, I didn't think I'd actually go to jail. I thought the cops would feel sorry for me. Kid living on the street, wanting to eat. But nah, they didn't care. And the store owner was adamant about pressing charges. He wanted to see me rot.

So here I am. Two months in this shithole. This will probably be the rest of my life: either living on the street, begging for money just to survive, or prison. At least there's a bed and food here.

After Benjamin and I escaped that house, we lived on the streets or snuck into abandoned houses to find shelter where we could.

When you've lived in the gutter for most of your life, you grow accustomed to it. The smells. The taste. And after a while, you come to realize that you're the smell that you've been running from. And by that point, it's too late to escape it.

Griffin rounds toward the edge of the table, Ryan seated on the corner. And right before the asshole looks up to see if the guards are watching, he flings Ryan's plate of pasta and the spaghetti flies all over his lap.

Griffin and his friends cackle while Ryan inhales harshly, staring down at the mess.

The pulse in my neck throbs like it wants to rip through my skin. I want to do some damage. I want to hurt those guys.

They tried this shit with me when I first got here, but that all stopped when I beat Griffin to a pulp. No one talked to the guards. It's not how we do things in here. Rats die.

Ryan needs to fight back too. Teach Griffin a lesson.

Griffin grabs Ryan's hair and leans real close. "I'd watch your back when you're sleeping, pussy. I've got a little present for you."

With a snarl, Ryan suddenly jumps to his feet, about five inches taller than Griffin, and he punches him in the face. Ryan's eyes enflame, and it appears as though someone has taken over his body, like he's someone else. Deadly. Scary as hell too.

Kids start to pay attention, rising from the tables to check out the next big fight. The guards don't care unless someone is about to die.

"Fight, fight, fight!" the chants start.

Griffin throws his arms in the air and grins. "About to give you a good one, boys."

His dark eyes fill with rage as he swipes the blood from his nose, while Ryan looks like he's about to lose it on him.

Good.

It's time.

With a growl, Ryan rushes for him, and they exchange punches. The asshole ends up underneath and struggles to remove something from his pocket while taking hit after hit.

My attention stays glued to his hand, though, and I slowly see what looks like a toothbrush.

But attached to it is a razor blade.

"Fuck," I mutter, knowing I have to get involved. Can't see the

new kid cut up like a fucking turkey.

As Griffin inches his hand toward Ryan's thigh, I walk over and step on his fingers. Griffin screams as the shiv punctures his hand and I drive it deeper into his flesh.

Ryan's gaze darts down to what I'm doing, and when his eyes land on me, a little smirk crawls over his face.

"Fuck you!" he bellows as he throws another punch to Griffin's nose before jumping to his feet.

Griffin screams, and the cheers of the other kids have the guards rushing over.

"You fucking punks!"

One grabs Ryan, and the other grabs me by the collar of my white t-shirt.

"In the hole you both go," he scoffs. "Where you belong."

The other guard lifts Griffin up. "Didn't your mother teach you not to play with sharp objects?"

The guards laugh. They're bullies just as much as any of the assholes here. They live for making our lives hell.

"What's your name?" Ryan asks as we're dragged away.

"Holden. Holden Morrison."

"Ryan Quinn."

Patrick thanked me in person for my bravery. He was the only visitor I ever had in that shithole.

And he's also the reason I became Hudson Mackay. He gave me a new identity and helped Benjamin with the same. Benjamin became known as Brooks Bardin. But we aren't those people we once were. We're different now.

Patrick gave me a fresh start. Someone finally gave a fuck about me. I wasn't used to that. I kept wondering when he'd leave me back on the street. But he never did.

He got me out of prison early and got my record expunged just to clear Holden's name. He agreed that I shouldn't have been arrested in the first place. But some people see the world in black and white rather than the shades of gray that some are unlucky to be born into.

Patrick said he saw something in me, and that once he dug into my past and why I was arrested in the first place, he wanted to help me.

All we wanted was to eat. Brooks and I had been without food for two days and we were desperate. But a crime is a crime, and I was thrown into a hole for starving.

Patrick welcomed me into his home with his five children. Fed me. Clothed me. But more importantly, he trusted me.

I owed it to him. Still do.

I became his lawyer. Then I became the best lawyer for people like him. My firm is one of the top criminal firms in New York City. I take on the cases no one wants, and I make good money doing it.

Hadleigh says she's proud of me. Though I wonder how proud she'd be if she learned of the kind of people I help put back on the street. All the bodies I've helped hide, all the ones I helped extinguish.

My wife isn't like me. She's a teacher, molding the minds of first graders, while I help those who've committed the worst sins. We may be different that way, but it's our love for one another that makes us the same.

My eyes go to the door of our master bath, the water buzzing, her on the other side. With a rough sigh, I stare down at the latest letter I've written her.

I don't know why I write them if I never intend for her to read them. But in a way, it's as though I'm confessing my sins to her even while she'll never know of them. Not if I can help it. Finishing the last few sentences, I leave it on my lap, remembering the day I first saw her ten years ago.

It was the best thing to ever happen to me, even though the circumstances were less than ideal. She had her own demons she was battling. But I was there to help her. And I've been there ever since.

She was twenty when she walked into the firm I was working for at the time. I had graduated law school and was waiting for my bar results when I saw her picking on her nails in the waiting room.

She looked terrified, and once she met with one of the partners, I realized why. She was looking to divorce her abusive husband. A man I've been trying like hell to find so I can end him like I couldn't back then. But to this day, I don't know where he's disappeared to.

He made her life hell, and it took her a lot to save every penny and get an attorney. But it wasn't enough, so Patrick paid for it as a favor to me. She had no idea. She thought the firm took her case pro bono as part of a program they had. I didn't want her to think she was charity. She would've refused the help.

But the Quinns are my family. And family protects one another. Patrick tried to find her ex too, but it's like the asshole vanished. I hope he stays that way.

The shower turns off, and I quickly fold up the letter and seal it before slipping it into my briefcase and dropping the case on the floor.

As soon as the door opens, she's there smiling at me, and my heart damn near skips a beat. Because no matter how many days or years she's been my wife, she still takes my breath away.

A towel's draped around her curves, another tucked neatly around her chestnut-colored hair. She gives me a wicked stare and a smirk spreads across my lips, my arms bent behind my head as my gaze gives her body a leisurely swipe.

"Like what you see, do you?" Her brow tips up, matching the slant of her full pink mouth.

"You bet your ass I do." My hand lowers, gripping my thick and heavy cock through the comforter. "So how about you come over here, and I'll show you just how much I love it?"

She stands where she is instead with a glint in her hazel eyes as she removes the towel from her hair and squeezes it around her strands. A smile bends across her lips, and my chest swells because I love her so goddamn much.

If only I could give her a baby.

A fist curls behind my head, not wanting her to see it, to know how badly it kills me to listen to her cry month after month each time she finds out she isn't pregnant.

Only Brooks and her best friend, Elowen, know we're dealing with infertility.

It becomes harder on us when friends and colleagues ask us why we don't have children.

Are you guys planning to have a baby?

When are you going to knock her up, Hudsonbro?

She brushes it off or says things like, "It'll happen when it's meant to." And that has some getting the hint. But I know her heart, and I know it destroys her to hear those questions, even though she fights like hell not to show it.

Hadleigh was meant to be a mother. She has the purest heart and the kindest nature. I know she's trying not to give up hope, but after three years of trying, I think she's almost there.

And me? I just want to be there for her. To see her through this, whether we have a child or not.

Because Hadleigh has always been enough for me, and I'm alright knowing that I'm not enough for her.

"What are you thinking about?" she asks as she finishes drying her hair and throws the towel over the chair as she struts over to me with her long, tanned legs, eyes gleaming with flecks of golden honey.

Her hand stretches toward my bare chest, long fingernails running down the center and in between my abs.

My muscles contract, wanting her touch lower. Wanting her naked, legs spread as I stare into her eyes while I make love to her, hard and deep, just the way she likes it.

With a quick jerk of my hand, I tear off the towel that keeps her perfect body out of my view.

Reaching between her legs, my fingers climb up her inner thigh while she squirms and tugs her lower lip with her teeth.

I let my thumb brush between her slit, teasing that pretty pussy with my eyes locked on hers.

"So beautiful," I groan when her mouth parts on a low and throaty moan. "My little butterfly."

"Oh God, Hudson," she gasps when I force my palm against her clit, making her ride it.

"The way you're looking at me right now…" I growl, low and deep. "…has me wondering how many times I can make you come, just so I can get you dirty all over again."

And before she can say a word, I grab her hips and flip her onto the bed, her squealing replaced by her hungered moans as I fit my body over hers, grinding my cock into her warm center.

"It's been too long since I've been inside you." My voice grows thick with longing.

"You just fucked me this morning. Bent over the kitchen table." Her sultry laughter mingles with a moan.

"That was over ten hours ago, angel. Way too long for a man to go without his wife."

Her eyes grow soft, matching the beauty of her smile. She's always had a breathtaking one. It always made me feel at home.

And with my cock lined against her entrance, I thrust fully inside with a single stroke, swallowing her gasping groans of pleasure, needing to get lost in her for all my life.

Three

HADLEIGH

His hand's wrapped around my throat, eyes clashing with mine as he pounds inside me, making my whole body undulate with pleasure. Whenever we're like this, lost in each other, there's nothing else I think about. Nothing but how he makes me feel: cherished, wholly and completely owned.

Before Hudson, I didn't know what love was. I was stuck in a marriage with a boy who used me as his punching bag. Who hurled ugly words at me every chance he got.

I met him in college through friends, and things were great at first. So great that when he asked me to marry him after six months, I foolishly said yes. But soon after that, my life took an ugly turn.

Tanner began to take his angry tirades out on me. He hated when the guys at school talked to me or looked at me. It was always my fault, and he let me know it whenever he could. And since we both dormed in college, he followed my every step.

He was smart. He knew just where to hit me so that no one suspected a thing. His father was a police captain of our town, so going to the cops was out of the question. I was trapped in every sense of the word.

My mother wasn't pleased when we got married. She said I was too young, and of course she was right.

I had just turned nineteen. But at the time, I didn't want to see it. Not until it was too late. By that time, I couldn't tell her what was happening. I was far too ashamed.

So, when I saved a thousand dollars from my job at the library, I went to a law firm out in the city to get a divorce. I couldn't let Tanner find out. Because I knew what would happen if he did: I'd die.

Once he was served with papers, he was angrier than I ever saw him.

But Hudson was there for me from the moment I stepped into that office. His sparkling blue eyes were so kind when I sat there and told him and his boss what was happening. And when I got nervous, all I had to do was look at him to feel a sense of calm.

When I rushed out of the office, Hudson ran after me to ask if I had a place to stay. And instead of letting me continue to live at a run-down motel like I had been, he paid for me to stay at a beautiful hotel.

Once the divorce was finalized, Tanner disappeared. I was hoping he was dead, and I felt guilty for even thinking such awful thoughts, but I was still afraid of him. I was afraid of his family too. They had money and power, while I had nothing.

Hudson and I remained friends for a year before we began dating. And though I was afraid to trust again, my heart trusted him. Nine years later, I've yet to regret my decision.

Often, I wonder if us not being able to have kids is somehow my fault. That marrying Tanner and what he did to me caused me to become infertile. Though the doctors have found no medical reason for our inability to conceive, I still think I'm to blame.

I love Hudson with all my heart, and a life with him is better than any fantasy I could've imagined. But just once, I want to see those two red lines. To know that we created life. But every month, that dream becomes harder to imagine. What if we never have that?

Hudson's lips fall to mine as he consumes my gasps of pleasure, his fingers cinching around my throat as he deepens his strokes.

"I love you, butterfly," he groans, teeth marking the curve of my jaw as my toes curl, aching for release.

I like it when he calls me "butterfly." That special name brings me warmth.

He began to call me that after I was free from Tanner. It was a reminder that I was no longer stuck inside a cocoon that I was forced into. I was able to fly, to set my own path in life.

And now that name just reminds me of Hudson's love for me. His constant devotion. His commitment to our vows.

He kisses me hard, nipping my bottom lip right before he rises on his knees. Grabbing my hips, he flips me roughly onto my front and forces me on all fours. I can feel the crown of his cock nudge inside me.

"Fuck, baby, how the hell are you so goddamn tight?" His mouth drops to my shoulder, teeth marking my skin right before he enters me hard with one stroke.

He grabs a handful of my hair, holding me hostage while slamming his hips with a vengeful need, as though he's trying to get as deep inside me as he can. The sound of skin on skin only hastens my desire, needing to come undone in the safety of his arms.

With his other hand, he flicks my clit, and as soon as he does, my body explodes like fireworks, tingles and heat spreading throughout my limbs.

"Yes, oh God… Don't stop!" I scream as the pleasure pounds through me. But instead of easing, he takes me faster and harder.

"You're gonna be a good girl and come one more time." He rubs my clit between two fingers, pressing his body into mine while I try to fight the intense sensation in my core.

"Oh God, I—I can't…" The words die out in my throat.

He chuckles against my ear, all deep and raspy, and in one quick move, he slips out of me and slides his face under my body until it's right beneath my pussy.

"What are you…fuck!"

Hands palm my ass as he holds me captive around his mouth, his tongue snaking out, rolling around my sensitive flesh.

"You're gonna come on my face, angel, before I make you come around my cock again."

Then he's pushing his tongue flat over my clit and forcing me to ride it. Fisting the sheets, I bask in the sheer intensity of what he's doing to me, ready to combust through my body. He slaps my ass with a roughened palm, growling against me, making me quiver and beg him not to stop. And when he sucks my clit into his mouth, I'm lost.

"Hudson, oh God!" I scream out as he forces every drop from me, fitting his tongue inside me, tasting everything until all he knows is me.

When he's through, when he throws me onto my back and sinks inside me once more, I give him everything as though for the first time.

Because every day with him is like falling in love all over again.

"Who would you have married if it wasn't me?" I ask him, my legs tangled with his beneath the soft comforter wrapped around us.

"Uh, no. Absolutely not playing that game." His chuckle is gravelly, his fingers rolling up and down my spine as he gazes down at me.

"Oh, come on," I tease, cupping his stubbled jaw. "I know there had to be someone you liked from college."

"Never, Hadleigh. I've never so much as looked at another woman since I looked at you."

"Liar," I scoff and swat him on the chest. "You want me to believe that there has never been a woman to catch your eye, even at work? With their fancy designer dresses?"

His eyes grow with unbridled affection, and he raises himself to kiss my forehead.

As he does, I close my eyes and smile.

"I have you." He perches back and stares fondly. "Don't you realize by now..." His thumb brushes across my lips, his touch causing a shiver to race up my spine. "No one in this world could ever live up to you." His eyes bore into mine so intensely, my stomach tightens. "You were always everything I needed. Then and now."

There goes my heart... Thump, thump... Playing a melody only a love like ours can create.

"Fine." I arch a brow. "I'll play, then..."

I purse my lips, loving the look of envy appearing in his gaze. My Hudson is crazy possessive, and it excites me every time he is.

"If I didn't marry you, I'd have ended up with..."

His eyes round, and mock horror fills them. "Hadleigh Mackay, you better not finish that sentence."

"Why not? Jealous?" I bite the inside of my bottom lip to stop from laughing, and with one swift move, he flips me under him.

"Insanely, stupidly jealous." He rocks his shaft against me, already growing hard and begging to own me again. "I don't want to imagine you with anyone else."

Silently, our eyes lock, lost in each other, and my heart lurches from how deeply I feel connected to him in this moment.

"You're mine, butterfly," he vows. "Mine to love. Mine to *fuck*. Mine to cherish." He cups my jaw and kisses me hard across my mouth. "For all the days I have left."

"There will never be anyone else." I softly pepper his mouth with kisses. "You'll always be my first and last love."

"And you were always my only love, and that'll never stop." He peers at me with a look I can't name. Like he's saying *goodbye* or *I'm sorry*.

Something catches in my gut—this undeniable, unexplainable sense of fear that somehow, we're not meant to have forever.

Not meant to have anything at all.

With one arm tucked around him, my head resting on his firm chest, I click on the TV, wanting to find a movie to watch before we go to bed.

As I flip through the channels, the words *BREAKING NEWS* in bright red pop up across the screen and it instantly has my attention.

I don't typically watch the news. It depresses me. But with the police tape around what looks to be a large dug-up area, I decide to find out what happened.

Hudson slowly sits up as I increase the volume, the voice of the newscaster rising as she glances behind her at the four police officers.

"Two days ago," she starts, "as a construction crew was digging up this area behind me, they made a terrifying discovery. What authorities have told us so far is that the remains of two bodies have been found. The identities of these individuals haven't been revealed yet, but officials tell us that they're working hard to find out who these two people were. We were told it appears that the bodies have been buried for a long time, begging the question, how did they end up here and why? Back to you at the studio, Tom."

They start talking about the weather while I shake my head.

"Wow, that's crazy. This is only a couple of hours from us," I tell Hudson, peering up at him.

His unblinking expression is glued to the screen.

"Hudson?" I call, cupping his cheek.

Yet his gaze stays glued to the TV, as though he's lost in thought.

"Are you okay? Was that one of your cases?"

"What?" He snaps his eyes to me, his face tense.

"That story. Is it one of your cases?"

I never really ask him about his work. I know it's confidential, and I don't particularly want to hear about the tough cases he takes on.

"No." He forces a smile. "That area looked familiar," he whispers as he stares at the TV, his eyes distant once more.

A chill scurries up my back. This isn't like him.

"Familiar how? Like from your childhood?"

That's another thing he's very quiet about. He rarely ever talks about his life back then. I know he didn't have it easy. His parents died when he was young, and he was forced to live with an uncle that wasn't good to him.

"What?" He returns his attention to me, a crease appearing between his brows.

But he barely sees me, still lost in his head. The way he gets when he's got a lot on his mind.

"Yeah… Uh, another life," he goes on as he grabs the remote and flips on a random movie. "Anyway, are you ready for your birthday tomorrow?"

He relaxes back on the bed and tucks his arm around me. It's obvious he wants to change the conversation, and I let him.

"I am." My fingers run up and down his six-pack, my head pressed to his shoulder. "Not quite sure how I feel about turning thirty, however."

He chuckles, tilting up my face with a finger under my chin. "You're beautiful, baby. Not a day over twenty."

"I love how you lie to me," I tease.

His face passes with intensity, but just as quickly, it disappears. Something twists in my gut. But I push that unease away.

Again.

"It's going to be fun. Low-key, just like you wanted." He kisses my forehead, and that unease simply vanishes when he's gazing at me the way he is now. Full of affection.

I never cared about my birthdays before Hudson came along. I never did much of anything. My mom was a single mother, so money was always tight, which meant birthdays included pizza and cake with a few friends. As I got older, I didn't do much celebrating either. Didn't seem important.

But even with the blessed life Hudson and I have now, I still don't like to go crazy. So tomorrow, when I turn thirty, it'll just be a dinner at our place with Elowen and Hudson's best friend, Brooks, plus Leighton and Henry, a couple we met while vacationing in Turks and Caicos a few years back. They so happened to live a few blocks away from us in the city, and when we met, we instantly hit it off.

"Thanks for arranging the party," I tell Hudson, kissing him once.

His hand drifts lower until he's cupping my behind, squeezing it as he groans. "Next year, I'll take you on a trip anywhere you want."

"It's okay." My lips softly stroke his. "Our schedules are crazy this year. It's not your fault it didn't work out."

"I know." He sighs. "But you come first, and I want to give you everything, baby. Everything and more."

I drop my head against his beating heart, my arms tightening around him. "You already gave me that, Hudson. You gave me you."

He cups my nape, fingers splicing through my hair as he jerks my head back, his gaze searching mine. "I love you, Hadleigh. Don't ever leave me."

My heart jolts. "Why would I ever do that?"

And that heavy, unexplainable feeling I had before washes over me again as I stare into his crystal blue eyes, searching for an answer that never comes.

four

HUDSON

At work the following day, I stare at my laptop, watching that news broadcast again and again.

Someone found the bodies.

What if they connect the murders to us?

Brooks and I may have been young, but we weren't stupid. We made sure to wear gloves we found in their garden shed. But if there's any of our DNA still on the bodies, we're fucked.

My office door opens, and Brooks, who works as my paralegal, marches in with a smirk on his face. But as soon as he takes in my serious expression, his features tighten.

"What's wrong?" He shuts the door and proceeds to sit across from me, taking a spot on the leather chair.

Pressing two fingers into the bridge of my nose, I wordlessly turn the laptop toward him and play the video.

Through his dark eyes, he processes every second of what I've been watching for an hour. And for a moment, there's fear within them. He edges closer, his attention still glued to the screen.

"Shit…" Momentarily, he glances up at me before he continues watching.

I shake my head, my pulse pounding in my ears. "If this comes out, I'll lose everything."

"Don't worry," he attempts to reassure me. "The bodies are nineteen years old, and we cleaned up well. No one will know it was us."

His chest climbs higher with every breath, as though he doesn't believe what he's saying either.

"You don't know that." I grip a fistful of my hair. "Fuck!"

"You need to calm the hell down before someone hears you." His eyes sternly scold me as he goes on. "We're not the same kids we once were. You have connections now. It'll be fine."

"We don't know that."

Taking a deep breath, I drop my face into my palms.

"I can't lose her," I tell him, my throat constricting until I find it difficult to breathe. "I can't lose Hadleigh."

"That woman loves you. She'd forgive you for anything."

"No, she wouldn't." I run a hand down my face. "She doesn't know me. Not really. Not who I really am."

"You make yourself sound like some fucking gangbanger." He laughs.

I hit him with a cold glower. "You know the things I've done. Do you really think Hadleigh would want a man like that, especially with everything she's been through with Tanner?"

"Screw Tanner!" He waves off my concern. "You're not him, and you never will be. So shut the fuck up and get out of your head."

But getting out of my head is impossible. All I can picture is her face as she finds out the things I've done, then and now.

"I think I'll talk to my detective contact. See what he knows before I disappear and lie low."

But of course, I'd never leave Hadleigh behind. If anything, I'd take her with me. Make her understand that I'm still the man she fell in love with.

"You know you'd never leave." He folds his arms over his black dress shirt. "I mean, shit, you've got yourself a penthouse apartment bigger than my damn house, a gorgeous wife, a great job, and more money than God himself. Why the hell would you ever want to leave that?"

I release an exhausted exhale. "None of those things matter if I don't have Hadleigh. What if I end up in prison for the rest of my life?"

"Please…" He snickers. "You're Hudson fucking Mackay. Snap out of your pity party. They'll find nothing. We did nothing."

His expression is hard and unbending. Yet it doesn't stop my unrelenting worry. Because something in my core tells me that my life is about to implode. That everything I've built will crumble.

What will happen to Hadleigh if I'm dead or in prison? I have money in a safe, and she knows the combination. But what about the rest? How can I leave her alone? Other than Elowen, she has no one to depend on.

My heart physically hurts.

"Promise me you'll take care of her if something happens to me," I tell Brooks.

He jolts his head back. "You're scaring me, man. What the hell are you planning to do?"

"Nothing. But just in case something goes wrong, I need your word that if I'm not here to watch out for her, you will be."

"Jesus…" He runs his fingers through his black hair, shaking his head incredulously.

"Come on, you're the only person I can trust. Just tell me I don't have to worry."

He pinches his temple, eyes concentrating in thought. But seconds later, he says, "Fine, yeah. Of course. You know I will."

I nod with relief.

Brooks has always been more brother than friend. And in every sense of the word, we *are* brothers. Ever since we met when we were ten, he defended me against our adoptive parents, and I protected him in return. We were the only thing each other had, and we knew it.

A knock sounds at the door, one belonging to my secretary.

"Come in," I tell Adalyn, who's been with me for a couple of months now.

Pushing the door open, she advances inside, her high stilettos clacking as she approaches with a large yellow envelope in her grasp. "Sir, this was delivered to you. Marked urgent."

"Hi, Adalyn." Brooks grins flirtatiously from her left, and her cheeks grow with color.

"Hi, Brooks." She bites the edge of her bottom lip.

I take the mail from her. "Thanks, Adalyn. You may go."

I barely look up, starting to open the flap. Clearing her throat, she nods and turns on her heels before rushing out.

"Stop flirting with her, asshole." My eyes narrow at him.

"How else am I supposed to fuck her?" A wide grin stretches across his smug face.

"You're not supposed to. That's the damn point. I don't need a sexual harassment suit, so don't fuck the new girl. Or any woman in my damn firm, for that matter."

After I found out about him and my previous secretary, who quit when they broke up, I told him it couldn't happen anymore. Not when it affects my firm.

He scoffs while I start to pull out a paper, expecting to find something for one of my cases, but instead…

My pulse turns erratic, an ominous pounding in my throat.

Words appear in thick black ink, and I hold air in my lungs as I read them again and again and again, hoping maybe they'll change.

This can't be happening.

"What's wrong?"

Brooks's concern does nothing to stop me from staring at the note, the words haunting me, heartbeats racing frantically in my chest.

> I know who you really are, Hudson Mackay. Or should I say Holden Morrison? I know where you came from and what you did all those years ago. I'm coming for you. And there's nothing you can do about it. Except run as fast as you can.

I flip the envelope to the front, hoping for a postage stamp, but there's nothing. This was personally delivered.

My hand jumps to the phone and I buzz Adalyn's line, putting her on speaker.

"Yes, sir?"

"Who gave you the envelope?"

"I-is something wrong?" she stammers.

"I need to know *who* gave it to you." My words are a sharp bite.

"It was our usual delivery carrier. Do you want me to call the post office and find out?"

"Fuck!" I scrub my face roughly with a palm. "No."

Pressing a button, I end the call. Whoever wanted me to get this made sure to somehow slip it to the post office. And with the bodies that were just discovered… This was planned.

"Hudson? What the fuck is in that letter? You look like you've seen a ghost."

Reaching over, I extend a hand and give it to him, and as I do, something slips out from the envelope still in my grasp.

While he snatches the letter, I reach down to the floor beside my feet to grab whatever fell, and when I see what it is, my heart stops beating.

In my hand is a photo of Hadleigh leaving work, oblivious that someone was following her, taking her picture.

"Holy shit," Brooks mutters, reading the note. "This is bad…"

But all I do is stare at my wife.

Anger churns in my gut. I did this. I've put her at risk just by being with her.

"Look, let's not panic yet." Brooks drops the letter on the edge of the desk. "I'm sure it's one of your clients who didn't get off or something. Probably one of their people just trying to scare you. I mean, they would've named me too if they knew anything, right?"

"Maybe…but they're following her." I flip the photo around, and his eyes expand.

"Motherfucker…" Anger twists his face.

Hadleigh's family to him. Of course he's pissed.

"We have to find out who's doing this," I say. "There has to be a way to trace this."

"We will." He tilts his chin. "This isn't about us anymore. They've involved *her*."

Five

HADLEIGH

The pregnancy test stares at me on the sink in our master bathroom, while I count down the minutes until my heart breaks all over again.

Every month. Like clockwork.

I don't know why I even bother anymore. But that's the funny thing about hope. Just when you think you've lost it, it's there to remind you that you haven't after all.

Anxiety pools in my gut because I want to believe that this month will be different. That this month, against all odds, we will get our miracle.

I know Hudson struggles more with my pain than with our infertility. And maybe I'm the one who wants the baby more, and that's okay. Because I know if we ever had a child, he'd be the most amazing father.

He's brought up adoption, but I want to grow a child inside me. I want to feel that. I want to be the one to bring our baby into this world.

We've been through multiple failed rounds of IVF. It just wouldn't take. So the doctor gave us the option of donor eggs, a surrogate, or naturally trying again with the help of meds. I chose the latter. Neither of the other two options felt right. Not yet.

Another minute passes as I gaze at myself in the mirror: my hair perfectly straightened, the edges hitting my shoulders, my makeup dark and sultry. I run my palms down the black knee-length fitted dress covering my body.

Everyone is going to be here for my birthday soon, and I swore to myself that if the test is negative, then it's okay. I'll be okay. I won't cry. Just another month of disappointment.

Elowen is the only other person I can talk to about this. She allows me to vent and cry, just so I don't have to do it in front of Hudson all the time.

I don't know how he's not sick of it by now. But I try. I put on a brave face every day, and I bottle up my emotions until the next month when the agony starts all over again.

A cruel, never-ending cycle.

"Hey, butterfly," Hudson calls, knocking softly. "Are you alright?"

"Yes." I clear my throat. "Just fixing my makeup."

He chuckles. "You're beautiful, Hadleigh. Never needed it at all. But take your time. I'll finish setting up the table."

"Thanks, baby," I tell him, doing my best to keep it together.

I've been in here for a while, and I didn't tell him why. I think he forgot about it this month, or maybe he didn't want to remind me.

I didn't want to tell him I was testing today of all days, though. But I just knew if I didn't, I'd be thinking about it the entire night.

My cell vibrates across the sink, the alarm turning on, informing me the wait is over. Closing my eyes, I take slow, deep breaths.

It's going to be okay. You're going to be fine, no matter what.

But when I open my eyes to look down at the test and only see one bright red line, my emotions come spilling out like a waterfall, an unending river of agony. And I drown in it, suffocating on my silent sobs.

One by one, I let the tears fall, each stinging more than the last. This deep-seated pain is something I should be used to by now. But it's impossible not to feel the hurt cut like a knife.

I gasp with a cry as the truth really hits me.

I'll never really know what it means to have my own baby.

I'll never know how it feels to experience that first kick.

I'll never give birth.

Never hear my baby cry as they storm into the world.

I'll never have any of it.

With the test in hand, I slide down onto the floor and sob. I sob so hard, I know I've ruined all my makeup.

But right now, I don't even care.

HUDSON

"Hadleigh?" I rush over to the bathroom again, knowing I definitely heard her cry as I passed the bedroom.

It's suddenly quiet in there, yet I just know she's weeping on that floor and I'm not there to hold her.

"I'm fine." She attempts to sound like her whole world isn't falling apart, but I know better.

I know exactly what day today is: the earliest day she's allowed to test. Of course it had to fall on her birthday, of all fucking days. I wish it wasn't today. I wish she could've enjoyed her birthday without being reminded. My Hadleigh deserves more than this.

"I know, angel. I know." A ragged sigh escapes my lungs. "Open the door for me. I just wanna hold you."

That has her sniveling, causing my own heart to break.

And when the door clicks open, I find her with thick black mascara running down her cheeks and her black eyeliner smudged, but none of that matters. I just need to hold her.

"Come here, baby." I open my arms for her, and she rushes into them.

I tuck her against my beating heart, wishing there was something I could do to make it all okay. Make it so she's not hurting anymore.

"I'm sorry." My voice is raw and thick with emotion. "If there was a way, you know I would give you everything."

"I'm the one who's sorry, Hudson." She sniffles, forcing her head back to look at me. "You deserve better than this."

Clasping her face with both palms, I stare straight into her broken eyes.

"Don't you ever say that again. I love you with all my heart." I kiss her forehead, closing my eyes, my mouth perched there for long, aching seconds. "I don't deserve you; I never have, so if anyone deserves better, it's you."

"Hudson…" she pants, her hand clasped around the side of my neck.

But before she can go on, the doorbell rings, causing her to gasp.

"Crap, what am I going to do with my face?" She grimaces, wiping under her eye, black makeup staining her finger.

"Stay here. I'll deal with them." I give her one last kiss across the corner of her mouth. "Take all the time you need. They'll wait."

"Thanks." A wrinkle forms between her brows. "For everything."

With one last look and a small smile, I start to head out the door. "Hudson?" She pauses.

I turn to her over my shoulder. "Yes, baby?"

"Do you think we should stop trying?"

Her eyes shimmer, and my pulse rams in my throat because I don't know how to answer that.

"Only if that's what you want."

She hitches a shoulder, sniffling. "I don't know *what* I want."

"Then we don't decide right now."

"Okay." Her mouth quivers. "Let me go and make myself presentable. But they're all going to know I was crying."

"If they ask, I'll shut them up. Don't worry about anyone else but yourself."

She nods. "Yeah, okay."

"I'll see you in a bit." I hit her with a wink before heading toward the door just as another ring of the bell comes through.

"Come on, man!" Brooks shouts. "Stop fucking and open up. We're all waiting over here."

I shake my head with a chuckle as I reach the door and unlock it, and there is Brooks, along with Henry, Leighton, and Elowen.

But he's not alone. He brought a *fucking* date.

I form a glare at who it actually is.

He shrugs and throws an arm around Adalyn.

"Hi...uh...sir. I hope it's okay I came. Brooks insisted." She smiles shyly at him, her long black hair in a high ponytail.

"Of course it's fine," Brooks adds, rushing past me through the door, clasping me on the shoulder.

"Where's the birthday girl?" Leighton asks, holding a blue Tiffany's box in her hands.

"She's getting ready. But come in, everyone. Make yourselves at home."

They all shuffle in while I lock back up, and with my cell, I turn on the Bluetooth speaker and play soft music, the volume set low.

"I just love your place," Elowen gushes, staring out onto the cityscape from our fifty-second story four-bedroom penthouse.

I sometimes sit back and wonder how a kid like me got to have all of this. I consider myself lucky to have it, but I'd give it all back for a chance to give Hadleigh a baby. The money, the job…none of it can replace that.

But truthfully, I don't know if I even have what it takes to be someone's father. Mine was never much of a dad, too busy drinking and beating me. And Mom ran off when I was three. I was too embarrassed to tell Hadleigh all that, so I told her my parents were dead and that my uncle took care of me my entire life.

I'm a fraud. She definitely deserves better.

After my father died from killing himself while driving drunk, I lived with my uncle—who, like my dad, didn't have a paternal bone in his body. So, when I was six years old, he gave me up to foster care, and I went from home to home, never knowing stability. Never knowing what a family was until Hadleigh. She has been the only true family I've had.

As much as Patrick has been like a father to me, no one comes close to what Hadleigh has given me. And I'm afraid that once she finds out about my past, she'll be gone.

"Who wants a drink?" I move toward the bar at the end of the den, with Brooks and Henry joining me while the ladies settle on the gray velvet sofa overlooking the city.

"I'll have some wine if you have some," Elowen says.

"Red or white?"

"Red, please."

"Same for me." Leighton tosses her long, wavy deep blonde hair back, throwing one leg over another.

"Want something, Adalyn?" Brooks asks, pouring himself a cranberry and vodka.

"Sure." She blushes as their eyes connect. "I'll have whatever you're having."

"Sure thing, babe."

While I grab the wineglasses and pour the women their drinks, I near him.

"Why is she here?" I whisper directly into his ear.

"Because I like her?"

"You go through a new woman every week. Don't mess this up for me. Not after you caused the other one to quit."

"Not my fault she thought we'd be married after one week." He chuckles.

"It *is* your fault. Stop messing things up for me."

He snickers. "Yeah, okay. Got it." He roughly walks past me. "Hey, Adalyn. Hudson says we can't date."

I drill him with a sharp look. If I didn't want to make a scene, we'd have a fight right about now.

"Oh, uh…" She grabs the drink he brings her and swallows half of it. As she clears her throat, her deep brown eyes land on me. "I'm sorry. We promise to keep it professional. Maybe you can make an exception?"

She slants her head and grabs his hand as he settles beside her.

"Yeah, boss…" Brooks grins, his almost black eyes full of amusement. "Pretty please."

I don't know what has gotten into him, but I'm not in the fucking mood for his shit today, of all days.

Henry marches over to Leighton and hands her the glass of wine I poured.

"Thanks," she mutters, snatching it up, barely looking at him.

Curiously, I glance between them. The tension is thick as he lowers onto the sofa opposite her, even though there was plenty of room right beside her.

"So, where's Cassidy?" I snap my attention to Elowen, asking about her five-year-old daughter.

Her husband left her for his secretary last year and barely ever comes around, even to see his own kid. I don't understand how he can do that. Not only to Elowen, but to his own child.

It took a lot of convincing from Brooks not to find her ex and beat the shit out of him. I wanted to. He deserved it. He had everything, and he pissed it away for a fuck. Last anyone heard, the woman left him for someone else. Karma is a bitch.

"Oh, she's with my mom." Elowen's dove-gray eyes shimmer when the topic of her daughter comes up. "She's still talking about the time you guys took her to that water park." She tips the glass to her mouth. "She's crazy about her uncle Hudson and aunt Hadleigh."

"We love her too." I smile tightly. "Maybe we can all go in a few weeks when my current workload eases up a bit."

"That'd be great."

"You work too hard," Henry interrupts us.

"Yeah, maybe he should do what you do." Leighton snickers, her eyes narrowing. "Skip around on work to do things you shouldn't be doing."

Everyone goes silent.

Henry glares at her, a hushed battle between them. "If you didn't want to come with me tonight, then you should've stayed home."

"Maybe *you* should've!"

Just as I'm about to get myself a shot of tequila to suffer through another one of their fights, the bedroom door opens, and relief washes over me once I see my beautiful wife approaching. A snug dress hugs her curves like it was made for her.

She's exquisite. Absolute perfection in every sense of the word.

And I feel sorry for our friends to not have what we do.

"There she is!" Elowen jumps to her feet, while I meet Hadleigh halfway, wrapping an arm around her and kissing her temple once she's near.

"Thank God you're here," I whisper. "Leighton and Henry were about to go at it."

"Oh, no. Not again," she mutters while glancing at our guests and forcing a smile.

"You look stunning, baby," I tell her.

"Are you sure? Are my eyes red?"

I shake my head.

"Okay, good." She breathes a sigh.

"What took you so long?" Leighton heads over to her, and the two women embrace, followed by Elowen.

"Happy birthday, sweetheart."

Brooks nods, and Henry wishes her the same.

Hadleigh's attention goes to Adalyn. She's never met her, so I'm sure she's confused.

"This is Adalyn," Brooks offers. "She's Hudson's new secretary."

"Oh!" Hadleigh grins and advances toward the woman, reaching out a hand in greeting. The two shake.

"It's so nice to meet you." Adalyn purses her mouth and offers a small smile. "You're even prettier than in the pictures Mr. Mackay has all over his office."

I should probably tell her she can call me Hudson here, but fuck it. I don't want her to. Feels too personal.

"So, how's my husband treating you?" She flicks me a playful gaze while I pour her some wine.

"He's a great boss. Best one I've had."

"Well, he better be." Hadleigh laughs, her eyes on mine once more. "Or else he's going to hear about it from me."

"Would never want to disappoint my wife." I stride over to hand her a glass of red wine.

As she takes a large gulp, I swing my arm around her hips and kiss the top of her head.

Brooks gags. "You two make me sick."

Adalyn tsks at him. "Be nice. I, for one, think it's sweet."

"Yeah, yeah." He finishes his drink and gets up to get himself another.

"Oh, did you ever find out who sent you that envelope?" Adalyn asks, her eyes widening.

Brooks freezes as he stares at me, and I feel the weight of Hadleigh's intense gaze before she asks, "What envelope? Did something happen?"

"No." I shake my head, chuckling, hoping she doesn't start to worry. "Just work-related nonsense. Anyone hungry?" I turn toward the room. "We catered from Keens."

"Yes, please!" Leighton starts for the dining room, and we all follow.

As we do, Hadleigh lifts her mouth toward my ear. "Are you sure everything's okay?"

"Never better." I hug her close to my body. "Especially when I have you."

HADLEIGH

After dinner, the ladies and I chat, seated back in the den, while the guys congregate by the bar.

My mind is still on what Adalyn said, and I didn't miss the way Hudson reacted to it. Like he was keeping something from me.

I don't like being kept in the dark, especially if Hudson is in danger.

I may not ask him about his cases, but I know he represents some high-profile clients, and not all of them are innocent.

What if someone is after him? It wouldn't be the first time. Last year, he had a client he couldn't get off, so a friend of the client sent Hudson death threats. Hudson had to get him arrested for it to stop.

Sometimes I worry that something will happen to him. Whenever I hear stories of judges and lawyers being killed when criminals come after them, it terrifies me that he's next.

"Are you doing okay?" Elowen whispers softly beside me. "I know you said you wouldn't test today, but I know you better than that."

I shrug. "I'm as okay as I can be."

Which is not okay at all. But I smile anyway, because that's all I can do. Pretending is the only way to survive.

"I'm sorry," she goes on, glancing at Adalyn and Leighton seated across from us, lost in their conversation about some celebrity scandal. "I shouldn't have even brought it up. But as soon as I saw you walk out, I could just tell you were upset."

"Don't apologize." I squeeze her hand. "I know you're being a good friend."

Her eyes travel to Brooks, but he's barely paying her any mind. She's had a thing for him for a couple of months, but he's never noticed her. Or maybe he has and she's not his type, which would be crazy since she's beautiful. She's got curves for days and the kindest personality. She'd do anything for the people she loves. It's too bad her deadbeat husband didn't see that.

As soon as my mind goes to what he did, my body fills with disdain. I had to pick her up off the floor last year after he walked out on her. As though the affair wasn't bad enough, he had to leave her like she meant nothing. Like six years of marriage meant nothing at all.

"I can't believe Brooks brought Hudson's secretary," she remarks. "You'd think after the last one, he'd know better."

I roll my eyes. "You know how he is. You can do way better."

"I'm not into him," she denies a bit too vehemently.

"Oh, of course not." I wave a hand, my lips twitching. "I was just saying. You know, in case…"

She sighs. "Fine, yeah, I like him. It's obvious I know just how to pick 'em."

"Brooks isn't all bad," I say under my breath. "He just has some more growing up to do."

"And I'm not going to wait around for that to happen. I have Cassidy to think about."

I give her hand another squeeze.

"You think I'll ever find someone?" she asks, melancholy weaved through her words.

"Of course I do." I stare into my best friend's eyes, seeing her worth, hoping she knows it too. "When you're really ready to open up your heart again, I promise, there will be a man who will love you like you deserve."

"I don't know if I believe that, Hadleigh. I don't know if I'll ever have what you and Hudson do."

HUDSON

"How the hell are you guys still so in love after all these years?" Henry angles in close around the bar, a glass of whiskey in hand. "What the hell is your secret?"

"Loving her is my secret."

My eyes travel to the far end of the room, where my wife doesn't see me looking at her. But I can't help it. She's all that I see. It feels like just yesterday that she walked down the aisle and we swore to love one another. But that was six years ago already.

"Damn, Brooks is right. You two are nauseating." Henry pours himself another drink. "Tell me at least that you're fucking around on her." He chuckles. "Make me feel a little better about my marriage."

"Sorry, can't do that."

"Is he serious?" Henry asks Brooks. "Not even at work?"

"Our boy Hudson is a different breed. He doesn't even know other women exist. His dick only ever gets hard for Hadleigh."

"That's right, it does." I smirk. "I don't need anyone else, or I wouldn't have married her."

Marriage is sacred. It's something I was taught when I was young, and it's something that stuck with me.

Patrick was the one who drilled this in my head. To him, marriage is a bond that can never be broken, especially by infidelity. The thought of cheating on her never even crossed my mind.

"I mean, I get it…" Henry adds. "Hadleigh is a beautiful woman, but there are a lot of beautiful women out there, especially in the city."

"But none of them are Hadleigh, and I'd never cheat on my wife. *Period.*"

"You're a better man than me." His laughter deepens, and it's then I realize he must've had another affair, and that's what the fight with Leighton was about.

Fucking idiot. I told him the last time to stop it. It took a lot to save their marriage. But maybe Leighton will finally have enough. I may like Henry as a friend; I just don't appreciate how he treats his wife.

"Maybe if you put that effort into actually fixing your marriage and not fucking around on her, you'd actually have a shot at making it work," I tell him.

"What's the fun in that, though?" He takes a swig of his drink, a stupid grin on his face. "You have to see the girl I met. Twenty-one, tight-ass body…"

"Stop." I fix him with a glare. "Not in my damn house."

"Fine. Shit." He raises both palms. "I was just saying, I can share…"

His gloating expression widens, and my rage only intensifies.

"I'd even let you have her first." He winks.

In an instant, I grab a fistful of his shirt, my heartbeat pounding, my teeth bared like an animal as I near my face to his. "If you ever disrespect my wife again by suggesting I fuck around on her, I will kill you."

My chest rises and falls to my battering breaths as Henry's eyes pop. He's never seen me this way. Never had a reason to. Until now.

"Relax," Brooks whispers into my ear. "You need to chill."

"What's going on here?" Hadleigh asks as the ladies start to approach us, and it's the reason I drop my grip off of him.

"We're fine." I force myself to calm down and throw in a flicker of a smile.

Her brows gather inquisitively.

"I think it's best we leave before things get more heated." Henry starts to rise, his sharp blue eyes full of quiet wrath.

He's lucky I didn't do worse.

"Come on, Leighton. We're leaving," he informs her.

"Uh, okay. Bye, Hadleigh." She gives her a quick hug. "Happy birthday again. I hope you like the necklace."

"I'm sure I will. You really didn't have to."

"Of course I did. I'll talk to you tomorrow." She adjusts the strap of her handbag around her shoulder. "Bye, Elowen. Bye, Adalyn."

Waving to the two women, she rushes after Henry, who's already out the door.

"What happened?" Hadleigh asks me.

I grab both of her hips and bend my mouth to hers, stroking her lips softly with mine. "He suggested I sleep with someone else like he was. I'm sorry, butterfly, but I lost it. Because no one gets to disrespect you like that."

"Oh, Hudson." Her features soften. "That's the sweetest thing

I've ever heard."

Then she's the one kissing me, and I don't care who's here to see it.

Seven

HUDSON

The next morning, I place sausage and eggs onto Hadleigh's plate, then prepare my own, carrying both to our kitchen table.

"Thank you." She takes her seat while I go and settle across from her.

I hate the late hours I've been working lately, not getting home until nine or ten at night. I want to be here with her instead of in the office. To spend time together for as many hours as we can. But there's nothing I can do about that. My clients demand more of me than those of other firms. They need special attention, and I'm the one they come to for that.

I can't say I hate what I do, which probably makes me a bad person in the eyes of the world. But the only opinion that matters is my wife's. Though I'm sure she'd agree with everyone else if she were to find out about the beatings I've given, the murders I've sanctioned, the ones I watched happen and did nothing about. It's why she can't find out. She'd never forgive me.

Hadleigh's in the dark about a lot of what transpires in our life. She knows Patrick and the rest of the Quinns well, but she has no idea who they are. She has no idea that I represent members of the Mob as well as other organized crime syndicates, nor that they even exist.

The Quinns know not to say anything in front of her. It's for her own good.

Hadleigh's closest to Iseult Quinn, Patrick's oldest daughter. But Hadleigh has no clue that Iseult is the best Mob enforcer the Irish have. She's killed more men than her three brothers combined.

And I know that should anything happen to me, Iseult would be there for her. But the Quinns live in Massachusetts, too far to really watch over Hadleigh the way Brooks can.

"How about we go to dinner tonight after I get home?" I ask as she pops a piece of sausage into her mouth. "I'm going to make sure to be home at seven thirty tonight."

"That would be great, but are you sure? I don't want you to do it if you really can't."

I pull her hand from across the table and bring the top of it to my mouth. "You always come first, butterfly. I'm sorry if it doesn't seem that way with how much I've been working lately. But I swear you're the only one that matters to me. I'd throw it all away for you."

"Hudson…" She smiles, gaze softly searching mine. "I know that. But I never want you to feel it's either me or work. I know this is your job and it's not easy to run your own firm, especially as well as you do. So never worry that I'd ever make you choose."

I shake my head, my eyes closing for a moment. "I don't know what I ever did to deserve you, but whatever it is, I'll keep doing it for the rest of my life."

"You better."

She grabs her mug full of the sweetest coffee known to man. With the amount of sugar she adds, it may as well be considered dessert. But it's one of the many things I love about her, the things that make her my Hadleigh.

We finish our breakfast, and I take her plate to rinse both before I wrap my arms around the small of her back and mold her body to mine.

Our gazes tangle and a slow-growing smile appears on her face.

"Keep looking at me like that," she says, "and we'll both be late for work."

I groan, arching my hips so she can feel what she does to me.

"That wouldn't be so bad, now, would it?" My voice turns gravelly as I drop my lips to her jaw, kissing along the curve of it before I take her mouth roughly.

Her hands climb into my hair, and I don't care if she ruins it. I want her to.

We both part breathlessly, and I slant my forehead to hers.

"I'm going to miss you, angel. I'll try to call you during your lunch break."

"Okay," she whispers hoarsely, her exhales heavy.

Seconds pass until she speaks again.

"You promise you're not keeping anything from me that may hurt you, right?"

I jerk back, searching her nervous gaze. "Why would you ask that?"

"I don't know. Just been worried about you lately." She sighs. "Promise that if something's going on, you'll talk to me. I don't want to be kept in the dark."

"I promise."

I hate lying to her. But it's better if she doesn't know anything. My life could hurt her, and I'd do anything to keep her safe, even if it means keeping her away from the truth.

As soon as I finish responding to some emails at work, there's a harsh knock on my door.

"Come in," I say before Sanders, one of my partners, marches in, a stern look on his face.

"We have a serious problem."

Fuck. As if there isn't enough on my goddamn plate.

"What is it?"

"Someone has been altering billing on Salazar Perez's case."

"*What?*" I lean in, elbows hitting the edge of my desk as I narrow a concentrated stare. "That's not possible."

He drops a blue folder on my desk. "I personally triple-checked before I came to you just to be sure, but it's true. Someone has been billing more hours, and his people know about it. And let's just say they're not pleased."

I lean back into my chair. "Well, I sure as hell didn't do it! And I'm the only goddamn person working on his file."

If this is true, if Perez gets a whiff of disloyalty, I'm as good as dead.

Perez is the leader of the most dangerous Colombian drug cartel, and I've been handling some of his business in New York. To the world, his uncle runs the cartel, but he's the true leader. Vicious and never shows mercy. Crossing him is a death sentence.

"I know that," Sanders goes on. "That's why I wanted to tell you as soon as his right hand called me yesterday. I assured him it had to be a mistake and that you would personally see to it that it was cleared up." He sighs harshly. "They didn't seem appeased. I don't know what the hell to do."

Sanders is one of the few partners who knows exactly what we have to do for these people. I had to trust a few of the partners working here, and so far, they have been nothing but loyal.

"Fuck!" I slam my fist on the desk, taking deep breaths. "Who could've done this?"

How the hell am I going to make it right with Perez? Once he thinks you've crossed him, there is no negotiation.

Opening the folder, I look through the hours we have billed him, and it all has my signature. Obviously forged. But by whom? We hired two new attorneys, and then there's Adalyn...

"Thanks for bringing this to my attention, Sanders. I'll personally call Perez and discuss it with him."

"Be careful..." He gets to his feet and heads toward the door.

As he does, Adalyn is there with another yellow envelope. My pulse instantly kicks up.

"Sir..." She proceeds toward me, extending her hand. "This just came for you."

My heated stare rises toward her gentle one, and I continue to look at her, trying to figure out if she really could be behind this. She has access. She inputs the hours into our computer system.

But why would she do this? What does she have to gain?

"Thanks." I grab it from her, hoping that this time it's actually legal documents.

She quietly turns to leave while I open it, removing a single paper. One that instantly reminds me of the other.

As I hold it in my hands, the same thick black ink meets my gaze.

My pulse batters in my ears as I read the words, knowing for certain that someone is truly after me.

You're still here. Didn't think I actually meant it the first time? If you don't leave, I will tell the world what you did all those years ago. Would the partners stand beside you? Would Hadleigh love you then? Maybe we should find out.

I swallow thickly, breaths ravaging through me. Reaching inside the envelope, I expect another photo of my wife.

But instead, I feel something cold and grainy, almost like dirt...

Yet there's something circular and hard there too, and when I take it out...

"Fuck!" I jump off my chair, my heart shooting into my throat as the item in my grasp falls to the floor.

I instantly recognize the blue topaz ring. The same one my adoptive mother wore on her finger as we buried her. The same one she used to hurt us with every time she punched us.

Someone got it off her body. Someone went to the burial site. The same person writing these notes.

But who?

A million thoughts run through my head all at once.

Who could be doing this?

Why do they want me to leave?

Is it the cartel?

Is Perez fucking with me as payback?

It would be like him. He loves mind games. And he'd have the resources to get the ring undetected.

Taking out my burner from my pocket, I shoot off a text to my detective contact. He may know something about what the local precinct found by way of evidence on the dead bodies.

HUDSON

Those two bodies found in Windy Pine.

Any leads?

Bouncing my foot, I wait, staring at the screen, needing him to reply before I lose my fucking mind! Minutes stretch until a ping comes through.

DOUG

Got a buddy working it. Says the bodies are clean, but they're still digging. Why? You working it?

HUDSON

Nah. I was just curious. Comes with the job. Thanks, man.

DOUG

Don't mention it. Tell the wife I said hello.

HUDSON

Will do.

Pressing two fingers into my temple, I quiet the anxiety filling my veins before picking up the ring I dropped. Placing it back into the envelope, along with the note, I stick them back in my briefcase.

At least there is nothing tying me or Brooks to the bodies.

We're safe. For now.

Needing to get it over with, I dial Perez. Two rings, and he answers.

"Nice of you to call, lawyer man. Was wondering when I'd hear your voice." Icy humor flits through his tone, as though he's taunting me.

"It wasn't me," I inform him. "I need you to know that. But I will find out who it was, and you will have his name."

Quiet seconds pass. "I believe you."

But I don't think he does.

"I'd never ruin my reputation like that for money. You know that," I remind him.

He chuckles. "Relax, relax. You sound too stressed. I trust you to get to the bottom of who the thief in your firm is. But I swear, Hudson…" I can make out the rough sways of his exhales. "If I don't get a name by tomorrow morning, there'll be nothing left of your firm. Or you."

I grit my teeth until my jaw aches, my fist balling until my knuckles go white against my thigh.

"I need more ti—"

He hangs up before I can finish.

"Fuck! Fuck! Fuck!" Over and over, I slam a fist on the desk. "How the hell am I going to find this all out by tomorrow?"

I realize I'm going to have to break the promise I made to Hadleigh about coming home on time and taking her out on a date. I drop my face into my palms, my chest tightened. I know how much she truly was looking forward to a night out together. It's been months since we have done that, and now I'm failing her again.

Knowing I have to call her and disappoint her, I retrieve my cell from my pocket and press on her name.

The phone rings and rings until her voice comes on and I promptly leave a message, my heart hammering as I do.

"Hey, butterfly. I miss you. I hope your day is going well."

Shit, I can't do this. My silence echoes as I let out a harsh sigh.

"I'm so sorry, baby, but something urgent came up at work and I won't be able to be home early. If it wasn't time-sensitive, I'd be with you, but it's a life-and-death kind of situation, so I have to stay late. Please forgive me. I know I ask that a lot, but I'm sorry. I love you, Hadleigh. So much. I'll see you at home tonight."

Hanging up, I stuff my cell back in my pants pocket and press the intercom button on my work phone, calling Brooks's office.

"Hey, what's up?"

"I need you in my office. It's important."

"Alright. Coming."

A few seconds later, he's here, a stern look on his face when he sees mine.

"Close the door. We have a problem."

His brows furrow as he shuts it with his foot. "What's going on?"

"Someone in the office may have forged some billing numbers on Perez's case. We have today to figure out who it was, or we're all done."

His eyes enlarge.

"Shit…" he mutters, lowering slowly onto the chair across from me. "What do you need me to do?"

"Pull everyone's computer logs, for starters, and check who accessed the billing files."

"Then what?"

"Whoever went in there has to have done it. And they'll have to answer to Perez."

"He's going to kill them."

"They should've thought of that before they did what they did. Now, whatever happens is on them."

Eight

HADLEIGH

Melanie, a fellow teacher and friend at my school, sips on her iced coffee while I take a bite of my turkey sandwich.

"We have to plan a girls' night..." She dabs a napkin to her mouth. "I feel like it's been forever."

"That's 'cause it has." I laugh, my eyes on the students in the boisterous cafeteria. "It's either you're busy or I'm busy, but maybe in two weeks?"

"Sure!" She flings a hand through her long blonde hair, reminding me of rays of sunlight glowing in the afternoon sky. "I actually have nothing to do that week. Maybe we can hit up that rooftop restaurant that everyone raves about?"

"The Ribbon Room."

"Yeah, that's the one." Her blue eyes gleam. "You think Hudson can get us in?"

She gives me a salacious grin because she knows he can.

"I'll see what I can do." I pop a knowing brow.

Hudson knows many important people in the city, like the owner of The Ribbon Room, who owns multiple restaurants around here. But that particular place is incredibly difficult to get a reservation for, so knowing the owner is quite helpful.

"Mrs. Mackay?" One of my students approaches from my right, holding a small white envelope.

"Yes?" I grin at his sweet face, his reddish hair curling around the top of his forehead.

"This is for you." He extends the hand with the envelope toward me.

I take it, looking kindly down on it, thinking he probably wrote me another note.

Glancing back up at him, I ask, "What is it?"

"A man at recess said to give it to you."

A sweeping cold rush races through my body.

"What man?" My voice drops with a shudder, my eyes widening as Melanie gasps lowly beside me.

"He had black hair and sunglasses, and he was holding a black baseball cap."

I swallow the thick ball of dread forcing itself up my throat. My hands tremble, the envelope almost slipping from my grasp.

"Are you sure it—it was black?"

All the hairs on my arms standing up. Because once upon a time, that was all he wore. That damn black baseball cap.

"Yeah… Uh, are you okay, Mrs. Mackay?"

"U-umm…" My words trail, body breaking out in hives. "What did he say, sweetie?"

Attempting to keep my voice steady backfires. Maybe it isn't him.

Black hats are common; so is black hair. It could be a coincidence. But my gut says otherwise.

"I'm gonna get the principal," Melanie whispers, starting to rise.

"He said for me to give this to my nice teacher. He even knew my name. Mommy says not to talk to strangers, so I didn't, but he squeezed the envelope through the hole in the fence. You know where the seesaw is? And then he ran."

I place a shaky palm on his shoulder. "You did so good telling me all of that. You can go back to eating your lunch now."

His brows draw. "Are you okay? You look sad."

I force a grin. "I'm okay. Don't worry. What are you eating for lunch?"

"Mommy packed me mac and cheese and a brownie." His eyes return with their youthful innocence while tears burn behind my eyes.

"That sounds delicious! How about you go finish that, okay?"

"Okay!" He rushes back to his table.

And with my hands shaking, I start to open the envelope and...

"Oh, God," I whisper, unable to stop the fear bathing my body.

Inside is a simple postcard. On the front is the name of the city where I met my ex-husband, Tanner.

And on the back are nine little words written in thick black ink that send a shudder down my spine.

Hi, sweetheart. I've missed you. I'll see you soon.

And that's when I know for certain.
He's found me.

After I got the note, I called Hudson at work. He didn't answer his cell multiple times. Not even a quick text back, which isn't like him. But Adalyn told me he had left for a meeting, so I'm hoping that's why.

With the postcard in my grasp, my foot bounces on the floor, the fear undulating throughout my body.

It's already past ten, and Hudson is still not home. The phone rings while I keep leaving voicemails and texts.

I've heard the one he left me, so I knew he'd be home late. But what worries me is that he still hasn't called me back. He always calls me back eventually.

My heartbeats slam in my rib cage, fearing that maybe Tanner found him and hurt him. What if he confronted him at work and they got into a fight?

Oh, God...

I call him again. And again.

"Hudson, please call me back." I leave another message. "Tanner has returned, and I'm scared. Please just call me back."

Hanging up, I dial Brooks's number. He answers immediately.

"Hey, Hadleigh. What's up?"

A woman's giggle interrupts him.

"Shh," he tells her, clearing his throat.

"Have you talked to Hudson tonight?"

There's shuffling as he answers. "Not since he left the office. He had a meeting with a new client. Why? Is everything okay?"

"I don't know," I whisper. "God...I'm scared, Brooks."

"Hadleigh? Tell me what's happening." His tone rises with alarm.

"He hasn't answered any of my calls. And today..." I gulp down the fear. "Today, Tanner handed a postcard to one of my students. I'm...I'm afraid he's going to hurt me, or maybe he hurt Hudson already."

"Shit," he mumbles. "I'm on my way. Stay put."

"Okay." When he hangs up, I'm more afraid than I was before. Because Brooks sounded worried too.

By two a.m., the cops have arrived at our place, and I'm crumbling to pieces.

Brooks is talking to them while I sit on the couch, unable to grasp the fact that my husband has vanished.

Detective Tompkins is on his case, her stern expression drifting toward me as I look up at her. She doesn't like Hudson; I knew the second she arrived. Maybe she doesn't like defense lawyers. I can imagine he's probably stepped on her toes once or twice. But I hope that doesn't hinder her from doing her job.

She's listened to the voicemail he left me. And so have I. Until I memorized every word. It was as though he was saying goodbye without even knowing it.

"We're going to find him." Brooks comes to sit beside me, three other cops standing around taking notes after they have looked through his home office.

"Where could he be? Why won't he call?" I sniffle.

He drops a heavy palm on my shoulder. His silence is thick, and what it means is clear: *because he's dead.*

I grow violently ill at the thought, my body surging with icy fear, because a life without Hudson is no life at all.

"Mrs. Mackay?" Detective Tompkins calls as she approaches, a notepad in hand, her deep, dark sandy hair coiled in a tight bun, her eyes dark and murky.

"Yes?" I swipe under one eye and straighten my spine.

"Your ex-husband, Tanner. You say you've had no contact since you divorced?"

"That's right. Not until that postcard I gave you."

"And it was definitely his handwriting?" Her brows tighten.

"It was. I'd recognize it anywhere. I have no doubt it was him."

She nods, jotting that down. "We'll be talking to him."

"Good luck finding him." I roll my eyes. "He's been hiding. Maybe overseas. His family has money. If he were smart, he'd go back there."

"Well, let me worry about that. Just so you know, my officers have attempted to track Hudson's cell phone. Though it still rings, there's some kind of block that keeps us from finding his location. It's purposely done."

My stomach drops. "Oh, God... Does that mean someone has him? Did someone kidnap my husband?"

Brooks's hand remains clasped to my shoulder, squeezing a little. "You're telling me with all the resources at your disposal, you can't undo whatever's preventing his phone from being tracked?"

"That's exactly what I'm telling you." Her brow lifts a fraction. "But we'll keep trying. And if either of you hear from him, call me."

She reaches into her pocket and hands us both her business card.

NATALIA TOMPKINS
DETECTIVE
FIRST GRADE

I'm almost sure first grade denotes that she's at her highest level.

"Thank you." I hold the card tightly in my grasp. "Please, find him." Tears line the rims of my eyes. "He's my whole world."

She nods solemnly. "That's what I intend to do."

Nine

HADLEIGH
FIVE DAYS LATER

It's funny how the world just keeps spinning even while your own remains still.

An unmoving bend in time that you don't feel because every second of it is pure agony.

I force myself to go to work, even with the bloodshot eyes. Even while I go to the ladies' room during lunch and silently break down into pieces. No one says anything except how sorry they are and how they hope Hudson is found safe.

Nausea swirls in my gut as I heave into the toilet at home, Elowen holding my hair as I pant, unable to stop. This illness has been going on for two days now. My stress is affecting me so much, I can't do anything about it.

I keep imagining different scenarios. Was he killed and left somewhere? Is he all alone, bleeding in some alley? Is someone torturing him?

I grab a towel from the hanger and wipe my mouth, my hands falling to my knees as Elowen rubs my back.

"Please go see a doctor. I'm worried about you," she says.

I breathe out a harsh exhale, straightening myself.

"I'm fine. Just stressed." My voice is hoarse, and I cough before picking up the water bottle from the sink, taking a few small gulps.

"Well, you should go. Just in case. Can't hurt," she goes on, worry evident in each word.

But I don't need her to worry about me. I'm not the one who's gone.

"Elowen…" I give her a harsh stare. "Please." My chin quivers and tears bathe my eyes. "Not now, okay?" I blink back the moisture building.

She purses her lips and her face relaxes. "Okay. Whatever you want, I'm here."

She hooks her arm into mine, and together, we exit into the living room. She helps me settle on the sofa, and I grab my phone from it, seeing a missed text from Leighton.

LEIGHTON

Henry and I are thinking of you. Let me know if you need anything. I'll drop off some food tomorrow if that's OK.

HADLEIGH

Thanks. You don't have to, but thank you.

LEIGHTON

Are you kidding? Please don't thank us. I'm here for whatever you need. OK?

He will come home. I just know it.

HADLEIGH

I appreciate it.

LEIGHTON

Talk soon. Hang in there.

Hang in there. That's funny.

I'm barely surviving. It's like I'm standing at the edge of a cliff, just waiting to fall. This pain in my heart is indescribable. Unimaginable. And I hate to think I'm giving up, but I just don't know what to think anymore.

The more days a person is missing, the less chance there is that they're alive. That's what I read online, at least.

"Was that Leighton?" Elowen turns on the TV. "She keeps asking me about you. We all care about you, Had—"

But she freezes midsentence when Hudson's face jumps on the screen.

A flush of adrenaline tingles through my body, my breathing heavier, like the air has gotten thicker.

"Top criminal lawyer disappeared without a trace five days ago," a voice says. "Mr. Mackay has represented a lot of high-profile clients…"

"Shit, I'm sorry." Elowen quickly switches channels, but the damage has already been done.

Seeing his beautiful face has ripped my heart right open, and sobs break from my chest.

He's gone. He's really gone.

Something happened to him.

Something bad.

And I may never know what.

Ten

HADLEIGH
THREE DAYS LATER

E lowen won. I'm going to the doctor.
The nausea has only gotten worse in these last few days,
to the point where I have started to worry.

As I head into my car, opening the door, a text pings through. Settling into the seat, I hope it's the detective with something new.

They have come up with nothing so far. No leads.

After Hudson went to the meeting with a new client the day he disappeared, they were able to trace his steps to a subway. But after that, they lost him.

The thing about the city is, it may be small, however, it's pretty easy to disappear in the hordes of people. The only good thing is, they haven't found a body. But that could also mean whoever did something to him doesn't want him found.

Nausea returns to my gut at the thought.

No. He has to be alive. I can't give up.

With fresh tears springing into my eyes, I shatter across the wheel, my hands gripping it until my fingers ache. Minutes pass as I unravel, stricken by so much grief, I don't know how I'll survive it.

Needing a distraction, I check who texted and find Iseult's name. Her family is like family to Hudson. They're worried sick about him and are using their financial resources to find him.

As soon as I met Iseult, I liked her. She's not one of those pretentious women I've come to meet living the life I do. She's down-to-earth and rough around the edges. But the kind of rough that also has a soft side. She doesn't show it to many, but I've seen it. I consider us friends, even though I don't see much of her, being that she lives in Cherry Grove, a town in Massachusetts.

From what Hudson told me, the Quinns are one of the wealthiest families on the East Coast. Patrick Quinn built each one of his kids a home on the land. He owns acres of it.

Sometimes when she comes into the city, where she has an apartment, we get lunch together and catch up. She doesn't have many friends, except her younger sister, Eriu, and someone named Kora that I met once or twice.

She's getting married in a week, and I've never seen her this happy, which for her, is saying a lot.

ISEULT

> Are you feeling any better? Because I'm about to come there and drag your ass to the doc.

HADLEIGH

> I've already heard enough from Elowen.

So...I'm going. You can all leave me alone.

ISEULT

When?

HADLEIGH

Now.

ISEULT

Well, good, then.

Seconds stretch, and I see her typing, then stopping. Like she's afraid to say the wrong thing. Until the next text finally comes through.

ISEULT

We're still looking. My father will never give up. I'll never give up. You hear me? Never.

HADLEIGH

I need him back. Please find him.

ISEULT

You have my word. But, Hadleigh...

I know what she's going to say, and I don't need a reminder that I may get nothing but his body.

HADLEIGH

I have to go. Running late for my appointment.

ISEULT

Call me after. Let me know you're okay or
I'll drive to New York.

HADLEIGH

Promise.

Throwing my phone into the cup holder, I start the car and head down the driveway.

My doctor returns to the room, while I shiver in a blue gown, hating that I even came.

Her bright red lips spread into a stiff smile before she scratches the deep, dark brown skin of her throat, as though she's nervous to tell me whatever she's about to.

Dr. Layne has been my doctor for ten years. She's not one of those physicians with no bedside manner, so if she's about to deliver some awful news, like that I'm about to die or something, she'd definitely be nervous.

"Just tell me. Whatever it is. My life is as bad as it gets."

She sighs, her brows pulling in concentration. "I've been praying for you and Hudson. When I saw the news…" Her eyes close, and she shakes her head. "I'm really sorry."

"Thank you." My mouth tightens. "So, am I dying?"

"No." She laughs. "It's actually nothing bad…"

But her face tenses.

"So why do you look as though you're about to drop a bomb?"

"Hadleigh…" She takes my hand, her eyes pinned to mine. "You're pregnant."

A hysterical laugh bubbles out of me until I can't seem to stop.

"I'm serious. You're not that far along, but you're definitely pregnant."

An icy rush drowns my entire body.

"What…? No." I shake my head violently. "That's not possible. We've been trying but…I… No!" I cry. "You're wrong!"

I can't do this without him. He has to know. He has to be here.

Tears burn behind my eyes while her hand squeezes mine.

"I know this isn't how you wanted it to happen, but Hudson will come back. I believe it. He will come back to you."

"What if he doesn't?" I murmur, my vision clouded as I take in her gentle expression.

"Then you'll be the best mother to that baby because that's who you are, Hadleigh. Strong."

"I don't feel strong right now," I whisper.

"We can't be strong all the time. Sometimes we have to let others be strong for us. And you have an army of people holding you up. Lean on them."

I nod, dragging in a long breath. "Are you sure?"

"Very sure. Schedule an appointment with your OB as soon as possible."

"Okay." I swipe a hand down my face as she pats my knee and starts to rise.

"Hang in there."

As soon as she walks out the door, my hand curls around my stomach. "We'll be okay, little one. Somehow, we'll be okay."

Because what other choice is there?

I stare at the six pregnancy tests in my bathroom, and they all say the same thing.

Pregnant.

My heart's heavy. Breaking. Because as much as I've wanted a child, I've wanted it with Hudson. I wanted to share this with him.

"I don't want to do this without you."

Tears well in my eyes as I whisper the words out loud. Being pregnant with our child hurts more than I ever imagined.

With a scream, I swipe the tests, watching them scatter across the ceramic floor.

A heaving sob shakes my chest, and I sag against the wall, wishing this was a dream. Wishing I could go back to the time he was here.

If only I'd kissed him longer. Touched him just one more time.

But now it's all gone, and I'm left here picking up the pieces his absence left behind.

Eleven

HADLEIGH

"**C**ome on. You have to actually buy food so you can eat it," Elowen says as she hooks her arm through mine, leading me down the cookie aisle the following day.

Who cares about cookies? I can barely force myself to eat.

Being here instead of my home is like being stuck in hell. But worse. Other than going to work, which isn't much of a choice, all I want to do is stay in bed.

Has Hudson eaten? Is someone feeding him wherever he is?

I have to believe that he's okay. The alternative cuts like a knife. But it's nearly impossible to continue to stay hopeful. Hope won't bring him back to me.

I know in my gut that the man I fell in love with would never allow me to worry this way. He wouldn't want to do anything to hurt me. He'd do everything in his power to let me know that he was out there.

But he hasn't. There have been no signs at all.

And that alone is terrifying.

"I'm not hungry."

Through my large sunglasses, I stare at an aisle full of double chocolate chip cookies. They're my favorite. But right now, they look as appetizing as dirt.

Elowen grabs three packs of them and throws them into the shopping cart.

"Just in case," she remarks, adding some biscotti cookies too.

She knows everything I like. I should've just sent her shopping for me instead of going out myself.

Everywhere I go, something reminds me of Hudson. Even stepping foot into this store instantly took me back to the one time he was kissing me and we knocked into the produce aisle, both of us hysterically laughing. Got some dirty looks too. But we helped clean up the mess together, grins on our faces. Because we were together and we were happy.

"I'm going to make you my famous mac and cheese for dinner, followed by those pecan pie bars you like." She pushes the shopping cart with one hand while dragging me with the other.

"Elowen. Please." I stop mid-stride. "Go home. Go be with Cassidy. I don't need a babysitter."

"Cassidy is having fun with her cousin, so stop trying to get rid of me."

Huffing, I don't say another word.

I know how people see me. I know I look like a ghost of who I once was. And with every day, I lose even more of myself, not knowing how much more there is left to lose.

As we round the corner to enter the next aisle, we almost run into a woman with long black hair and eyes almost as dark.

"I'm so sorry!" she says, laughing nervously.

And I realize I know her.

"Adalyn?"

"Mrs. Mackay? Is that you?"

I nod, and her face instantly turns into a frown. She places a hand on my forearm. "We've all been thinking about you. We miss him so much at the office."

"Thank you."

Brooks said Hudson's six partners have taken over his cases, so at least the firm is doing okay.

"Between Mr. Mackay and Evan missing..." she goes on. "The firm is a sad place la—"

"Evan?" I question, completely confused. "Who's that?"

"Oh, right." She smiles tight-lipped. "I forget you don't know all the people who work for Mr. Mackay. Evan Kresten is one of the attorneys. He went missing around the same time."

"What? I had no idea."

Are they connected somehow? Why haven't the police mentioned it to me?

I intend to find out.

"Yeah." She purses her lips and nervously peers down at her feet before looking back up at me. "Well, I should be going. If there's anything you need, please reach out. Brooks knows how to get in touch with me."

Not sure what Hudson's secretary can do for me, but I get that she's trying to be helpful, so I force a smile.

"Thank you."

"Okay, well...I'll, uh, see you around." She gives us a wave and starts past us.

"That was kinda weird," Elowen whispers.

"What was?"

"The fact that she's shopping here when she lives downtown."

"She does?"

"That's what I heard Hudson say when we were at your place for your birthday."

That *is* weird. She's a good thirty-minute train ride away from us.

"Whatever. Who cares? Are we done yet?"

I just want to be in my bed, holding Hudson's t-shirt—the one that still carries the smell of his cologne—drifting into the distance with each passing moment until I lose that too.

Twelve

HADLEIGH
THREE DAYS LATER

Morning sickness is actually not morning sickness. Sometimes it's an all-day kind of thing, and in the past few days, it has gotten worse.

My OB did confirm that I am, in fact, pregnant. She told me how wonderful it was that the meds she gave us worked this time. That we were lucky.

Except we weren't a *we* anymore.

It was just me.

Sure, I nodded and smiled at the right moments. But I can't get to the point of feeling truly happy. Because how can I be while my husband is gone? How can I celebrate this miracle we've been given while he's not here to celebrate with me?

Flipping on the TV, I lean into the sofa, removing my cell and scrolling to one of my favorite photos. One of us after a Broadway show last year. We were so happy in the selfie. Him beside me as he took it, the lights of the city gleaming behind us. Feels like another life now.

I'm barely focusing on the TV, hearing a reporter talking about the weather when I decide to shut it off.

But I stop instantly as one says, "The body of Evan Kresten has been found in the Chelsea Piers."

I know that name. How the hell do I know that name?

"Mr. Kresten was an attorney working for the missing lawyer, Hudson Mackay."

Oh, God. That's right…

"The police are investigating all possible connections between these two events. We will return to this story as it develops. Back to you in the studio."

This can't be a coincidence. The two have to somehow be related. What if…

No…

But the thoughts won't leave me alone. Because what if that's where Hudson's body is too?

That damn detective hadn't even mentioned anything about Evan's case. She's been avoiding my calls the last couple of days, and maybe this is why. Maybe she knows more than she's been saying.

I've called her almost every single day, and the first few times, she'd return my messages, telling me they hadn't found any new evidence. But then she stopped returning them. She doesn't yet realize how persistent I can actually be. I don't want her to ever forget about my husband.

Her phone rings again and again until her voicemail comes

through.

"This is Detective Tompkins of the first precinct. Please leave your name and number and the reason for your call after the tone."

"This is Hadleigh Mackay, calling you again. Please call me back. I'd like an update on Hudson's case, as well as to discuss something else with you. Thanks."

With a frustrated groan, I hang up and dial the one number I dread calling every day. But it's the only way I can still talk to him. And maybe by some miracle, he's actually listening.

Hudson's phone rings as it always does, as though someone is taunting me, keeping it on to tease me with the fact that he could be alive. Maybe it's his kidnapper. Maybe he's got Hudson locked up in some basement and has kept his phone charged just so he can see who's calling.

The loud ringing continues for a few more seconds before I hear his voice.

And the pain? It's soul crushing, right down to the marrow of my bones.

"This is Hudson Mackay. Leave your message after the tone."

Beep.

"Another twenty-four hours has gone by without you in it, and I don't know how many more of them I can do."

I force down the pain gripping each word, but I fail, and a gasp breaks free.

"If you're somehow hearing this, please give me a sign that you're safe. That I can see you again soon. Because I can't go on not knowing if you're dead or alive, Hudson. I can't live this way."

I sniffle.

"If someone else is listening, let my husband come home. Please! I need him."

A small sob escapes from my chest.

"I need him so badly and…"

My words crack as I try to force them out, hoping they're enough to convince whoever has Hudson to let him go.

"And so does our baby," I cry softly. "That's right, Hudson. We're having a baby. Just like we always wanted. Come home to us."

I wait there, gripping the phone in a tight fist, crying through the line, not knowing if someone's listening on the other side.

Brooks shows up the next day with some gift cards to restaurants nearby and more groceries, even though the last set I bought are still lying in the fridge.

"He'd want you to take care of yourself," he tells me, handing me a bowl of tomato soup he just warmed up.

Silently, I wonder if I should ask him about Evan.

What happened to him? Who could've done it? How are Evan's and Hudson's cases connected?

Settling on the chair in the kitchen, I take the bowl and force myself to take a spoonful into my mouth. The steam rises, and the aroma does nothing for me. Nothing tastes the same, smells the same. It's as though the world has lost its color, shadowed by my far-reaching pain.

The warm liquid sluices down my throat, and before I know it, I've eaten half. Brooks leans against my counter and pops a brow, gesturing toward the bowl.

But I can't tell him that I'm afraid to finish it just in case I throw up. I'm not ready to talk about the baby. My mother doesn't even know. I haven't answered her calls. A simple text to tell her I'm alive is the only reason she hasn't hopped on a plane from Denver to come to New York.

"I'm full," I tell him, pushing the bowl away.

"Look, Hadleigh…" He comes to sit across from me, pulling the chair for himself. "I know you're hurting. I am too. He's my best friend." His expression turns pensive. "But killing yourself isn't going to bring him back. You need to stay strong and take care of yourself so you can have the energy to keep looking."

I snicker. "Other than scouring the internet and calling hospitals and morgues, I haven't done a damn thing. I'm useless."

My teeth snap against one another, the pain radiating into my jaw.

"It's worse, you know. Not knowing?" My lashes flutter to a close as tears throb behind my eyes.

"I'm so sorry," he breathes. "If I could switch places with him, I would."

Staring back at him, I find sincerity bathing in his eyes. I don't think I've ever seen Brooks look this intense. He cares a lot about Hudson and me. I've always known that, but in this moment, I actually see it.

I must admit when I first met him, he wasn't my favorite person. He was loud, liked to party a little too much. There was always a new woman attached to his hip too. And though he hasn't settled with anyone yet, he's toned down his partying a lot.

Maybe Adalyn will be good for him. She's very much his type: tall, slender, dark hair. Needing to switch the subject, I decide to ask about her.

"How's everything going with Adalyn?"

He leans back and his mouth twitches with a glint in his gaze. "I like her. She's fun."

I let out a small laugh. "Oh, Brooks, are you ever going to put a ring on some lucky girl's finger?"

He inhales sharply, his face losing all traces of that smile.

"Maybe one day." He hitches a shoulder. "But right now, I'm where I'm supposed to be."

"Stuck babysitting me?" I scoff.

"I'm not babysitting you, Hadleigh. I'm checking in on you. That's all. That's what Hudson would've wanted and what he would've done for me had the tables been reversed."

I nod. He's right. Hudson would've done the same.

"Have you heard from Detective Tompkins? She keeps dodging my calls."

"She's avoiding you?" His expression turns irritated.

"Yep." I look him dead in the eyes. "And after I just heard about Evan being murdered, I definitely want to speak to her."

His brows rise and momentary shock settles on his features. "You saw the news…"

"Yes. And I found out he was missing through Adalyn. I ran into her at the supermarket a few days ago."

His stare narrows. "She never said anything to me."

"She told me that Evan went missing around the time that Hudson went missing. And today I find out they fished his damn body out of the piers, Brooks!" I can't even finish the sentence without my emotions clogging my throat. "How could you keep this from me? It could all be connected to Hudson!"

"Fuck…" he rumbles. "Because of exactly this reason. Look how much more worried you are now. I didn't want you more upset, and neither would he."

My heart races, and anger settles in my gut. "Look, if something has to do with Hudson, I don't want you keeping it from me, do you understand? I need to know everything."

He sighs heavily. "Okay. I promise from now on, I'll tell you what I can."

"No, not what you can. *Everything*. Okay?"

A heavy feeling pummels inside my chest.

"Hudson's dead, isn't he?" My face falls into my palms.

"Don't think that way. Don't give up on him."

Swiping the back of my hand under my eyes, I stare at him once more. "I'll never give up. I'm going to get him back. There's no other choice."

My vision clouds with the misery I've come to know these last ten days.

"Come on, let's go for a drive," he says.

"Where are we going?"

"You'll see."

With Brooks seated beside me, I wait for Detective Tompkins to speak to us. Brooks figured she couldn't avoid us if we went to the precinct. And he was right.

She walks over to the waiting area, a blue file in hand, her hair in that tight bun I saw her wear when she was in my apartment when we first met.

"Mrs. Mackay. What can I do for you?"

Brooks and I rise to our feet.

"Anywhere private we can talk?" I ask.

"Sure." She extends an arm, leading the way to the back, and opens the door to a corner office.

It's clean and simple. An unassuming brown desk at the far end of the wall with a couple of chairs before it and a black leather sofa to our left.

"Please have a seat," she tells us, pointing to the chairs.

As we settle, she does too, placing the folder down on the desk before she opens it.

"So, you're here for an update, I presume."

"Well, yes. Seeing as you've been avoiding me, we decided a face-to-face is best."

An indifferent smile curls around one side of her mouth. "I'm afraid we've hit a wall with your husband's case."

"How's that possible?" I throw a hand in the air. "How is one of the best police departments in the country not able to find one lawyer? Not even a body!"

She leans forward, eyes angled to mine. "Because if your husband is purposely hiding, then we'll never find him."

"What the *hell* does that mean? Are you saying my husband left on his own? That he's made me worry about him all this time without letting me know that he's alive and okay? Is that what you're saying?!" I take a deep breath, my chest tightening. "If you think that, then you don't know Hudson at all."

Pausing, she concentrates her attention on me. "Respectfully, I think you're the one who doesn't know Hudson."

"You better stop talking..." Brooks's nostrils flare. "You do not get to speak to her like that nor do you get to tarnish his name."

She laughs wryly before narrowing a gaze. "Do either of you have any idea who he really is? The kinds of things he's been accused of? Not proven, of course." She grins. "People like him know how to bury their skeletons."

"That's enough! You hear me?" Brooks's tone continues to simmer, like a kettle bubbling until it explodes. "I don't give a *fuck* who you are. You will shut your damn mouth."

I get his anger. I'm angry too. Hudson was his best friend. They've always had each other's backs.

She chuckles, entertained by his display. "Wait. You work with him, right? The paralegal?" She tilts up a thick brow. "You must help him cover up his dirty work. Is that why you're so upset?"

He rises, bending his torso over the desk, his tall frame towering over her. "If that's what you think, *Detective*, then maybe you should be afraid of me."

He breathes slow, their eyes battling one another as though in a duel.

"Let's just go, Brooks," I say, knowing she won't be of help anyway.

In that instant, she gives me a glance.

"It's very obvious you hate my husband. So maybe I should reach out to the mayor and let him know how bad you are at your job. He's a friend of Hudson's, and I'm sure he'd love to know the kinds of things you're saying about him."

"We're threatening now?" There's a hint of humor on her features. "All I was trying to do was help you get to know your husband better. Let you know he's not some innocent lawyer. He's got ties to the Mob. Did you know that?"

"Shut the hell up," Brooks adds.

But she ignores him, her eyes seared to mine.

"The Mob?" I burst out a laugh, because nothing has ever sounded so ridiculous. "That's really low, Ms. Tompkins. Even for you."

I purposely didn't call her a detective. She sure as hell isn't one right now.

"It *would* be funny…if it wasn't true." She leans into the back of her chair while Brooks rights himself, the rage splitting through his entire face. "But unfortunately for you, it is. Whether you believe it or not, you didn't know your husband as much as you thought you did."

My pulse batters in my ears. I hate her. I don't think I've ever hated anyone until now.

But even as I fight it, her words echo in my head.

You didn't know your husband.

Could she be right?

"You really didn't know, did you?" she goes on, her eyes inquisitively turning to slits.

"Know what?" My heartbeats quicken.

"That your husband is dirty."

"Hudson wasn't dirty!" Brooks fires out. "Ignore her, Hadleigh. She's lying."

But she snickers and goes on. "He *was* dirty, no matter what Mr. Bardin wants you to believe. Your husband worked for the Mafia, the Mob. All of them. Did whatever they wanted. Gave up people for them to murder. Did you know he's the reason Evan was murdered? That he gave him up to the Italians, or fuck, maybe the cartel. Criminals talk, and we'll eventually get one of them to snitch."

"No…" I whisper, my stomach turning. "Hudson would never…"

"That's enough!" Brooks grabs my hand and forces me to stand, pulling me toward the door.

But behind my shoulder, she continues. "He's paid off prison guards to get people killed for these criminals. His hands are smeared with other people's blood, Mrs. Mackay. Open your eyes."

"No! That's not him!" I force my hand away from Brooks, shaking my head, while everything inside me rattles.

"Hadleigh, let's go," he urges. "We'll get a real detective on his case."

"Good luck," she mocks, rocking back and forth. "You don't have to believe me, Mrs. Mackay. But everything I'm saying is the truth. The only problem is we haven't had enough evidence to nail him."

"You're lying." I breathe in and out, advancing toward her with a heavy pulse. "So much easier to make up a story to fit your own agenda instead of having proven facts. I want another detective on his case."

"Any detective here would tell you the same thing." She drops her elbows on her desk and stares at me, her eyes cold. "But unlike your husband, I'll do my job. I know how to do that without compromising my integrity. Now, excuse me. I have work to do."

"Next time she calls you…" Brooks addresses her. "You answer her, or we'll keep showing up every fucking day. You hear me?"

"Get the fuck out of my office." Her face contorts.

"Gladly."

Turning on my heels, I wonder if I messed up Hudson's case by coming here.

Thirteen

HADLEIGH

B rooks has just dropped me off back home, and the first thing I do is call Iseult. She'll be honest with me about Hudson. If he's been doing anything illegal, I'm sure Patrick would've told him not to. He's like a father to him.

"Hey," Iseult answers. "You never told me what happened at the doctor, by the way."

I sigh. "I forgot. I'm sorry, but I'm fine. Nothing bad."

"Well, fuck. I will have you know I was very worried, and I'm never worried about anyone outside my family."

I let out a faint laugh. "Thanks for the compliment."

"Who says I was giving you one?" She's all serious, but I can just picture her amused expression.

"Thanks for making me laugh, Iseult."

But even laughter hurts. Because I don't want to laugh or smile or be happy.

I want to hurt.

I want to feel his gaping absence every single day until he returns to me and calls me *butterfly* just one more time.

But in the back of my head, I hear that detective's voice.

Could Hudson really be hiding out somewhere? What if he can't contact me because he's afraid of getting tracked? If he really did disappear on purpose, then he'd have to be close. He'd want to be somewhere he could reach me just in case.

"Can I ask you something? And you have to tell me the truth."

"Uh, okay…" Her tone turns guarded. "I mean, it depends on what you're asking."

"It's about Hudson."

"What about him?"

I gulp down the nerves because even asking her this sounds ridiculous in my head. A few seconds pass before I gather the courage to say the words out loud.

"The detective told me Hudson's dirty. Said some awful things, like that he works for the Mob. Have you heard anything like that?"

"She what?" Iseult clears her throat.

"Yeah. I mean, I know there's no way he could do the kinds of things she claimed, but I wanted someone he knew to tell me that it's bullshit."

"Of course not. Tell that detective to shove that shit up her ass. In fact, I'll come down there and do it personally."

"Uh, no need."

Iseult's definitely easy on the eyes, but not afraid to stand up to anyone, so I know she'd walk into that precinct and flip that detective's desk upside down, and I wouldn't even need to ask. But I don't want her to get into trouble because of me. Nor would Hudson.

"Okay, but if she says anything else, make sure you tell me

immediately. My father would want to know. Hear me?"

"Yeah, of course." I pinch the bridge of my nose, frustration overtaking me. "How's the search going on your end?"

"We are still looking. Nothing yet." She lets out a deep sigh. "I wish there was more we could do."

"Me too, Iseult. Me too."

His phone rings and rings, and I've come to hate the sound, knowing in the end I won't get to hear his voice talking back to me.

I've left a message every single day since he's been gone, hoping that hearing me will make whoever is listening feel sorry enough to let Hudson go.

Someone has to be listening. The voicemail box would've been full by now. But it isn't.

I can't let myself believe that he's dead. My heart cannot accept it. I don't think it ever will.

"This is Hudson Mackay. Leave your message after the tone."

Beep.

"Hey, baby. I miss you. I don't know how to go on without you. Yet I'm somehow doing it. But it feels like I'm drifting through time instead of living. It hurts so much not having you here, not having you go to my doctor's appointments with me. She said I'm around nine weeks pregnant now. I heard his heartbeat. And a blood test revealed we're having a boy. A son. *Our* son. Can you believe it?"

Tears gather at the edges of my eyes. He would've been so happy. A trembling smile curls my lips, and I stare down at my small belly. No one can see it yet, but I'll have to start telling people, and I hate it. That's when it really becomes real.

"I want him to look like you," I go on. "I want him to have your heart and your passion. Your determination to do everything for those you love. I want him to be like his father, even if his father may never ever meet him."

Before a sob can break free, I hang up, and with my hands cupping my face, I cry. I cry so hard it could wake the angels and the devil too.

How could this happen? How could he just disappear?

I never even got to say goodbye. I wasn't ready to.

Closing my eyes, I lower to the sofa, recalling the first time Hudson ever kissed me. It was our first official date, something I go back to whenever I think about us.

I run my hands down my jeans, buttoning a simple white blouse while waiting for Hudson to pick me up from my studio apartment in Brooklyn.

Why am I crazy nervous? It's just Hudson. I know him. He knows me. Nothing about this is weird.

We've spent the entire year keeping our friendship platonic, even while I began to have intense feelings for him. So much so, I'd have dreams about us together. But he never so much as made a move.

I think he was afraid I wasn't ready after Tanner, and maybe he was right. But I'm ready now. I'm not afraid of falling in love. I'm not afraid that Hudson could turn out like Tanner because I know he's nothing like him.

There were signs I missed with my ex-husband. Things I didn't want to admit then. I don't see those things with Hudson. Not yet, at least. Not ever, hopefully.

Hudson has been my support system. He drives me to work at the daycare every morning and picks me up when he gets out of work early. And on weekends, we're always together. Broadway shows, restaurants, or a simple night at home. Other days, he comes over to cook for me or we order in and watch a movie together. Seeing him has always been my favorite part of the day.

But taking this next step is terrifying. Being friends with someone you have feelings for and then dating them is scary. What if it ruins our friendship? What if we realize we have no chemistry and then I lose him?

But when he asked me out the other day, I knew I wanted to say yes, so I did. And now, here we are.

Beep.

The intercom buzzes, and my eyes pop wide as I realize he's here. With a final look in the mirror, I brush my fingers through my long hair, add another swipe of red lipstick, and step out toward the elevator.

When I hit the button, the doors open, and I dash inside, heading for the lobby. A short ride down, and I'm proceeding toward the curb, where he's waiting for me, leaning against his white BMW coupe.

As soon as his eyes land on mine, a giant grin spreads across his face, that gaze gleaming like the sun. And in this moment, I want to run into his arms, skip over the awkward dating, and fast-forward to the part where I marry him.

Because looking at him, I know he's my destiny. My home away from home. A place that's safe and warm and altogether ours.

"There she is…"

He takes a few steps toward me while I do the same, until his arms wind around my back, his eyes boring into mine.

"You're so beautiful, Hadleigh," he rasps, his lips a breath away.

My stomach somersaults the more he looks at me. And when the back of his hand brushes down the side of my face, shivers run up *my spine.*

"Thank you." My cheeks heat up as his lips curve, his gaze growing heavy-lidded.

"Never thank me for telling you the truth, butterfly."

My heart hammers the more he stares at me with hungered prowess.

"You don't know how long I've waited to hold you like this," he breathes.

The way he feels for me is right there, in his eyes, and all that doubt from minutes ago about ruining our friendship vanishes.

"How long?" An exhale roughs out of my lungs, my gaze dropping to his lips while his go to mine.

"From the moment I met you, I just knew we were going to be together. I don't know if you believe in soulmates, Hadleigh, but I know you're mine."

"I like being yours." I sink my lips closer, and his jaw clenches, the hollows beneath them accentuating deliciously.

"Are you sure?" His warm breath mingles with mine while he strokes my mouth with his, sending a shudder between my thighs.

"I want you," I confess. "Please...please kiss me."

He clasps my face with both hands and stares deep into my eyes. "You never have to beg for a thing, angel. You're safe here."

Then he kisses me—hungry and hot—one hand sliding into my hair, the other wrapped around the side of my throat, his thumb pushing up my jaw to deepen our connection. He spins me around and pins my body up against the car, his muscular form molding into mine. His groans reverberate down through my limbs, sending a heady jolt into my core.

And I know in my soul that I'll never have a kiss like that again. Not this passion. Not this intensity. Because Hudson Mackay was meant to be mine too.

Pain pulses within my eyes, and I realize I'm crying.

He's truly gone.

And when he disappeared, he took it all with him. That passion, that life we planned…it's all gone, leaving me in the shadows of the love we once had, not knowing if we'll ever get it back at all.

fourteen

HADLEIGH

There's a visitor at my door the following evening, and I almost don't let them in because my appearance would scare a person.

I doubt it's Elowen. She never comes unannounced. And Leighton usually calls. With all the marital problems she's been having with Henry lately, I don't always see her.

As I get to my feet from the sofa that's been my home for the last two hours, nausea hits my gut, and I take deep breaths to quiet the unease. I can't wait until this morning sickness is finally over.

The doctor guesses maybe a couple more weeks. But I read online that for some it lasts for all of their pregnancy. How the hell does someone deal with forty weeks of this?

Once I feel the nausea lessen, I step toward the foyer, nearing the door before I peek through the peephole.

Brooks is there with bags, staring straight ahead. He shopped for me again, which is incredibly sweet because I sure as hell had no plans to. But I'd rather he didn't. He has his own life to live. He doesn't need to feel obligated to watch out for me out of some duty to Hudson.

I'm better off on my own, anyway. No need to bring anyone else down into my despair. Though he's upset about Hudson, it's not the same. It never will be.

When I open the door, he grins at me.

"Took you long enough."

"Sorry. Tired." I glance down at the bags. "What are you doing here?"

"I bought you some microwavable meals, just in case it's three a.m. and you're craving a White Castle cheeseburger."

"And let me guess. You got some." I force a polite smile, and my stomach growls.

"Two boxes." He chuckles. "And not the small ones, either. Now, may I come in so I can throw these in the freezer? Then I promise I'll leave you alone to your PJs."

He gives me a once-over, but not the dirty kind. Like he's teasing me.

"I guess that'll be acceptable." I force another smile as I move out to the side to let him pass.

He heads right for the fridge and begins to unpack everything, and by the end of it, my freezer looks overly stuffed. But things I can simply heat up is how I survive.

"You really don't need to do that, Brooks," I tell him as he shuts the fridge door and picks up the now-empty bags, bunching them up.

"I know I don't have to, but I want to." He swipes his gaze down my body, his brows knitting. "When was the last time you ate?"

"Um, maybe seven in the morning?"

He shakes his head and sighs. "Sit. I'll make you something."

When I arch a brow in challenge, he gives me a stern look, his mouth dancing with a small grin.

"You need to eat, Hadleigh. I'm worried about you."

"Fine." I release an exasperated breath. "I'll eat. But you don't have to worry about me. I'm a big girl."

"I know." His expression softens. "But I'm here anyway. Now, how about some grilled chicken with mushrooms, sautéed in that balsamic sauce you like?"

My hand stiffens against my thigh. That was Hudson's specialty.

"Did Hudson teach you how to make that?"

"No, sweetheart." He chuckles, shaking his head. "*I* taught *him* how to cook. He was a good student."

"He was good at a lot of things." I sigh.

He nods. "That he was. It's not the same without him." His eyes strain with sorrow. "I miss him too."

His jaw clenches as he pivots toward the stove, kneeling to remove a pan from the shelf under the oven. Once he does, he gets out all the ingredients he needs while I watch him, hoping he can be done soon and leave.

Thirty minutes later, there's a steaming plate being placed before me. It smells good, but I'm a little afraid to eat it. Never know if my stomach will agree with it.

But I grab the fork he handed me and try anyway. Lifting the knife, I cut a piece of the chicken. Placing it in my mouth, I start to eat while he grabs a plate for himself and joins me on the opposite side of the counter.

"How is it?" he asks as the first bite hits my mouth.

"Amazing…" I almost groan because it does taste good.

His mouth spreads into a grin. "I'm glad to see you enjoy it."

We continue to eat in silence, and when I take another bite of the mushroom, a violent attack of nausea hits me out of nowhere.

Quickly, I grab my glass of water and force the awful feeling to go away. But the more I drink, the worse it gets.

Dropping the glass with a clank, I push the chair back forcefully and rush for the bathroom.

"Hadleigh?" Brooks's thundering footsteps follow me close behind. "Hadleigh, Jesus!"

Reaching the toilet, I let it all out.

I feel his hand against my back, another holding my hair in his clasp. "It's okay. You're okay."

I can't seem to stop. I knew eating was a mistake. There are some things that the baby really isn't a fan of, and apparently mushrooms are another. Once I feel better, I grab the towel he's handing me and wipe my mouth.

My heart races uncontrollably. I can't believe this just happened. What am I going to say?

"Are you okay? Do I need to call the doctor?"

"Yes. I mean no." My hand rushes down my face.

My back is still to him and it's like I can't face him, afraid if I do, I'll spill my deepest secret. And I don't even know why I'm hiding it anymore. What does it matter if our friends find out now or once I'm showing?

"Talk to me, Hadleigh. What's wrong? Are you sick?" His voice drops, like the thought somehow pains him.

I shake off his sentiment, and when I turn to face him, the words begin to trickle out. "I'm not sick. Not exactly."

He stares questioningly at me. Waiting…

"I'm…I'm pregnant."

He jerks back a step, his eyes growing large. "Wh-what? How? I thought…"

"So did we, but somehow…" A heaviness forms in my throat, pummeled with emotions. "I found out a few weeks ago."

"Hadleigh…shit, I'm sorry." His palms hit my shoulders. "I can just imagine how hard this has been for you on top of everything else. I wish you would've told me."

"I haven't told anyone. You're the first person."

His expression grows softer. "Whatever you need. Anytime you need. I'm here for you. You shouldn't be going through this alone."

I sniffle from his sincerity, and one by one, the tears trample down my cheeks, lost to my misery.

His arms enclose around me, and he holds my crying form against him for so long that by the time he lets go, I no longer know what time it is at all.

Fifteen

HADLEIGH
ONE MONTH LATER

The days have bled into one another, the weeks disappearing in a blink of an eye, and yet he's still gone.

No sign of him.

Not one shred of evidence pointing to where Hudson is—dead or alive.

I have considered going to a fortune teller. One of those TV ones that claim they can see your future in a deck of cards. I know it sounds ridiculous. I've never believed in such things, but right now I'd believe in anything.

Driving down a long stretch of road, I head home from a yoga class in Brooklyn. I hate driving there. There's always traffic. With Hudson being gone, I haven't attended the class I normally go to near home, not wanting the women who know me there to say anything about what they saw on the news. I don't want their looks of pity. I don't need a daily reminder of what I've lost. But at this school, no one knew I was his wife. I could forget for an hour.

When I make a right turn, down a one-way residential street, a set of tires come screeching down behind me. There's a car in front, but it makes a right turn, letting me head straight, and instead of the one in the back slowing down, it guns faster.

"What the hell?"

My heart rate speeds up. I want to stop to let him pass, but that's impossible with the cars parked on each side.

I look through the rearview mirror, and think I see a man.

But as soon as I catch sight of what he's wearing, my body breaks out in a shiver, hairs prickling through the length of me.

The man, whose face I can't see clearly, is wearing...a black baseball hat.

The same kind Tanner always wore.

"O-oh my God..."

I speed up, hoping to lose him, but he only goes faster. Fear closes its hand around my throat.

He wants to kill me. He came back to finish what he couldn't back then.

I click on my cell and tell the phone to dial the police.

"911. What is your emergency?"

"Hello, someone is driving after me. I think it may be my ex-husband. He keeps tailing me, and I'm terrified he's trying to hit my car. Please send help."

"Can you stop on the side of the road and wait with other people around?"

"I...I can try."

Making a random left turn, I watch as the black sedan makes one too. But this is a two-way street, so maybe I can lose him.

"He just followed me again. This is intentional. He's trying to hurt me." I let out a gasping pant as fear for my baby makes it hard to take my next breath.

"I'm sending help to your location. Don't hang up."

"Okay." I swallow the dread as I attempt to pull over.

But the other vehicle makes no attempts to stop. Instead, he goes faster.

My eyes widen, chest heavy, and before I can slide out of the way, he slams right into the bumper.

My face hits the wheel, all air leaving my lungs.

There's honking, so much honking.

"Ma'am? Ma'am, do you hear me?" the police dispatcher's words echo.

Then everything goes black.

Lights flicker through the slits of my eyes, a beeping sound ringing through my head.

Groaning, I push open my lids, finding a blaring light above me. As my surroundings come into focus, I realize I'm in a hospital room, an IV sticking out of my arm.

"My baby!" I spring up to a seated position, my heartbeats rapping against my ribs.

It's as though I've been doused awake by the knowledge that something could've happened to our child, the one piece of Hudson I have left.

I see Brooks, Leighton, and Elowen rush toward me. I try to concentrate on their faces, but my pulse races so quickly, I grow dizzy.

"Hadleigh!" Elowen appears beside my bed. "You're awake. Thank goodness."

Her brows tug, and she grabs my hand and squeezes it.

"Th-th-the baby..." I choke. "How's the baby?"

"Baby?" She snaps her head back and her curious eyes concentrate on me.

"I'm pregnant," I croak out.

"Oh my God," Leighton whispers.

"Pregnant?" Elowen's chin trembles. "Oh, Hadleigh. I'm so happy for you."

Her arms jump around me, and she embraces me tightly, sniffling back her emotions.

"The doctor hasn't said anything yet," Brooks answers.

"How far along are you?" Leighton approaches with a single step.

"About three months."

"That's wonderful." A smile flutters on her face, but there's also concern there.

Elowen settles on the edge of the bed, still clasping my hand.

"We've been so worried about you." Leighton closes her eyes and sighs. "I'm sorry I haven't come around as much as I should've. Everything with Henry has been crazy. But I...uh..." Her shoulders drop. "I'm divorcing him. Already started the process."

"Good for you."

She deserves to be happy, and staying with a cheating son of a bitch won't get her there.

I reach out a hand for hers. "Proud of you."

"How's your head?" Brooks asks, a muscle popping in his jaw as he looks me up and down.

"What's wrong with my head?" I reach up, my fingers tracing my forehead, and I feel the gauze there.

"You slammed it when your car spun. Fucking gonna find whoever did that..." His eyes flash, anger curling in every one of his features.

The accident starts to come back to me. The chase. The man in the black baseball hat.

Tanner.

Fear claws its way through my bones, my body dancing with a shivery chill.

"The police will want to interview you," Brooks adds.

"It was Tanner. I think." My words are sticky in my throat. "He was following me. He wanted to hurt me."

He nods tensely, and in his eyes, all emotions have vanished other than his rage. "The police said they heard your 911 call. They're investigating." An exhale ravages out of him.

"Can't say I have much faith in them right now."

"If it was Tanner, if he did this, he's going to wish he'd never returned."

From his icy glare, I believe him.

"Mrs. Mackay," someone calls.

I look past Brooks to see an older woman with shoulder-length gray hair, a white coat hitting her knees.

"I'm Doctor Malone. How are you feeling? Any dizziness, nausea?"

"A little."

"You had a mild concussion. We will leave you overnight for observations, and if you're fine tomorrow, you may go home."

"How's my baby?"

She smiles. "Doing just fine. Perfect heartbeat."

The biggest relief washes over me, and I blink back the thick tears welling behind my eyes.

I didn't lose him.

I didn't lose the only piece of Hudson I have left.

The day after, I'm released from the hospital and Brooks is the one to drive me home.

Opening my door, I walk inside feeling much better than I did yesterday, though I still have a headache. All I'm thankful for is that both the baby and I are alive.

"Go lie down and rest," Brooks orders, holding the mail I retrieved from my mailbox in his grasp.

"I think I'll go sit on the sofa. Maybe drink a cup of tea."

"I'll go make you one." He looks at me warmly.

I admit it's nice to have someone here after such a terrifying accident. I can't get those last few moments out of my head.

The entire ride home, I saw it as though it was happening all over again. The baseball cap, the face hidden beneath it, the way he sped after me, the feeling of whiplash...

My hand trembles on my lap, and I curl my fingers to stop the anxiety battling within me. I didn't see his face, but I just know it was him. It's as though he wanted me to know it was.

Clearing my throat, I force myself to look at Brooks, to think of anything but my ex.

"Thanks. I don't know what I'd do without you."

He waves off the sentiment, his mouth curving up one side. "We're family, Hadleigh. It's what family does for one another."

"Well, thank you anyway. I appreciate it." I lower onto the sofa. "Could you hand me the mail? Want to check it before I fall asleep."

"Of course." He brings the stack over to me, then hurries off into the kitchen.

I hear him shuffle in there while I open the first piece of mail, finding a bill for some of my OB visits. As I open one after another, I find that the last one has no return address.

But my name is scribbled in thick black ink.

A shiver shimmies up my arms. Starting to tear up the flap, I remove a piece of white paper and carefully unfold it.

As I do, my eyes widen in crippling horror when I scan the words.

In Tanner's handwriting.

"No..." My lungs constrict, my hand clawing my chest as I read it over and over until my eyes bleed.

Horror and dread twine in my gut because for one moment, I hoped I was wrong. That the man in the car wasn't him. That he wasn't back.

I wanted so badly to forget about him, and I hoped he forgot about me.

But Tanner doesn't want to forget.

He wants to make me remember everything. He wants to punish me. To hurt me.

Or worse.

To kill me.

I enjoyed the run-in we had. How's your head, Haddy?

Tears swim in my eyes.

That name. That damn name I've fought like hell to erase from my memory. Erase the voice that gave it to me.

But he's found me. After all this time, he's back.

My pulse quickens and my fingers quake around the edges of the paper.

Tanner loved to call me Haddy. I hated nicknames and he knew it. So he used it on purpose, to show me he owned me no matter what.

"Alright, your tea is ready." Brooks marches back in, holding a mug in hand, and when he takes in my expression, his movements slow. "What happened?" He quickly places the cup on an end table beside me. "You look pale, Hadleigh. Do I need to call the doctor?"

"No," I whisper, trying to find the right words, but every single one I conjure up makes me ill.

Between Hudson being gone and the pregnancy, I didn't want to think about Tanner. But now he's forced me to think about him. Forced me to remember all the ugly things he did to me. Said to me.

I growl low in my chest, balling my hands and tossing the paper violently on the ground.

Brooks kneels to pick it up. "Tell me what's wrong."

He straightens the paper, and his eyes grow, his burly chest expanding with one sharp, quick inhale.

"It's Tanner," I breathe.

"What?" he spits out through gritted teeth.

Tanner definitely has to be involved with Hudson's disappearance. The time that I got that first note from him felt too coincidental.

The cops have yet to tell me if he was found and interviewed, but even if he was, I bet he'd have found a way out of it. He's charming. Conniving. Everyone always believes Tanner.

"That fucking prick…" His voice sizzles with promise. And it makes me feel just a little bit safer, like I'm not alone.

I swallow past the lump in my throat. "I just want him to leave me alone."

"When I find him, he will. Don't you worry." He grabs my hand and brings the top of it to his mouth, his eyes falling to a close.

As soon as I feel his lips there, I yank my arm back on instinct. Because anyone else's lips on me like that, no matter how innocent, feels like I'm drowning in betrayal.

"I'm so sorry, Hadleigh." He sighs, his body sagging a little. "I hope you didn't take that the wrong way. I shouldn't have…"

He scrubs a hand down his face, and I instantly feel like I just turned an innocent act into something bigger.

"It's okay." I force a smile, hoping not to make an awkward situation worse. "I'm just extra on edge with everything going on with Tanner and not having Hudson here with me." I curl my arm around my belly.

"No, it's not your fault. It was mine. I overstepped, and it won't happen again."

Wordlessly, I pick up the mug and begin to sip, hoping I don't say anything else. Other than Elowen, he's the only other consistent friend I have. I can't ruin that.

"If it's alright with you," he says, "I want to start taking you to your doctor appointments. I don't want you having to go alone, especially with that asshole running loose."

I nod. "That'd be great. Thank you."

If I'm being honest, I was nervous about getting into the car by myself. Having someone there is safer.

"We have to go see that detective," he continues. "Tomorrow, maybe. I don't know why that prick hasn't been arrested yet."

"I'm sure it's because his parents paid off the cops."

"Is that right?" he scoffs. "Well, money doesn't solve everything."

Sixteen

HADLEIGH

Two days later, we're back at the police station, sitting across from Detective Tompkins.

"What can I do for you two today?" Her attention jumps between us.

My nerves skitter up my throat and my mouth flutters as I attempt to find the right words.

But Brooks is there, giving my hand a squeeze. "We're here to find out what the hell you've done about Tanner Cutwright. Have you even bothered to look for the son of a bitch?"

He stares at her with brutal force while her chin twitches a fraction.

"I would love to speak to Mister Cutwright," she drawls. "If we could find him."

I suck in a quick exhale. "So you don't even know where he is?"

"His family hasn't seen him for months, they told us. Neither have his friends. If he's in New York, he's doing some job of hiding from us."

"That scumbag went to her school!" Brooks bangs a fist across her desk, but she doesn't even flinch. "He gave one of her students a fucking note, and you're saying you can't find him?"

She inclines her chin. "We tried to verify that, and other than the child, whose parents haven't let him speak to us, we have no witnesses. We can't be sure it was him." She crosses her arms across her small chest, and this time when she gazes at me, her eyes soften just a little.

"Of course it's him! Who else would it be?" I spit the words out, completely sick of all of this.

They can't find Hudson. They can't even find Tanner. Can they do anything right?

"I *am* sorry, Mrs. Mackay. I wish I had better news. Believe it or not, I want to solve your husband's case as much as you do."

"Right," I snicker, my temples throbbing, a buzzing sound ramping in my brain.

Brooks slowly climbs to his feet, removes the letter from his pocket, and smacks it right on top of her desk. "He sent her another one."

Her eyes narrow as she casts him a glare, her hand snatching up the paper.

She shakes her head as she reads it, then looks up at me. "The problem is, nowhere does it say it is from him. But we will verify the handwriting."

When I open my mouth to tell her it definitely has to be him, she holds out a palm to stop me.

"I'm not doubting you. But as far as proof goes, this won't help me arrest him. If you see him, if he says or does something, call the police, take a photo if you're able to safely do so, and I can try convincing the DA to grant you a restraining order."

I nod, my body sagging. I'm tired. So damn tired. All I know is that Tanner will never stop. He'll torment me within the bounds of the law until I break.

Brooks gets to his feet. "If he does something again…" He drops both palms against the edge of her desk and leans in. "She won't need your help."

"What does that mean, Mr. Bardin?" Her gaze turns deadly.

"Wouldn't you like to know?"

He grabs my hand, and I rise, following him out, looking back at her unhappy expression as we go.

ONE WEEK LATER

I hate time. I hate that it passes. I hate that it vanishes without Hudson beside me. And most of all, I hate that I can't pause it, just long enough to get him back.

Because in my heart and in my soul, I know he's still out there, just waiting for me to find him and bring him home.

To us.

My arm instinctively wraps around my small belly, easily concealed with a loose shirt. But I have to start telling more people. I know that. Every time someone new finds out, it's like a cut to my already bleeding heart.

Yesterday, I told Melanie at school. She hugged me and told me how happy she was for me. What a great mom I'll be. I thanked her at the right times, smiled at the right moments, but inside, I was seething. Furious that the happiest moment of my life is blinded by sadness.

"You seem quiet," Iseult tells me, glancing my way from the driver's side.

When she called yesterday to tell me she was stopping by and taking me with her to visit her family in Cherry Grove, I didn't want to go. But you can't say no to someone like Iseult. She'll hound you until you have no choice but to accept whatever she's offering. I know this was her way to check in on me, to distract me long enough to forget why my life has been in shambles, and I love her for it.

"Got too much on my mind."

"Well, one minute with my shit show of a family, you're bound to forget your woes for at least five minutes." Her peacock eyes play as she cracks a smirk.

I laugh dryly. "Five minutes out of my head is a blessing."

"Then it's a good thing I'm taking you with me." She winks. "I'm still waiting for a thank-you."

She does all she can to get my mind off Hudson. Iseult doesn't do well with her own emotions, let alone someone else's. And she hates it when the people she cares about are hurting. She may not say it to your face, but she'll do anything to see those who matter to her happy. Iseult's heart is bigger than she lets on, and it's the most special thing about her.

"So, where's Gio?" I ask, seeing as how they've only been married for a couple of months, and I'd have expected him to travel with us.

"Oh, my lovely pain-in-the-ass husband went to Cherry Grove yesterday to help my brothers with something."

A laugh escapes me. "Pain in the ass already, huh?"

She grimaces as she glances at me before returning her attention to the road. "I mean, I thought we're friends, Hadleigh. Why didn't you warn me how annoying living with a man can be?"

"I'm sorry." I let out a small laugh. "Sometimes I'm an awful friend."

"Well, clearly. I mean, the man has the audacity to constantly cook for me, insist on feeding me, because apparently I don't have my own damn hands." She rolls her eyes. "Oh, to make things even worse…" She flings a hand in the air. "…he even runs me a bath every night, with, uh…a respectable amount of bubbles."

She clears her throat, which has me chuckling.

"Oh, you keep laughing," she warns, her expression deadpan yet hilarious all at once. "But if you tell anyone about that, I *will* have to kill you."

My laughter grows as her eyes turn to slits. "I promise I will absolutely never tell anyone about all those bubble baths you have with your husband."

She bows her brows while I bring my fingers to my mouth and pretend to zip them up.

"And…" she goes on, making a left turn, releasing a hefty sigh as she does. "He's always telling me I'm beautiful, to the point that if he weren't my husband, I'd have killed him by now. Because, I mean, it can't be normal to tell your wife she's pretty all the time, right? He must be insane. That has to be it. I married a lunatic."

I swear she looks terrified, even though I've never seen her afraid of a thing.

She once swore she'd never get married, but Gio wasn't having it. I knew that from the moment I saw the way he looked at her, the way he longed for her from across the room, even while he was arranged to marry her younger sister.

But Gio had no plans to obey anyone's plan for him. He made his own, and he made it with Iseult. He was exactly what she needed.

It warms my heart to see her happy. Because she *is* happy, even while that terrifies her.

"He doesn't sound like a lunatic at all. He sounds like a smart man. Someone who picked an amazing wife. So I fail to see the problem."

"That *is* the fucking problem!" She flips one hand in the air, using the other to turn the wheel as we ease to stop at a red light. "He's too good to be true! It's not normal. And..." She scowls, twisting her mouth to the side. "I kinda like being married to the idiot." She shakes her head and looks up at the roof for a moment. "What has become of me, Hadleigh?"

"Aww..." I slant my face sideways. "You're all grown up."

"Oh, shut up." She sniggers, swatting the back of her hand against my shoulder.

"It's a good thing, Iseult." I squeeze her forearm just as she eases down the road once more. "Marriage is beautiful and powerful. And when you've found the right person like you have, it's also special. Your love is special. So don't you dare be scared. Instead, hold on to one another in this cruel world." My heart tightens, a raw ache settling in the middle of my chest. "It's what I did."

Her eyes glaze over when she looks at me, then her demeanor shifts into something lighter. "No more sad shit. As soon as we get to my father's, we're taking some shots."

Um...should probably tell her that I can't exactly do that.

A few more minutes dwindle by, and we're pulling down a narrow road, toward a secured gate. The two men there nod at her and the doors instantly open to let us through. Driving down the rest of the path, we come into acres of land. A towering mansion in the center with more windows than I'm able to count greets us. Slightly smaller properties extend down each side.

Iseult and Gio decided to move to New York and live at his home in the suburbs, but she still comes to Cherry Grove a lot.

Easing into the driveway of her father's place, Iseult shuts off the car. Before we go in, though, I drop my hand on the top of hers.

She turns to me curiously.

"There's something I have to tell you."

Oh, God. I can't believe I'm doing this.

"What is it?" A line creases between her brows.

"I'm just going to say it because if I start thinking about how to say it, I'll lose the courage. I just—"

"Hadleigh, just tell me before I go crazy with worry. And believe me, you don't want to see me crazy."

I drag in a long, shallow breath.

"I'm pregnant." The words sound more like a whisper.

Wrenching her head back, she peers down at my belly. "What? How? I mean is it his…"

"Yes, of course it's his! How could you even ask me that?" My heart races at the mere fact that she thought I'd betray the love of my life.

"I'm sorry, that was stupid of me." She sighs. "I'm so damn happy for you."

She throws her arms around me and brings me tight against her.

"But I'm not." I confess the words out loud.

"What?" She pivots back, appearing confused.

"I know…" My voice drops. "It makes me seem like the most ungrateful person in the world. But I just miss Hudson and want him here for this." I sniffle as a wave of emotion hits me. "Without him, celebrating a child doesn't seem right."

"I'm so sorry." Her eyes glean with compassion. "So…no shots, then?"

I sniffle back a laugh. "Shut up, let's go in before I change my mind."

"You don't have to tell anyone." She opens the car door.

"They're all eventually going to find out." I follow her out.

"Keeping it a secret now seems pointless, you know?"

"I'm good with whatever you want to do."

I nod as we stride down toward Patrick's home, and the knots in my stomach grow. We make it up the three stone steps, and as soon as we're before the door, Gio opens it, a huge grin on his face when he sees her, his dark eyes swimming with affection.

"There's my gorgeous wife." His gaze glides down her body, and she rolls her eyes.

"Stop doing that." She strolls past him. "Stop calling me your wife every chance you get."

He doesn't let her get far, grabbing her wrist and pulling her flush against him.

"What happened, bambina?" His voice goes all sultry as their eyes clash, his knuckles rolling down her cheek. "Already forgot all the times I made you beg for it last night? Want me to remind you? Right here up against the wall?"

Her chest flails.

"We have company." She gestures toward me with a tilt of her head.

He grabs a fistful of her hair and brings her mouth to his, stroking his lips against hers. "I think you like a little company."

"Gio…"

"There she is." He smirks right before he kisses her, hard and fast, groaning as his other hand winds around her lower back.

Breathlessly, he stares at her intensely while she mirrors the passion in his gaze. And I'm not sure if I should pretend I don't exist so they can continue having their moment or scurry out of view.

"Hey, Hadleigh." Gio finally realizes I exist. "Sorry about my wife." His mouth curls salaciously. "She can be a little temperamental sometimes. It's a constant state of making the woman fall back in love with me, ya know?" He yanks her closer as she attempts to escape. "But a man has to try. Isn't that right, baby?"

She grimaces, but I don't miss the little twitch on her lips.

"Fuck, I love her." He grabs a handful of her fiery red hair once again and gives her a quick kiss.

"I'm glad you guys have each other," I tell them as an ache pounds in my chest, missing Hudson all over again.

Iseult instantly gives him an *are you kidding me* face, like they're hurting me by being happy. And sure, in a way, it is painful, but I couldn't be happier that she found someone who completes her like Gio has.

Gio's expression grows tight as he reverts his full attention to me. "I'm very sorry about Hudson. We're all doing everything we can. In fact, I want you to meet with my friend Grant Westbrook. He—"

"Westbrook? Like the phone?"

He chuckles. "Yep. Same bastard."

The Westbrooks own a cell phone company—among other things, I'm sure. They're an incredibly wealthy family. I had no idea Gio knew them.

"Anyway…" he goes on. "He knows what's going on and is trying to see how he can help track Hudson down, but he may need your help to fill in some blanks about Hudson's past."

"Okay, yeah." My heart skips a beat, and fresh hope swells in my chest. "I'll do whatever needs to be done. Just let me know where to go, and I will see him as soon as he wants."

"Good. I'll have Iseult text you his info."

She quickly removes her phone and starts typing. "Done."

She smiles just as a ping arrives to my phone.

"Thanks. I'll call him tomorrow."

Maybe this is it. Maybe I'll finally find him.

"Come on, let's go say hi to everyone," she says.

And together, they start further into the house while I stand there wondering…

"Do you think he's still alive?" The question rolls out before I can stop it.

They both turn toward me. Iseult's mouth quivers while Gio's features bloom with concentration.

"I don't know," he admits. "But I hope he is. He's a good man."

"I hope so too." I cradle my belly.

His eyes drop to the movement right before they expand.

"Oh…shit," he mutters when he catches Iseult's crestfallen expression.

Now, another person knows the truth.

The following day, I ride up the elevator to the thirtieth floor, hoping Grant can help me locate Hudson. His office is in Midtown, not a far trip from my Upper East Side apartment.

The doors open, and a woman with short auburn hair greets me with a smile. "Name, please?"

"Hadleigh Mackay. I have an appointment."

"Of course, you may proceed straight ahead into Mr. Westbrook's office. He's ready for you."

"Thanks." I turn on my heels and head a few short steps toward the double brown doors.

Turning the knob, I push it open, seeing a man my age. His bright blue eyes are a bit darker than Hudson's, and he greets me with a welcoming grin, his dress shirt a deep shade of plum.

The city glistens behind him, the floor-to-ceiling windows allowing for a breathtaking view.

"Please have a seat, Mrs. Mackay. Would you like anything to drink before we start?"

"No, thank you. I just appreciate you seeing me so quickly."

I called him hours ago, and he made time for me.

"Of course." He runs his thick fingers through his jet-black hair. "Any friend of Gio is a friend of mine."

"You don't know how much this means to me. The police haven't been much help thus far."

"Well, the police operate within the colors of the law, but me? I trample across that line just a little." His mouth lines with a wicked smirk. "Now, if that bothers you, I won't be able to be much help."

"No!" I rapidly shake my head.

I don't care how many laws he has to break. I'll help him.

"How you do what you do is none of my business. I just want to find my husband for my sake and the sake of our baby."

"Baby…" His stare widens. "I see."

"Yeah, I can't have this baby alone."

"I understand. I'll do everything I can."

"So, Gio said you wanted me to fill in some blanks about Hudson?"

"That's right." He crosses his arms against his chest. "I was hoping to get a hold of any possible journals or appointment books or even laptops he's used that the cops haven't taken. Sometimes there are clues there that everyone misses."

"I'll look through his home office. I'll get you anything you need."

"Good." He nods. "But, Mrs. Mackay, I need you to understand that I may uncover things about your husband you may not want to hear. Are you prepared for that?"

My heart pounds. "I know my husband. Whatever you could tell me doesn't scare me."

He leans back and stares for a second. "Everyone wants to

believe that, but it's not always what happens. So I want you to be prepared just in case." His unwavering gaze deepens. "How well did you really know him?"

My mind spins, circling through every memory we shared, and with all the confidence I can muster, I say, "Well enough to know that he'd never leave me willingly."

"Let's hope you're right."

In that instant, I hear Detective Tompkins's voice say, "*You didn't know your husband.*"

And I start to wonder if she was actually right.

Seventeen

HADLEIGH

A s soon as I arrive back home, I rush for Hudson's study, finding everything just as he left it.

The cleaning lady comes every two weeks to keep the dust at bay. But I haven't stepped foot inside since he's been gone. Too afraid of the emotions it'd invoke. But right now, my focus is on finding whatever Grant needs to help locate Hudson.

Rounding the corner of his desk, I settle on his black swivel chair, running my fingertips against the cold black leather before I'm opening the top drawer.

Spotting two files, I take them out and look through them, not finding anything remotely helpful. Two legal motions in one folder and a memo to a partner in the other.

Closing one drawer, I go into the other. Everything is neatly stacked, with more folders than I can count. I remove them all, going through each one, then the ones in the opposite drawer until there's a stack of useless papers in front of me. The police have his home laptop, so I can't go through that.

Getting to my feet, I go to the floor-to-ceiling bookshelf, running my fingers over the gold letters of a thick book on corporate law. My heart sinks into my stomach when I realize I have nothing. Not one shred of information to give Grant.

Frustration overtakes me until my body is screaming, needing to break something, to destroy something.

With a deafening shout, I rip the book out of the shelf and toss it on the floor. And before I know what's happening, I grab another, hurling it across the room while my pulse pounds, my body humming with rage and fear and loss.

Without another bloodcurdling cry, I remove book after book, throwing each one across the room, wanting to rip the pages, wanting to destroy everything. A heavy book hits a vase on the shelf on the opposite side, glass shattering everywhere.

"How could you leave me?!" I snivel. "How?!"

Tears burn within my eyes, tracking slowly down my cheeks as I forcefully yank another book out, throwing it hard on the floor.

And as I do, something falls out of it.

With my chest heaving, my eyes blurry, I kneel to pick it up, realizing it's an envelope.

With my name on it.

In Hudson's writing.

I lower to the floor, my heart bleeding as I open it, needing something, anything from him. Needing for him to find a way back to me somehow.

Slowly, I unfold it and see the date from eight months ago. As I begin to read it, I can't help the tears that fall, one after another.

Dear Butterfly,

I once read that one's wedding should be the lowest point of their marriage. That every day after should be better and better. And I know for a fact that a life with you has been the highlight of my life. Every day, I wonder how our love can become stronger, and with each passing year, somehow it does.

I can't really tell you where I read this or if I'm subconsciously making it up, but I swear someone smarter than me said it. We can always pretend I'm that smarter person. I don't mind.

I laugh, swiping my nose as I continue.

I have many regrets in my life. But being your husband has never been one of them.

Have I been a good one? Have I told you I loved you enough? Did I show you enough?

I hope that in these years together, I have been enough. Because you have been everything.

I need you to know that no matter what happens, I'll always love you. No matter where I go or when, I'll find you and I'll always watch out for you, even when I'm not here to do it myself.

If soulmates exist, I know you're mine. You always were, from the moment I met you.

A shiver races up my back. Why did he write that? Why did it sound like he knew he was leaving me?

You're my family. The only person I have in this universe, and I'm lucky that you've chosen me to be yours.

I don't even know why I'm writing these letters when I never intend for you to read them. But in some way, it makes me feel good to pretend I'm spilling everything to you. A purge, so to speak. Maybe one day I'll have the guts to give these letters to you, but for now, they'll stay in hiding, like I have been.

The only person who's known the real me is Brooks. I have wanted to tell you so many times. I'd rehearse it in my head, but every time I tried to get the words out, I'd see you walking away, and I couldn't, Hadleigh. Because I can't live without you. Not in this world, and not in any in between.

But I need you to know who I am. I need you to know that I'm a killer. I never intended to murder anyone. But nineteen years ago, when I was sixteen, I did.

What…? My breath catches.

I wish I could tell you it was the worst thing I did, but I'd be lying. But here in this letter, I only speak the truth. Because you're not here to see my shame.

And that's not all.

There's more I've been lying about.

Like my identity.

You've always known me as Hudson Mackay.

But I used to go by another name. I was once Holden, but he died with my sin, only to be reborn into someone much worse.

And I'm sorry you had to marry him.

Hudson

Gasping, I feel my hands shake, my body full of tremors as I try to wrap my head around what I just read. Because there's no way Hudson wrote that. No way he spent years of our life using a name that wasn't his, talking about killing someone?! Hudson would never hurt a fly. He was gentle.

With me…

Thump.

Thump.

My heartbeats pound, fear skirting up my spine.

In this moment, I remember the way he grabbed Henry on my birthday. The way he sounded…

That was someone else, wasn't it? That wasn't Hudson.

But I brushed it off. He was defending my honor, after all.

But what if I was just blind? What if I was seeing what I wanted to see?

What if he really did work for the Mob?

You didn't know your husband.

I realize now, she was right.

There's a knock at my door the next day while my cell goes off simultaneously.

Staring at the ceiling, the letter Hudson wrote crumbled in my fist, I ignore both. I was up all night, racing thoughts getting in the way of sleep.

How could I sleep when my entire world—entire *marriage*—was a lie?

He wrote those words. It was his handwriting.

He lied about so much. What else has he lied about?

"Hadleigh!" There's a louder knock on the door. "Open up! I'm supposed to drive you to the doctor today, remember?"

"Crap," I mutter, rubbing my face with the back of my hand.

I completely forgot about it. But I don't want to look at Brooks, knowing he knew all of Hudson's secrets and kept them from me. That's what Hudson said in the letter, isn't it?

The only person who's known the real me is Brooks.

With my pulse slamming in my ears, I jump off the bed and sprint toward the door. As soon as I open it, I find Brooks standing there with a soft smile on his face. The one he's come to wear for me.

But once he sees my expression, that same smile vanishes.

"What's wrong?" His brows gather.

When he takes a single step forward, grabbing my hand, I yank it back, anger surging in my gut.

"How could you lie to me?!" My voice is harsher than he's ever heard.

I don't feel like the same woman I was before I discovered the letter. The hurt has taken over and refuses to let me go.

"Hadleigh? What's going on?" He takes another step and my eyes narrow.

Clenching my teeth, I give him my back and let him follow me inside. The door slams closed, his footfalls getting nearer.

My breathing gets louder. I'm too furious to speak. How could he keep me in the dark, especially since everything Hudson's been hiding could very well have something to do with why he's missing?

Or dead...

But I don't let my subconscious win. I have to continue to believe Hudson is alive. That there's a chance he can come back to me.

Two hands fall to my shoulders, and I have no energy to fight them off. I'm close to losing it completely. Breaking into pieces I won't have the strength to put back together.

"What did I do?" he asks with a barely there whisper. "Talk to me. I don't want you stressing. I read it's bad for the baby."

He read about that? The sting to my chest comes swiftly, wanting Hudson to be the one who's reading about my pregnancy. Wanting his hands on me. Yet he's not here. Instead, all he's left me with is secrets and lies.

I turn around to face Brooks and level him a glare. "He wrote me a letter. Did you know that?"

He shakes his head very slowly, eyes inquisitively taking me in. "What sort of letter?"

I scoff. "The kind that told me that his real name is Holden. That you knew! That he murdered someone when he was sixteen! That there were other things he's done." My exhales lurch out of me. "He told me you're the only one who really knew him! And you kept it all from me! I told you to tell me everything!"

"Hadleigh…" His voice drops, his face sagging.

And I know instantly: it's all true.

I rush toward him, face inches from his, tears welling in my eyes. Raising a clenched fist, I slam it against his chest.

"Why?" My chin trembles, vision clouded. "Why didn't you tell me once he disappeared? You had so many chances after! Why did you keep the truth from me? I deserved to know! This could've helped find him!"

In a flash, he grabs my wrist, cinching his fingers, his charcoal eyes boring into mine as he yanks me closer. He grinds his jaw, staring heavy with emotion.

"I'm sorry." He sighs and his harsh expression softens. "He's my friend, and it wasn't my place to tell you."

I tug my arm back, and he lets it go.

"What else are you keeping from me? What else was he hiding?" I move backward, my throat clogged with betrayal.

He shuts his eyes and runs a hand down his face. And when he stares back at me, it's through the eyes of a broken man.

"Tell me! Tell me who he killed! Tell me everything, Brooks. Please," I cry, my resolve shattering even more.

"Hadleigh…" His strides cut through the distance until he's in front of me again. Taking my hands in his, he looks me right in the eyes. "Fuck, I can't believe I'm about to talk about this. But I can't lie to you now that you know. Let's sit down, alright?"

My heart still races and my body shakes with adrenaline, but when he tugs my hand toward the living room, I follow until we're both seated.

He turns to face me, and with a quick glance up to the ceiling, he starts to speak. "I met Hudson when we were ten. We were both in the same foster home, and—"

"Wait a minute…" I hold out a palm, stopping him. "Foster home?" My gaze widens. "Hudson told me he lived with his uncle after his parents died."

"No." He shakes his head. "His uncle gave him up when he was six."

"Oh my God." My teeth sink around my lower lip, my heart breaking for a little boy I never knew.

To be a child, to feel unwanted…what that must've done to him.

"Eventually the couple who fostered us adopted us. Things were great at first. Hudson and I got along once we got to know each other. Marcella and Pietro were nice to us too. Their house was big enough for both of us to have our own room. We were happy. Neither of us remembered being happy." His mouth slants up a fraction, melancholy gripping his gaze. "But then things slowly got worse."

My stomach sinks, anticipating the worst. "What happened?"

"It started subtly. First they'd yell at us if we didn't finish our dinner or if we made a mess. Then the yelling turned to beatings and starvation."

"Oh my God…" I clasp a hand around my mouth.

"I don't know if I should be telling you this." He releases a rough breath. "I don't like seeing you this upset."

"No. It's fine." I shake my head. "Please, continue."

He sighs. "They'd beat us. Lock us up in our rooms and not let us out for days sometimes. Other than a bottle of water, they'd leave us nothing. Once they decided to let us out, they'd smile as though they were giving us a gift. That bitch used to pat us on the head and tell us to behave so she didn't have to do that to us again."

His nostrils enlarge and his eyes cast in the distance, as though he's remembering.

"I'm so sorry." My face crumbles, and on instinct, I lower a palm to his forearm, feeling heartsick for what he endured. What they both endured.

He stares down where my hand meets his flesh, and his chest grows with a deep, silent breath.

"Don't be." He stares back at me. "We survived. They didn't." A cold grin tugs up both corners of his mouth.

My stomach turns. Those people sound like they deserved it; still, the thought of ending anyone's life makes me sick.

"We endured years of their abuse," he continues. "Trying to defend the other when one of us was getting hurt. But all that did was get both of our asses kicked and then locked up in our rooms. By the time we were sixteen, we were bigger than them. Stronger, too. So, we decided enough was enough. We both did it."

My pulse speeds up, picturing how they could've killed them, but I don't need to know. "And the bodies...?"

"We buried them. But right before Hudson disappeared..."

His eyes grow distant again, and I scurry closer.

"What? What happened?"

"The bodies... They were found."

I gasp. "Did they find any evidence? Does someone know?"

"I don't think so, or I'd be arrested. But Hudson found out when he saw it on the news and showed me. Two bodies being dug out."

"Oh my God! I remember that. We saw it together. And the way he appeared... I—I just thought it was work-related. But then he reassured me it was just the area that looked familiar from long ago. I took his word for it. I should've pressed. I—"

"Hadleigh, no. Don't do that." He clasps the top of my hand with his. "He would never have told you. There were plenty of times I urged him to tell you, that you'd understand, but he was afraid the truth would make you run."

Would I have? I may have been upset about him not telling me his real name, but I don't think I'd have been mad at what he did. He was just a child who was abused most of his life. How fair would it be of me to judge him for that?

"And Holden. Why did he change his name?"

"We both did. I used to be Benjamin Hansley. Patrick helped both of us start a new life, to leave that part of our past behind us."

"Patrick?" Stunned, I blink back.

He nods slowly. "Yeah, the Quinns are powerful people. They're *the* Mob, Hadleigh. They have connections, and those connections helped Hudson."

"My God..." I swallow down the bile rising in my throat. "So the detective wasn't lying..."

"She wasn't." He shakes his head. "I just couldn't tell you. I'm sorry."

He looks sorry. I can't blame him for that. It wasn't his mess. It was Hudson's.

"It was Patrick who paid for him to go to college and the best law school," he continues.

"How did Hudson meet the Quinns? He always told me it was from work."

"Fuck, I feel like I'm betraying him by telling you all of this." He presses two fingers into his temple. "I don't want you to hate him, okay? He did what he thought was right. He loved you. His only mission in life was to keep you safe."

"I know that." A fragment of a smile trembles out of me. "I'd never doubt that. None of this changes anything. Hudson will forever be the love of my life. Nothing can take that away, but I need to know everything."

He nods. "What you two had is special."

"Have," I correct him. "What we *have*. He's not dead." Tears sting my eyes at the thought. "I will find him, and we will work through everything. Together."

"Of course." He squeezes my hand. "I have no doubt that he's out there trying to fight his way back to you."

"Thanks, Brooks. I appreciate you being here."

"No need." His thumb rubs circles over my knuckles. "Always."

I clear my throat, gently sliding my hand out of his grasp. "So, the Quinns…"

"Right… After we got rid of our adoptive parents, we lived on the street and had to steal food just to survive. Unfortunately, one time, that got Hudson thrown in juvie for a few months—"

"Juvie?" I run a trembling hand through my hair.

"Should I stop?" Concern fits his dark eyes.

"No, don't you dare."

"Alright." He nods, looking at me like I'm this fragile thing that'll break at any moment.

But I'm not some weak woman, and I hate that it's how Brooks sees me. How Hudson saw me too.

"Patrick got him out of prison early because Hudson saved the life of another kid, who ended up being Patrick's nephew, and that's how it all started."

My head spins, trying to process it, trying to remember Hudson through new eyes, while knowing all this about him. "And at his job, did he ever kill anyone? I remember the detective said Evan was killed because of him."

"No, he never killed anyone. Not directly…"

"So he was somehow involved?" My voice drops, eyes growing. "He got Evan killed?"

I can't stop shaking.

"Hadleigh, you need to understand…he's the lawyer to the Mafia, the Mob, the cartel… Fuck." He laughs dryly. "He represented the scariest motherfuckers you'd ever meet. So yeah, sometimes he had to do some things he wasn't proud of to save his own ass. Don't judge him for that. He was doing his best. It's the hand that he was dealt, and he played his cards the best he could."

I can't believe this. He got someone killed. How many others were there?

I start to rise. "I just need time to process all of this."

Moving toward the kitchen, I hear Brooks's footsteps behind me.

"Take all the time you need. This is a lot. I get it," he replies as I reach into the fridge for a bottle of water. "Were there any other letters?"

Slowly facing him, I take a big sip before I answer. "No. Should there be?"

He shrugs. "I was just wondering."

I consider that for a moment, and I realize there very well could be more hidden somewhere.

"How could I know nothing about the man I married?" I muse. "I feel so betrayed."

But I instantly feel guilty for even thinking such thoughts, because no matter what, I still love Hudson with all my heart, and I'll never stop.

Does that make me a bad person, to love someone who was involved in awful things?

"You'll get through this. You're strong." His mouth flickers. "Now, how about I take you to that doctor's appointment? You'll be a little late, but I'm sure the doc will still take you."

"Yeah, I'll call them and then get changed. Thank you for taking me." I inhale a deep breath. "With Tanner still out there, I'm just…"

Afraid.

"Always. Never have to ask. You're family, and family always takes care of each other. Hudson taught me that."

After I return from the doctor, I head back to Hudson's office. Books lie scattered across the floor. Releasing a weighty sigh, I attempt to start cleaning the mess I created.

It's then I recall what Brooks had said about the letters—that there could be more—and maybe they're here, waiting to be discovered.

As I pick up a book, I start flicking through the pages, hoping to find another letter. But six books in, I'm close to giving up.

Grabbing another, I head for the shelf. But as I do, something falls out of it.

An envelope.

My name written in Hudson's handwriting.

My limbs shake, my pulse slamming in my throat.

I don't know if I'm ready to read what else he wrote. But before I know it, I'm ripping off the flap, removing a folded paper and reading the words over and over until I know them by heart.

Eighteen

HUDSON
SEVEN MONTHS AGO

Dear Butterfly,

You have no idea that as I'm writing this letter,
I'm also staring at you while you're dancing with
your headphones on, wiping the dinner table.

Fuck, you have a nice ass. And after I'm done
writing, I plan to bend you over that table,
grab that soft hair in my palm, and fuck you
until we're both breathless.

But for now, I'll just stare at you and thank the universe for giving me you. The worst thing is, I know you deserve better. I just hope you never realize that.

You're nothing like me, and that's a good thing. I know your heart, and it's beautiful. Everything about you is.

You'll be an amazing mother one day, and I want to believe that you will be, with or without me.

I know how much pain you're in, wanting a child the way you do. The disappointment and grief you go through every month. And fuck, baby, I want to tell you we should stop. That it's not worth the agony you suffer. But I can't say those words out loud because I know you'll hate me for them.

And here in my letters, I can be honest. I can tell you that I never wanted to become a father. I never wanted a child of my own. But when we met, I fell in love for the first time, and I swore from that moment that what I wanted didn't matter. I wanted to live my life making you happy because that made me happy.

You're like the key that opened my heart and

gave it life. Because before you, I was walking through hell. No hope. No real future. But you gave me both. And now... I want a baby, Hadleigh. I want one so goddamn bad, it hurts.

I want a little you and me. I want to hold him or her in my arms. I want to have another person to protect. Someone I know I'd love just as much because they would be half you.

So I'm sorry, Hadleigh. I'm sorry we can't have that. Maybe it's the universe punishing me for everything I've done.

A murderer.

A sinner.

Maybe some aren't meant to have it all. Maybe you're better off without me. Maybe if I wasn't around, you'd meet someone else and you'd have that child with a man who deserves you more than I do.

But it kills me to even imagine another man touching you. The things I want to do... Fuck, Hadleigh. Maybe I'm too selfish to ever let you have it all. Because you're my everything, and I want to be yours.

Forgive me.

Hudson

I fold the letter up and stick it in my briefcase, hoping to hide it in one of the books in my office. Hadleigh barely ever steps foot inside. She never even goes near the shelves.

As soon as she turns around, she yanks her headphones off her ears, her hair in a short ponytail, her cheeks slightly pink, face bare from makeup.

Beautiful.

Like a perfect sculpture molded in the heavens and gifted to me on earth.

My heart does that thing it always does when she looks at me with that affectionate grin, her eyes gleaming with love. So much of it, I can feel it fill my veins.

"Hey, handsome. How long have you been there, staring at me like you're about to eat me for dinner?"

I chuckle, slowly rising, nearing her as she pops a brow, and throws a palm on her hip.

Looping my arm around her, I pull her body up against me. "Dinner. Dessert. It's all the same when it comes to you." I drop my lips to the corner of hers. "I'd devour you for every meal if I could, baby, and die with the taste of you on my tongue. You're everything I need. Without you, I'm a starving man."

She moans under her breath, moving her hips against my growing erection, her lips brushing slowly with mine in the most seductive way. "I could never let my man starve."

"Is that right?"

No one knows the real Hadleigh behind closed doors. The way she begs. The way she takes my cock. How rough she likes it. I like having that woman all to myself, knowing she's that way with me alone.

I nip her lower lip, and before she can utter a word, I flip her around and bend her over the cold table. My palm presses into her cheek as she groans while I roughly yank down her sweats.

"Fuck…" I growl when I find her bare. "I love it when you don't wear panties."

"Why's that?" She tries to sound all innocent while she gyrates her hips as my hand slides between her warm thighs, my palm working her clit.

She's wet and slick against my rough touch.

"Because it makes it so easy to get inside you, and I love getting inside you." I drop my lips to her shoulder, my teeth grazing her skin while two fingers slowly thrust, inch by inch.

She cries out my name, begging me for release.

"Watching you come is my favorite thing." I raise up her simple white t-shirt, my lips peppering kisses up her spine. "You're gonna come for me again and again, aren't you, butterfly?"

"Yes," she gasps with a croaky moan when I pinch her clit.

"That's a good fucking girl." I ram my fingers back inside her, slow and deep. "Give me one before you come on my tongue."

When I curl my fingers and hit her G-spot, her hands tense and spread across the table, her face turned to me, her moans louder.

"You're so goddamn beautiful," I husk out, rounding my hand around her throat, fastening my fingers over her erratic pulse.

Bending myself over her body, I take her lips in a brutal kiss. While I slam my fingers deeper, my tongue dances with hers, those feminine sounds of pleasure twined with my own animalistic need.

My thumb plays with her clit while I suck her tongue into my mouth, growling as she comes undone, spilling across the floor like only I can make her.

I push off her, flipping her around onto her back, and grab the backs of her knees. Lifting her pussy to my mouth, I feast on my wife the way a husband should.

HADLEIGH
PRESENT DAY

The tears run free as I read the last sentence of his letter, recalling in vivid detail the way we made love that very day. I remember it well.

The way he took me and owned me and cared for me. He always did that. Put me first in all aspects of our life.

I miss him. I miss him too goddamn much. I ball that letter up and I cry long and hard, wanting to go back in time and relive all the good days and even the bad, just for one more moment.

Nineteen

HADLEIGH
THREE DAYS LATER

M ore days have come and gone, and I've done all I can to accept the things Hudson said to me in those letters. Both of them are now safely tucked in my nightstand, where I can read them whenever I miss him.

I never did find any others, but I hope there are more. It's all I have of him.

I listen to the voicemail he left me every day. Still call his phone to hear his voice. And I still unravel when I hear him. Still break down when no one ever answers. When no one ever calls back.

I phoned Grant and told him I didn't find anything that could help him in his search. Maybe that makes me an awful wife. But the last thing I want to do is get Hudson or Brooks into legal trouble.

If giving Grant that information could land them in prison for murder, then how did I really help? It's best that no one but the three of us knows what happened all those years ago.

Grant swore he'd do everything in his power to find Hudson, and I know like everyone else, he's trying his best.

The Quinns have been unable to find him either. And seeing as how all these people are looking for him and unable to get any answers, it worries me. Maybe, just maybe, his body is undiscoverable. Knowing what I know now, that wouldn't be a stretch.

Sitting on my sofa with a fruit smoothie in hand, I dial Iseult's number, needing to ask about the stuff I learned about the Quinns.

Not that I doubt Brooks, but I want to hear her say it. I want her to admit she lied to me when I first asked.

Now, a normal person who learns that her friend's family may be the Mob would say nothing at all, but at this point, normalcy doesn't exist anymore. My husband has another identity, he and his best friend are killers, and my husband is friends with criminals. Life is great. Why not make it worse?

But if I don't say something, it's going to eat at me, and I'll never be able to be myself around her.

"Hey, Hadleigh. Is everything okay?" It sounds like she's driving, the air whooshing around her.

"Can we talk? It's important."

"Hold on, let me close the damn window. I probably sound like I'm in a tunnel."

Seconds later, that sound is gone.

"So, what's going on? Who do I have to kill? Is Tanner writing those fucking notes again, because I swear to God, I'm gonna…"

A shiver races up my spine. "Uh, no. This is not about Tanner."

Stillness echoes between us while I find the right words.

"I found a letter from Hudson." Pause. "He…he told me

everything."

Silence. Thick, heavy silence.

"Iseult? Did you hear me?"

"I mean, sure, I heard you. But I have no fucking idea what you're talking about. Told you what? Is it something to help us find him?"

My heart speeds up, ramming against my rib cage. "It's about your family."

How the hell do I say it out loud?

"What *about* my family?" Her tone goes darker than I've ever heard it.

My gut tightens and a tremor runs past my limbs.

"You didn't tell me the truth about who your family is. How you met Hudson." A weighty sigh leaves my lungs. "I know about juvie, and I know… I know your father is part of the Mob." I whisper the last part. "I know you lied to me when I asked you if Hudson was involved with that…stuff."

"He's what?" She acts all nonchalant, but I'm done buying everyone's bullshit.

"Stop that! I'm sick of everyone hiding things from me! I expected more from you, Iz. I expected you to level with me, especially after I lost Hudson."

She huffs out a breath. "This really isn't a conversation I'd like to have on the phone, but I'm nowhere near New York, and I have a feeling you're not in a patient mood."

"Not even a little. So start talking."

"Look at you, being all demanding and shit. I like this Hadleigh. More of her, please." Even with everything going on, she somehow manages to make me smile.

"Come on, Iz. Just tell me. Is any of it true?"

"Fuck me," she mutters. "Fine. But remember you asked for it. I'm not going to sit here and deny it anymore. I, for one, told

Hudson to tell you, but he didn't think you could handle the truth of our world. So yes, Hadleigh, my family is exactly who you think they are. I'm officially welcoming you to the family. I'd hug you and offer you a shot, but I can't do either, so here we are."

"Oh, God," I groan. "So it's true?"

I swallow past the thick ball of nerves stuck in my throat.

"Iseult Marino, are you seriously telling me that your family is the actual Mob? Like, *the* Mob?"

"I mean…there's only one Mob, so…yeah. We're it, baby."

"Jesus! What else are you gonna tell me? That you're some crazy assassin who murders people for a living?"

"Actually…"

"No!" My eyes widen as I shake my head, disbelief clouding my vision. "No way. Izzy, no way in hell…"

My head spins. She can't be.

But a lot makes sense now. Her *fuck you* attitude. The way she carries herself, like she can snap you like a twig. That's because she can! I can't figure out if I should be afraid of her or turned on.

"I could lie to you," she goes on. "But I think we're all tired of that, aren't we?"

"No. I—I mean yes." I huff, placing the long-forgotten smoothie on the end table beside me.

"Okay, look, you can't say a word to anyone. You understand that, right? Now that you know, you have to pretend you don't. Having this knowledge is dangerous. It's why Hudson didn't want you to know."

I run a shivery hand down my face. "It's obvious he didn't want me to know a lot of things. Is there anything else I need to know?"

"Yeah. My husband is in the Mafia," she throws out as though she just gave me a weather forecast.

"Oh! Well, that's great! At least he isn't in the dark like I've been my whole marriage."

"You can't think that way. Hudson did what he had to. He loves you."

"I know that." I release a defeated exhale. "It's just been a lot. Between why he went to juvie, how your father gave him a new name, then this whole thing with your family."

"Wow, he really told you everything."

I don't want her to know that Brooks told me the things about her family. Don't need any of the Quinns coming after him for being honest.

"So, how many have you, you know…" I don't want to actually say the word murdered.

No big deal. Just asking a friend how many people she's taken out.

"Come on, Hadleigh," she chuckles. "You don't ask a woman that."

Of course not.

Because that number is probably high.

THREE WEEKS LATER

I can't believe I'm a couple weeks from halfway through my pregnancy. The days just flash on by while I'm stagnant, living in the past.

But I'm trying. I force myself to go out to eat with Elowen. To see friends when I can. I smile and laugh and do all the things people expect you to do so you can pretend you're not dying inside.

But I am dying.

Slowly withering away.

Once I get home, it's instant regret. How can I laugh or smile or live my life while he's out there somewhere? What kind of person does that make me?

"Are you okay?" Brooks asks, making a slow right as we head back to my home from my OB appointment.

"Yeah. I'm just, you know…" I raise both shoulders.

It feels like a lie to tell people I'm okay when I'm clearly not.

"I know." His eyes grow sympathetic. "You never have to explain it to me."

The one good thing is that the baby is doing well. He has all his fingers and toes, his heart is strong, and he's passed all the tests so far. It's surreal seeing him on the sonogram. Seeing his little legs moving inside me. Hudson would've loved to be there. Knowing he wanted a baby, that I wasn't the only one who wanted us to have a family… My heart physically aches.

And there I go, thinking about him again.

But it's impossible not to. He's been the center of my world for quite some time.

Brooks's phone goes off, and he puts it on speaker. "Hey, Adalyn."

He grins, his eyes lighting up. I'm glad that things are still going strong for them.

"Hey, babe! Are you coming to pick me up?"

I tilt my head toward him.

He whispers a curse and digs two fingers into his eyes. "Ah, damn it. I'm so sorry. I completely forgot."

Her sharp intake of breath is hard to miss. "I told you I needed a ride to pick up my car from the garage. You *told* me you'd help! What the hell? Where are you?"

"Ugh, look, I needed to drive Hadleigh to the doctor, and now I've gotta go and put a crib together for her."

She laughs bitterly. "Are you fucking kidding me right now? You're with her *again*?! You're with her more than you're with me! I swear, sometimes I wonder why the hell we're still together!"

My mouth pops open. I had no idea I was interfering in his relationship. Of course I didn't! Because I've been selfish, allowing him to be there for me constantly. That has to stop.

"Adalyn, I'm sor—" he attempts.

Click.

"Brooks…"

"Don't say a word. This isn't your fault." His eyes remain on the road. "She's grown too clingy lately. Talking about marriage and kids. I mean…" He scoffs. "I haven't known her that long. I don't know if she's the one or anything." He glances at me then. "How did you know Hudson was the one?"

A huge grin spreads across my face, and my body warms. I stare distantly, wrapped in the memories of us.

"It was the first time in a long time I felt safe."

He sighs. "Can't say Adalyn makes me feel much of anything lately. If anything, she scares the fuck out of me."

"How so?"

"I don't know. She's just been too obsessed lately. Wants to know my every move."

"She's probably just upset you're around me a lot. I mean, from that phone call, it was obvious."

"I don't care. If she can't be the least bit understanding about the situation, then I don't need her."

"What are you saying?"

"I'm saying I'm gonna end it with her. Don't want to waste any of her time or mine."

"But you seemed so happy with her. I hope this isn't because of me."

"Of course not." His brows furrow as he glances at me for a moment. "It's because of her." He pulls the car into park across from my building. "Now, let's get that crib assembled."

I realize he wants to change the subject, so I let it go.

"Sooo…" I slant a brow. "Are you sure you know what you're doing?"

"I mean, I think so." He offers me a crooked smile and laughs.

"You think so? Should I be afraid?" I follow him while he clicks a button on his remote and shuts the car.

"With me? Probably." He chuckles deeply as we stride across the street.

Together, we head up to my place, where another man is going to help me set up my baby's room, while I'm wishing my husband was doing it instead.

TWENTY

HADLEIGH
THREE MONTHS LATER

"**I** can't believe how cute you are pregnant." Melanie scoffs playfully. "When I was pregnant, I looked like a whale who swallowed a whale. But you? Seriously, a damn supermodel."

"Yeah, okay…" I waddle and settle onto the sofa. "A supermodel. Sure…" Snickering, I take a sip of my ice water. "My feet look like two balloons. I just want this baby out, and I still have nine weeks left."

Iseult settles beside me, swallowing her wine while throwing an arm around me. "I hope you know those weeks are going to go super slow."

I narrow my gaze at her. "Wow, are you trying to help or make me feel worse?"

"I'm just saying, when my aunt was pregnant, she told me that the last few weeks are torture."

"Again, not helping." I grimace.

"I'd say I'm sorry, but..." She shrugs with a laugh. "Hey, at least you look like a supermodel…with beach balls for feet."

"You're terrible." I shake my head with an amused glare.

"Yeah. You still love me, though." She tilts up her chin with a raised brow.

"Not at the moment, I don't." I switch over to my virgin piña colada and take a big gulp, looking around my place.

The apartment has been decorated for a baby shower thrown by Elowen, who's currently trying to make her daughter, Cassidy, eat.

I didn't expect a party. It was the last thing on my mind, but Elowen insisted, saying that after everything I've been through, I deserved to celebrate.

Watching my coworkers and friends—all ten of them—having a good time makes me glad I decided to have the shower.

The doorbell rings, and when I attempt to rise to my feet to see who it could be, Iseult clasps a hand on my knee.

"I'll get it, you sit and let those poor feet rest."

"Alright, fine. You win."

"Didn't seem like much of a fight." She laughs, getting to the door, and when she opens it, I find my doorman there.

"Hello, Mrs. Mackay." He waves as he peeks past Iseult. "I have a delivery for you."

"Thanks, Willie." I wave with a grin as he hands Iseult an envelope.

"You guys have a good day and a great party." His brown eyes crinkle at the corners. "Congrats again, Mrs. Mackay."

"Thank you," I tell him.

He says goodbye to Iseult, and she closes the door behind him, heading toward me and handing me the envelope.

And when I look down at it…

"No," I whisper, staring through disbelieving eyes.

Because on it is my name.

In his handwriting.

All air leaves my lungs as I fight for breaths that never come.

"Uh, excuse me." I slowly climb to my feet, growing lightheaded, losing my footing and almost tripping against Iseult.

"Hadleigh?" Iseult calls.

But I barely hear her, moving past her. "I'll be right back. Just gonna use the restroom."

Leighton and Elowen appear beside me.

"Are you okay?" Concern fits through Elowen's features. "Who's the letter from?"

"I don't know," I lie. "But I want privacy as I open it."

She nods. "Alright. You tell us if you need anything."

"I will."

With my heart beating in my throat, I rush into the bathroom and shut the door, needing a moment with my husband. To celebrate our baby with him, even when he's not here to do it with me.

Did he know? Is he out there, watching over me? At the thought, anger rises to the surface. Why would he do that? Why would he not come back?!

Unable to hold on another moment, I rip open the letter and a rush of emotions bathe across my skin. This letter… It's from over a year ago.

Why did he send it? Why did he want me to have this one? And why now?

Dear Butterfly,

I did something awful today.

Konstantin, one of my clients, is the head of the Russian Mafia. Brutal as he is savvy. And today, he needed my help identifying a mole in his organization, someone who's been feeding the feds information. I was to use my resources to uncover who it was. And I did.

Today, I found out it was a cop. His name was Jerry. And I gave Konstantin the name. Then I watched as he butchered the man until he begged to die.

My shaky hands grip the paper tight, my pulse hastily beating against my ribs as I go on.

This is who I am, Hadleigh. I won't pretend I didn't know what would happen once I gave the guy up. I knew. But it was either him or us, and Konstantin wouldn't hesitate to hurt you for my shortcomings.

It wasn't the first time I've played a hand in someone's death. There were too many, butterfly. Far more than I can count. It's what I do. It's what I'm good at. And I'd say I'm ashamed, but I'm immune to it now. I just want to come home to you every night. That's all that matters to me.

Does that make me a bad man? Maybe you're
better off without me. Maybe I should've let
you go a long time ago.

Hudson

With my chest heaving, I slowly fold the letter up and return it back to the envelope, needing to call him, to scream and beg for him to come back.

Because this means he's alive, right?

It has to. Who else would send his letter?

I should care more about what he's done. But my mind is focused on finding him first. Then I can be mad at him. For lying. For doing things he shouldn't. But now isn't the time for that.

Dialing my voicemail, I hear him, and the tears? They don't stand a chance, running wildly down my cheeks.

"Hey, butterfly. I miss you. I hope your day is going well. I'm so sorry, baby, but something urgent came up at work and I won't be able to be home early. If it wasn't time-sensitive, I'd be with you, but it's a life-and-death kind of situation, so I have to stay late. Please forgive me. I know I ask that a lot, but I'm sorry. I love you, Hadleigh. So much. I'll see you at home tonight."

Life and death…

Is he staying away from me to keep me safe? Or keep himself alive?

Gritting my teeth, I scream silently until the walls around me shatter, until tears cascade down my cheeks.

He's gone. He's really gone.

When will I accept that?

Almost seven months without him, and every single day I still hope he walks through those doors.

Hanging up, I call his number. The phone rings and rings as it always does, and my heartbeats echo when the deep baritone of his voice comes through.

"This is Hudson Mackay. Leave your message after the tone."

Beep.

"Hey." I sniffle. "It's me again. I got the letter that you sent. Why did you send that one instead of writing another? Did you keep that one? Did you know it was my baby shower today? Are you watching me? I hope you are. I hope you're okay. I hope you're listening to my messages."

My words crack, chipping away at my resolve.

"I picked a name for our boy. I'm going to call him Holden," I cry. "Because I'm not afraid. I'm not afraid of your past or what you've done. Because I love you, Hudson. With all my heart. And our son is going to know you and love you too. No matter where you are or what happens, he'll know his father, and I hope one day you'll know him too."

Hanging up, the phone clasped in my hands, I let the pain consume me. I let it wash away the joy.

Minutes pass, and my cell rings, startling me. In my shock, hope blooms as I wish it was Hudson. But when I peer down, I find Detective Tompkins's number there instead. We rarely speak now because Hudson's case is now considered cold.

No trace. No new evidence. Nothing.

That's what they're saying. But I know what she's thinking: Hudson is a bad man who crossed someone worse than him, and that person got rid of his body.

But I refuse to believe it. Because my husband is alive.

"Yes?" I answer her, trying to make myself sound like I'm okay.

"I have some news."

My pulse batters.

"Okay…"

Please just say it.

"I wanted you to know, Tanner was arrested."

My pulse thumps violently like it's trying to break from my throat. "W-what?"

Is that why I had stopped hearing from him months ago? The last note I received feels like ages ago. I had hoped maybe he'd come to his senses and decided to leave me alone.

"When? For what?"

"For assault in Georgia. Don't know what the hell he was doing there, but he got into a fight with someone at a bar and almost killed him. I spoke with the sheriff there, and he's going to be locked up for a long time. You can breathe easier now."

My eyes flutter to a close, tears trapped in my lashes. Because I'm not breathing any easier.

"Are you there?" she asks, almost too softly for her.

"Yes. I'm here. I'm always here."

Alone.

I could tell her about the letter, but if Hudson sent it and it's not safe for him to return, maybe telling her isn't a good idea.

"Well, I wanted you to know that part is over. You can go down there for the trial if you want to face him."

"Thanks, but I don't want to see him." My fingers snap around the cell, and as the seconds drift, silence barraging between us, I say, "Don't stop looking. Don't give up on my husband."

"Mrs. Mackay—"

"Just don't." My voice shatters. "Don't say it's over. Because for me, it'll never be over. He's going to come back to me. To our baby."

"I hope he does."

But nothing in her voice says she believes it.
Come back to me, Hudson.
Please.
Please, come back.

Part Two

AFTER THE STORM

Twenty-One

HADLEIGH
A LITTLE OVER FOUR YEARS LATER

The rays of the golden sun spring across my windowsill, the laughter of a child I never thought I'd have ringing behind me with a man who's been like a father to him.

The years may have tempered my aching heart, but it still bleeds, drops trickling everywhere I go. Tattooing his memory everywhere I touch, smell, taste. He's in everything.

Lost, but never forgotten.

I never did find Hudson. No one could. The Quinns, as well as Grant, have turned the world upside down, turned every rock, uncovered every trail.

But there was nothing there.

Not a single pebble to hold the secrets of what truly happened.

What took him away. Why he never chose to come back. Because I still believe in my heart that he's out there, alive and well.

Maybe he did walk away because he felt he wasn't good enough for me. Maybe this was his way of leaving without facing my rejection. But I wish he'd talk to me, because then I'd have the chance to prove to him that with us, there's no rejection. There's only love.

And I still love him.

With my whole heart.

I often wonder if I'll ever get the answers. If I'll ever know the truth.

I sit here every day, doing what I can to hold it together for the sake of Holden, my four-year-old son.

He reminds me of his father, not just because of those baby-blue eyes or chestnut hair. But it's in the way he laughs, the things he loves to eat. In the little things, the memory of his father lives on.

I kept that promise to Hudson, that his son would know him. That boy knows everything about him. He could spot him in a room if it ever came to it. Which it probably never will.

Never getting closure is the hardest thing I've ever gone through. It's like a gaping hole filled with hours and hours of wonder, of hope, of longing. Dreaming of things that never quite come true. Yet I sit here believing that maybe one day he'll walk through that door and tell me he loves me again.

Except he doesn't know this door. He's never been inside this house. Never marked these walls with his memories. He's a stranger to them.

After I had Holden, I decided to buy a house in the suburbs, not far from the city. I wanted our son to have a large yard to run in, and the city had too many reminders of what was for me to stay there any longer.

We still own the penthouse. I didn't want to sell it. Getting rid of it would, in essence, be getting rid of Hudson and everything we shared. So it's still there, collecting dust, hoping he returns one day.

"Mommy!" Holden rushes over to me just as I kneel, extending my arms for him.

And when he slams against my chest, I close my eyes and sigh.

Pure contentment. Pure love.

I kiss his forehead, glancing behind me at Brooks with a baseball bat and glove in hand. "Have fun at the park, you two."

"Come with us!" Holden's sweet voice and bright eyes get me every time.

"Uh…" I glance between my son and Brooks, unsure if I should be there.

"Come on, Mommy." Brooks's mouth curves, his eyes daring me to refuse.

Something in my gut stirs, but I lock it away because I'd never betray my husband, no matter how much time has been cemented between us.

Brooks has been my rock. Without his help with Holden and his friendship, I'd have felt alone. He bought a place not far from us so he can be here if we ever need him.

Being a single mom has been hard. I still have Elowen, and Leighton on occasion, but they no longer live close, so I can't depend on them for emergencies. Iseult and Gio aren't too far, a good hour away, but they have their own life.

"Yeah, Mommy!" Holden grins, his voice carrying that endearing sound of childhood. "You can watch me! I'm really good!"

"I know, sweetheart." I brush my hand down the back of his head.

"We'll make Mommy play with us." Brooks wags his brows, and I instantly feel guilty.

Was it my fault he never found someone after Adalyn? Was he

spending too much time with us? He's never actually told me there was something between us, but it's this unspoken, weighty thing. Something I feel and see, but refuse to touch.

I can't seem to move on. I can't make that leap. It feels wrong. I'm Hudson's wife. I always will be. Going to the park with them feels like we're this family that we aren't.

If I'm right about Brooks's feelings for me, I don't want to somehow lead him on, either. But the look on my son's face… How can I turn him down?

"Alright." I plaster on a huge grin, my palms clasping both sides of his cheeks. "Let me grab my shoes."

"Yay!" Holden jumps up and down. "Can we get ice cweam after?"

He looks up at Brooks, and I shake my head. He expects me to say no because he hasn't had dinner yet, so of course he goes to Brooks, who can never say no to him.

Brooks laughs. "You know I can't override Mommy, right? It's whatever she says."

He catches my gaze and winks. My cheeks warm, and I clear my throat, narrowing my eyes at my little boy.

"That's right. I'm the boss in this house, mister." I tap him on his nose. "But just today, we can have ice cream before dinner."

His little mouth drops open, his eyes popping wide, and he squeals, rushing for my thighs and holding on to me with all his might. "You're the best mommy ever!"

"Yes, she is." Brooks's voice drops to a husky beat, his eyes slipping from my eyes to my lips. His jaw locks before he snaps his gaze back to mine.

I fumble my fingers through my hair, the edges hitting my shoulders as I rush toward the foyer closet to slip into my sneakers.

Going is a bad idea. I should stay here, where I'm safe from whatever has been happening between us lately. I hate that I feel it. That warmth between my thighs, the sensation of needing a man.

I haven't been with a single soul since Hudson, and I try not to think about the future, but it comes anyway.

How long do I stay alone? Will it be like this forever?

At night, I let my mind take me to those intimate moments between Hudson and me, when I can let go, when the release shoots through me. But afterward, when it's over, I realize how alone I truly am, and I grab a pillow and cry into it.

"Come on, Hadleigh. You can do it," Brooks eggs me on, while I get ready to throw a ball toward him.

Now, my sports skills are as good as my drawing skills, which means they're nonexistent. I can barely catch or throw. My kid is better than me, and that says quite a lot.

"Come on, Mommy, throw it. Don't give up! That's what you say to me."

"You're right, buddy." I bend my knees and give him a determined stare right before I throw the ball as hard as I can.

They both cheer as the ball flies in the air, almost halfway toward Brooks before it gives up and lands between us.

Well, so much for trying.

"Again, Mommy!" Holden claps.

"I don't know, buddy…" I look over at him to my right. "I don't think I'm very good at this."

"Don't do that." Brooks fixes his blue baseball cap, his bicep flexing, and I force myself not to stare at it.

Because that's wrong. Very wrong.

"Try again." He runs toward the ball and hands it to me, and as our fingers brush, tingles prickle my flesh.

I quickly grab it and move a few steps backward, forcing a cool smile. He returns back to his spot, waiting for me to throw it again.

My son gazes at me with excitement. My little wonder. The spitting image of his daddy.

And when I throw the ball this time, I let it all go. It sails, faster than it ever has, soaring through the sky, and once it gets closer, Brooks hits it, and it goes flying.

"Yay, Mommy!" Holden cheers while Brooks rushes for me, lifting me up in the air, flipping me over his shoulder.

All of us are laughing and having such a great time, I get lost in it. Lost in this moment.

Until I see *him*.

Chestnut hair.

Eyes as bright as the sky.

It can't be him.

He wouldn't know we're here.

But what if he did? What if he came for us?

Brooks is still laughing, not realizing I stopped seconds ago.

"Put me down," I tremble out, unable to peel my gaze from the man who I know to be my husband.

He's walking toward us a few feet away, a bottle of something in hand, a grin on his face.

"Put me down!" I yell. "Hudson!"

Brooks stills. "What?"

"Just put me the hell down!"

He flips me back to my feet and I'm rushing toward him, screaming his name.

"Hudson! Oh my God, Hudson!"

"Mommy?" I hear Holden call, but I ignore everything except *him*.

But as soon as I'm in front of him, I inhale sharply.

Because the man? He isn't Hudson at all.

I pant with a sob, tears swimming in my eyes as I practically collapse onto the grass.

"Are you okay, miss?" The man's blue eyes are darker, hair lighter. He isn't even as tall.

I gasp as my chest lurches, pain battering through my body until I feel it coming: the emotional turmoil. The dashing of hope.

"Miss?"

"She's okay." Brooks is there, arms circling around me from behind. "I've got it."

The stranger nods, a puzzled looked fitted on his face before he's walking away.

"Mama?" Holden's sadness creeps through each letter of that word I've come to love. "Are you okay? Do you miss Daddy again?"

"I'm okay." I blink back tears, faking a smile I've come to perfect over the years. Kneeling down, I clasp my hands around his face. "I just thought I saw someone I recognized. But I was wrong."

"Daddy?"

My heart tightens, my chin trembling.

"Yes," I admit, not wanting to lie to him.

His thumb reaches for my face, and he wipes across my lower lashes so tenderly, new tears well in my eyes.

"Don't cry, Mommy," he says. "Daddy loves us."

I throw my arms around him and hold him to my chest. "Yes, he does, baby boy. Yes, he does."

The day has come and gone, the night fitting across the sky while Brooks finishes up dinner with Holden's help. Macaroni and cheese, as the little one requested. And Brooks would do anything for him.

It doesn't hurt that Brooks likes to sneak some carrots in there without Holden knowing. Because getting this child to eat his vegetables is a feat.

"Alright, ladies and gentlemen." Brooks grins, holding on to a large oval platter. "Dinner is served."

He places it down in the center of the table, while Holden helps bring a basket of freshly made bread.

"Here you go, Mommy." He hands it to me, hopping over to help Brooks with the napkins while Brooks fetches the bowl of Caesar salad.

He even made the dressing from scratch. In the past, I really had no idea he was such a good cook. But over the years, that became clearer.

"Come on, little man." Brooks lifts Holden in the air and places him on the chair between us.

"What are we having for dessert?" Holden proceeds to ask, a sly little grin on his face.

"Broccoli," I tease.

"With chocolate?" His eyes grow elated.

I grimace. "Would you actually eat broccoli with chocolate?"

"Yeah!" He nods with rounded eyes sparkling. "But I would hide the broccoli in my pocket."

"You little…" I ruffle his hair as Brooks laughs, adding a piece of bread and the mac and cheese to Holden's plate, then does the same thing for mine.

"Thank you," I say. "This looks amazing. You're too good to us."

"Anything for family." He pours himself some food, and together, we eat.

I'm glad Holden has Brooks. He adores his uncle. And we *are* family, no matter the blood that courses through our veins.

Brooks has been every bit the uncle to Holden. He taught him how to play baseball, spends time with him. They do so much together, I don't know how he'll take it when Brooks eventually settles down and isn't a part of our world as much. Not sure when that'll happen, but it will happen eventually. He's not going to want to stick around here indefinitely.

Except he might. Because he wants you...

The thought comes instantly, and I shove it away.

It doesn't matter what he wants. I'll never go there. Not with him. Not with anyone.

Ever.

When dinner comes to an end and we've managed to clean everything up, Brooks carries an exhausted Holden to bed.

"Give your mommy one last kiss before we go brush those teeth," he says, moving him toward me.

"Goodnight, sweetheart." I kiss my boy on his forehead and each one of his cheeks.

"Goodnight, Mommy. I love you."

"I love you more."

He giggles, waving to me while Brooks carries him upside down, over his shoulder. That man will be a great dad someday. He's surprised me. I never saw him as a family man before.

While they disappear, I go into the kitchen and pour myself some wine, waiting until Brooks goes home so I can get in bed and read Hudson's letters and call his phone like I do every night. It's like a daily ritual.

The cell still works. Still rings the same way it did back then. As though nothing has changed. Yet everything has.

If Hudson is still watching us, I wonder what he thinks of Brooks being in our lives. Would he like it? Would he hate it? But I don't know, because he's not here to ask.

"He's going to be out cold in five."

I quickly turn to the sound of Brooks's deep baritone.

"Oh, God. I didn't hear you back there." A shy laugh slips out. "Thanks for doing that. He really loves you."

"And I love him too." He shuffles a step, staring down for a moment, before he's looking at me again. "Hadleigh...look..."

And the way he says my name...I just know.

This won't be good.

"Don't." I hold out a hand, my brows furrowing. "Whatever you're about to say, just don't say it."

"Please, Hadleigh."

He takes a step forward while the glass of wine jitters in my grasp. Because I know that whatever he wants to say will ruin everything.

Staring down at the floor, I hear him speak, unable to look at him.

"I know I'm not Hudson. Hell, I'll never be Hudson." He laughs bitterly. "But I care about you. Maybe more than I should. But I can't help it. I can't help how I feel about you, Hadleigh." He treads another step, footfalls heavy. "I tried to fight it. I swear I did. But I can't fight it anymore."

He reaches his hand for mine, but I pull it away.

"Not without at least telling you how I feel."

I shake my head, my pulse racing faster. "I'd never want to hurt you, Brooks. But I can't. I can't date anyone, let alone you. You're his best friend and brother."

"Don't you think I know that?" Pain and conviction course through his tone. "But it's been years, Hadleigh. *Years!* When are you going to finally allow yourself to be happy, whether it's with me or someone else? You have to let him go."

I smile bitterly. "I don't know how to do that. How do you say goodbye to the love of your life?"

"I don't know."

He sighs, cupping my face with a palm, and I let it stay there, searing through my skin, calling me a sinner. It's been so long since I've felt a man's hands on me. Since I felt wanted and desired and cared for. The back of my nose throbs, because I don't want to feel what I do right now. I don't want to like his hands on me.

"But what I do know is that I want to give us a try. I want to see where this goes, because I know that even though you won't admit it, you feel something for me too."

My heartbeats explode in my chest, so much so I grow lightheaded.

How can this be happening? Why did he have to confess that? Doesn't he realize I can't give him what he wants?

"Please, look at me," he demands, tipping up my chin with his thumb. "I know you may never love me like you loved him, but I'm okay with that because I'll love you enough for the both of us."

Gently, I grab his wrist and pull his hand away. "You don't know how badly I wish I was strong enough to move on. But I can't." My shoulders drop with a weighty sigh. "Because my heart will always be his."

His jaw clenches as I go on.

"I don't even have closure. I don't know if he's dead like everyone wants me to believe or if he's still out there. And if he is, then I'll wait for him."

He digs two fingers between his eyes, frustration overtaking him. "And how long will you wait for someone who's never going to come back?"

"You don't know that." There's a tight edge to my words.

"Hadleigh, you have to face the facts. He's gone. He's dead. He's never going to come back. And you can either accept that or live your life regretting that you never let yourself live."

Anger curls in my gut until I'm practically shaking. "I think you should go."

How dare he say that to me? He doesn't understand what I've gone through. The kind of agony I've lived with. He's never loved. He's never lost. And he should be grateful for that.

"Don't be mad at me. Please…" His face falls, consumed by his own pain.

"I'm not," I lie. "I just can't do this. I can't speak of this again. Okay? If that's too much for you, then maybe you shouldn't be around us so much anymore."

"You don't want me to come by anymore?" He looks as though I just about broke his heart.

"I didn't say that." I huff out. "We love having you. You're our family too, Brooks. But that's as far as it can go. I just can't, okay? With anyone."

He nods. "Understood. I'm sorry. I shouldn't have said a word."

"It's alright. I'm glad you did."

"Liar." He smirks. "You look anything but glad right now."

"That's my regular face. See." I narrow a playful stare.

"Goodnight, Hadleigh." He gives me a lingering look.

"Goodnight, Brooks."

I walk him toward the door, and as he goes, he stares back at me one last time.

For a little longer than he should.

Twenty-Two

HADLEIGH

Elowen pours herself some iced tea as we sit on my porch the next day, watching our kids play.

Cassidy is nine now and so great with Holden. She's like a big sister to him. She throws him a football while he giggles, running after it, throwing it back at her.

"I can't believe he admitted he had feelings for you," she remarks, taking a sip of her drink. "I mean, we all saw it. Have to be blind not to see it, but to actually tell you… Wow."

She glances at me while I turn all the way around toward her.

"It's bad. Really bad." I shake my head. "How am I supposed to face him after that?"

"With your head held high." She shrugs a single shoulder. "You can't control how he feels. You did nothing wrong."

"Didn't I, though?" Guilt pours salt into my wound. "I allowed him to spend time with us. Too much time. And now it's a mess."

"It'll be fine. You'll see."

But I'm not so sure.

"And Adalyn? Is he definitely done with her? I mean, I know it's been a while, but they still work together, so that's gotta be awkward."

"I haven't heard him mention Adalyn in years, so I'd guess he never started anything back up. I don't ask, though."

That's completely not my business. That's on them to figure out. What I care about is how Hudson's firm is doing, and it's still flourishing. He'd be proud. Though Brooks says the heart of it is gone without Hudson there.

He was always the center of the room whenever he walked into it. People gravitated toward him. It was his charm. He had it in spades, and I loved watching him command a room without so much as trying.

Tomorrow night, I'm supposed to attend a benefit honoring him that the partners are hosting at the Garden Skylark hotel, overlooking the city skyline. I have to wear a gown and put on makeup, which I really do not want to do.

Because I don't want to go. I don't want to see a large photo of Hudson staring back at me. It hurts too much. Even seeing his photos around our home is a painful reminder that he's gone.

Elowen stares contemplatively, her eyes giving me that look that tells me she has more to say, but doesn't want to.

"What is it? I can see your mind stirring."

"Well…"

"Oh, no. Here we go." I roll my eyes.

"You don't even know what I'm going to say."

"Yes, I do. You're going to tell me to go out with him."

"Crap, I think we've been friends for way too long." She laughs.

"But yes, I *was* going to say that because, Hadleigh, you have to live your life." Her dove-gray eyes grow sad, her head slanting toward her shoulder. "You can't do this to yourself anymore. I love you too much to let you."

I puff out a breath, dropping the back of my head against the rocking chair. "I don't want anyone. I'm fine by myself."

Lies. I'm lonely, and I hate that I'm even thinking such thoughts. My son should be enough for me.

"I'm living my life for Holden now." I glance back at her. "And if it means being alone for the rest of my life, so be it."

"Come on. Hudson would never want that for you."

I snicker. "Well, we'll never know, since he's not here to ask, now, is he?"

She shakes her head, appearing defeated. But Elowen and I are different. She wants someone to replace that bastard ex-husband of hers. I don't.

There was a time she wanted Brooks, but that ended years ago. She's met a few guys, but none of them were the one.

"I knew Hudson." Her lips purse as she releases a weighty sigh. "He'd want you to be happy. He loved you unselfishly."

Not according to his letter. He didn't want to see me with anyone else. I can't do that to him.

I won't.

"Wow, Mommy!" Holden's eyes light up. "You look pwetty!"

"Thanks, sweetheart." I kneel in my bright green floor-length gown and kiss his forehead. "You be good for Iseult, okay?"

"Oh, don't worry about us." She waves a hand in the air, scooping him up in her arms while I rise to full length. "We're just gonna hang back, drink a couple of pints, maybe start some fires. No biggie. Right, bud?" She gives him her palm for a high five.

"Yeah!" He slaps her hand. "What's a pint, Aunt Izzy?" His little brows knit.

"Oh, God," I mutter. "Maybe I should stay home."

I really wouldn't call Iseult to babysit. Don't get me wrong, she's an amazing mom to her three-year-old fraternal twins, and she adores Holden and he loves her just the same. But knowing what I know now, it makes me nervous.

As soon as she heard I was in a bind with no one to watch him, she volunteered. Gio's home with the kids and she had nowhere to be, so I agreed.

Elowen was my first choice, but she had plans, and Leighton is out of town, so Iseult was it. And I'd never hire a stranger to watch him. Hopefully, Holden doesn't learn how to become an assassin by the time I get back.

"Shut up and go," she scoffs. "We'll be fine. Just ask Sophia how awesome I am at babysitting."

I laugh nervously. Sophia is Gio's niece, who's now about Cassidy's age.

"I don't think she'd be objective. She likes you too much."

"And why do you think that is?" Her mouth bends at the corner, her auburn brow arching a fraction. "Because I was the best sitter she ever had."

"Fine," I say, hating the thought of leaving him alone. This is the first time I've had to unless he's at preschool. "One last hug, and then Mommy's gotta go."

While he's still in her arms, I grip him tightly against my chest and kiss him one last time. "I love you, kiddo. Mommy will see you tomorrow."

He nods while Iseult surreptitiously whispers something in his ear. His giggles bubble out of him while his eyes hold mine.

"Oh, you two better tell me what that's about," I tease, loving the look on my son's face, his eyes lit up like the stars at midnight.

"She said as soon as you leave, we'll eat ice cream and—"

"Hey, shush!" Iseult playfully locks his mouth with her palm while his giggles ring free and unrestrained.

He's happy. He's really happy. I thought I somehow failed him, living in my own grief and hoping it didn't affect him.

But right now, locked in this moment, I realize it hasn't. Not really. He's okay.

Maybe one day, I will be too.

Arriving at the gala, I slip out of my car, handing the keys to the valet. And as I move toward the glass double doors, my eyes connect with Brooks.

We haven't spoken for a couple of days since he told me how he felt. He didn't call. I didn't either.

I was hoping he wouldn't come today. But there he is, wearing a tuxedo, walking over to me with an older couple I recognize. Robert Allen is one of the partners, and I've met him and his wife, Cheryl, a few times at events the firm has held.

"Hadleigh, darling!" Cheryl approaches me, kissing both of my cheeks, her black hair coiled up in an intricate design. "You look extraordinary! Doesn't she, Robert?" She smiles through ruby-red lips.

"Yes." He politely nods, his kind hazel eyes greeting me. "We're happy you could make it."

"Thank you. Me too."

My throat grows tight; I want to run away. I know they're going to bring up Hudson, and it's going to hurt.

"Yes, we're so glad." Cheryl gives me a pitied look, the sides of her eyes wrinkling as she assesses me. "Hudson was a great man. He's deeply missed."

And there it is.

"Yes, he is." I nod. "Well, excuse me. I…uh, need to use the ladies' room."

I start heading toward the entrance, hearing her say, "Well, alright. It's good to see you."

When I begin to open the door to the hotel, a body towers behind me.

"Hadleigh, wait." Brooks's voice rumbles.

"Hey, nice to see you," I say as soon as I stride inside, him now beside me.

Making my way to the event room, I hope to find the nearest bar so I can drink this night away as quickly as possible. I figure I'll stick around until they make the presentation honoring Hudson, then I'll make my escape.

"You look amazing." His gaze stays on my face.

"Thanks. You too." I quickly turn and look straight as we step inside the expansive room. The last thing I want to do is give him any wrong ideas.

Music surrounds us, something slow and rhythmic. The space is dimmed, countless amounts of tables and people dressed in tuxes and gowns all around us.

"I'm sorry that they ambushed you like that." He moves closer to my side just as we make it to the bar.

"I expected it." My mouth flickers into a barely there smile, a finger in the air as I call over the bartender, ordering a cosmo.

"Hadleigh, can you look at me? Please?" His heavy, warm palm lands on my forearm like an intrusion. "I wanted to call you, to talk about what happened, but I didn't think you'd want to hear from me."

I sigh, my resolve cracking in two. "Brooks...I just don't know what to do with all of this. Can we stay friends? Is that possible anymore?"

"It is. Just friends. I promise."

I nod, though I don't know if that's something we can do. But I don't want to shut him out of our lives either.

"Is Adalyn still single? Maybe you two can—"

"Fuck no!" He snickers. "She's nuts. She's around somewhere, probably plotting my death."

He orders a whiskey neat, tipping up the glass into his mouth before placing it back down.

"She's still not over the breakup. So what does that tell you?"

"So, she wasn't the one, then?" I laugh.

"Definitely not."

"Well, I'm sure you'll find her one day."

He gives me a long look, eyes staying on mine for stretched, torturous seconds. "Yeah, I hope so."

The song changes to an upbeat one.

"How about a dance?" He offers a carefree smirk, marching back a step, holding out his hand for mine.

I grimace. "Uh, I don't know."

"Scared?" He chuckles, the way he once did when things between us seemed easier.

"Me? Scared?" I scoff. "I'm just afraid you wouldn't be able to keep up with me."

I finish the rest of my drink, the alcohol slipping a warm veil of heat over my flesh before I walk toward him.

"Let's see what you've got." I lead him to the dance floor, his laughter rumbling behind me as we sneak past a group of people and start to move.

With my arms in the air, eyes closed, I let go, feeling the melody, the energy of the room. The song changes, and we continue, his hands on my hips from behind, swaying together, forgetting my problems. Forgetting everything.

He spins me around, and twirls me once, twice, until I land hard against him.

Our eyes clash.

His hands slowly ride up my arms.

His breaths leave his lungs in hurried paces, his gaze dancing between my mouth and my eyes. Before I realize what's happening, his lips brush against mine, the taste of them mingled with the whiskey on his breath.

"Hadleigh…" he whispers all husky, and my pulse races, filling my ears like beating drums.

"Hudson…" I groan, my heart beating faster, imagining it's his hands in my hair, his mouth stroking my lips.

But suddenly, I realize what's happening and I wrench myself away. As I struggle to pull air into my lungs, my eyes fill with tears. I shake my head, trembly fingers skating across my lips.

"I—I—I'm sorry."

I spin on my heels and rush out of the room, whispers growing louder around me, so many faces looking at me. I wonder if they're thinking what an awful woman I am, kissing a man who isn't my husband on the night he's being honored.

As I rush toward the restroom, I slam right into a woman, and when I look up at her, I immediately recognize her. She hasn't aged much since we last saw one another in the supermarket.

"Adalyn, I'm sorry. Excuse me."

She scoffs as I brush past her. "I knew you wanted him."

Slowly, I pivot, inching closer to her, my heartbeats fluttering.

"Excuse me?" My cold, icy tone matches the glaring anger that pours from my eyes.

"Don't pretend to be all innocent with me, okay?" Her face warps into a snarky expression, making me want to claw it out of her.

I've never seen her this way. But then again, we're not friends.

"I just saw you kissing him!" she shrieks. "I knew you had your sights set on him while we were dating." She grits her teeth and nears her face until only a couple of inches remain between us. "If it wasn't for you, we'd still be together."

"I don't know what you thought you saw, *Adalyn*. I have no interest in Brooks. He's a good friend. That's all. What you saw was a misunderstanding, so back the hell away from me!"

"Yeah," she laughs callously. "A misunderstanding with your mouth. How convenient."

"You need to go." Blood rushes to my head, but I can't afford to make a scene. "This is highly unprofessional, so I suggest you stop now before things get worse."

She throws her head back with a cackle. "And what are you going to do? Get me fired?" Her charcoal eyes grow darker. "Go ahead, *bitch*."

"You little—" I hiss.

"What the fuck is going on here?" Brooks bellows from behind me.

"Oh, look. It's you." She gives him a long glare. "Came to finish what you started on the dance floor?"

"Walk away, Adalyn." His chest rises and falls heavily. "Before I have you escorted out. And believe me, you don't want that. The partners will fire you."

She chuckles and shrugs her shoulders, the thin strap of her turquoise dress almost slipping off. "Let them. I hate this job anyway."

She starts heading backward, but as she goes, she narrows a devious gaze, a snarl flicking past her upper lip.

"Hey, Hadleigh. Get any letters lately?"

"What?" A shiver chases up the back of my neck. "How do you know about—"

"Get the hell out of here, Adalyn!" Brooks barks, marching toward her.

"Happy to." She gives us both a wave with her fingers before she's rushing toward the exit.

"What the hell was that?" I ask him. "How did she know about the letters?"

"Maybe she heard me talking about it on the phone with you when I was still with her? Either way, fuck her. If she ever bothers you like that again, let me know, okay?"

"Yeah..." I exhale roughly, needing to return home.

There's no place for me here. I'm over it. Hudson wouldn't care if I left.

"I should go home. I'll...uh, talk to you later."

When I attempt to walk away, his fingers encircle my wrist, and he gently tugs me to him. His eyes burn with unspoken promise, his tongue snaking out for a swipe across his full lips.

I shouldn't be looking at them. I should drag myself away before he kisses me again. Before I let him. He cups my jaw, and I hate the tingles racing up my arms.

"I'm not sorry, Hadleigh. I'm not sorry that I'm falling in love with you. How could someone not fall in love with you?" His thumb brushes across my mouth. "Tell me you feel this too."

My stomach tumbles.

But I can't. I won't. Because whatever I feel for him is a mere fragment of what I once felt for my husband. This is just loneliness and lust twined into one.

His other hand curls around the small of my back, and he pulls me closer until my chest is pinned to his. "Tell me this isn't just in my head."

"Brooks, I—"

My phone rings in my handbag, and relief washes over me. He lets out a harsh breath and drops his hands from me as I dig inside and fetch it out.

Curiosity plagues me when I find Grant's number on the screen. It's been a while since I've spoken to him. There was no reason to. He had nothing on Hudson.

My heart beats so quickly, it feels as though I'm going to pass out.

"What is it?" Brooks asks.

"It's…it's Grant." My lashes flutter as I gaze up at him.

His eyes grow. "Answer it."

But I'm afraid to. Ripples of fear hit me all at once.

What if he's found Hudson?

What if he's dead?

What if it's really over?

"Hello?"

"Hadleigh?" Grant's deep voice booms with urgency. "Where are you?"

"I'm at a gala in the city. Why? What's happening?"

"Can you come to my office right now?"

"Yes, of course."

I'm already rushing out, Brooks following me to the valet.

"Just tell me. Is he…" A throbbing pain hits the back of my throat.

He releases a whoosh of a breath. "I found him, Hadleigh. He's alive."

Twenty-Three

HUDSON

I settle back on the swivel chair in my office, staring at a picture of my parents, the white frame sitting on the corner of my desk.

Both of them are now gone. I'd miss them if I remembered them.

It's been years since they passed, and I only have myself to blame.

If I hadn't been driving, they'd still be here. I wasn't drunk. I know it was an accident, a bad one, but I can't help but carry the blame.

I have a faded scar on my forehead and shoulder from it. Apparently, I hit my head so badly that I lost my memory. It's like with the blow to my head, it all got erased.

Every shred of who I once was, now gone.

No matter how hard I try, I can't seem to recall a damn thing.

Not my parents, not my friends, not even things I once liked. I had to relearn everything.

My doctor can't give me answers, either. He says with memory loss resulting from trauma, it's difficult to say when or if I'll get it back. But it doesn't look promising. With each passing year, nothing's changed.

I know my name, though. My ID says I'm Preston Kramer, the current mayor of Cedar Hills, South Carolina, after the last one died a few months ago. I moved to this tiny town for work right before the accident. My parents were visiting me from Florida when we got hit by a truck driving the wrong way.

I was lucky that I still had my job after I recovered. I was an executive assistant to the previous mayor. Before that, the cops told me I lived in a different state, working for local government. I have no other family that anyone could locate.

I'm alone.

Life before I became the mayor was good by all accounts. Nothing tells me otherwise. And apparently the people of Cedar Hills liked me, since many of them urged me to run. So I did, not realizing I actually had a shot of winning.

But outside of my work, I don't have much of a life.

My home is big enough for a family, yet I don't have one. Not sure why. Can't remember any of my past relationships. And since I came out of the hospital all those years ago, I haven't had any interest in anyone.

My next-door neighbor and friend, Sheldon, says that I told him I dated a woman right before my accident, but we broke up when she cheated. Can't say I'm mad I don't recall that particular bit of info. She left once she had the affair and moved in with the man she was fucking. Nice, right?

I wonder if she's the one I keep dreaming about. This familiar gnawing feeling fastens to me whenever I see her. Though her face is blurry every time she comes to me, like I'm underwater, still, it feels like in my heart I know her.

As soon as I wake up, she's gone, like she was never there at all.

And I'm left wondering if I'm clutching on to something that isn't there just because I want to remember everything so badly.

My mind is fucking with me. But the doc said that if something feels familiar, to lean into it instead of fighting it. So that's what I try to do. But nothing ever felt like home except when I see her in my dreams.

"Who are you?" I wonder out loud, my finger running over the black resin statue of a butterfly sitting at the center of a globe.

I don't know what about it spoke to me, but as soon as I saw it at a local mom-and-pop shop, I knew I needed it. And for some reason, every time I stare at it, I find comfort and peace.

I just want to remember—everyone and everything.

But I can't. I'm trapped, standing outside of my own recollections, like a stranger to my own thoughts, my own demons.

When those demons come for me and I'm forced to face them, will I even know what I'm staring at?

I press two fingers into my eyes, recalling when I woke up in the hospital with no recollection of who I was, not knowing who Sheldon was, who my boss was.

I held on to that anger, the unfairness of my situation. I didn't want to be around anyone for months after that. They didn't know me. They couldn't have. Because *I* didn't know me.

But over the years, it's gotten easier. I was grateful to be alive. And some of the people in my life, like Sheldon and Sergeant Peters, gave me fragments of myself back by filling in the gaps with their memories of me. They made me accept the version of my life they knew.

What other choice did I have?

I had nothing else.

Sheldon is the only real friend I have in this place. He's a realtor in town and single like me. He prefers going out more than I do, though. I much prefer to stay home.

Just as I'm about to turn on my laptop for the day, there's a loud knock on my door. Speak of the devil…

"Sheldon," I greet him.

He inclines his chin in return, settling on the leather chair across from me.

"Look what I got us for tomorrow night." He slaps a pair of hockey tickets in front of me. "Front row."

He grins while I stare down at them before returning my attention back at him.

"Damn, how did you score those?"

"A friend of a friend." His smile widens, fingers rolling past his dark brown hair. "You in?"

"Hell yeah. Not like I have anything better to do."

"Ain't that the truth." He chuckles. "You need to stop being a fucking hermit and come out with me and the boys sometimes."

"Maybe."

But I have no intention of that.

"Damn, you don't even lie well. I thought politicians were supposed to be good at that."

"Shut the fuck up," I snicker, balling a piece of paper and throwing it at his head.

But he catches it, laughing as he places it down on the desk.

"I'm serious," he continues. "Just one night. I bet you'd actually get laid."

Shit. Sex isn't even on my mind. My focus is on trying to find all the parts of myself I've lost. To get back to the man I once was.

Losing yourself is like being in the dark, and the only light is through those holding the matches. But I'm tired of relying on everyone else to tell me things I don't remember. I want to remember. I want the pain, the joy, and all the shit that comes with life. I want it all back.

Sheldon shakes his head and starts to get up when my intercom rings. I lift the receiver to my ear.

"Sir?" Julie, my secretary, says. "There's someone who's been waiting to see you without an appointment. I told her you had a meeting, but she insists on waiting as long as it takes. Says it's personal." Her voice lowers. "Do you want me to call security?"

"Does she seem dangerous?"

"I don't think so?"

She sounds unsure, and I can't blame her. In my line of work, batshit crazy comes with the territory. But sometimes you can't see it at first.

Last month, a woman claimed I fathered her baby and tried to extort me. Luckily, the lawyers took care of her.

"Did you ask her for her name?"

"Of course," she whispers. "It's Hadleigh. Hadleigh Mackay."

"Mackay?" My brows furrow thoughtfully.

Why does that sound so familiar?

I gaze out, wracking my brain for answers. I know that fucking name.

But how?

"Yes, sir. That's what she said."

Fuck!

I ball a fist and press it into my thigh, attempting to keep my breathing normal even while everything in me flickers with rage.

I hate this feeling of being lost in my own head.

"What do you want me to tell her?" Julie continues.

"I'm gonna go," Sheldon interrupts, getting to his feet. "Gotta get back to work."

I lift a hand to say goodbye, but he's already out the door.

"Send her in, Julie. I'll get to the bottom of this."

"Alright, sir." She drops the call while I place the phone back and fix my silver tie.

And as I rise, attempting to slip on my suit jacket to appear more professional, *she* walks in.

Comfort and peace and absolute breathtaking familiarity.

It's that feeling of knowing a person before you actually do.

It's the same way I've felt every time I dream of the faceless woman. And I wonder if it could somehow be her.

Is she from my past?

Someone I knew from before…

My heart ceases to beat as I stare, unable to peel my eyes off of her. This beautiful woman with a name that sounds all too familiar, with a face that men would wage war for. Honey-colored eyes, her deep brown hair framed around the sharp edges of her face, the tips flicking against her shoulders.

She's the most exquisite thing I've ever seen. Refined beauty with those long legs covered up by a pair of tight jeans, a loose off-the-shoulder white t-shirt that accentuates her tanned skin.

But it's her eyes that hold me. A calming wave of the unknown, begging me to take a dive.

Before I can ask what she's doing here, she quivers where she stands, staring at me through widened eyes, tears filling them as she takes not one, but two steps forward.

Her shuddering hand reaches for her mouth, cupping it as she continues to look at me as one would look at a ghost, fear and awe unmasked within her features.

"H-how…how could you?" A sob breaks from her perfect pink

mouth. "How could you leave me for all this time?"

I tilt my head in confusion, staring at a woman whose heart is breaking right in front of me, but I have no idea what she's talking about. Or how I can make it better. Because I want to. And I don't know why.

"Answer me, Hudson!" Tears burst from her eyes. "Tell me how you could abandon us and our marriage! To do what?" She pants, throwing a hand in the air. "To live some alternate life? Did you even ever love me?" Her bottom lip shakes with a small sob. "Or was it all a lie?"

Married?

Love?

My head's spinning, thoughts running wild.

She must be crazy. That has to be it. She probably heard about the accident and figured she could come here and pretend to be my wife and get money from me.

Because I looked myself up. I never had a wife. And my name was never Hudson.

I should tell her to leave. She means nothing.

But when I try to get the words out, to tell her that whatever she's planning isn't going to work, her eyes water over once again. And all I want to do is hold her. Hold this beautifully broken stranger in my arms and tell her that any man who'd leave her is a fool.

"Answer me!" she demands, rushing toward me, slamming a small fist into my chest.

Those eyes glisten with anguish, begging me to give her something I simply can't.

What answers could I have? I'm a man crumbling, on the verge of his own collapse. I'm not the one she's looking for.

Because no one's looking for me.

I'm alone.

Her eyes narrow with silent wrath even as her pain seeps through her pores.

"Are you really just going to stand there and not say a word? Was our entire life together a lie?" Her harsh voice gives way to heartbreak, losing the strength it just carried.

I didn't even know we had one.

The more I look at her, the more this unrelenting need to take her pain away takes hold, like I'd destroy the entire world just to see her smile. I bet it's a beautiful one. And my heart longs to see it.

Before I know what I'm doing, I rise to my feet, wrapping my arms around her and holding her close to me, as though my arms are welcoming her home.

My eyes close on instinct, and this feeling of happiness washes over me. But it doesn't make sense because whoever she is, I don't know her.

Right?

With two palms against my chest, she pushes off me a fraction, her brows knitted.

"You don't get to hold me like that without explaining it all to me." She swipes under her eyes with the back of her hand. "I deserve answers!"

With a sigh, I move back a few steps, and the more distance there is between us, the more my heart craves to be near her.

"I'm sorry," I say, forcing myself to return to my chair. "I'd love to help you, but I have no idea who you are."

Twenty-Four

HADLEIGH

I gasp as those treacherous words leave his lips. My heartbeats echo hastily in my rib cage as he stares at me as though I'm nothing but a stranger. A forgotten piece of his past that never truly mattered.

But how can I believe that after everything we shared? The man I married may have lied about everything else, but he'd never lie about his love for me. He couldn't have.

So what is he doing? Why is he acting as though he doesn't know me?

"What the hell are you talking about?" I breathe. "Hudson, whatever this is, please just stop it! Y-you're scaring me."

"Who's Hudson?" His expression turns stoic, and I can't help the bout of anger that simmers in my blood.

"God damn it!" I shout. "Enough! Just stop this! Okay?"

I shake my head, unable to believe this is the reunion I once dreamed of.

"I found your letters in your office, and I read the one you sent. I know about everything, and I don't care. Do you hear me? You don't have to hide from me anymore."

He doesn't say anything, just looks at me through those intense blue eyes, reminding me of the way he looked at me once upon a time, when our love was there.

Untarnished.

But now? It's almost out of reach.

My hand slowly reaches out, needing him to feel it. To remember. Inch by inch, my fingers grow near, as though I'm afraid he'll vanish. When I clasp my palm around his cheek, his rough stubble grates my skin like it once did. And instead of pushing me away, he leans into my touch and takes a long, pained breath as his eyes slowly shut.

And that breath, that one single breath, it sears into my soul like a silent connection between two people who were once each other's world.

But now I don't know what we are.

"I don't care, Hudson," I repeat, hoping he looks at me again.

His chest rises, and when he gazes back up at me, my heart flips.

"You and me, that's all that ever mattered. I still love you…" My thumb brushes over his mouth, and he kisses it, setting my heart on fire. "…so much."

I pant, tears running like two wild rivers down my face. My pulse rings violently in my ears, feeling his mouth on me after all this time… My God. I want him so much it hurts.

"There wasn't anyone else. No one but you."

He sighs, wrapping his fingers around my wrist, and my skin instantly tingles. For a moment, I bask in the hope that he'll tell me he's sorry for leaving. That he loves me. That he's done with the lies and wants to come home.

But instead, he slowly removes my hand and lowers it to my side.

"Ma'am…" He rolls his armchair closer to his desk. "If you need help, I can help you. I have a lot of resources at my disposal. But I can't pretend to be someone I'm not." He runs his fingers through his thick hair. "My name is Preston Kramer, and I'm the mayor of this small town. I've never been this Hudson you're looking for."

My chest grows heavy, unable to withstand the weight of my broken heart.

"W-why are you doing this?" I stammer, feeling as though I may pass out.

"I'm trying to help you. So, if you give my secretary your information, I can reach out to the authorities on your behalf, and we can locate your husband."

Bitter laughter escapes through my lungs. "That'd be difficult, since *you* are my husband."

"That's impossible."

"Is this some kind of cruel joke? Do you hate me so much that you'd pretend you didn't know me just so you can be done with me?" I dig a finger into my throbbing temple. "You're killing me, do you understand that? You may as well take a knife and slice out my heart, because this hurts worse than when I didn't know if you were dead or alive." Angrily, I swipe away at my eyes. "Because now, I realize you never loved me, did you?"

"Fuck!" he roars, slamming a fist against his desk.

I jump a step, completely taken aback by the rage slithering through his features. His face twists as he shuts his eyes, his knuckles going white with how hard he squeezes his hand. And when he peers back at me this time, it's softer.

"I apologize, but you have to leave now."

"What?" I gasp. "No!"

"I'm sorry you can't find your husband, but I am not him. I promise you that. I've never been anyone's husband. Now, if you'll excuse me..." He presses some buttons on his laptop and ignores me.

My throat swells from the aching he put there.

"I don't know why you're doing this, but I won't let you," I vow. "I'll always be here to remind you."

"Remind me of what?" His eyes find me then, filled with the same affection I once saw.

"That you love me."

As I reach into my handbag, I remove something and place it in front of him.

He stops moving; his body stills as his eyes take it in, a finger tracing the image.

I wish more than anything for him to say something, anything, to show me that I've gotten through to him. But instead, he says nothing at all.

And it only breaks my heart all over again.

HUDSON

I can't seem to look away, eyes glued to the photo of her. And the man beside her with a wedding ring on his finger?

Is me.

It's my face. My eyes. My smile. But it's like I'm looking at a stranger.

I look happy, though, and so does she.

And her smile? I knew it'd be beautiful.

But how is this possible? How could I have been married to someone and never known about it? How come she never came for me until now?

"I don't understand any of this…" My voice drifts. "May I keep this to get it verified?"

"You need to verify that I'm your wife?" A dour laugh rises out of her. She holds out her hand, a single solitaire wedding ring on her finger. "You gave me this."

"I don't remember that, and you wouldn't be the first woman who wanted me to believe I was hers."

Her teary eyes pin to mine.

"You—you really don't know me?" she cries.

I shake my head.

"Oh, God…" she pants as her palm slowly extends.

And for the second time, she holds my face within her soft hands. Utter serenity washes over me. This tender touch. This feeling of floating even while I'm grounded, unable to understand why I'm feeling what I am in this moment.

"What happened to you?" she whispers.

I'm instantly envious of whoever she thinks I am, because I know in my heart that to be loved by this woman is something every person lives for.

But no matter how much I wish I were him, there's no way I can be.

She's not my wife, and I'm not her husband.

Twenty-five

HADLEIGH

I didn't want to leave. I wanted to stay in that office until he had no choice but to admit who I was. But the more I tried, the angrier he got, so I decided that leaving and returning the following day was a better idea.

Finding the only motel in town, I check in and settle on the bed, throwing my face down into my palms.

As soon as Grant called me yesterday, I went home after meeting with him and told Iseult what was going on. No one believed it could be him. But I had to find out.

Once I did, I let everyone know it was him.

Sort of.

Could he really not remember anything? How? Why?

Nothing's making sense.

Brooks was going to come with me, but I had to do this alone. So instead, he was kind enough to stay at my place and take Holden to school so I can be here.

And thanks to Gio, I was able to take one of the private planes his family owns instead of flying commercial.

I hate being away from my son, but I can't have him here. Not if his own father could reject him. No, I have to do this alone. I have to get to the bottom of what's going on before I get our son involved. I just hope it doesn't take me forever to convince Hudson to come back.

If he's pretending not to know me to protect me from something, he won't stop until he's pushed me out. But I won't let him. Our son deserves better. *I* deserve better.

I'm going to get my husband back. No matter what.

Removing my shoes, I lie back on the bed and dial Elowen's number, needing her help. She's off today from her job as a nurse in the hospital.

One ring, and she answers.

"Hey! So, what did he have to say?" she quickly bursts out. "I've wanted to call you, but I knew you'd call when you could."

I blow a breath. "It's bad, Elowen. He's saying he doesn't know me."

"I'm sorry, what?!"

The tears come, dragging me into a puddle of my despair.

"Yeah, he said his name was Preston Kramer. He's the mayor down here. And he doesn't..." I sniffle back. "He doesn't know me."

"Is this a joke? It has to be a sick, cruel joke. In either case, I'm about to head down there and give him a damn piece of my mind."

"I don't know if he really doesn't or if he's lying to protect me. But I did look him up, and he is the local mayor."

"What the hell..." she whispers while everything spins in my own head.

It doesn't make sense. How can he be two people? He has been the mayor for the last few months, and he seems to be liked here.

Is this where he's been living since he disappeared?

But that doesn't explain why he can't remember me. I don't even know what would be worse: him actually not remembering, or him pretending he doesn't.

"Can you do me a favor?" I ask her.

"Anything."

"Can you go to my place and log into my laptop? I want you to email me the wedding video highlight I have on my desktop. Brooks is at work, or I'd have asked him."

"Of course. I don't mind at all." She pauses. "Are you going to show it to him?"

"Yeah. I plan to go back to his office tomorrow and make him watch it. And if he still says he doesn't remember, then I'm going to have to figure out why. Because he *is* Hudson, even if he forgot."

HUDSON

"Tell me everything you remember from when we first met."

Sheldon stares as I ask my question, curiosity settling behind his brown eyes. He pulls his swivel chair closer to me as we sit beside one another at the bar after the hockey game.

I didn't want to come, but I didn't want to waste a moment to speak to him, and the game wasn't the place for that. Of all the people in the city, he's the only one who really knows me.

He takes a swig of his beer. "What's going on?"

I let out a harsh breath, picking up my own beer and drinking the entire bottle. As the liquor pools in my gut, I slam the empty glass down.

"The woman who came to see me today, after you left…"

"Fuck…is she claiming you're her baby daddy like the last one?"

"No. Worse. She's saying we were married, and she seems adamant."

"What?"

I slowly nod. "She thought I was lying to her when I said I had no idea who the hell she was. Because I don't."

"Shit. Do you think it's possible you were married before…"

Before I lost my memory, he means. Before I moved here.

I reach into my pocket and remove the picture she gave me. He stares at it wordlessly for a few seconds.

"Well…that definitely looks like you. Think it's fake?" He catches my eye.

"I plan to find out. But…"

"But it looks real," he finishes for me.

"Yeah."

God, if I was married, why did I leave? Why would I have two names? I have to talk to her. I have to know more.

"Well, I didn't know you before the accident," he explains. "I heard about it through people in town, but that was it. We met maybe a few months later when I moved here. You kept to yourself. I never saw you with a woman, and I've definitely never seen her before. Because, shit, if you had to be married to anyone…" He chuckles with innuendo. "She'd be a damn good choice."

I elbow him in his ribs, not liking how he's looking at her. "Shut the hell up."

He chuckles. "Well, you sure as fuck are acting like her husband already."

Am I?

"Look," he goes on. "The cops found all there was to know about you before you came here, and there wasn't a wife. So I wouldn't let this mess with your head. She's probably lying."

"Yeah, maybe you're right."

"I'm always right." He flings a finger in the air, calling for the bartender. "Now, how about I get us another round?"

"Fine, whatever."

Not like I'm driving home. May as well enjoy it.

Seconds later, when the drink's placed in front of me, I lift the bottle to my mouth, and as I do, my eyes drift to the end of the room.

Sitting around the bar, a drink in her hand, is none other than the woman who called herself my wife.

She can't see me, but I can see her face quite clearly, staring at nothing at all, still in the same clothes as before.

She plays with the fork in her hand, a plate of pasta in front of her. But it appears untouched.

My first instinct is to walk over there and tell her to eat. I'm sure she's stressed, looking for that husband of hers. Maybe I can head over there and have the conversation we should've had when she came into my office before I kicked her out like an asshole.

I'm afraid the more I talk to her, the more things I'll discover that I may not be ready to hear. But being afraid won't stop the truth.

"Excuse me," I tell Sheldon, getting to my feet.

"Where are you going?"

He follows my line of vision. "Shit, is that your so-called wife?"

"Yeah. I mean...fuck. I don't know." I scrub my face with my palm. "I have to go talk to her. Get more information."

"Be careful." He stares solemnly. "You have no idea what brand of crazy she is."

"I'll keep that in mind," I mutter, picking up my drink and finishing it, because I sure as hell need the liquid courage right about now.

Before I even take a step, a man around my age holding a beer pulls up a chair beside her. Once he starts talking to her and those gorgeous eyes of hers look at him and she smiles, something in me snaps.

My gut twists like someone is turning a knife inside it while I wait there, watching her. She nods at him, and before I know what I'm doing, I'm marching forward. Faster and faster.

When the bastard's arm curls around her back and she flinches, I snap his hand back.

"Fuck!" he bellows, before he realizes someone's there. "What the hell, man?"

He yanks his arm away, and I realize he isn't anyone from around here. Must be a passerby.

"Get your *fucking* hands off my wife."

Her attention snaps to me, and her chest rises with a rapid inhale. And when our eyes connect and hope springs in her gaze, I realize what I've said and done.

I made her believe I remembered.

I'm such an asshole.

I don't know why those words came out of my mouth. Because she's not my wife. No matter how good it would feel to have one. There has to be an explanation for all of this.

The man's rushing away, but neither one of us is paying much attention to him, lost in each other. In this palpable feeling that's almost so real I can touch it.

"Did...did you remember?" she asks with bated breath.

"I..."

Shit, what do I even say?

Sorry, I think you're beautiful and something made you feel all too familiar. But no, I still have no fucking clue who you are.

Hating the idea of hurting this stranger, I still decide to settle on the truth because that's all I have. "I'm sorry, I don't. It just looked like you needed help, so I…"

"Oh." Her face falls, and she blinks a few times as though trying to suppress the hurt I put there.

"Are you staying in town?"

"Yeah, for now."

I nod even as her sad eyes make me want to rip out my own beating heart. "At the Leeway Motel?"

"Yeah. Didn't seem like there were many options here." The corner of her mouth winds up.

"Yeah, we're small. Everyone-knows-everyone kind of place."

"A far cry from where we lived…" Her eyes grow distant.

But I purposely don't ask where that is. I don't want to know.

"Would it be alright if I sat down?" I move even closer. "Maybe buy you a drink?"

My heartbeats hammer as though the idea of her saying no already hurts.

She inhales a long breath. "Sure."

The way that one word leaves her lips, it's like she's tired. Mentally exhausted. If I could just find her husband.

What if you really are *her husband?*

But that's what I'm afraid of, isn't it? To realize I don't really know who I am. That I don't know anything. Nothing but a room with darkness.

I once thought I wanted the truth. Now I seem to be running from it. But I can't live in the dark, either.

"You say I'm your husband," I start. "But how did you lose him? Where did you think he went?"

She sighs deeply. "About four and a half years ago, you went to work and never came home."

You.

Fuck. She really believes I'm him. The picture in my pocket burns…

Because I do look like her husband, don't I?

"Everyone has been looking for you, unable to find you. Until just the other day, I got the call from a friend of a friend. He found a local story of a mayor in a small town who saved a woman and a baby from a burning car." She blinks back tears. "And it was you." Her lower lip quivers. "Even with your memory gone, you're still the man I remember. Helping those in need. You were always doing good when you could. Taking pro bono cases. Always donating money to some charity. Always trying to help."

Why do I want to tuck her on my lap and tell her not to cry? Why does she hold so much familiarity? Why do I want to know everything about her?

"Saving them was just instinct. I was there, and the woman was screaming for help, so I did what I had to do."

She smiles affectionately, her hand reaching for my fingers, threading hers through mine, and my heart does that thing again. It flips right there in my chest. Instead of pushing her hand away, I hold it tighter.

"Not everyone would do that," she assures me. "Not everyone would risk their own life to save someone else's."

I brush off her compliment, wanting to know what else she can tell me. "What did I do for work?"

"You're an attorney. A criminal attorney. You started your own firm, and it's still in operation."

My pulse races because even though my head doesn't want to believe what she's saying, somehow my heart does.

I don't like this feeling. This inability to control my thoughts. I don't want to believe her. If she's telling the truth, it means I walked out on my wife and left her.

Why would I do that? What would make me break her like that? Because she *is* broken.

And if I'm her husband, I'm the one who made her this way.

HADLEIGH

I can't believe he's here, looking at me like I'm part crazy. Like I'm making it all up.

How can I make him realize that he *is* Hudson? My Hudson.

My first real love and my last.

The father of my son.

But I can't tell him about Holden. Not yet. It'll only push him further away from me.

The fact that he's asking me these things means he wants to find out more. But a child? That would probably terrify him. So I have to be careful. I'll tell him when he's gotten to know me more.

And even saying that to myself hurts so badly. I close my eyes and force my lungs to breathe for me, to let me live through these horrible moments where the love of my life doesn't know me. While I sit here and pretend that I'm not dying inside. Not screaming for him to remember.

But I need him to remember.

I need him back.

"I want to show you something." Reaching into my handbag, I take out my cell phone.

As I start it up and open my email, I play the video of our wedding. The words *Hadleigh & Hudson* with the date we wed jump on the screen until it cuts to me and Elowen, my maid of honor, drinking champagne and laughing.

Slowly, he moves in closer, his gaze stuck to the screen. I watch him as he watches these moments from our past. And I hope like hell it sparks something in him.

Elowen pops on the screen, giving a toast. "Hudson, you're about to marry the best girl I know, so if you hurt her, just remember I know where you live." She tries to look all scary, but instead bursts into laughter. "Okay, but seriously, I love you both, so be good to one another and have lots of sex!"

She giggles, and I swat her shoulder.

"My mom is going to hear that!"

The video cuts to him and Brooks then. Beside me, I hear his audible intake of breath as he continues to focus on the video. Brooks helps him with his bowtie, both of them grinning for the camera.

"I love you, Hadleigh. I can't wait to be your husband."

His smile is soft, and my tears gather with quiet fervor as I watch the man I love promise he loves me back.

But now, there's nothing left between us.

Like the aftermath of a wild storm.

Like the barren trees after the leaves have left their nest.

"Turn it off," he breathes.

But I don't. I let it play. Until we're on the screen and I'm walking down the aisle toward him. The face of the man who once loved me breaks with a grin, full of raw emotions.

That was him. That was my Hudson.

"Turn it off!" He says it louder this time. "I—I can't." His voice cracks.

I instantly stop it, not wanting to hurt him.

"It's okay. I know this is hard." I place a comforting hand on top of his, needing to wrap my arms around him and never let go.

He cuts me with a glare. "You have *no* idea how any of this feels."

"You're right. I'm sorry. I don't."

I only know how it feels to miss you.

I take my hand back and awkwardly place it on top of the bar. "Do you know how you lost your memory?"

"Car accident." He moves back the few strands of hair falling across his forehead and points to a small scar I hadn't noticed. "I have another on my shoulder. Docs told me I was lucky to survive."

I shake my head with confusion. "None of this makes any sense. When did this happen?"

"A little after I moved here, about four years ago."

"I just don't understand." I push the plate away from me, turning toward him. "We were happy. We loved each other." My jaw aches, and tears sting the backs of my eyes. "I want you to know that. I want you to know we were happy."

"I don't know what to think." His stare deepens into mine for a moment, his Adam's apple bobbing. "I don't remember you. I don't remember anything from before."

Every time he says that, it's like a fresh slice of pain.

"Believe me," he goes on, his tone low and husky. "I'd love to remember you if I could."

My heart lurches, because the way this man is staring into me, it's the same way my Hudson once did.

And I feel it happening again, the deepening of this connection between us that's been there from the moment I was his and he was mine.

His thick fingers slowly reach out.

And I wait there with bated breath, wishing he'd touch me.

As his strong, masculine palm cups my cheek, I feel it everywhere. Like I'm floating. Like this powerful feeling is filling the marrow of my bones.

"Did I make you happy, Hadleigh?"

"The happiest," I whisper with the barest smile.
Because it's true.

Twenty-Six

HUDSON

I keep thinking about last night. Reliving the video of her wedding. The man she married looked exactly like me. He moved like me. Talked like me.

He *was* me.

But no matter how hard I try, I can't recall a single detail about her or our supposed life together.

I made her happy. There's that at least.

I had a tech guy in the office verify the photo she gave me, and he said it's real.

But it's still hard to accept that I'm this Hudson Mackay. Some bigshot attorney from New York City, or at least that's how it sounded.

Picking up my cell, I stare at her number. The one she gave me, and I gave her mine in return. It felt right for her to have it for some reason.

With a sharp exhale, I force myself to get some work done, placing the cell down and retrieving a file from my desk drawer.

As soon as I open it, I hear Julie shout, "You can't just go in there!"

"Watch me!" a woman grits almost violently, but it's not Hadleigh.

"Best you let my daughter do what she wants, aye?" An older man laughs. "She's not much for the rules."

Before I can even rush to my feet to see what the hell is going on there, the door flies open, so hard it's as though it's about to come off its hinges.

"Who the hell are you?" I snap, gradually rising.

"I swear to God, Hudson, you'd better stop this shit before I kill you."

A woman with rich crimson hair falling over her shoulders looks as though she's ready to do as she promised. Her bright greenish-blue gaze gleams with rage, while an older man with pale green eyes stares at me with fondness.

She called me the same name Hadleigh did. But I don't recognize either one of them.

"Ma'am, are you threatening a government official?" I settle back down in my chair.

"Ma'am?" She laughs sardonically. "Please..."

A hand flings in the air with a roll of her eyes as she marches forward, brazenly taking a seat directly in front of me.

"I don't care who the hell you're pretending to be. Because I know who you really are." She raises both feet on top of my desk, thigh-high black leather boots connecting hard with the wood. "I'm here to tell you, you're done with this charade. You're coming home to your wife and—"

"Iseult." The man's sharp tone causes her to look back.

She clears her throat and glares daggers at me.

"Why the hell are you doing this?" she asks as though I should have some clue what she's referring to. "I know you always put her first and wanted to protect her, but this has gone on too long. Whatever you're running from, we can help you."

"Look." I lean my elbows onto the desk and stare at her just as hard as she stares at me. "I have no idea who you or the old man are, so I think you should go now."

His gray brows jolt playfully. "Old?" He laughs, striding to take the empty chair beside the woman. "Shite, I'll have you know I've still got it."

His thick Irish brogue is hard to miss. He appears to be in his sixties, about the same age as my father was when he passed. The harder he stares at me, the more uncomfortable I get.

"You really don't remember anything, do you…"

I shake my head.

He assesses me through a thoughtful gaze. "I'm Patrick. Patrick Quinn, and this is my daughter, Iseult."

"Are you with her? That woman, Hadleigh, who came to see me?"

"That woman, Hadleigh?" Iseult glares with a sarcastic laugh. "Are you serious right now?"

"Yes, I'm damn serious." Boiling with fury at her tone, I grind my teeth until pain radiates through my jaw.

Patrick gives me a poignant stare. "Yes, I know your lovely wife. But I knew you first. Saved you from juvie after you helped someone that meant a lot to me. I took you into my family. I made you mine." He curls a fist and presses it to his chest.

"Juvie? I've never been to juvie. This has to be some sick joke."

"No joke, son. You didn't have an easy start in life."

"That's for sure." Iseult snickers, and I pitch her with a scowl.

My attention returns to Patrick. "Son?" Confusion stamps through my thoughts. "I had a father. And a mother. They died a few years ago."

"No." He laughs dryly. "Those people aren't your parents. Your mother was a deadbeat who ran off when you were three. Last I checked, the drugs killed her. And your father? Well, he was no better. A drunk who killed himself in a car wreck." Leisurely, he works the gray and black stubble of his beard. "Your uncle took you in for a year before he realized he couldn't take care of you, so you lived in the system your whole childhood. You had no one but us. And when you met Hadleigh…well, that woman was your life." A grin spreads over his face. "So I refuse to believe that you left her willingly, which means someone did this to you. To *us*." His jaw clenches.

My heartbeats slam in my chest as he gives me pieces of a past I have no connection to. Other than this woman who claims to be my wife, I don't feel a thing. Hudson is as much of a stranger as these people are.

"I don't understand any of this."

I lift a picture of my parents, the ones I was told were mine, and I concentrate on them. They look so much like me.

"These are my parents." I show them the photo.

Patrick takes and examines it, then looks back at me, shaking his head. "These aren't your parents. Who the hell told you they were?"

"The police. Sergeant Peters."

He scratches his salt-and-pepper hair at his temple. "I don't know what happened to you or how you ended up here, but you're not who you were made to believe you were." His expression turns ice cold. "We don't know why you left her and your entire life, but we've all been looking for you. I hope you know that. She has *never* forgotten you, not even for a moment. Never gave up hope that you were still alive, still out there. Even I had given up, but Hadleigh? My God, she's a strong, stubborn woman." He smiles, his eyes deeply scrunching at the sides. "But never did she imagine that the man she loves would forget her. So, whatever the hell is going on, we're gonna figure it out and help you remember, because that woman was the love of your life."

His words are like brick after brick of unrelenting pain.

Her face appears to me, and I want so badly to trace her by heart, to recall in vivid detail our life together, but it's just not there anymore.

Lost.

Buried underneath a stony rubble that I can't climb out of.

"What the fuck…" I grasp the sides of my head, a migraine splintering in between my eyes.

"We're going to help you figure this out, aye?"

"I don't know who to believe anymore." Rage spirals through the pit of my stomach. "I can't make out the lies from the truth. How do I know you people aren't the ones lying?"

"Please…" Iseult rolls her eyes.

"In our line of work, you'd be right." The man nods. "But I swear to you on the lives of my children and my grandchildren, I'd never lie to you, Hudson. You *are* my family, and family never gives up on each other."

"I don't have a family."

"You do. You just don't remember them."

I track back to what he said. Something I brushed over.

"What line of work?"

"What?"

"You said 'in our line of work.' What work is that?" My pulse drums in my ears.

"Just tell him, Dad." She huffs out. "Maybe it'll jolt his brain."

She must be close to this Hadleigh, because the way she's staring at me could cut glass.

"No, he's not ready." He shakes his head, but his eyes stay on me. "I gave you enough. For now."

"Have you looked yourself up?" Iseult asks, placing her feet back onto the floor. "I meant you as in Hudson?"

I shake my head. It wasn't something I was ready to see. Because deep down, I knew I was him as soon as Hadleigh showed me that photo.

But admitting that my entire life is a lie wasn't something I was willing to accept. Because that means someone betrayed me.

And it all began with that accident.

As soon as those two left my office, I got into my car, driving to the local police station.

Sergeant Peters was there on the scene during my accident. He was one of the officers who told me about my parents.

I buried them.

But the casket was closed.

The medical examiner said they were in such bad shape that an open casket wouldn't be possible.

Those first few days and weeks after the accident are all a blur.

Arriving at the precinct, I park the car in one of the spots in front of a small brown two-story building. Opening the door, I head out toward the entrance.

Two locals walk out to greet me, and as soon as I step inside, Sergeant Peters is there, speaking to one of the deputies.

"Mayor!" He marches up to me, rolling his fingers through his thick, black mustache. "What can we do for you on this fine day?"

"Can we talk in private?"

"Of course." He extends an arm. "Follow me to my office."

We move down the station and reach the last door on the left. He's the first to go in, and when I follow him inside, I close the door.

He rounds his desk and lowers into the black armchair.

I decide to stand, too much adrenaline coursing through me to sit still.

"You have my full attention, Mr. Mayor. How can I help?"

"I need the file from my accident. I need to know what happened again."

He inclines his chin and narrows a gaze. "Did something happen?"

"No. I just wanted to see if something in there sparks my memory."

He nods. "Are you starting to get some of it back? Because that would be somethin'."

"I may be," I lie, just to see if he reacts.

His jaw clenches right before he grins. "Well, that's fabulous news!"

"My parents. Have you met them before? Spoken to them?"

"I did once when you first moved here. They were fine folks."

Fuck. He just lied to me.

Unless Patrick and Iseult were the ones who lied.

"Thanks. I'm sure they were… So, about that file."

"Oh, yes, of course." He throws both hands in the air, starting to get up. "I'm really not allowed to do that, but since you're the mayor and all, I can make you some copies and—"

"No copies. I want the actual file. Now."

"Okay, okay. I understand." His brows gather. "This is important. Losing yourself like that…" He purses his mouth and shakes his head with pity. "Gotta be awful."

My chest tightens. I don't need anyone's pity.

"Anyway…" He shrugs. "Let me go and get that file for you." Moving toward the door, he turns. "Give me a few, alright? Gotta go to the archives in the basement to fetch it."

"No problem. I'll wait here."

My body pulses with anxiety, hoping that the damn records give me some proof as to who's telling the truth and who isn't.

As he goes out the door, I take out my cell and click on the search engine. I type out his name, and as the results pop up, so does his face.

My face.

Hudson Mackay.

Prominent Manhattan lawyer disappeared without a trace.

Grieving wife of Manhattan lawyer pleas for his safe return.

Is he dead or alive? The mystery behind Hudson Mackay's disappearance.

Headline after headline appears before me.

I head over to the video section and immediately see Hadleigh's face. Clicking on the video, I let it play, my heart shattering as she comes on, standing in front of a podium, tears welled in her eyes.

"My husband has been missing for two weeks now. Please, if anyone knows anything or if you have him, I *beg* you, please let him come home," she cries. "We have set out a one-million-dollar reward for his safe return. No questions asked. I just want him home safely."

A man's hand clasps her shoulder, and I realize I recognize him as the man from the wedding video. My best man. And I want to know why he's touching her like he's got a claim to her.

Because she isn't his.

She's mine.

My bout of anger intensifies. Like the time I found that prick touching her at the bar. But this time, it's worse. He knows her. He's been around her all this time that I've been gone.

I instantly hate him.

I want to rip this man's hand off for touching her, and I don't even know why. As she cries, he wraps his arms around her, holding her too close for a man who isn't her husband.

He's taller than her, dark hair and eyes. Nothing special about him. Except the way he's looking at her. Like she's his.

My pulse beats savagely the more he touches her like she belongs to him.

My breathing intensifies, my vision sharper.

Are they together? Has he been warming my side of the bed? But she said she hadn't been with anyone. I remember as she said it when she walked into my office and told me she was mine.

"Who the hell are you touching her like that, asshole?" I grate through clenched teeth.

My heart rams like a fist in my chest and I don't even pay attention to the cop that's now talking in the video, too focused on his palm riding up and down her back.

Why the fuck am I getting this worked up? She isn't mine. She doesn't mean anything. Even if she once did, even if all of this is true, I can't remember her, so why the fuck am I this jealous?

Because for some inconceivable reason, you want to be the man with your hands on her instead.

"Here we are." Sergeant Peters strides back in, interrupting my thoughts.

Turning off the video, I stuff the cell back in my pocket.

"Thank you." I take the orange file from him.

"Of course. You let me know if I can help you in any other way, you hear?"

"I appreciate that."

"Don't mention it, Mayor. We all hope you get what you're looking for."

So do I.

Twenty-Seven

HADLEIGH

S taring at the phone, I find a couple of more missed calls from Brooks, and a text too. I meant to call him, but with everything going on, I just haven't been able to.

BROOKS

> Are you OK? Let me know if you need me down there.

HADLEIGH

> As OK as I can be.

BROOKS

> How long are you planning on staying? Maybe I should talk to him. Maybe it'll jolt some things.

I consider that. They do have a history, and maybe having someone else who's been in his life would help somehow. But I also need more time alone with him.

HADLEIGH

I'll let you know. I don't want to overwhelm him.

BROOKS

Of course. Whatever you need. I'm here. Does he know about Holden yet?

HADLEIGH

No. But I will tell him. I know I have to.

BROOKS

Yeah, the old Hudson would want to know. Maybe that's what he needs to come home.

HADLEIGH

You're right. Thanks for being so good about it all with everything…you know.

I don't want to actually say the words out loud, but he did admit his feelings, and I just don't want there to be any problems between the three of us.

BROOKS

Hadleigh, come on. I love Hudson. And I love you. As a friend. That other stuff, it's over now. Can't wait to see him. I'm happy for you. Really.

HADLEIGH

Thank you for everything you've done for us.

BROOKS

Always.

Once I'm done, I dial Elowen's number, needing to hear my little boy's voice. Two rings later, and he's on the other side.

"Mommy! When are you coming home? I miss you." His crestfallen tone has me immediately wanting to jump back on a plane and rush home.

He's with Elowen for a few nights while she's off from work. It's a good thing she doesn't have to be at the hospital every day.

I felt bad inconveniencing Brooks. He's already done so much for us over the years. I didn't want him to have to take off work early just to stay with Holden.

"I'll be back very soon, buddy. I promise."

He's silent for a moment, and it makes me feel like the most awful mother in the world. How could I have left my son to go chasing dreams that may never come true? Hudson could very well never remember me.

What if he never does? How long do I stay here hoping?

"I don't like you not being home with me, Mommy," he says with a sigh.

I can just picture him pouting. When I spoke to him last night to say goodnight, he kept asking where I was, so I told him I had to take a trip for work. I didn't know what to say. I very well couldn't tell him the truth.

"Oh, buddy. I know. I miss you too. But I promise when I get back, we'll do a dance party followed by ice cream and a movie, okay?"

"Yay!" He instantly perks up. "Can we get cotton candy too?"

"Well, of course. Duh!" My body warms.

I'd give that boy anything he wants. But the one thing that will matter most is having his father.

If only I could make him want us.

"You're the best mommy ever and ever and ever!" He sounds like he's bouncing, the words slipping out almost out of breath.

"I hope you're being a good boy for Elowen."

"I'm always a good boy."

"Of course you are." A smile fastens to my face, and I feel it in every inch of me.

"Love you, Mommy. I'm going to play with Cassidy now."

"Have the best time."

I hear him rushing off before Elowen's voice comes through. "So, any updates? Did he remember anything yet?"

"No." I inhale long and deep. "But I did show him the wedding video, and he got really upset, which made me so sad."

My heart tugs as I recall the moment he made me shut it off.

"He'd always watch it on his phone. He'd tell me he liked the reminder of the day he became the…" My voice catches with an ache. "The luckiest man in the world," I cry, a sob breaking from my chest.

"Oh, Hadleigh. I'm so, so sorry. I wish I was there to hug you. This really isn't fair."

He may have forgotten me, but I'll do everything I can to help him remember.

But what if…

What if my best isn't good enough?

"What do I do?" I blink back the moisture building. "What do I do if no matter what I try, he doesn't remember? Doesn't want me anymore?"

"Then you make him fall right back in love with you," she says like it'd be the easiest thing in the world. Like with a snap of a finger I can make it come true.

"I'm a complete stranger to him! I don't even know if I'm his type anymore."

That pang hits me right in the middle of my chest. Because until this moment, I hadn't even grasped that it could be possible.

"Oh my God..." My voice drops. "I may not be his type anymore."

"That's ridiculous," she scoffs. "Any man with eyes would want you."

"You don't know that." I shake my head even while she can't see it. "What if it's really over, Elowen? What if this is goodbye?"

She doesn't say anything, while I wait, wondering how long one holds on before they realize that there's no one holding you on the other side.

What if he lets me fall?

And what if this time I stay on the ground and never get back up?

HUDSON

I look through the file the sergeant gave me for the second time and still see nothing that could help me figure out who lied to me and why.

There's even a photo of a black coupe completely smashed. Says it's my car. That my parents were both deceased on the scene. I even looked up their names again last night, and it says what it did years ago: that they died on that day. Though I still don't see anything about an accident, which isn't a big deal. Not every accident or death is reported on.

But it gnaws at me. Makes me wonder if I've been played with all this time.

Stepping out of my office, I head for the diner a couple doors down. We don't have much here, but one thing we do have is some great coffee. This small, picturesque town is the kind of place people come to raise children in.

And I suddenly wonder why I didn't have any with Hadleigh. Or maybe we do…

Maybe right now, in this very moment, there's a child out there wondering why his father doesn't love him.

Fuck.

The very thought is like a punch to my chest. Because that one thought terrifies me instantly. But what sort of father would I be anyway? I don't have experience with children. I don't even know if they like me. Sure, I've met a few being the mayor, but it's not the same thing.

I pause mid-stride, right in the middle of the block. And I shut my eyes, picturing that beautiful woman who feels like something I once had and lost.

Staring at her is like that feeling of emptiness only she can feed. This sensation of knowing you're missing something, but unsure what that something is.

Did she even mean it when she said I made her happy? Because I hope I did.

After I combed through the file of the accident, I spent the previous night thinking about everything I've learned in the last few days.

But in the end, all thoughts led to one place: her.

I wanted to know what her favorite color was, what she liked to do, what kind of music spoke to her. Most of all, I wanted to see her. To talk to her again. Even while it makes no sense. Because at the end of it, what do we have? She lives in New York, and I live here, miles away. I don't plan on leaving. Hell, I'm getting too far into my head. I don't even know for certain if anything she said was the truth.

Yet even my own subconscious laughs. Because how much more proof do I need? I saw the *New York Times* announcement of her wedding to Hudson. I saw how happy he looked.

You made me happy too, Hadleigh.

I know in the marrow of my bones that she did. I don't need to remember that to know it's true.

I've never felt lonelier than I do now. To have been loved, yet not recall the way she touched me. The way I kissed her. The way we danced. I know we did. We danced for long, beautiful minutes, wishing it could be hours. Because with her, minutes probably felt like seconds.

In her arms, I was once home. But now I'm just as much of a stranger to her as she is to me.

I scrub my face and start back on my way, a few tables set up in the front of the diner. But there's one that's occupied. Brown hair in the sunlight, woven with strands of golden, auburn lights. I can't stop staring because I know it's her—the woman claiming to be my wife.

As though attuned to me, she turns her head behind her, a thin pale blue strap of her dress adorning her shoulders.

That's new.

I like it.

"Huds—" Her face breaks with a grin before it falls. "I mean Preston."

"Mrs. Mackay." I nod in greeting, glancing down at her blueberry tart and coffee. "Enjoying yourself?"

I move around to face her, noting more of the pretty V-cut dress she's wearing. Her breasts are visible enough for me to notice them.

To wonder what they feel like.

Taste like.

"I…uh, yes, I am. Would you like to join me?" she asks, all doe-eyed and blushing cheeks.

Would like to do a lot more than join you. Like have a taste of you for breakfast.

With a tightening jaw, I attempt to calm my cock from growing harder than it already is right now. The thoughts currently racing through my mind would scare a woman like her. This sweet, innocent woman.

I shouldn't join her. I should leave this woman alone and not give her false hope.

"Sure," I say instead, cursing at myself for being weak, but I can't stand the idea of disappointing her.

Pulling out the chair, I lower onto it and stare at her as she awkwardly glances at me. My gaze peeks lower, down the length of her as discreetly as possible. My hands tingle to trace up her knee, the one currently visible and begging for my palms to ride up between her thighs, spread her over this table, and taste her.

Jesus Christ. What the hell is wrong with me?

She's your wife. She wouldn't deny you. You have every right to take her bent over this table.

I bet her hair is as soft as it looks.

My dick throbs, and I scold myself for thinking what I am right now. But I can't deny it. My body feels her just as much as my heart does.

Yet it wouldn't be right. I'd be using her. And after I fucked her, I'd break her heart, because I don't intend on going back to a life I don't remember.

"New dress?" I ask before I can stop myself.

"Yes…" She glances down at herself with a smile, then peeks back up. "I picked up a few things at the local shopping center. I was glad they had something for me."

"It's nice."

"Really?" Her face lights up.

"Yeah." I nod. "Really. He was a lucky man, your husband."

What the hell am I doing? Someone needs to shut me up right the hell now.

She picks up her coffee and tastes a few sips, peering up at me beneath a set of long, dark lashes and sighing deep.

"I don't know how to do this, Hudson. Preston. Hell, I don't even know who you are!" She laughs bitterly. "But I can't stand another minute of you saying *he* as though my husband was someone other than you."

She leans toward the edge of the table.

"*You* are my husband. Only you." Her words shudder out of her. "I don't know how not to get off this chair and jump into your arms like I once used to." Pain claims her eyes. "But now I'm afraid of saying the wrong thing in case it scares you away. I never scared you, Hudson. And you never scared me. You were the one who made me feel the safest in this world, even when I felt helpless after my divorce."

"Divorce?" My pulse pounds.

There was someone else?

"I was married to a really bad man. Then I met you." She smiles with so much sadness, it aches through my marrow.

"Did he hurt you?" The question leaves my lungs through gritted teeth.

She doesn't say anything, but the way she drops her gaze answers my question. Everything within me snaps, and I almost jump off my seat, my body vibrating with rage.

"Hadleigh…"

The way her name comes out of my mouth. I can't explain it. It's all too familiar, yet it's distant at the same time.

"Did I kill him?" I snap, failing to keep my cool.

I don't even know where all this anger came from. Because I've never hurt a soul. Not that I remember… But if someone laid a finger on her, they don't deserve to live.

She grabs my hand from across the table. "No." Her head slants against her shoulder. "But he won't be a problem anymore. He's in prison in Georgia."

"Not good enough." I steel my spine, keeping my expression hard.

She laughs bitterly, a huge grin appearing.

"What's so funny?"

Tears shimmer, trapped in her lashes, and her chin quivers. "You remind me of him—my husband. It's what he wanted to do to him too."

"Well, then he should've fucking done it."

She swipes under her eye.

"I've missed you," she whispers, agony dripping through her tone.

What those words just did to my heart…

Fuck.

"Were we close?" Unable to peel my gaze from hers, I fasten my fingers around her hand, my heartbeats quickening.

"We were." Her throat bobs. "You were always the person I wanted to talk to. The one I told everything to. Because I love you, Hudson. No matter the years. No matter that you don't remember me. I *still* love you. I don't know how not to." Her mouth thins. "So sitting here and pretending that I'm not crazy in love with you, that

I haven't spent years in hell missing you, it's killing me! And I don't want to die, Hudson. I want to live for us and our family."

Family? Does that mean there are kids?

I should ask her. I should get the truth. But at the last minute, I chicken out. I don't want to know. I don't want children I can't remember.

"I wish I could give you more." I pull my hand back. "But this is all I have right now."

She exhales sharply, like she's giving up hope on me. I would if I were her. She's waited for me long enough, and all she got is a stranger.

"Tell me about us," I whisper.

And that has her eyes illuminating with surprise. "You really believe me?"

"It's still hard to wrap my head around it all, but yeah, I think I do."

"Good." She nods with a tiny, broken smile. "Because I'm telling you the truth."

"I met some of your friends." I cross my arms over my chest.

"What friends?"

"Patrick and Iseult."

"Oh! They didn't tell me they came by."

"They were interesting." I arch both brows.

"Well, once upon a time, they were your friends too."

"And I actually liked them?" I grimace, hoping to make her smile. "That woman has got to be insane."

She laughs instead, a big, beautiful laugh that sets every inch of my heart ablaze. "Yes, Hudson, you adored them. Both of them."

And this time when she says that name, I want to be him. I want to know his life. His love. The way he gave that to her. I want to know it all. Feel it all.

I continue to stare, unable to peel my eyes from how beautiful she is, how good. I can practically sense it radiating out of her.

"Tell me about us," I ask again. "Tell me what kind of couple we were."

"The kind that laughed. The kind that held each other through the difficult times. The kind that never went to bed angry. The kind that made love fast and slow because the way you loved me…there was nothing like it in the world."

I scrub my face roughly. Because the thought of being inside this woman is doing things to me I'm not proud of.

"What's wrong?" she asks, tucking my large hand in her small one.

"Wanna know the truth?"

"Always."

I laugh sardonically, right before my face hardens and I lean in, my fingers tracing up the top of her hand until every hair on her arm stands in attention. Her eyes pop as she drops even closer to meet me, and if I grabbed the back of her neck, I could take her mouth and worship it.

"I can't stop thinking about fucking you."

Her eyes and her mouth widen simultaneously, and she shivers as I go on.

"From the moment I saw you, I've wanted to, Hadleigh. I wanted to take you bent over my desk, while you called me by another man's name."

She gasps as I go on.

"And I swear, I have *never* wanted to be another man so goddamn much in my life."

Her chest rattles with uneven breaths, her eyes unyielding from mine as she suddenly laughs and cries all at once. "I don't really know whether I'm supposed to be sad or turned on right now."

That has me chuckling too. Feeling so carefree for the first time in my life. Is that what his life was like? Was it easy? Did she make every moment feel like it was a gift?

I peer into her eyes for long seconds that may as well be minutes. Or maybe I wish they were hours because I want her.

Right here. Right now. I just want to kiss her and have her kiss me back.

"I don't know if you believe in soulmates, Hadleigh, but I know you're mine."

As I go on, she silently gasps, awestruck as her gleaming eyes bore into mine.

"I don't know why I feel the way I do, and I don't even want to know. Because for the first time in a long time, I feel something. I feel it in my core. And I feel it for you."

Tears shimmer in her gaze, her mouth trembling into a gentle smile.

I don't even know where all that came from, but I just knew I had to say it.

"Mister Mayor," someone calls just as her lips tremble with something unspoken.

When I begrudgingly look to my right, I find Dolly, the owner of the diner, strolling out of the entrance. Both of us straighten and fidget as though caught doing something bad.

Dolly swipes the sweat from her brow. "So good to see you visiting us this fine morning. Can I get you something?"

"Coffee would be great, Dolly. Thank you."

"Sure thing." She scratches the grays around her temple, grinning at Hadleigh. "And who might this lovely lady be?"

"She's, uh...."

"A friend." Hadleigh forces an easy smile, stretching out her hand toward the woman.

Dolly takes it in hers while giving me that look. The one that says she thinks Hadleigh should be a lot more than just a friend. She's always telling me I need to date, get married, have some kids. Little does she know, I'm already married.

"Just a friend, huh?" There's an obvious glint in her eyes, and no one needs glasses to see it.

"Yes, Dolly," I grumble. "Just a friend. Don't get any of your ideas."

Hadleigh laughs affectionately.

Dolly, though? She scoffs.

"Well, Mister Mayor, you ain't foolin' anyone. I was watchin' you two through that little window over there." She points to the store. "And you both seemed mighty friendly to this lady."

"We have a little bit of history," Hadleigh explains.

With that, my wife looks at me, and my chest echoes with unending beats. The ones she created. And in her eyes, it's like I'm worthy of her love. But I'm not. I'm a soul lost, unable to find his way back home, hoping she's the one to take me there.

"Mm-hmm." Dolly nods thoughtfully. "Now, I hope you invited your *friend* to my son's wedding this evening. Five p.m. sharp." She inclines her chin, fixing her floral blue apron.

Shit. I completely forgot about the wedding.

"You forgot, didn't you?" She tsks.

"No?" I grimace.

She gives me a disapproving look.

"Five p.m., Mayor. Better be there. Both of you." Dolly gives me a poignant stare.

"I'll be there." Hadleigh gives me an excited look. "Sounds like fun."

"Our weddings always are. Wear your comfortable shoes." With a wink, Dolly pivots and returns back to the diner.

"She seems sweet." Hadleigh's face brightens. "I can see why you like it here."

Would you ever move?

Hell, what am I doing thinking about shacking up with her anyway?

Because she's pretty and you think she's your soulmate? And you can't seem to stop thinking about her, no matter how hard you try?

"Yeah, she's real sweet." I snicker. "Especially when she tries to set me up with women in town."

She inhales sharply and her eyes widen. "You've dated?"

"Not since the accident. But…" I can't get the words out, not with the heavy flood of tears gathering in her gaze, slipping between her lashes.

"Just say it," she breathes, her heart shattering. "You…you were with someone."

But I don't want to. I don't want to hurt her.

"Hudson! Tell me!"

"I don't remember, God damn it!" I grab her hand and tug it against my chest. "I don't remember, Hadleigh," I whisper. "I was told there was someone I dated right before my accident, but we broke up after she cheated."

"Oh, God," she sobs, trying to rip her fingers away from me, but I hold them tighter. "Let go."

"No. Fucking listen to me!"

She continues to cry silently while I attempt to find the right words to keep her heart from breaking further.

"I don't remember her. And I haven't been with anyone from the time I had my accident. So please, don't," I plead, my voice cracking to the beat of her heart. "Don't run. I don't want you to."

I raise her hand and place it against my cheek while her lower lip shakes and tears flood down her face.

"I meant what I said in your office. I haven't been with anybody," she snivels. "I couldn't do that to us. And if you have… I know you don't remember me, but I just…God, the thought hurts so much."

"I'm sorry, Hadleigh. If I could, I would undo it all. I would go back and remember everything. It's like I lost the plot to my own story." I release an exasperated breath. "I don't know if I'll ever get it back."

"Where does that leave us?" She waits, devastation building in her eyes.

"I don't know," I answer earnestly. "But I want us to be friends."

I want to hold on to you somehow.

Because for some strange reason, I think the woman I've been dreaming of…

Is you.

Twenty-Eight

HADLEIGH

F riends? He wants to be friends?

Ha! Okay, yeah. I can't just be friends with my own husband.

How will that even work? Does he introduce me to his future wife? Do we all live together happily ever after? The very thought of him being with someone continues to make me violently ill. Just like it did hours ago at the diner.

I can't face him again. I can't see him and appear as though I'm not falling apart. Because I don't know how not to.

When he said he felt as though we were soulmates, when he repeated the exact line he once said on our first date, I wanted to die. My heart was ripping into pieces because something inside him was fighting to come out. Was fighting to remember, to feel, to be who he once was.

It's there, I just know it. If only there was a way to get it back.

After he told me we could be friends, all I could say was okay. Because what else *could* I say? Saying no could mean goodbye. Could mean letting him go for good.

I can't do that. At least this way, I can find a way back into his heart. I can fight. I can claw until he wants me like he once did.

But I don't know how long I can stay here to do that. I can't leave Holden for weeks or months.

It's as though I'm caught between two worlds: my life in New York and the one currently here with the man I love.

Would he ever go back? Would he leave this new life behind for another one? Maybe telling him about Holden would convince him instead of terrifying him? But I'm afraid to take that chance. I need more time.

Slipping on a simple black pencil dress and low-heel pumps, both of which I found at the same store where I bought the powder-blue dress, I stare at myself in the mirror.

My hair's styled straight, my eyes slightly smoky, a nude lip and a hint of blush.

Will he like what he sees?

Should I even be going to the wedding? I don't know these people. This new life of his.

But I want to be near him. I want to talk to him. To look at him. Just be around him. That's enough. Just having these little moments is enough. Because I once longed for them, begged, and cried for just one more moment. And I'm not about to let it go.

There's a soft knock on the door, and my pulse instantly kicks up just like it did that first time he took me out on a date.

Except this isn't a date. This is…I don't even know what. But my heart doesn't know that, beating triumphantly.

Grabbing my handbag, I hurriedly slip my phone into it before I head toward the door. With a deep breath, I open it and smile.

But as soon as I see him, my mouth drops and the heaviness in my chest grows tighter. Because the man in front of me is the most handsome man I've ever seen.

I almost forgot how incredible he looks in a tux.

He exudes masculinity and power, and that cologne he has on has me squeezing my thighs together.

I instantly feel underdressed.

"You look beautiful." He smirks, making my gut flutter.

"You...uh...you look handsome. Really handsome."

"This old thing?" His smirk deepens, and with it my emotions pound through me, because in this moment, I find him: the charming man I married.

"I really hope I'm not underdressed."

"You could wear a garbage bag and you'd look more beautiful than anyone in the room."

My chest swells with a quiet breath.

He just said that.

To me.

It's something he'd have said back then. I can't believe he just said it now.

"That's so sweet of you, but then again, you always were. You always made me feel like I was beautiful. Thank you for that."

His jaw tenses, and he uncomfortably clears his throat. "We should go before we're late. Wouldn't want to hear Dolly when she's pissed."

"I think I kind of do, though." I laugh as I step out and shut the door, hoping to dance with my husband like we once did.

The drive only lasted five minutes to the garden wedding. Tables are decorated with small pale pink and white flowers, a band set up at one end. There was a church ceremony earlier that we didn't attend. It was meant for the family, Hudson told me.

There are maybe fifty people here at the reception, much different than the large weddings we're used to in the city. But I like this. It's intimate.

"There you two are," Dolly gushes, rushing over to us.

Hudson gives her a quick hug, not looking my way. Not even in the car. He was quiet the entire time.

I hug her before she pulls back, inspecting me up and down. "You look gorgeous. Doesn't she, Preston?"

"Yep. Gorgeous." He grips his jaw anxiously, like the thought of admitting I'm pretty to someone else somehow makes this more real.

I hold back the laughter that's dying to burst out. The whole thing amuses me at this point. Because if I didn't laugh, I'd stand here and cry in Dolly's arms.

"Is Sid around?" Hudson asks.

"Oh, yes. My dear husband is grabbing a beer by the bar over there." She points behind her.

"Okay. Well, I'm going to go and say hello. Excuse me, ladies."

"Sure. I'll keep Hadleigh company."

He starts to strut away, but stops mid-stride, glancing back at me behind his shoulder. "I'll be right back."

Something resembling a smile appears on his full mouth. Then he's off, marching across the room.

"My goodness, is it hot in here or what?" Dolly asks with inuendo, and I turn to look at her with a scrape of a laugh.

"I don't know if it's like that. Not anymore..." The last few words escape me with a whisper, and I don't know if she even heard.

"Honey, that man is crazy about you. I've known him long enough to tell you that. And this woman doesn't lie. I'm too old and grumpy for all that nonsense, so hear me." She clutches my hand and stares right into my eyes. "You grab that man and don't let him go."

Trying.

"He's happier around you. I saw it with my own two eyes at the diner. He's too good of a man to be alone the way he's been." She purses her lips and shakes her head, dropping my hand.

"He's never been with anyone since you've met him?"

"Not that man." She scoffs. "And believe me, I've tried like hell to set him up. But there was always one excuse after another. And I've always wondered why." Her mouth winds up. "Now I know."

"What do you mean?"

"Well, I believe there is a special person for everyone. I believe that some people are lucky enough to meet that soulmate, and I have a strong suspicion that you may be that person for him. That his heart has been dormant, just biding time, waiting for you to come and snatch it up. And here you are." Her face splits with a widened grin. "So, you keep that good man close to you, you hear?"

An ache pillages my throat. Because once upon a time, that's what we were. He always reminded me of that. Swore that I was made for him, and he was made for me.

"He's never told you about any woman?" I ask. "Not even before the accident?"

"A woman? Heavens, no. I sure didn't see that, or hear about it. And I've lived here my whole life. If there was someone from before he came to live here, she must not have been that important."

So there could've been someone else. My gut knots at the thought.

"How do you two know each other again?" Dolly's eyes thin.

"From another life," I breathe.

"Well, hopefully together, you can create a new one."

When I stare across the room, I find him staring back at me, and that longing feeling in my gut springs to life, hoping for that too.

Twenty-Nine

HUDSON

Sid is talking, but I don't hear a word. It's impossible to when she's gazing at me that way, asking me to remember. To let her in.

But I can't see her in the darkness.

I can't find my way out.

And I need her. I know she's the one who holds the compass that leads me back home.

The more I stare into her eyes, the more my heart wants to remember every single portion of our life together.

I couldn't handle how breathtaking she looked when I picked her up, thinking she was anything but beautiful. Every woman here pales in comparison.

"Mayor, you hear what I said?" Sid chuckles. "Or you gonna keep gawking at that woman who you should be asking to dance instead, before another fella does?"

They could try.

"I'm not much of a dancer," I admit.

Never had a reason to. Don't even know if I'm any good.

"Neither was I until Dolly came along."

When I glance over, he's got that look in his hazel eyes that says I'm a fool.

"If that lady isn't a reason for you to dance…" He scrubs a hand through his gray beard. "…then you're just about hopeless. And Dolly would have my neck if I didn't try to convince you. So, if she asks…" He takes a step forward and drops his face near my ear. "You make sure you tell her I did all that I could." He takes a swig of his beer as he moves back.

I shake my head. "Don't worry. I'll make sure I tell her." I continue to watch Hadleigh as Dolly palms her shoulder, then hurries off with someone else.

Not even a minute later, one of the local cops approaches, and her gaze jumps between me and this asshole.

They keep talking, and my pulse keeps accelerating. I don't know what the hell is happening, but I'm no longer in control of my own damn body. Not when there's a man standing way too close to my wife.

"Better hurry off before good ol' Martin steals your girl, Mister Mayor." Sid's amused chuckling reverberates through his body.

But my feet are moving already, Sid's laughter growing fainter with every footfall.

"So nice of you to offer me a dance," Hadleigh tells the young deputy. "But I—"

My heated gaze instantly cuts her off. Her mouth parts as she finds me towering over her from her right.

"M-mister Mayor." Martin nervously fumbles, reaching out a

hand that I don't shake, glaring at him instead.

"Move along," I bark out. "She's with me."

"Oh! I'm sorry, sir. Ma'am. I...uh, didn't know." He starts backward, almost tripping over his own damn feet. "Sorry again, Mister Mayor. You have a splendid day."

"I'm with you, huh?" She pops a sassy palm on her hip, her brow curving as she scowls. "Didn't seem like it with you being on the other side of the room, clearly avoiding me."

"I wasn't avoiding you," I lie right through my teeth. "I was catching up with Sid."

"About what?" She narrows an unconvinced stare.

Fuck. I have no idea. I was too busy staring at you.

"Fishing."

"Hmm. You fish now?"

"I don't know what your Hudson did, but Preston fishes." My mouth twitches.

She lets one of those breathtaking smiles slip, and I just about ask her to marry me. Twice, I guess.

"Maybe you can take me sometime."

Would take you anywhere you want to go, beautiful.

"You want to learn how to fish?"

"Maybe." A sultry, shy grin paints across her lips.

"My God, you're trouble," I breathe, my heart racing right out of my chest, her gaze locked with mine.

What is it about this woman that makes me want to never let go?

"You used to love it when I caused a little bit of trouble." Her tone grows all lustful, and my dick pulses in my slacks.

"I bet I did."

Her eyes bore into mine, and I want to stay like this for as long as the world will let me.

"Dance with me." I curl my arm around her hips like it belongs there and pull her flush against me, staring down at her lips like they belong to me too.

"Thought you'd never ask." She sighs, like being here with me is all she ever wants.

So I drag this damn woman onto the dance floor and hope like hell I can dance.

Her hands twine around my neck as she longingly stares into my eyes just as my arms coil around the small of her back. And together, we move in sync, as though our bodies have done this before. As though our hearts have sung this song, melted in the lyrics of this obvious passionate chemistry simmering between us.

We dance slow, our eyes lost in one another, and this overwhelming sense of emotion comes through me, and I tug her just a little closer. I can feel eyes on us, but I don't seem to care. The rest of the room disappears, and all I see, all I know, is this woman whose love for me could be felt for miles.

With the back of my hand, I brush the softness of her cheek, and she melts into my touch.

Her brows knit, her shallow breaths growing faster as my mouth gradually sinks lower until I'm near enough to kiss her, to taste this slow-growing addiction.

My lips stroke hers, her breath minty and warm. And she moans, a sexy little feminine sound that I want to bottle up for when I'm alone in bed, stroking myself, wanting her to do it instead.

How would it feel to get lost in a woman for once? To want and be wanted the way I'm wanting her right now?

"Hudson…" she breathes.

And that one word is like spilling water to fire, reminding me I'm not who she wants me to be. I don't know him. I don't share his memories. His passions. I don't share anything with him. I'm not who she wants. I'll never be him.

Because she wants someone who's already dead.

I immediately roll back, realizing what a colossal mistake this would've been. She's hurting, and I'd be taking advantage of her pain for my own pleasure. What kind of man would that make me?

"Hudson, please." She's pleading for what I can't give.

"I—I'm sorry. I just can't." I attempt to press her face into my chest so I don't have to see the hurt in her eyes.

But instead, she shoves me off.

"No! You don't get to do that." Her features are consumed with anguish. "You don't get to hold me like that after you just..." Her shoulders tremor with harsh breaths. "I—I can't be here."

She forces her fingers into her eyes before she looks at me again.

"Maybe everyone was right. Maybe I should move on. Maybe this is really…" She sniffles. "Really over." Her chin rises while she fights to steady her emotions. "Maybe I should forget you the way you forgot me."

Those words shouldn't hurt the way they just did. But something about them, her forgetting me… I don't ever want to be forgotten by her.

Before I can get a word in edgewise, she's storming off, catching the eyes of many of the guests—including Dolly, who's looking at me like she's going to have my head if I don't fix whatever I just broke.

As I rush after Hadleigh, only a yard away, she enters the adjacent restaurant that's attached to the garden. The door bangs shut behind me as I slowly march after her through a long corridor.

The place is empty, the staff taking care of the guests at the wedding instead. It's quiet here too, the music fainter, except the clicking of her heels.

"Get out of here, *Preston*!" She pivots toward me, and I realize calling me by my name was meant to hurt. "I don't want to look at you right now!"

"I don't know what you want me to do, Hadleigh! I'm not him!" I storm down some of the space between us. "Maybe I was once, but I'm not anymore."

"Yes, you fucking are!"

She rushes over, cutting more of the distance until only a foot remains wedged between our hearts.

"I'm sorry you don't remember. I'm sorry about whatever happened to cause you to forget, because God, Hudson…" she cries. "I want to know so badly, and I want to hurt every single person who took you from me, but you *are* him. You're my husband, even while you don't remember. But see, I remember everything. For the both of us."

Those last few words are said with a whispered breath, her eyes slamming with fresh tears.

"Fuck!" I clutch the top of my head with both hands, my pulse drumming.

"If you don't feel anything for me, if you don't want to try, then tell me right now, and I'll go. I'll go back to our penthouse in New York City, and you'll never have to look at me again."

Tell her. Tell her that you don't want that. You want her to stay here with you.

But as she waits for me to do just that, I can't seem to make the words come out.

She shakes her head with a silent cry. "You know what? Screw this!"

Roughly, she wipes under her eye with her fingers. And this time, the woman staring back at me is not fragile, she's strong.

"Maybe I should go out there and take Martin up on that dance, and if I'm lucky, maybe he'll feel me up." She crosses the rest of the way until we're chest to chest. "Because God knows I haven't been touched by a man since you've been gone. So maybe it's time I really forgot you."

But as soon as she brushes past me, I grab the back of her throat and throw her up against my hard body.

"See, the only problem with that is..." I growl as I walk her backward until her spine hits the wall. "The thought of you with another man makes me want to do very bad things."

Her breathing quickens as her mouth parts, staring wild-eyed as I press my heavy, throbbing cock up against her belly.

"What kind of bad things?" she pants.

"The kind that involve blood, Hadleigh. Because seeing you with someone else makes me want to rip out his heart."

She groans from my words, from the way I'm grinding against her. My fingers spread into her hair, and I yank her head back, clutching the softness in my fist.

"So, to answer your question..." I let my other hand fall, an index finger slowly tracing up her bare thigh. "I do feel something whenever you're near. I thought we already established that at the diner. I don't know why. It makes no sense to me. But I'm tired of fighting it." I drop my lips to her ear. "So, if you say I'm your husband, maybe it's time I fucked you like one."

"Oh, God..." A sultry, gasping moan escapes through her mouth right before I flip her around and roughly yank up her dress, exposing her perfect round ass.

I step back to admire the view, but when she attempts to move away, I slap her ass hard, leaving a nice handprint. "Never said you could move."

She gyrates, groaning for me while I keep her in place, forcing my palm against the back of her head while she stares at me, longing and desire intensifying in her gaze.

My wife likes it rough, and apparently, so do I.

I grab a fistful of her ass with my other palm. "You're goddamn beautiful."

"S-someone could see us in here." Her words are uneven, fear and excitement there too.

And she's right. If I turn around, I can see into the garden. If someone decides to peek or if the staff comes in here for anything, we'll definitely get caught. But the kitchen is all the way on the other side, and there's another entrance for staff.

"Let them."

I spank her again, my need growing the more I look at her, the more she makes those little sounds that are making me so damn hard; I don't remember ever feeling this way.

I let my palm slip between her thighs and cup her warm, wet cunt.

As I push my body back up against hers, my mouth drops to her ear, two fingers slowly running on both sides of her clit.

"Did someone forget her panties?"

"It's a habit I can't seem to break," she cries out with a hiss. "Oh my God, I've missed you. Please, I need this."

"Does my wife need to come?"

I don't know why I'm doing this. Why I'm playing this game I'm not a part of. But I can't seem to stop.

"Yes, please," she begs but I need more.

"Then tell me exactly what you want. I need to hear those filthy words come out of those pretty lips. Then I'll let you come. On my fingers."

I suck her lobe into my mouth.

"On my tongue."

My lips pepper kisses down her neck.

"On my cock while you're taking every thick inch of me."

I stroke her clit faster, making her whimper louder.

"Is that what he did, Hadleigh? Is that what your husband did for you?"

I thrust three fingers inside her until she screams, and I pound even deeper.

"How many times did he make you come before he fucked you? Because I want more than what you gave him." I curve my fingers while she writhes and moans, so wet she's dripping down my hand. "I'm jealous of my own damn self because I want to be the one to give you more."

"I love you," she rasps, turning to catch my gaze. "I love you as Hudson, as Preston…"

Her brows furrow while I keep up the pace even as my heart beats unevenly, not able to hear those words, or accept them. The need to run overwhelms me, but there's this gnawing feeling of wanting to stay too.

Her pussy quivers as she tries to finish the words. "I don't care who you are. I just love—"

No. I can't hear her say that. Before she can finish, I slam my lips against hers and I kiss her with a raw hungered need, taking this woman with every bit of desire I've been drowning in.

Of course, I wanted to hear her tell me she loves me. But she can't say that when she can't be sure she can love the man standing behind her. I couldn't listen to that and make myself believe she could accept me as I am.

I deepen my strokes while my tongue snakes with hers to a rhythm all our own.

Her hand finds the back of my head, pushing me deeper into her mouth while her body trembles, my thumb working her clit as I fuck her with my fingers.

She feels damn good.

Warm.

Intoxicating.

Altogether mine.

And when I flick her clit this time, she falls, and I'm there to consume all her cries of pleasure, groaning as I suck her tongue into my mouth.

"Perfect," I whisper huskily, kissing her trembling lips one last time.

Before she comes down from her release, I drop to my knees and fit my head between her silky thighs, keeping her facing the wall while both palms clutch her ass cheeks.

"Oh God, Hudson…" She peeks down at me. "I need a minute, please."

I chuckle with a growl. "You aren't getting one."

Then my mouth is on her, sucking her clit against my flattened tongue.

"Yes…" she moans, her hand fisting my hair as I lick and suck and taste.

Feeling this woman quiver around my tongue is an experience I don't ever want to forget. My tongue slips inside her, then rolls around her center until I know she's close.

"Hudson, I can't… It's too much!" She yanks my hair as she cries out his name, the man I don't remember.

But this time, I don't fight it. I let it take me, let it drown me until I pretend that I am him. Anything to have her in this moment.

The tip of my tongue circles around her faster now until she cries out, slapping a hand over her mouth as she comes. I growl against her pussy and taste every drop she lets me have.

A door suddenly opens from a distance, and that instantly has her gasping.

Rising slowly to my feet, I place a finger against her lips. "Shh."

She nods while I lower her dress, making sure she's covered.

Unfortunately.

"Can you believe the way he was touching her," one of the ladies in town says, probably coming in to use the restroom. "I mean, my goodness. What do I have to do for him to touch me like that?" She laughs.

"I know, right. Where did she even come from? Does he know her? Is that what they're sayin'?"

"That's what I hear."

"Lucky bitch."

I try to fight a smile while she silently laughs, her shoulders softly rocking. She's so beautiful. So familiar. And there goes my heart, telling me things I can't quite hear.

Yet, somewhere in the distance, I feel the whispers of forgotten words and endless promises.

Can I give her that? Can I somehow learn to be the man she needs me to be?

"We should go." Her chest rises and falls with uneven beats of her heart, but I don't want to leave, not if it means I get to leave without her.

My chest constrains with feelings too great to put into words. I stroke the curve of her jaw with my knuckles, cupping it in a rough palm, and without my eyes leaving hers, I lower my mouth against her shuddering lips and kiss her.

And I've never felt more—more of everything.

Taking my time, I kiss her with unhurried passion, wanting her to feel it—this aching in my bones—swearing to give her something I don't even know if I'm capable of.

Because I don't know how to fix it.

I don't know how to take us back to how it used to be.

thirty

HADLEIGH

"**W**ait a minute," Iseult remarks over the phone once I'm back in my motel room. "Are you telling me he went down on you after saying all that, and instead you're here. Talking to me. And not fucking his brains out?"

"Yeah, basically." I laugh with a groan, falling backward onto the bed, staring at the ceiling.

Of course, I'd very much love to be fucking Hudson right now instead of thinking about it. My God, it's been so long that I'm not even sure if I remember what to do.

But when he touched me, when he was filthy and crude, yet tender and loving? That was Hudson.

My Hudson.

He may not remember who he was, but inside that soul of his, there are pieces of him burning through, begging to make themselves known.

Maybe that's what it'll take for him to come back. Being around me. Being himself without knowing it.

But what if I'm just wishing for something that'll never happen?

She snickers, snapping me out of my thoughts. "You better find out where that man lives and make him finish whatever the hell he started."

Crap. I don't even know his address. I mean, I'm sure I could find Dolly and ask her. But then what? Invite myself in?

"And what if he turns me away?" I ponder. "I don't know what to do, Iseult. Do I go back home? Do I move here with Holden? And if I move here, what if he still doesn't want us?"

"Please." She scoffs like I just said something ridiculous. "The man just went down on you for basically everyone to see. It's safe to say he wants you."

"You know what I mean."

"I know…" Her voice grows sincere. "I hate this for you. For both of you." She quiets for a moment until she sighs. "I used to look at you and Hudson and secretly feel jealous. Because I wanted that. I wanted what you both had." She roughly exhales. "And seeing it destroyed this way? Fuck. It makes me want to find whoever did this and kill them."

I don't say anything in return. Because what is there to say? She's right. Our love was destroyed, and I want to kill them too.

"You there?" she asks.

"Yeah."

"My father and I have been looking into this sergeant in town, Sergeant Peters."

"How's he involved?"

"Hudson told us he's the one who told him some fake-ass couple in a photo frame on his desk were his parents. Why the hell would he do that?"

A chill scurries up the back of my neck. Like a phantom I can feel, but not see.

"Daddy Dearest wants to quietly get our people to investigate him," she explains. "He thinks that's where we need to start, while I'd prefer to use my fists. Guarantee he'd talk faster that way. What do you think?"

"Do whatever you have to do."

She gasps in mock horror. "Holy shit. Hadleigh Mackay didn't say no. I like it."

"Someone lied to him. Someone did this to him. To us. And I want them all to pay. So yeah, do whatever you have to do." My heartbeats hammer until the sound fills my ears.

I want to scream. To cry. To break everything. My fingers curl, and I squeeze them against my palm until my nails bore into my skin.

"I don't blame you. I would too. I'd fucking beat Peters to a pulp until he talked. But my father thinks if I do that, I may tip off whoever else is involved."

My pulse fires up even faster. "You think there is more than one?"

"Oh, definitely. This is not something just one person cooks up. My guess? It was planned well. And we will figure out by who and why. Just need some time."

"You have time. Because no matter what you find, it won't bring back his memories."

"He's going to remember, Hadleigh. He has to."

I press two fingers into my temple. "I don't know about that. He said he got into an accident, which supposedly caused his amnesia, years ago, around the time he disappeared. Which means he's had no recollections of me or any of it for all these years. So if nothing has returned in all this time, I don't think it ever will."

Her silence speaks volumes. She agrees with me. And it guts me because I so badly want to be wrong.

"Look," she finally says. "I'm not going to sit here and feed you bullshit. It doesn't look good. But he's back. Maybe not like he was, sure. But he's still here. He's alive. There's a chance for a new kind of life for you guys. And if he doesn't decide to come back with you, I will drag him myself."

I let out a small laugh. "You know, now that I know your real identity, every time you threaten murder or violence, it has a whole new meaning."

"You'll get used to it. Eventually."

While I attempt to find a comeback, there's a soft knock on my motel door.

"What the hell?" I mutter, jolting to a seated position.

Who could that be? I made sure the staff knew I didn't want cleaning service. There's even a sign on the door that says so.

"What happened?" Iseult questions with alarm. "Are you okay?"

"Someone's knocking."

"Shit, I bet it's him coming to finish you off."

"Finish me off?" My laughter bubbles out. "Like murder?"

"No, you ass, not like murder. I mean unless we're talking about your vagina…then maybe you could use some murdering."

"Oh, shut up. I bet that's not even him. I bet it's Dolly coming to check on me after the way I left her son's wedding."

I start to slowly climb to my feet, adrenaline coursing through me as I approach the door, hoping it's him. Hoping he really did come back for me.

"Who could blame you? The mayor had just defiled your revirginized vagina. Maybe she's here to tell you she got a view of the show."

"Oh my God, Iseult. Don't even joke like that!" I whisper-shout, getting closer to the door until I look out the peephole. "Shit," I pant. "I have to go."

"Wait, who is it?"

But I hang up and quickly pull the door open, stunned at the person looking back at me. "Hey. What are you doing here?"

HUDSON

"What do you think I should do?" I ask Sheldon after dropping Hadleigh off at her motel.

All I wanted, though, was to invite her over to my place. To hold her. And kiss her again. To help me feel like for once, nothing is missing and everything is right where it's supposed to be.

But I stopped myself before I could get the words out. Because until I know that she can accept me as I am, that I can be what she needs, I can't do that to her.

I haven't told Sheldon about what I discovered about Sergeant Peters. That he could be involved in what happened to me. I don't want to accuse anyone of anything just yet. Not openly, anyway.

I need time to figure out what happened. But how? I have no leads. I have nothing. Patrick Quinn has sworn to help me, and it feels like he's on my side. If Hadleigh says I can trust these people, then I trust her.

"You're asking me for my help on women?" Dropping into the sofa, he scoffs. "Have I ever given you sound advice?"

"No...but maybe you should start the fuck now because I'm losing it, man." I lean against the wall, shutting my eyes and gripping the back of my head. "I can't stop thinking about her. And I've tried, believe me."

"Well, you'd better stop trying, 'cause I don't think there's a point."

When I return my attention to his, he's smirking.

"A man doesn't simply forget a woman that looks like that."

I flay him with a glare. "Yeah, you better stop thinking of her the way you are right now."

He throws a hand in the air. "All I'm saying is, you have to decide. Do you let go of everything you've built here? Or do you let her go instead?"

And let that asshole who was cozying up to her on the video have her? Fuck no.

This is more than jealousy. I don't want anyone else to have her because *I* want her instead.

It's irrational. I know that. She's a stranger in every sense of the word. But she's this pull of energy I can't explain. This magnetism that I can't escape. And with every hour, it grows stronger. Until I can't hold on.

"So, you're saying I should leave and move to New York?"

"Not what I said. But it's an option. Can you really be who she wants you to be?"

Of course I can't. But going to New York may jog my memories. *Or make you regret remembering.*

I don't know why that thought even came. What would I be afraid of finding out?

Stepping off the wall, I start toward the door. "Gonna go see her."

His grin is cocky as hell. "Glad to be of service. And maybe this time you can get her off without almost everyone at the wedding finding out."

"Fuck…" I pinch my eyes shut for a second. "How'd you find out?"

I didn't tell him, and he wasn't there. He wasn't able to attend. His grandmother needed help after breaking her hip, so he spent the day with her out of town and has just returned.

"Dolly's niece supposedly heard you two, and you know how she has a big mouth. Dolly was happy with the news, though." He chuckles harder.

"Jesus Christ," I mutter. "Don't tell Hadleigh. She's gonna run the hell out of here if she finds out."

"Well, better pack some bags, then." He extends both arms across the sofa. "Just in case she does."

But could I leave my job? The people here? Could I leave it all behind for something I don't know?

But on the other hand, could I leave her twice? Could I really hurt her that way?

As soon as I arrive at the Leeway Motel, I ask the receptionist for Hadleigh's room number.

See, most places wouldn't give you that information. But when you're the mayor and the people all know you, they would do just about anything for you.

Standing in front of room twelve, still in the early hours of the night, my knuckles hover an inch from the door. My heart races, unable to knock.

What the hell is she going to say when she sees me here? Will she even open the door?

I don't know. But I have to try. I have to talk to her.

"Screw it." I lightly tap.

Seconds drift, and I don't hear anything. So I do it again until footfalls and hushed voices come through the other side.

Who the hell is there with her?

I knock louder, practically banging down the door.

Gradually, it begins to open until I see her. Same black dress. Beautiful…

Was she really mine? There's no way in hell I left her on purpose. She consumes me. Undoes every unconscious emotion residing inside me.

"Hadleigh, we should—"

But as soon as those words slip out, the rest instantly vanish because a man walks up to stand beside her.

Anger churns in my chest, hands dropping to my sides, forming fists of tension.

The man from the videos is here.

With her.

With my wife.

Looking too comfortable.

Fuck!

He assesses me as my expression grows turbulent, ready to physically remove him.

I instantly hate him, and I have no idea why.

The more I stare at him, though, the more something in my gut stirs, like there's something familiar about him. Something I don't like. Yet I can't place him, and it's killing me.

But it's probably all in my head. He wants to fuck my wife. Of course I hate his guts. And I'm sure he feels familiar because I saw him in the wedding video.

"Holy…" he whispers. "It's really you."

His eyes round, and he's staring at me like he knows me. But I guess he does.

"What's he doing here?" I grit, not giving him any attention.

Her mouth nervously fumbles. It's so easy to tell how

uncomfortable she is. Gently, I clutch her wrist and drag her right past the threshold.

"We need to talk." I pitch him a glare. "Privately."

"Uh, Brooks, give us a sec," she tosses behind her shoulder even as I continue to pull her out.

I don't want her anywhere near him.

"Okay." His brows gather, and he gives me a suspicious look. "I'll be right inside if you need me."

"She won't need you."

There's an edge to my voice that he catches, his mouth flickering with a faint smile.

"Shut the door," I snap at him, and for a second, his nostrils flare up.

Let him say something. I dare him.

"Just close it, Brooks. Please." Her eyes plead for him to listen.

One look at her, and the motherfucker softens. "Alright."

As soon as he does, I inhale a quick pull of air before I push her up against the wall, palms flat beside her face, eyes searing into hers.

"Did you *fuck* him?"

"Brooks?" Her face twists with hurt at the accusation. "Are you crazy? I've never slept with anyone!" she whisper-shouts. "Least of all your brother!"

"Brother?" My muscles go rigid. "That asshole who was looking at you like you're his was my damn brother?"

"Yes, Hudson!" she murmurs. "You guys were best friends too. You were adopted together at ten, he told me. You lived together until you were almost adults."

"No way. I refuse to believe it. I'd never be friends with that asshole."

She shutters her eyes for a second and shakes her head. "Brooks may have his flaws, as do all of us, but after you were gone, he stepped up for…uh…for me. I don't know what I would've done without him."

The words stab me in the chest because I hate them. I hate knowing he was there when I wasn't. That he was cozying up to my wife while I was here, forgetting her with every passing day.

But I'm here now. Whatever's left of me is hers. And I'd rather die than watch him take her.

Hadleigh's mine.

I can learn to fall right back in love with her. Wouldn't be so hard. Just look at her.

I cup her jaw, and with ravaging breaths, I graze my mouth with her soft lips. "I'm sorry." My forehead meets hers. "I shouldn't have been so rough with you. I just hate seeing you with someone else."

She twines her arms around my neck. "Ditto."

She sighs, and that broken little sound only causes the pain in my heart to deepen.

"There was no one else, Hadleigh."

"That you know of," she breathes. "Let's not, okay?"

She pushes me back a bit to look at me.

"I don't want to imagine you with another woman. It makes me sick."

Her face falls, and she stares down until the back of my hand is there under her chin, forcing her to give me those eyes.

"I'm so sorry," I tell her. "You don't know how badly I wish I could undo all the pain I've caused you. I'd do anything to give us back the years we've lost."

Her palm fastens around my forearm. "Nothing we can do about that. All we have are the years we haven't yet lived. And we can have them, Hudson. Together." Her thumb draws circles on my skin, causing it to tingle. "If you're willing to try. If you're willing to—"

I'm willing to do anything for you.

And instead of words, I kiss her, letting it consume us both—these feelings in me that just won't go away.

There's nothing soft or unhurried about the way I take her. My hands in her hair, fingers slicing through the softness as I tell her that I want it. I want it all. I don't know how we'll make it work, but we'll figure it out.

I've been alone all these years, not knowing the right woman was there in my memories, slipping through the cracks while I lay down to sleep. Because I know in my heart she's the woman I've been dreaming of.

It has to have been her all along.

She moans into my mouth, and a deep-chested growl rumbles in my throat as I pin my body to hers, wanting her bare, my hands, my lips tracing every gorgeous inch of her. I want to finish what we started at the wedding, and this time I won't let her go.

Not ever.

My palm wraps around her throat, feeling her pulse slam against my flesh while my other hand slips down to her upper thigh, forcing the dress higher, inch by inch, wanting to feel her grow wet against my fingertips, wanting to hear her call me Hudson.

Never liked the name Preston anyway.

But as I do, as I suck her bottom lip into my mouth, the door opens, and the bastard clears his throat.

"Sorry... Uh, Hadleigh, there's a call for you."

I growl against her lips at the sound of his voice while she attempts to drive me off her, but fails.

Reluctantly, I give her room to breathe, but still have my body right up against her.

Her cheeks grow pink, and I like seeing that.

I force my grin to widen because that son of a bitch doesn't seem happy seeing the two of us this way.

"Who is it?" she asks, her voice hoarse and sexy as hell. "Is it Elowen? Tell her I'll call her later."

He grinds his jaw. "It's Holden. He's been calling for the last five minutes."

She inhales sharply, and fear fills her eyes. She stares at him as though looking for a lifeline that never comes.

"Shit…" he mutters. "I thought you told him."

Something eerie hits the pit of my stomach. It washes over me, like a tidal wave of dread.

I cup her face in both hands and force her to look at me and me alone. "Who's Holden, Hadleigh?"

But as I ask the question, I know that her answer is going to ruin us.

Thirty-One

HUDSON

"Who's Holden?" I ask her again, her eyes shimmering with tears she won't let fall.

"Hudson…" Her shoulders drop, and it's as though every single part of her wants to retreat, to hide from whatever she's about to tell me.

"I'll let you two talk," the bastard says, and I don't even look at him. "I'll tell Holden you'll call him back."

Then he shuts the door and leaves me with more questions than answers.

Hadleigh pins her eyes to a close, long lashes fluttering unevenly, breathing heavy while I back off of her, shaking my head.

"Tell me what the hell is going on." I exhale harshly, pacing back a few more steps.

She opens her gleaming eyes. "I wanted to tell you yesterday."

She chokes on a cry. "But I was afraid it'd scare you away, and I just…I can't lose you again." She swipes the moisture dripping down her cheek.

"Fuck…" I grip my forehead, forcing my eyes to close.

Because I know. Before the next few words slip, I know what they will be.

"We have a son, Hudson."

"W-what?"

I can't seem to breathe, even while anticipating the answer. My chest piles with invisible bricks.

Heavy.

Breathe in.

Breathe out.

"His name is Holden," she goes on while I palm my chest. "He's four, and he's beautiful."

Her words cut deep.

I have a son.

"Jesus Christ," I mutter, my pulse racing as I peer back at her. "This can't be happening."

"I'm *so* sorry." Brows drawn, she attempts to grab my arm, but I shake it off, unable to wrap my head around it all.

I have a son.

A son I've never met before.

A son I don't know.

A son who's been growing up without me.

I'm a stranger to him.

Then it hits me.

Brooks has been raising my son, hasn't he? He's been there when I wasn't.

My heart rips into shreds at the thought.

I give her my back, unable to handle the raw emotions pouring out of her eyes when I'm barely keeping it together myself.

"He's perfect, Hudson," she pants. "He reminds me so much of you."

I grind my molars, my entire body surging with anger. Not even at her. But at this whole fucking situation.

A soft hand lands on my shoulder, and I swear her touch burns.

"Please look at me," she pleads. "I know this must hurt, but I never meant to keep it from you. I hate seeing you in pain."

Her arms wrap around me, and she places her cheek between my shoulder blades.

And without hesitation, I grab her hands in mine and hold them against my beating heart.

"What's he like?" I whisper, even while what I really want to know is if he knows I exist.

But the answer could shatter me, and I'm not ready for that. Not when I'm ripping apart at the seams.

"He's funny. Sweet. Mischievous as hell." She laughs with tears bathing her breath. "He's my purpose for living. He's everything that's beautiful in this world."

My audible exhales and the twining of my fingers in hers are my only response.

"We struggled," she goes on. "You and I. We couldn't have kids for years, and then I found out I was pregnant right when you disappeared, and I hated it." She sniffles, and her heartache seeps into mine. "I hated the thought of having a child without you."

What she must've gone through all these years...

"I didn't want to celebrate anything, but I had Iseult and my other friends, Elowen and Leighton. And...and Brooks." She whispers that last part.

I squeeze her hands, because fuck, every time I hear his name, I hate it even more.

"They made me face every day. They made going on tolerable. Because I didn't want to for a long time. I didn't want to live without you."

"Hadleigh…" I bring her hands to my lips and kiss her knuckles. "I'm sorry you went through that alone."

"Come back," she pleads, burrowing her face into me, and tingles spread up my spine. "Come home to us. I want you to meet him. We can be a family like we were always meant to be."

My head swirls. I want that. But I can't just leave with her. It seems insane to just drop everything and go. I'm still trying to piece together what happened to me. I still have a job to do here. I can't just dump it all behind, can I?

And what if Holden hates me? What if he thinks I abandoned him and his mom? Then what? I can't handle that. The last few days have been blow after blow. I can't take anything more right now.

"Please, Hudson." She lets me go and turns to face me. "Unless you want me to call you Preston, because I don't care what your name is. I just want you."

With a longing gaze, my thumbs stroke away the tears gathering under her eyes. My God, she's breathtaking—beautiful, broken, and breathtaking.

But I can't.

"Hadleigh, I…fuck, I don't know anything right now." I pinch my eyes to a close, not wanting to witness the hurt I'm about to land at her feet. "I can't go back with you. I'm sorry. We just met. Just give me more time. Okay?"

She lets out a sharp gasp, causing me to look at her, and I instantly regret it.

Large tears form in her eyes, but I can't lie to her. I need to be honest. I need time to think it all through.

"I'm so sorry." I cup her cheek. "I want you. I do. This connection between us is too strong to deny. But I want to get to know you first, and I want you to get to know me. Because you don't know me, Hadleigh. You may think you do, but you don't."

She cries silently, her chin trembling.

"This isn't fair to you. I know that." My throat clogs, and anguish shoots up my bloodstream because I can feel hers. "I'm so sorry." My thumbs brush back and forth against her cheeks as she cries. "I wish I knew you like he did. I'd give anything to be the husband you once had, and it kills me that I'm not."

"I…I understand," she whimpers, and it shatters me—fucking *shatters* me—to know I'm making her cry.

"Fuck!" I step back and palm my mouth, balling my other hand. "And now with…with my son, our son… I don't know how to deal with all of this."

Her face drops, and she tries to hide the new tears welling as she nods. "It's okay. It wouldn't be fair of me to expect you to just drop everything you've built here and…" Her bottom lip quivers. "And come home to people you…you barely know."

"Jesus, don't cry." I clutch her face in both palms. "Please just don't cry, because you're breaking my heart."

"Mine's already broken," she whispers, placing her hand against my cheek.

"God…" I clasp the back of her neck and bring her to my chest, kissing the top of her head.

"Where do we go from here?" she asks softly.

"I don't know." My words are filled with the truth.

Because like her, I don't know where the road may lead. Or where we'll be at the end of it.

HADLEIGH

"He doesn't want to come back with me," I sob into Brooks's arms while he consoles me, holding me close as I let it all out.

I don't know what I expected after I dropped a bomb in his lap. I should've told him sooner, but I don't know if that would've changed anything. He may have refused to come back either way. But it's out now, and he can choose what he wants to do.

"It's gonna be okay, Hadleigh." Brooks slides his hand up and down my back. "With or without him, you'll be okay."

I perch back to peer up at him. "I don't think I will be." Angrily, I swipe under my eyes. "I don't know if I'll be able to survive this, not when I know he's out there not wanting to be with me anymore."

The thought hurts so badly, I drop my face into his shoulder and sob even harder.

"At least he still wanted to look at you." He chuckles. "He couldn't even stand the sight of me."

"That's because he thinks we're sleeping together."

"What?" His brows rise.

"Yeah. I did set him straight, but I think he still believes you're trying to get with me."

"I mean, I was..." He shrugs with a smirk. "Not anymore, though." His smirk deepens. "So tell new Hudson to relax a little, because I sure as shit know he won't want to hear it from me."

"Probably not." I grimace. "Give him some time. He'll come around."

He scoffs. "You know him as well as I do, and you know how stubborn he was. Doubt that has changed much."

A small laugh falls from me as I remember exactly that. "I have faith you two will find a way to be friends again."

Even if he chooses not to be my husband anymore.

He nods solemnly, staring out into the distance. "I'd like that. I miss him."

"I know." I huff out a breath, trying to calm myself down before I call Holden. "Thanks again for coming to check on me. You really didn't have to."

"Yeah, you already said that." He laughs. "But I wanted to. Elowen was keeping me updated, and she told me how upset you've been. I didn't want you to be all alone here."

My lips purse. "You've always been a great friend to us. Thank you. I know I've said that a lot, but I mean it. I really appreciate it all."

"Of course." He dismisses the sentiment. "Now, call your son." He picks up my cell from the bed and hands it to me. "He sounded upset."

"Oh, no! I'm such a terrible mom, aren't I?" Emotions hit the back of my throat as I grip the phone in my palm.

"No, you're not," he says sternly, grabbing my free hand in his. "That kid is damn lucky to have you. It's okay to leave him sometimes, Hadleigh. He's not gonna break. He's strong." His eyes stay on mine. "Just like his mother."

I nod. "Don't feel too strong right now."

My mouth trembles as I force myself not to cry again.

"But you are, Hadleigh. You've overcome so much, all for that boy." He holds my hand even tighter, and I wish it was Hudson instead.

"Thanks for the pep talk." I clear my throat, slipping my hand out of his, trying to keep my composure.

That's what I seem to be doing all the time. Attempting to keep it together even while everything before me is crumbling. Every day, I wished for Hudson to return, and now that he's back, it's as though he's still gone.

I cup my mouth with a pant, tears flooding over my vision. It can't all end like this.

"I know," Brooks says tenderly. "I'm right here."

He is, isn't he?

Before I cry on his shoulder again, I grab my cell and dial Elowen's number. She answers on the second ring.

"Hey. Dare I ask?"

"Is that Mommy? I wanna talk!" Holden bellows in the background, and my heart warms at the sound of his little voice.

"Hold on, buddy." Elowen manages to placate him for a moment so I can answer her.

"It's not going well." I sigh defeatedly. "He found out about Holden before I could tell him, and he's... He's just lost in more ways than one."

I picture him—the way he looked when he found out. He was so heartbroken.

"He doesn't know if he's ever coming back to us." My voice shatters, even while I try to make myself sound like I'm not falling apart.

"Oh, Hadleigh. I'm sorry."

"Me too." I nod. "Anyway, let me speak to my guy."

"Of course," she tells me. "Holden, it's Mommy."

"Mommy?" he fires into the receiver.

"I'm here, sweetheart. I miss you *so* much."

"I miss you too! When are you coming home? I wanna sleep in my own bed. Please, please come home."

The way he sounds. So sad... My heart clenches.

"Okay, baby. I'm coming home."

Brooks's eyes pop in response.

"Really?" Holden utters excitedly, and I can just see his eyes sparkle with joy.

"Yes, I'm done here. Mommy's coming home tomorrow, and I can't wait to give you the biggest hug."

"Yay! Mommy's coming home, Aunt Elowen."

"Oh? That's wonderful! May I speak to her?" A second later, she says, "Are you really leaving? Because I hope it's not because of me. I can keep Holden for as long as you need. My mom loves to hang out with him while I'm at work."

"It's not you. I know you'd help in any way I need, but it's not right. I've been here for a couple of days already, and sure I could stay longer but I don't know if that will help. I need to be with Holden."

Gio's plane is on standby. I can hop on it at any time. And that time is now. I'm done waiting for Hudson to come around while our son is left in the dust. I need to be home with him. Hudson will know where to find me if he wants us.

"If you're sure…"

"I am. I'll be home tomorrow."

But before I go, there's one stop I need to make.

Thirty-Two

HUDSON

The morning light seeps through my curtains behind me while I sift through memos at work the next day.

I barely slept. Spent all night thinking about Hadleigh and our son.

What does he look like? Does he have my eyes? My hair? Does he laugh like me? Like her? Does he think that fucking Brooks is his father?

No. She wouldn't do that, would she?

But I don't know her. I have no fucking clue who any of them are!

"Ahh!" I bang a white-knuckled fist against my desk, my black coffee rattling, drops spilling on the paper.

I see the smug look on Brooks's face when he first appeared at her door. Did he spend the night in bed with her? The very thought fills my blood with venom, poisoning my thoughts.

I kept wanting to go back there, throw her in my car, and drive her to my place. Even turned around to do just that until I realized how insane that would make me.

I have to trust that she's not sleeping with him. That she's being honest. But what right do I even have to tell her not to when I won't be her husband?

But I don't want her to move on. I just need more time to figure out how I fit into all of this.

As I grab a napkin to wipe away the few drops still lingering on the desk, my cell vibrates beside the cup.

When I pick it up, I find a number I don't recognize. Instead of sending it to voicemail, I answer it.

"Hello?"

"It's Iseult. Got a minute?"

"How the hell did you even get my number? I didn't give it to you for a reason."

She scoffs. "When the hell did that ever stop me?"

"You're crazy, aren't you? Like *real* crazy."

"Yeah, and? Tell me something I don't already know. But call me crazy with my husband around, and you might find yourself missing a limb or two. Or maybe your head. So, you know, watch your *fucking* mouth."

"Someone actually married you?"

"Hell yeah, he did. And he's probably crazier than I am. You once knew him. Giovanni Marino."

"Doesn't ring a bell."

"Pity. Now, can we talk? 'Cause I have news you aren't going to like."

That has my pulse battering. "What kind of news?"

"So, your sergeant friend definitely lied to you. That sweet old couple who you've spent years thinking are your parents are definitely not. They really did die in an accident around the same time as your supposed accident, and that car was theirs. But it didn't happen in your town."

"What?" My gut curls, heart beating faster with each word she utters.

"Yeah, the accident they were in was in a completely different area, a couple of hours from you."

"Are you sure? Because I have the accident report, and the location was here in town. It looked real. I…" I pinch the bridge of my nose.

"It's fake." She sounds so damn sure.

"Fuck! I don't know who the hell to trust!"

"Look, I know the new you doesn't like me very much, but we were once friends. I liked you, and believe it or not, you actually liked me. So trust me. Trust my family. We have never done you wrong. But someone else did. Someone had reasons to fuck with you, and we will find out who it was, and it starts with that sergeant."

"What are you going to do?"

This woman sounds determined as hell, like she's about to storm in guns blazing.

Who are these Quinns?

"Well, first, you're going to send me a copy of that report to a secure server, and after I verify that it's fake, I'm going to pay that sergeant a very *unfriendly* visit. Are you in?"

"Um, shit… Yeah. I am. I want answers."

"Then we'll get them. Just do me a favor?" Her voice lowers with a flicker of amusement.

"And what's that?"

"Don't tell my father. He didn't exactly approve of my plan, but I'm me, after all." She lets out a sardonic laugh.

And it makes me wonder even more who this family really is.

"Have you met my son?"

"Of course. He's an amazing little boy. I was babysitting him the night she got the call that you were found."

"Jesus... This is all so hard to believe. I've spent all this time thinking I was Preston, yet it's all been a lie, hasn't it?"

"Yeah, and it sucks. I'm sorry."

She sounds shockingly sincere, and she sure as hell doesn't come across as someone who ever apologizes to anyone.

"You got the raw end of the deal," she goes on. "But I need you to know that you loved her with every fiber of your being. She was it for you. You'd do anything to protect her, and you did. You protected her from this life. From everything. You cared so much about her, and it'd be a shame to see all of that just disappear."

"I just don't know how to go back when I've never been that person. Not that I remember."

"Look, I get it. This is messed up. But don't give up on her and on each other. Because if you break her heart, I'm gonna have to break yours."

"Already broken." I repeat the words Hadleigh said to me, both of us wounded with shards of a life we once had, blood spilling from the cuts that won't heal.

"Can you tell me everything about the life I've had?" I ask her. "I feel like you're the only person who wouldn't give a shit and tell me the truth."

"Ahh, you've come to the right place." She chuckles. "Just promise not to die of a heart attack. 'Cause both my father and Hadleigh would kill me, and then Gio would kill them. So yeah, don't die."

"I'll try." I choke out a laugh. "Now, tell me. Who the hell are you, really?"

"Have you ever heard of the Mob?"

"Oh…*fuck*."

HADLEIGH

My flight has been arranged for later this morning. But I can't leave without saying goodbye.

Not to Hudson. I can't say goodbye to him. Not in person, anyway. In my hand is a note I wrote to him. The one I hope Dolly gives him after I say my farewell.

When I arrive at her diner, the door chimes as soon as I advance inside. She's chatting up an elderly gentleman who's seated at a stool beside a small round table.

When her eyes find me, she grins, waving me over.

"Hadleigh!" She meets me halfway and circles her arms around me in a tight hug. "You sure left mighty early last night from my boy's wedding. Slept well?"

"Um…not really, no." My brows tighten, unsure of what she's insinuating.

Unless she somehow suspects something happened between Hudson and I…

"Well, rumor has it you and the mayor got hot and heavy when no one was watchin'."

Oh my God. My face instantly heats up.

She leans into my ear. "Except someone was."

I gasp as she weaves back with a wink and a sly grin.

"This is so embarrassing!"

My eyes grow like saucers as I scan the diner, finding some of the patrons glancing at me. And some of them were definitely at the wedding.

"Does everyone know?"

"Not everyone." She gives me a knowing expression, and I just about want to die. "Let's go talk outside." She leads the way and opens the door for me as we both exit.

"I'm so sorry!" I immediately say. "We were reckless. It was wrong."

Also very right, and I wish it were happening again.

She tosses a hand in the air and snickers. "Honey, I don't care. I'm glad, actually." Her mouth curls. "That man needed it. Are you off to see him?"

My heartbeats stutter and my expression grows solemn. "Not exactly."

"Oh?"

"It's not going to work out between us. It's too complicated and he doesn't want to try, so I'm going back home to my son."

"You have a child… I can see how that would change everything."

"It does, but things between us are far beyond simply that." I purse my lips.

"He's a stubborn man, but I wouldn't give up on him just yet."

"I don't know how to give up on him."

My lips quiver with a broken smile, and my heart aches so vengefully I want to cry. But I don't. Instead, I hand her the envelope for Hudson.

"Can you give him this? It's important he gets it."

"Why don't you go and see him? Then maybe you two can talk and figure this out." She takes my hands in hers. "You two belong together. I can just see it."

"We once did." My voice sounds small and weak. "I just don't know anymore."

Her eyes turn with sympathy, and she takes the letter from me.

"I'll make sure he gets it."

"Thank you so much." The backs of my eyes throb. "I'm glad he has you."

"Well, I owe him." She shrugs. "Not that I wouldn't watch out for that man regardless."

I stare curiously, and she realizes I have no idea what she's talking about.

"You hear about him saving that mom and baby from the car?"

"Yeah…" I narrow a gaze.

"Well, that was my daughter and grandbaby he saved." Her own emotions show on her features, and she dabs her fingertips under her eye. "I'll never forget getting that call, but thanks to him, they only had a few scratches after their car hit a tree."

"Oh, God," I whisper, recognizing her fear. "I'm glad he did that for you. It's who he's always been."

"He gave us a miracle. Will never stop thanking him for that. Anyway, I don't want to keep you from your little one. How old is he?"

"He's four." A smile stretches across my face.

"Oh, how I miss that age. You take care of him and get home safely. Where's home, anyway?"

"New York."

"Oh, you've got yourself a drive."

"I'm actually flying."

"Well, you come back and visit us with that little boy of yours, will you?" Her gaze shimmers with kindness. She reaches for a hug, arms tightening around me before she pats my shoulder and lifts Hudson's letter in the air. "I'll get this right over to him."

"Thank you."

Then I'm heading down the road, back to my motel, where Brooks is waiting to return home with me.

Thirty-Three

HUDSON

I told myself I was only stepping out of the office to grab a cup of coffee. But instead, I find myself in front of her motel room. And when I knock on the door, I realize it's open.

My heart falls into my stomach. Because I already know she's gone.

When I step inside, my muscles tighten. It's completely void of any signs of her.

Not a trace left behind. Even the smell has been wiped from existence. As though she was never here at all.

I move further and sit on the bed, fingers running over the comforter she once lay under.

I should've come sooner. I should've asked her to stay. To bring Holden here. But I didn't. I ran.

I knew she was going to leave, but I just didn't realize it'd be today.

"Fuck!" I drop my face into both palms and mutter in frustration. I should call her.

And say what?

Sorry. I just missed you, and I don't know, don't fuck Brooks?

That asshole's face appears right in front of me, and it's making me fucking insane imagining him with his hands on her.

"Looking for Hadleigh?" a voice I recognize muses.

I instantly look over, finding Dolly entering.

"What are you doing here?" I note the white envelope she's holding.

"Well…" She takes a step closer. "I saw you pass the diner and called for you, but it didn't look like you heard me, so I followed you." She looks me up and down as though with pity. "Not surprised where you ended up."

"Do you know where she is?" I rise.

"I sure do." She plants a hand on her hip and stares disapprovingly. "She left with a man who wasn't you, Mr. Mayor. Saw her driving off with him after she told me you don't want to be with her." She shakes her head. "So, I gotta know. Have you lost your mind?"

Have I ever.

I chuckle wryly. "In fact, I did lose my mind, Dolly."

"Well, you'd better fix that right up, because if you don't, she's gonna marry that man and you'll never forgive yourself."

Marry him? For that, she's gonna have to divorce me, and I sure as hell will *never* let that happen.

Peering at Dolly, I want to tell her the truth. At least the truth as far as I know it. But Iseult warned me not to trust anyone in town until we figure out what's going on.

She did tell me everything about my past. About the Mob and the Mafia. How I used to work for people like her and her family. The kinds of things I used to do. She didn't spare any details.

I'm glad she didn't. I don't know if I'm really processing it yet. Really grasping that the person she was talking about was me. But at least I know.

Maybe I ran off to keep Hadleigh safe. But that doesn't explain the sergeant lying to me about the accident or the fact that he never met my parents like he said he did.

When I don't say anything in response, Dolly extends her hand for me. "Here. She wanted you to have this before she left."

"What is it?" I take the envelope from her, my pulse shooting into my ears.

"No idea, but whatever it is, I hope it has a way for you to go find her."

I stare down at it, my heart racing, unable to open it.

When I look up, I say, "I think I messed up, Dolly."

"What man hasn't?" She shrugs it off with a smirk. "It's what you do with those mistakes that matters." She comes to stand beside me and throws an arm around my shoulders. "Now, how about you come back to the diner and I make you a big breakfast? Then you can figure out how you're going to grovel. Have a feeling you haven't eaten."

Who can think about that when the only woman I've ever caught feelings for left me, and it's all my damn fault?

As we start to head out, my phone in my pocket rings. And when I take it out, I find Iseult's name. I quickly answer it.

"Hello?"

"I'm on my way to you." Her tone is harsh and urgent, and it causes me to stop moving. "Do not breathe a word of this to anyone, but the sergeant is planning on leaving town. Tonight. Permanently."

"What? Why?"

Dolly's brows furrow as she looks at me.

"Probably because he's afraid you'll learn what happened. So, we have to get to him before he disappears. Can you keep an eye on him until I'm there? I'll need a couple of hours at most. My plane is ready to take off any minute."

"I can try."

"And, Hudson?"

"Yeah?"

I'm kinda getting used to people calling me by that name now.

"The accident report was fake."

"Shit…" I know in my gut she's telling me the truth.

"I'd watch your back. It could be anyone. Don't trust a single soul."

I peer at Dolly from the corner of my eye.

No…

She can't be involved. Can she?

I've been following the sergeant for miles, staying far enough back that he doesn't see me, and I don't think he has.

Iseult landed a bit ago and is on her way to meet me here. Then she plans on grabbing him and interrogating him in my basement. Hopefully, he tells her what she needs to know and then we can have him arrested.

He quickens his pace, turning a slight right onto a narrow road. Another car passes him as he slows down and drives into the parking lot of a now-empty tobacco store. It hasn't been used since I recall, and no one has purchased it yet.

Parking right by the entrance, he slips out, retrieving his keys and using one for the store. That's odd. I never realized he had the key to this place.

Once he's inside, I keep a few yards back and park my vehicle behind a row of large trees. Hopefully, that's enough for him not to catch sight of me.

Slowly, I creep around the shrubs to the right of the store, wanting to know what he's doing inside. Is he meeting someone? Is he planning something else to ruin my life?

My phone buzzes in my pocket, and when I take it out, I find a text from Iseult.

ISEULT

Five minutes out. What is he doing?

PRESTON

Just went into an abandoned shop in town. Might be meeting someone.

ISEULT

Good. Will do it there, then.

PRESTON

What do you need me to do once you get here?

ISEULT

Nothing. Just stand there and look pretty.

PRESTON

Never gonna happen. Hurry up.

Stuffing the cell back, I round the corner of the shop and stand under an opened window when his voice comes through.

"I'm not doing it anymore." He stomps around angrily. "No! You listen to me. I'm done! I did my part, and now it's time for me to take my money and go live a quiet life."

Seconds of silence stretch as he paces.

"He's asking questions! Soon, he'll ask the right ones and put it all together. And I ain't going down alone for this, do you hear me?!" His shouting echoes through the space. "You threatening me?" He chuckles humorously. "Because I promise you, I could destroy you with what I know, so don't try me."

As I continue to listen, Iseult is slowly making it across the road in a black hoodie and pants. I gesture with my hand to my ear, letting her know he's on the phone, and she nods as she approaches me, standing right next to me as we continue to listen.

"I said I'm leaving, and that's it. I'm done! You can't make me stay. I'm not telling anyone anything. I just want out! I already betrayed my oath to this town and these people. How much more do you expect me to do?!"

Iseult's teeth clench as she concentrates on every single word.

"Fuck you! I've got my bags already packed. Nothing you can do about it." Another few seconds of quiet. "I'm leaving."

"We're going inside in one minute." She reaches into her waistband and removes a gun, stretching her hand for me.

My eyes grow.

"What the hell do you want me to do with that?" I whisper. "I don't know how to shoot."

Her mouth quirks up, and she drops closer to my ear. "You do know how to shoot. I taught you personally. And if he fires first, you may not have a choice. So take the *fucking* gun, and let's do this already."

Jesus Christ. Is this really happening? Am I really about to go in there and interrogate the damn sergeant?

But he's involved. He had to be talking about me.

A crashing sound rings inside, like he threw something and

shattered it to pieces.

"There's only one exit out of here, except the window," Iseult observes. "You stay by it, and I'll go through the door."

She eyes me coldly. She's ruthless. One look at her, and that's not hard to see.

"If he so much as puts his hand on his waist, you shoot. Got it?"

I've never killed anyone. Not as the new me, anyway. But I'm here now, at the crossroads between my old life and my new one, and they're about to clash. It's either I save myself or get buried in the process.

And if I want to see my wife and my son, I have to take care of this first. I have to know what happened to me, and this is where it begins.

"Okay. I'm ready." I take the weapon from her.

With a single nod, she crouches down like a damn ninja, going around toward the door while I hide under the window.

The door creaks.

My heart races.

"Ma'am, are you lost?" Peters's jovial tone rings through, the one he wears for everyone else. "You aren't supposed to be here."

"Actually..." She laughs dryly. "I'm exactly where I'm supposed to be."

Looking through the bottom edge of the window, I find her raising her gun at him.

"Whoa..." He lifts both hands in the air. "If you want money, I've got money. You don't have to do this. Let me just get my wallet and—"

"Move back and sit the *fuck* down on the chair."

"Wh-what?"

"You heard me, Sergeant. Move!" One look at her, and no person in their right mind would defy her.

"O-okay. Okay." His words fumble out of him, fear coating each syllable. "I'll do whatever you want. Just don't hurt me."

He steps backward, almost tripping until he gets to the wooden chair and settles into it.

"You can come in now," she calls to me.

I immediately rush over. Seconds later, and I'm stepping inside. When his eyes meet mine, they grow with unparalleled fear.

"Mister M-mayor? What is this?" He takes in the weapon in my hand.

"I should be asking you the same question." Sweat beads at my brow, my eyes flashing with a slice of fury.

And I instantly want to kill him. The desire to end his life overtakes me until I'm one with it. He made me believe a lie. He pretended this entire time, and he *will* tell me why.

Iseult reaches into her pocket and removes a pair of zip ties. "Tie up his hands behind his back, then do his feet."

"Absolutely not!" the sergeant bellows. Instead of remaining seated, he jumps up to a stand.

But I'm right there, two palms on his shoulders, a glare fastened on my face as I force him back down.

"Who were you talking to?" I question.

"Excuse me? What are you talking about?"

Iseult mocks a laugh, removing her hoodie. "Okay, so…this can go one of two ways. One, you behave like a good little boy…"

She pats his head.

"…and tell us exactly what you and your friends have been up to. Or…"

She grins with cold, bitter darkness.

"I torture you until you cry for mommy and tell me exactly what I need to know anyway. See, me? I'd much prefer the second option, but I don't think you would."

His eyes bounce over to me, chest trembling with wild breaths. "Preston, wha—what is this?"

"No!" She shoves the barrel of her gun under his chin and forces his face up to her. "You talk to *me*. You look at *me*. You don't get to play innocent. Not in this room. We know you lied about his police report. We know there was no accident. We know those people you made him believe were his parents are not, in fact, his parents. Their names are May and Augustus Swander. Does he look like a fucking *Swander* to you?"

"I—I didn't lie. I swear."

She huffs and shakes her head. "What a disappointment."

She reaches down to her ankle and removes a flip knife. The blade gleams within the sunlight streaming from the window while his gaze fills with palpable fear, so thick you can taste it.

And in a split second, she slams the knife into the top of his thigh until not even an inch of the blade is visible.

"Ahhh! F-f-fuck!" His scream permeates the walls, blood oozing from his flesh.

"Holy shit…" My pulse slams in my throat.

"So…" she nonchalantly remarks. "If you don't talk fast enough, I'll pull the knife out and let you bleed out right here on this floor. I'm sure the people who paid you to lie to Hudson won't give a shit. But, see…"

She exhales all dramatically, flipping her long crimson hair off one shoulder.

"I care. Because if you die, I don't get answers. But…" Her expression turns thoughtful as she stares up to the ceiling and taps her finger against her temple. "But that also means you die, so I guess I'm okay with that. I can always get answers some other way."

His face contorts with pain, shoulders rocking with heavy panting.

"You know what, Hudson?" She lifts the pistol in her hand and shoves the barrel in between his brows. "How about we just kill him and dig through his house, his phone, his work? We'll find something on our own. We don't need him."

"Yeah, fine." I clear my throat, pretending I'm completely okay with all of this, but I'm not.

Even with everything he did, seeing him like this, I don't want him dead, even though I wanted to kill him only moments ago.

"P-p-please," he stammers. "I don't want t-to die. I didn't want to." He stares right into my eyes. "I didn't want to go along with it. But they gave me no choice, and I—I needed the money..."

He sobs openly while Iseult rolls her eyes with boredom.

"I don't have time for this!" She bends forward until they're face-to-face. "My husband kinda misses me, and he gets really annoying when he does, so if you don't hurry up, he'll come down here and finish what I started." She lowers her tone. "And you don't wanna see him when he's really angry. So I suggest you talk faster. I want names!"

She removes a second flip knife from her pocket and lines the blade against the side of his throat.

"Okay, okay, please," he pants, lining his attention to me. "I—I was just supposed to make you believe you moved here f-for work."

She pierces his skin, drawing blood while he tries to continue.

"Was supposed to make you believe you lost your memory because of the accident, that you were driving and...and your parents died."

With deafening heartbeats, I slowly grow closer to him. "What really happened, Antonio? How did I lose my memory? Who told you to lie to me?"

His inhales grow deeper, matching mine.

I'm *this* close to finding out the truth.

This close to knowing what really happened to me.

My throat goes parched, my hands tingling with adrenaline.

"It—it was—"

Zing.

"Get down!" Iseult screams as my brain tries to comprehend what's going on.

She shoves me down onto the floor as a second bullet fires from the window, right at Peters.

But he's already dead.

Because the first one hit him right in his forehead.

His eyes stare blankly at the floor while the sounds of my own exhales echo through my head.

Iseult fires a shot through the window, while I do nothing. I'm useless with a gun.

Who did this? Who was trying to silence him?

She rushes over to me, darting her vision up and down my body. "Are you okay? Are you hurt?"

I shake my head. "No...I'm fine. What the hell was that?"

"A sniper. Professional. This is a lot deeper than even I thought it was. We have to go to my father."

"What about the body?" I get to my feet, looking back at the sergeant.

"I'll send the cleaners. They'll make it look like a suicide."

"Jesus Christ!" I slap a hand over my face, unable to calm the hell down.

"Did you tell anyone about what we were doing today?"

"No. Of course not!"

"We need to go. Now!" She reaches into the sergeant's pocket to retrieve his phone. "We don't know if the sniper is still here, or if more are on the way."

She hurries out the door while I follow, realizing we stepped into a pile of shit we may not be able to climb out of.

Thirty-four

HUDSON

"**F**uck, Red, you drive me crazy," Gio cups both sides of Iseult's face as his brows tug, dark eyes capturing his fear and adoration for his wife. "I was so worried about you."

It's plain to see how much he loves her.

Did I love Hadleigh the same? Did I put her above everything and everyone?

I'm instantly envious. Not of them, but of myself. Of the man I once was. Of the memories I've carried, not knowing I even held them in the palms of my hands.

Yet, they're there. Silently relishing in the love we shared, keeping me warm without my even knowing the safety of them.

This feeling of emptiness hits me all at once. Like something I didn't know existed was ripped from my gut, and I lie here in the aftermath, bleeding with no antidote.

Because she's in New York. Without me.

Iseult looks longingly at Gio, throwing her arms over his shoulders, a smile dancing on her face. "If I didn't keep you on your toes, you'd get bored of me."

The back of his hand glides down her cheek as his eyes lock to hers with affection. "I could never get bored of you, baby."

He leans in and kisses her while she groans, her hands in his hair, both of them lost in the memories they're creating.

Gio's friend Grant clears his throat from his desk, but neither Gio nor Iseult seem to care. He gets off his chair and comes around to stand beside me.

"Get used to it," he whispers. "They're like fucking teenagers."

"Good for them," I say almost to myself.

"Eh…" I see his shrug from the corner of my eye, a hand running through his thick black hair. His blue eyes catch mine for a moment. "It's not for me. I don't want to be tied down to any woman. To be responsible for her."

His eyes close as he takes in a deep breath, then stares back at them.

I consider what he says, yet shake my head. "I don't know. I think it sounds nice…"

My chest grows heavy as Hadleigh's face appears so vividly in my mind, it's almost as though she's right in front of me.

Close enough to touch her. To hold her. To tell her…

To tell her I want to remember how it feels to be tied down to her. To be tied *with* her. I bet it was beautiful.

"Well, from what I've heard about you and Hadleigh, I'm not surprised you'd say that."

"I don't remember her."

"Yeah, but your heart does."

And at that, it beats faster, as though it knows something I don't.

"Alright, you two," Grant calls. "Stop making out, and let's figure out how to not die, okay?"

Gio grunts and reluctantly separates from his wife. Slowly, they both turn to face us. He curls an arm around her hips and tugs her to him as though the thought of her being too far hurts too much.

As soon as Iseult and I drove off from the scene in a hurry, we took one of their planes back to New York. When she called Gio, who apparently knew of her plans, he told her to head to Grant's office in the city.

Grant Westbrook is some bigshot tech guy who runs Westbrook Enterprises, a company that creates the most popular cell phone right now and produces microchips too. And by the looks of this lavish office, set on the thirtieth floor, he's definitely got money, and a lot of it.

The view of the city is visible from his floor-to-ceiling windows, and the fancy-ass artwork on the walls makes no sense to me.

"Alright, so the sergeant was paid by someone," Gio remarks.

"Yeah..." Iseult nods. "If only we had a second more, we would've had a goddamn name!" She shakes her head with marked irritation. "I can't believe I let that happen. Fuck!"

She flings off of Gio and paces.

"Hey, don't do that." Gio grabs her wrist and brings her up against him. "You did nothing wrong."

"Don't lie to me." Her eyes hold his as she goes on. "I messed up. I shouldn't have done it there. I should've taken him somewhere like I had originally planned."

"It was an empty space," I offer. "Nothing in the vicinity. There's no way you could've known that someone would try to take him out."

She glares tightly, obvious disappointment of herself in her expression.

"But it *is* my job to know these things." She slowly marches forward. "If I hadn't fucked up, we could've had the real culprits in our grasp. We could've found out everything. But I…" She places a palm against her chest. "I fucked up, and I own my mistakes. You got it?" She looks around the room at all of us. "I don't wanna hear shit from any of you about how this isn't my fault. You hear me?"

"Okay, yeah," Gio and Grant grumble in unison.

"Good." She tilts up her chin and a ghost of a smile falls to her mouth. "Now that we've established that…" She reaches inside her pants pocket and hands Grant the sergeant's phone. "It's one of yours. I want to know everything on it. When he woke up. When he took a shit. Everything, you hear me?"

Grant chuckles as he takes it from her. "You know I love you like a sister and I'd do anything for you. But even my phones can't tell you when someone takes a shit."

"Well…" She tilts a shoulder and her eyes play. "You have room to improve, then, don't you."

"I'll let my team know." He laughs with a shake of his head.

"Stop flirting with my wife before I kill you." Gio's hardened, unblinking stare says he's anything but joking.

"Aww…" Iseult tilts her head until it meets her shoulder. "I love it when you get jealous."

He grabs a fistful of her behind and throws her body up against his, their eyes hungry for one another. "Keep talking and you'll see what happens when I get really jealous."

"Here we fucking go." Grant groans and returns to his chair.

As he does, Gio's phone goes off in his pocket. When he takes it out and stares at the screen, his demeanor turns stoic.

"Shit, babe, your dad's calling."

"What?" Her eyes grow. "Don't answer it."

He scowls. "He's gonna keep calling."

"Why?" Her gaze turns to slits, appearing like two weapons.

He grimaces. "He kinda knows where you were and what you did."

"How!"

"Well…" He takes a step back as though he knows she's about to lose it. "I told Tynan where you were, and he let it slip."

"I'm…gonna kill you *and* my brother," she hisses.

"I know you don't remember my wicked wife before this," Gio says to me. "But when she makes a promise like that, she usually means it, and I usually like it." He smirks. "Isn't that right, bambina?"

She scoffs and smacks his chest with the back of her hand. "Do you know what you just did? My father is going to throttle me for going against him."

"Yeah, he will." He shrugs. "He's gonna yell a little, get all red."

His chuckling only makes her more irritated.

"But then he'll just wanna make sure you're okay."

She huffs. "Just shut up and answer it. May as well get the scolding over with."

She gives him another death stare, and he chuckles even more in response, handing her the phone.

With a dramatic exhale, she hits a button on the cell and throws on a grin. "Hi, Daddy. What can I—"

"Are you fucking kidding me, Iseult Gwendolyn Marino?!" His booming voice carries.

"Okay, Dad…" She winces, pushing the phone off her ear. "So you're a little mad. I can see that."

"Mad? Mad?! Shite! You went on a mission on your own. With no feckin' backup! Are you insane? Is that what's happening? Because I didn't expect that from you. You've got kids now, darling. Think about them!"

Her eyes close as she shakes her head. "I always do. I know I fucked up. I don't need you to remind me. Won't happen again."

He laughs dryly. "I'd be relieved if that was actually the truth."

"Let's not dwell on the negative, Daddy. Let's focus on the positive."

Gio snickers, and she widens her eyes in a silent scolding.

"And what positive thing is that? Hmm? Because I fail to see any. We got nothing to go on now, unless you want to interrogate his entire town and cause a panic." He snickers.

"Well…" She stares at me. "We have Hudson back, or whatever the fuck his new name is, and that sure as hell is positive." Her eyes narrow at me. "Wait, do you want us to call you Preston?" She makes a gagging face.

"Babe…" Gio throws an arm on top of her shoulders. "Your middle name is Gwendolyn. you're not in the position to make fun of anyone's name."

She flips him off, still holding the phone to her ear.

"Put me on speaker," Patrick interrupts.

She does as she rolls her eyes. "Okay, Dad, go ahead."

"Gio, I thought you were supposed to be watching out for her. How the hell did you let her do that on her own?"

"Come on, now. We both know no one *lets* Iseult do anything." He hugs her to him and kisses the top of her head. "I married her knowing exactly who she was, and I'm not about to change that."

She sighs and plops her head against his shoulder.

"Jesus feckin' Christ. Your mother would've been so happy, sweetheart," he tells his daughter, and I wonder what happened to her.

Iseult's eyes grow sad, but she blinks the pain away.

"I'm going to go see Hadleigh." I break through the tension, and all eyes go to me in an instant.

"Why?" Iseult concentrates on me, as though wondering if I've found those missing pieces of myself. The ones that once loved Hadleigh.

"Because whoever was after the sergeant could be coming after her, and I need to make sure that she's okay. That our son..."

"Aye," Patrick says. "You go be with your wife, son. She needs you."

"I can drive you there," Gio offers.

"Thanks." I pause. "She wrote me a note."

The envelope Dolly gave me is in my pocket.

"What does it say?" Iseult stares inquisitively.

"I have no idea." My heart sinks from fear of what awaits me.

"Well, I think you should find out before you see her."

I think she's right.

Her folded-up letter chars my skin, begging me to open it as I sit in the passenger side of Gio's Bugatti. I can't seem to make myself read her words. What if she tells me she never wants to see me again?

I called Sheldon a bit ago, needing to talk to someone who knows me. He told me going to Hadleigh was the right thing to do. That I needed to know more about that part of my life, and I was glad he said that. I needed the confidence.

I didn't tell him anything about the sergeant, though. The last thing I wanted to do was get him involved in whatever's going on.

I also had to call the office to tell them I'd be out of town on vacation for a few days. I didn't inform my secretary where I'd be. They don't need to know that. I don't know if anyone there is involved in the con.

"You gonna keep staring at that letter, or…" Gio quirks a brow.

"I can't make myself open it." My pulse speeds. "I don't even know what to say to her once I get there. Or how to make any of this right for either one of us."

"Take it day by day." He makes a sharp right as he glances at me. "You like her, right? So that's a start. Everything else will come if you want it to."

"I do. But fuck!" I slam my head against the backrest. "She doesn't deserve for her own damn husband to simply like her. And what if it doesn't work out? What if her son hates me? What if she hates this new version of me?"

He snickers. "Hadleigh loves the hell out of you. The only reason it wouldn't work out is because of you. So stop getting in your own way."

"Like that's possible."

He laughs. "While you two talk, I'll get you a rental car from someone I trust and set you up with a hotel nearby, so that way you'll have somewhere to stay in case you don't want to sleep at her house."

"I definitely don't think that'd be a good idea."

I have to start slow. I can't just show up there and demand to sleep in her bed. Or any damn bed that's near that beautiful woman.

God damn it.

I grip my eyes shut, needing to stop where those thoughts are heading, but I can't seem to.

Feeling myself getting lost, I envision our bodies tangled between the sheets, my cock deep inside her, that gorgeous body slick and needy beneath me.

"Read the fucking letter, man," Gio interrupts, and I clear my throat, as though he caught my illicit thoughts.

"Yeah, alright."

I start to unfold it, focusing on the words as I begin to read them, hoping they don't kill me in the end.

Dear Hudson,

It's not your fault. I hope you know I don't blame you for any of it. I know you couldn't have wanted to go. I know you'd never want to leave what we once had.

But even knowing all that, even knowing how much I still desperately love you, how badly I want to hold on to your heart, I have to let you go. I can't stay here another day, wishing for something you can't give me.

I've spent years refusing to give up hope, wishing upon every star that you were alive, that somehow you'd come back, even while everyone believed you were gone.

But you are gone, aren't you?

Whoever took you from us took everything. All the good days and the bad, all the shared memories we held on to.

They're all gone.

But the problem is, while they may have taken them from you,

I still carry them in my soul, and I can't forget them.

I can't forget when we met. How much you meant to me. How much you loved me in return. It hurts to be the only one who remembers. To be left in the ashes of the fire that we once burned in.

So I had to leave. I had to go back home to our son, who needs me.

Just know our door is always open. You're welcome here anytime. But you have to want us as badly as I want you. So, until then, Holden and I will be here waiting.

My address is below. I hope to see you soon. But if I don't, just know I'll be okay.

I'll survive it. At least this time, I know that you're alive. That will be good enough for me.

It has to be.

Love,
Hadleigh

My chest grows heavy with emotions I can't waft through while

I hold on to that letter with the tightest grip.

If there was a way to remember, to feel the way I once felt for her, I would do it.

But what if there's still a chance for us? What if she can truly accept me as I am? Maybe we can start again.

Would that be fair of me to ask? Would she want that?

Maybe it's time I find out.

Maybe it's time I get my wife back.

Thirty-Five

HADLEIGH

"**M**ommy? Can I go outside and practice baseball? Pleeease?" Holden clutches his mitt in one hand and a bat in the other.

"Okay, but only for a little bit." I throw some pasta into boiling water. "Dinner will be done very soon, okay? And it's starting to get dark."

"Okay, Mommy!" He rushes toward the glass door, leading from the kitchen into the yard.

I peek out the window, seeing him there while I make us dinner.

I've been back home for a few hours, and after he got to hug me for maybe an hour straight, I started on cooking. He was so excited to have me back home, and I was equally happy to be back with him. I've missed him more than words can even say.

But as I stare out at our son, running wild and free, chasing happiness, a part of me is still with his father. And that part hurts so badly because I want him here in this house, making it a home, staining these walls with memories of us together.

Most of all, I want Holden to meet the man I've spent countless nights talking about. I want him to laugh, to play, to know his dad. To know the man who gave him life.

But I don't know if that's ever going to happen.

I start on the meatballs, combining the ingredients in a bowl. After I'm done, I return to the pasta, seeing that it's cooked to perfection. Lifting the pot, I drain the spaghetti in the strainer spread across the sink.

I wanted to make Holden's favorite food, to make up for not being here for these past few days, and spaghetti with meatballs is what he asked for.

With a smile, I look out the window once again, expecting to see him playing.

But I don't.

There's eerie silence greeting me instead.

My heart plummets into the pit of my stomach as I drop the pot with a clank and rush toward the door.

When I come out, I find his bat on the ground.

My arms break with a feverish chill.

"Holden?"

I glance all across our expansive yard, not seeing him anywhere. Panic grips its ugly hand around my throat until I can't breathe.

Until I'm blinded by gnawing fear.

"Holden!" I sprint toward the gate, my entire body trembling. "Holden!"

But there's no answer.

He isn't here.

Someone took him.

Someone took my son.

HUDSON

Arriving at a sprawling two-story colonial, I stare out at her simple brown door, powder-blue window shutters greeting me.

The home is big, but not grotesque. It's got an inviting charm, set across bright green grass that smells as though it had been freshly cut.

A black SUV sits in the driveway, and I instantly know she's home. My pulse rams in my ears as anxiety overtakes me, not knowing if I should even be here.

But I came to make sure they were safe, and I plan to stay in the area until we can figure out who shot at us. Until then, I'm not going anywhere.

"You gonna be okay?" Gio asks.

I grab the door handle, still staring out the window. "Think so."

"Alright. You have my number if anything happens. I'll text you the info for the hotel and leave the rental here in an hour. I'll put the keys under that giant flowerpot by the front door." He points toward the purple hydrangeas.

"Thanks. I appreciate it."

"Yeah, well..." He shrugs. "You were my lawyer once, and you got me off on a lot of shit. So I owe you one."

"Do I even wanna know?" I chuckle lowly.

"Nah. Best you don't." He smirks, his dark eyes full of malice.

I start to get out.

"You think you'll ever practice again?" His question causes me to stop.

"Why?" I raise a brow. "Plan on committing more crimes while I'm gone?"

Amusement flitters through his features. "I'm a Marino. It kinda comes with the territory. And the other lawyers we've had were nowhere as good as you were." He gives me a long look. "Maybe I could knock the memories back into that big head of yours." A slow-growing grin travels to his face.

"Wish it worked that way." I sigh. "Alright, let me go before I change my mind."

"Yeah, get the hell out of my car."

I scoff, finally getting to my feet, and shut the door behind me.

As soon as he pulls away, I'm standing there all alone, nerves grating my insides.

"I can do this. I can knock on that door."

But I fail at convincing myself, rooted in place as flustered heartbeats echo through my rib cage.

My steps are heavy as I trudge across the grass, heading for the front door. When I get nearer, I register a loud clank from her yard and a baseball flies over the wooden fence, landing inches from my feet.

Bending down, I retrieve it, staring at it for a second before I rise. As I do...

"Hey, that's my ball! Give it back!" A little boy stands from the other side of the fence, staring at me.

His brows gather with frustration while my heart beats in agony.

Because I'd know that face anywhere.

That boy is my son.

I stare at the small child, brown hair curling at his ears, his soft blue gaze a replica of my own.

An ache pummels through me.

My son is standing right in front of me, yet he doesn't even know who I am.

He extends a hand for his ball, and I trail nearer, blinking away the torment.

I shouldn't feel this way for a child I never knew.

Yet I do. I feel everything.

This gaping hole stretches inside my heart, causing it to ripple in heartbreak.

I missed out on *years* of his life.

I missed out on everything.

And for what? Why? Who did this to me? Who hated me so much that they wanted to ruin my life?

As I approach him, he tilts his head, and then his eyes bulge.

"D-d-daddy?" His mouth parts. "Is that... Is that you?" he whispers.

He knows me?

He...he knows who I am?

An ache throbs in my throat as I get closer to the fence, stretching out my hand for his. He takes the ball from me, our fingers brushing, and it sends a tingle up my arm.

"Daddy!" He throws the ball behind him, and I reach for the latch and open the fence.

And this boy? He runs for me. He runs so fast, I almost stumble back from the velocity of it.

When he's safe in my arms, I kneel to his height and hold him against my beating heart. "Hey, buddy. It's me. I'm home now."

I cup the back of his head with my palm and never want to leave.

"Holden! Holden! Where are you?" a woman screams in fear from around the house.

A woman who sounds like Hadleigh.

Before I can separate from our son and explain why I'm here, she appears, tears running down her cheeks. And as soon as she sees me, she gasps, a quivering hand clasping around her mouth.

"Look, Mommy!" Holden exclaims as I straighten to full height, her eyes glued to mine. "It's Daddy. He found us like you said he would."

Emotions beat through and tears fill my eyes.

Her body trembles with quiet sobs as I take our son's hand in mine and walk toward her. And with every step, she cries harder, taking my broken soul with her.

"Hudson?" she snivels.

And when I'm right in front of her, I curl my arm around the small of her back and tuck her to my chest, our hearts beating in unison.

"I'm here now, Hadleigh. Don't cry, baby. Please, just don't cry." My fingers twist through her softened strands, my nose inhaling her floral scent.

Her arms rush around my neck and she breaks apart, sobbing against me.

And all I want to do is stay. Forget the world I left back home and get lost in her.

But things aren't always that simple, no matter how badly we want them to be.

Thirty-Six

HADLEIGH

He's here. He's really here. He came for us. And I'm not stupid enough to ask why, because what if I don't like the answer?

"Is this where we lived?" His gaze scatters around the large kitchen, while I nervously straighten up, hoping he doesn't care about the mess.

"No, we lived in the city. I moved here after you were gone."

He nods thoughtfully, hands in the pockets of his sweats. He's uncomfortable around me, while I just want to clasp my arms around him and hold on.

Hold on to the past. Find a new present. Create a new future.

But how do we start over? How do I make the man I love fall back in love with me?

"So, he knew about me?"

He pulls up a chair and sits around the kitchen island as we wait for Holden to return with his collection of Hot Wheels. He was so excited to show Hudson everything he has.

"Of course he did." I slip a few loose strands of hair behind my ear while I finish cooking the meatballs, glancing at him over my shoulder. "I made you a promise when you disappeared that our son would know you. That he'd know everything about his father."

His gaze dips down onto his lap, and his eyes fall to a slow close.

Turning off the stove, I say, "Did you think he wouldn't know who you were?"

He sits up straighter while I wipe my hands on the towel, moving toward him.

"I—I thought he'd think I left, that I abandoned him."

Rounding the corner, I grab his hand. How I've missed his big, strong hands... The way they made me feel safe...

His eyes tangle with mine, staring up at me with that tranquil blue gaze, like a wave of calming seas throwing me into chaos.

"I love you, Hudson. So does our son. Don't ever doubt that."

His chest heaves as his fingers wrap around mine, and he nods. "Thank you for that."

My heart feels as though it's ripping right out of my chest from the emotions pinned to his features. From the tragedy of this situation.

And without thinking twice, I throw my arms around him and hold this man tight.

At first, his hands stay at his sides. But that only lasts for seconds until I feel his masculine touch around my back, and it's like a warm current bathing me in its light.

His palm brushes up and down, and my eyes fasten shut, taking in the beauty of this moment, the fleeting seconds of blissful existence I haven't known in years.

I'm in my husband's arms, and he doesn't even realize how much it means to me.

"Daddy, look!" Holden comes rushing in, all red cheeks and bright grin.

And in his glistening eyes, there's so much love to give. His heart is full.

This is what I've wanted for so long—for him to meet his father, the man who gave me the world. Until the world took him away from us.

Hudson kisses my temple before separating from me, and I just about melt.

"Wow," he tells Holden. "Let me see what you've got."

I blink away the quiet tears making an appearance, while Hudson grabs Holden and places him on his lap.

I still haven't asked him what made him come back. Was it my note? Does this mean we have a shot of starting over? Or is this temporary? I still fear the answer.

"Uncle Gio said this one is rare!" Holden lifts a red and blue motorcycle, which he got in a set from Gio and Iseult.

This boy is obsessed with those little racecars. He has about two hundred of them we're always putting away after the day is done. He once told me that when he sees his daddy, they're going to race them together.

And as he hands one to Hudson and they race them on the counter, the cars tumbling to the floor, I just stand there, misty-eyed, watching my two favorite guys playing together like they should've all those years he's been gone.

"Do you play baseball, Daddy?" Holden peers up at his father as though he hung the moon.

"Well…" he considers thoughtfully. "I can't say that I do, but if you ever want to try fishing…" He looks up at me and holds my stare. "Maybe I can take you and your mom sometime."

My heart somersaults.

The way he's got those eyes on me is making every inch of my body heat up—tangled with want, with love, with ravenous desire.

"Yay! That's fun! Right, Mommy?"

"Yeah, baby," I reply, still staring at my husband, whose gaze turns sultry and heavy-lidded.

"Can we go tomorrow? Pleeease?" our son pleads. "I don't have school."

"If it's okay with Mom, we can." Hudson holds him just a little tighter.

"Then we can go? Because Mommy already said yes!"

"I did, didn't I?" I laugh. "Tomorrow, it is."

"I've never fished before. Do they bite? Will I get to touch a worm?" He gasps with excitement, the sparkle in his gaze matching his father's.

"Sure will." Hudson ruffles his hair.

"We can go to the lake a few miles away," I offer.

"Can we do a picnic too?" Holden grins, waiting for an answer. "With s'mores!"

"Of course we can," I tell him.

I've never seen him this happy. Never seen his eyes look this bright, as though the stars have caught them.

My heart beams.

Hudson and I stare at one another once more, our eyes doing all the talking while Holden drops his cheek against his father's chest.

"You're not leaving, right, Daddy?"

"Well...uh...I have a hotel room your uncle Gio arranged for me, but..." His eyes fill with uncertainty, as though waiting for an invitation.

"You can stay here," I offer freely.

Of course I would. He's my husband. He belongs with us, for

whatever time we have him.

But the thought of this being temporary only causes my heart to break.

"Are you sure?" he asks. "I don't want to put you guys out."

"There's plenty of room here." A small smile twines around my lips. "You can stay in whatever room you want."

And I very much wish that it was mine.

"Don't worry, Daddy." Holden tilts up his chin proudly. "You can sleep in my room. I can sleep on the floor just in case we both won't fit."

Hudson laughs, and I swear his eyes turn wet with emotion. "Thanks, buddy. You're a good boy. I can see what a good job your mommy did…without me."

Those last few words are said almost under his breath. But I catch them, catching the sadness perched in his gaze too.

He missed out on so much. He must've felt it just now. Really felt the void. But if he really knew, if he got his memories back, he'd really hurt.

And in this moment as I peer at him, I realize I don't want him to. I don't want him to be hurt that way.

"How about we eat?" I say, needing a reprieve from reflecting on all the years we've lost, all the pain trapped between the days we never got.

"Do you like spaghetti with meatballs, Daddy?" Holden gazes up with a grin.

"Do I?" Hudson jerks back. "I'll have you know that's my favorite."

My little boy gasps, whispering, "It's mine too."

HUDSON

There's magic here. In this house. In these walls. Echoing through the space around us.

I could get used to it.

Staring over at her as she tucks Holden into bed, I can't imagine everything she's been through, and yet she's a wonderful mom. It's in the way that boy looks at her, the way her eyes sparkle when she stares at him.

In these quiet moments, I continue to realize how much I've missed. How much we could've had together. How much I don't remember.

"Alright, buddy." She bends to kiss his forehead. "Time for bed."

"Daddy?" he calls, and every time he does, my heart beats a little faster.

"Yes?"

"Will you be here when I wake up?" His face grows with concern, and I do everything in me to hold it together.

"Yeah, of course. I'll be right here. And I'll make you breakfast. Whatever you want."

"Yay!" He practically bounces in his bed.

From the corner of my eye, I find her swiping under her lower lashes.

"You sleep well, okay?" I kneel and kiss his forehead too.

"Goodnight, Daddy." He yawns.

I'll never get sick of hearing that.

I have a son.

My son.

And he loves me.

Thirty-Seven

HUDSON

"**W**hat made you come to see us?" she asks, settled on her beige sofa, a cup of tea in her hand. Her nervous gaze fumbles between me and her mug.

I consider how to answer that. I can't tell her about Peters. That I only came to keep her safe.

But that isn't even the truth. That was just an excuse that gave me the push I needed to see her again.

With soulful eyes, she waits for me to tell her it was all because of her.

And it *was* all her. Of course it was. This woman who feels like every bit of the home I've never truly had.

"I got the note you left with Dolly." I scoot toward her, the sides of our knees almost touching. "I wanted to see you. I wanted to meet him."

"I hope we were worth the trip." She smiles tentatively, and it hurts me to see her glancing away from me, seeming as though she's at some fucking job interview.

"Don't do that." I take her hand in mine, my lips dropping to the top of it. "Don't act like that with me. Not after I've seen you naked. Not after I've heard the way you sound when you come, the way your eyes beg."

Her chest rises with a sharp intake of breath.

"Just don't, Hadleigh, because you *are* worth it. You'd always be worth it."

Her chin quivers, and she swallows harshly. "I'm glad you're here." She gives me a long look. "But how does Gio fit into all of this?"

"What do you mean?"

"Well, you said he got you a hotel room. Why?"

"Oh…"

Fuck. Think.

"Iseult stopped by to investigate, and they offered to take me to come see you."

"Mm-hmm." Her brows gather.

I hate lying but I don't want to scare her with the truth. "Gio got me a rental just in case I stick around for a bit."

Her mouth purses. "Wow, you guys have been busy."

Shit, I really hope she's done with the interrogation. I don't know how much more lying I can tolerate.

"They wanted to help."

"I'll be sure to call Iseult to thank them." She tries to snatch her hand back, but I keep it planted on my lap. "Would you like some tea?"

She attempts to get up, but I don't let her, pulling her hand closer.

"I don't want it now, or the first time you asked. Now tell me what's wrong."

"What?" Her voice rises an octave. "What do you mean? Nothing's wrong."

"Hadleigh," I clip. "I may not know you like I once did, but I can tell something's bothering you. Tell me what it is."

"Fine! You wanna know? Then I'll tell you."

I stare poignantly.

"I know you're lying. I could tell right away, and I'm done with the lies!" She throws a hand in the air. "I swore that when I found you, we'd be honest with each other. But you're *still* lying, even while having no recollections about how you'd do the same thing in the past." She sighs, all defeated.

"I'm only doing it to protect you."

"I've been hearing that bullshit all my life, and I'm sick of it!" she scoffs. "I know you don't remember, but you've been keeping me in the dark our entire marriage. Iseult told me she told you about your past. And you didn't trust me with any of it." She shakes her head. "You thought I was some fragile little thing who'd be afraid of you or the world you were sucked into. But I'm not afraid, Hudson!" Her eyes hold mine with resolve. "I'm not afraid. It's why I named our son Holden. I wanted to show you I was all in. That no matter what you did, I'd still be here, waiting for you to love me again."

Her voice breaks, and she yanks her hand away this time. I let her get to her feet, hating to see the pain etched along every line of her face.

I knew about my prior identity, because yes, Iseult told me everything. But I just assumed she named our son Holden as some sort of memory to me.

She sighs frustratedly, and paces back a few steps when I rise. I hate that she's trying to get away from me. Hate seeing the anger there.

I march forward, gaze fastened to hers until my arm curls around her hips and I bring her up against me. Without taking my eyes off her, I stroke her cheek with the back of my hand, taking her tears with me. I'd take it all if I could. All her anguish, all the hurt she's endured. But I can't do that.

"I'm…I'm sorry, butterfly."

She gasps, her eyes stricken wide as though she's terrified. "Wh-what did you just call me?"

"Did I say something wrong?" Confusion settles on my features.

"You just called me…" She clasps a hand around her mouth, large tears gripping her lower lashes as they topple down her cheeks.

"I—I called you butterfly…"

Is something wrong with that name? Did I miss something?

"Yes," she cries, throwing her arms around me as she sobs. "Yes, you did."

This ghostly feeling washes over me. Like I should know something I don't. But instead, I stay silent and let her cry while I hold her, letting her get it all out.

When she perches back, she swipes under her eyes. "I have to show you something. I have to show you the letters you wrote to me."

She grabs my hand, and together, we climb up the stairs until she's pushing open the door to her room, a large bed in the center, walls a pale gray. But my heart is too busy beating out of my chest to care about the details. All I want is to see those letters. To know what made her this sad.

She rummages through a dresser drawer, removing a large yellow envelope. Slowly, she walks back to me. "You may want to sit down."

And I do, taking the envelope from her outstretched hand.

Needing a second, I take a deep, shallow breath before I open the envelope and remove four pieces of paper.

As my eyes scan the text of the first two, I realize exactly why she cried. Why her pain seeped out the way it did.

Because in them, I call her "butterfly."

My heart grips in my chest.

Somehow, somewhere deep in my corrupted subconscious, I know her.

I know my wife.

Chills spread across my arms as I instantly remember the sculpture on my desk at work, the one with the globe and the butterfly sitting at the center of it.

"I knew," I tell her with my heavy heart beating to a violent crescendo. "I knew somewhere in that damn head of mine. I knew you were my butterfly."

Grabbing her hand, I kiss her palm as she gazes down at me with battering emotions.

"You did." Her lower lip wobbles as she nods. "You think maybe we can see a doctor here and get another opinion about your case?"

"Yeah, let's do that." I suck in a long breath, kissing her hand once more before my eyes scan the first two letters, not believing that I'm the same man who wrote these words.

I read the third, about being involved in the murder of some cop. I wasn't a good person, was I? I really did terrible things. How the hell does she still want that man?

I shake my head and look at the fourth letter, but this one... I didn't write.

It's from her.

I peer up. "You wrote me a letter?"

My pulse quickens, not knowing if I can handle whatever it says.

"Yes, about a year ago." Her lips quiver with a barely there smile. "I wanted a way to talk to you without always leaving you voicemails for God knows who to hear."

My head pulls back. "What voicemails?"

She sighs and sits on the edge of the bed beside me. "Your cell phone, the one you used to have, has remained on all this time. Someone must have it. Whoever did this to you, I assume."

"Jesus Christ." I rub a hand down my face.

"It wasn't traceable," she explains. "Or we would've found it."

I nod, needing to tell her about what happened with Peters. She's right, I shouldn't keep her in the dark. I don't want to be the man I used to be. I want to change. I want to do better.

"I lied to you," I tell her. "You were right."

Her brows shoot up.

"Sergeant Peters from my town was definitely involved. Iseult and I heard him talking about having enough and wanting to skip town."

"Oh my God."

"There's more. He was about to tell us who paid him to lie, and before he gave us a name, a sniper took him out."

"What! Oh, God! Is she okay? Are—are you?" Her eyes wander down the length of me.

"I'm okay; so is she. But Peters is dead, and so is any chance of us discovering what happened. At least for now." I shrug. "Iseult is resourceful, though. I'll give her that."

"So, that's why you came…" Her shoulders fall. "Not because you wanted to, but because you were, what? Worried about us?"

"Yes… No… I mean…fuck, Hadleigh. I came because I missed you in some crazy way. I wanted you to come back. And even before this shit with Peters happened, I went to your motel and found it empty. And you know what that felt like?"

"What?" she whispers.

Sitting so close, I can hear the quiet breaths she takes, feel the electricity shoot up my leg when her knee touches mine.

"It felt like I was dying inside, Hadleigh." My fingertips trace up her knee. "Like my heart was physically breaking, knowing you were gone. That it was because of *me*. My heart somehow beats faster when I'm near you, like it's only ever whole when you're by my side. So no, I didn't come here just because I was worried. I came because I wanted to see you again. I wanted to…" I brush her hair away from her eyes as I stare deeply into them.

"You wanted to what?" Her breath hitches.

"I wanted to…" My nostrils flare. "Fuck, baby. I wanted to do this."

Then I kiss her with a groan, those letters scattering to the floor.

She tumbles backward against the mattress, me fitting my body on top of hers. My hips grind between her thighs as I kiss her like a man who hasn't kissed a single soul until this moment because he's been waiting for her.

She cries out into my mouth while my lips move south, peppering down her neck, her pulse beating rapidly beneath mine.

My teeth graze her shoulder, her hand sinking into my hair as she whimpers and hisses when I bite her a little.

"Please, Hudson," she begs, making my cock jerk with those little whimpering sounds.

"What do you want, Hadleigh? What does my wife want?" I grip the back of her head, fisting her nape roughly while I kiss along her jaw, watching the way her eyes hungrily take me in.

"Fuck me…please…" She pants, her nails scoring along my scalp, one leg wrapping around my hip.

"Jesus." My eyes lock with hers. "You sound so good begging for my dick."

My free hand slips into the waistband of her leggings, slowly inching lower, not feeling her panties again.

"Oh, God," she moans.

"Is this for me?" A finger brushes between her wet and warm slit. "Do you like being bare under all these clothes? Is that what you once did for him?"

"Yes…" she whispers. "He used to love it when I didn't wear panties." Her tone's heavy with desire. "Would make him crazy."

I roll my index finger over her clit, making her groan.

"Is that right?"

I love that she's playing along. Love that she's not referring to me, the new me, as her husband. In some sick way, I like competing with the man I used to be.

Slowly, I work two fingers around her clit, making her sounds of pleasure grow the more I touch her, claim her, even though she's mine already.

In name.

In blood.

In every promise we ever made. The ones I don't remember. The ones I hope to one day.

"Look at me," I demand, clutching her hair while I start to inch inside her. "Such a perfectly tight little pussy. Think it's time I stretched it out."

I thrust my fingers inside her, swallowing her needy gasps with my tongue, kissing deep and hard as I drive roughly, wanting her to come for me before I make her do it again.

Her walls quiver and tighten around me, and I can feel how close she is. Just a little more and she'll—

"Mommy?"

Fuck.

Her eyes widen while I glance toward our son, rubbing his eyes while holding a brown teddy.

I don't dare stop, though, even as she fights the orgasm she's about to have.

"Hey, buddy. Go back to bed," I say, grinning like a motherfucker on Christmas morning because this right here, her and my son, it's the best damn gift I ever got. "We'll be right there to tuck you back in."

"What are you doing to Mommy?" he asks as I rub her clit and hit her G-spot simultaneously, making sure I conceal her body with mine.

"Mommy had something stuck in her eye." I glance back at her and smirk. "Daddy is just taking care of her. Isn't that right, baby?"

She bites her lower lip, her brows tightening. "Mm-hmm. I—I'm good, buddy." Her voice turns low-pitched and fucking sexy as hell. "I'll be right in to put you back to bed."

"Okay…" His expression narrows. "It's not a mosquito in your eye, is it, Mommy?"

Thrust.

"Remember when I had that mosquito that flew in my eye?" he asks with a giggle while she fights a moan.

Thrust.

"Oh my God…" Her eyes roll back while I fight the urge to kiss her, loving the panic and neediness playing on her features. "Yes, Mommy remembers. No bug. Maybe an eyelash. Go to bed, Holden. Please…"

"Okay, Mommy. I love you."

"I love you too," she pants.

"We both do." I give him a grin. "Good night, bud."

Fuck, she's so wet. Bet I can make her wetter.

As soon as he closes the door, I fasten my palm around her mouth and slam my fingers so hard, she screams against my hand.

"That's it. Scream for me. Let me hear how dirty you are."

She spills across the bed, soaking the sheets beneath her. My hand slides into her hair, and when I brush her clit again, she flinches, crying out for me.

"Oh God, Hudson! I can't stop…"

I want to hear her. I want to hear what I do to her.

Continuing, I rub her, adding another finger because she's about to come again. I can see it in her eyes.

"What a needy little wife you are. Think it's time I got to taste that pretty pink pussy again. Don't you?"

Before she can protest, I'm on my feet, roughly pulling her leggings down, throwing them on the ground.

"Spread your thighs nice and wide," I tell her while I pace backward and quickly lock the door.

She obeys, opening herself for me, showing me how wet she is, how beautiful.

"What else do you want me to do?" she asks, like a shy, sexy little vixen, fingers rolling in between her breasts.

I cup my rock-hard dick, hungrily watching her movements. "Sit up and take off the rest of your clothes, then lie back down and touch yourself. Show me how you did it all these years that I've been gone."

A moan slips from her mouth before she does what I asked, tossing the tank top at me, hand between her soft thighs as she clasps them.

"No, baby…" I shake my head slowly. "Not like that." I settle on the chair right in front of her feet. "I wanna see it. I want to watch as your fingers slip inside you. I want to see how you stroke that clit. How you like it. Show me, butterfly. Show me how you make yourself come."

"Hudson…" she cries, this time spreading her legs until each one touches the bed.

"I can't wait to be inside you. I can't wait to take what's been mine."

I stroke myself through my sweats, unable to hold my composure when she's so uninhibited, willing to give me this.

I didn't even know what I was capable of. How I liked it. Not until she came into my life. Not until she showed me what it can be like.

My heart beats louder whenever I'm near her, and it isn't this intense attraction that I have for my own wife. It's deeper. It's as though, no matter the walls created between us, I can still hear her soul beating in mine. As though every inch of my heart still remembers, still wants everything we once had. Even while my mind forgets.

I'd do anything to know her, to get back every folded-up memory, every song, and every dance.

But we can make new ones. We at least have that.

I want that. I want to be a part of her world. A part of their life. I want us to do it together. Hell, I don't even know what that's going to look like. But right now, I don't care.

She sinks two fingers inside, rougher now, pinching her nipple with her other hand, and fuck, I can't handle it. I can't sit and just watch.

Jumping to my feet, I grab the undersides of her knees, and she groans with anticipation.

Throwing both of her legs over my shoulders, I lower my mouth to her pussy and let my tongue roll up from entrance to clit.

She rises on her elbows, biting that bottom lip while I taste her, sinking the tip of my tongue inside, before circling it around where she's most sensitive.

"Yes… Don't stop…" She grabs a fistful of my hair. "I'm gonna come."

I growl against her needy flesh, palms gripping her ass now as I push her deeper into my mouth.

"Fuck!" she screams, falling back on the bed, her body jolting as the release hits her hard.

I don't stop until she spills every drop, wanting this to last as long as it can.

She starts to loosen her fingers around my head, and I give her core a kiss before I climb up her body and sink my tongue inside her willing mouth.

And fuck, is my wife kissing me back.

Her tongue strokes with mine to a perfect rhythm, and I bet making love to her is going to feel like I've reached the damn heavens.

"Mmm," she groans, lips dropping to the corner of my mouth. "I should go and check on Holden. Knowing him, he'll be waiting."

"How about you stay here and I go check on him? How does that sound?"

A smile widens on her face. "He'd love that." Then she grimaces. "Think I need to change the sheets anyway."

"Seems like my wife is a bit of a squirter." My smirk curls on one side as I kiss the tip of her nose and rise to my feet.

"Oh, God…" She slaps a hand over her eyes, her cheeks still flushed.

"Look at me." I remain standing over her, staring at her bare body, so perfect I ache.

She gives me those eyes again, shyly looking up at me.

"There's nothing more beautiful than knowing I made you come like that. I just hope you have extra sheets…" My teeth scrape along my lower lip. "'Cause after I put our son back to bed, I'm gonna make you come on my cock, over and over, until you give me everything I've been missing."

Her chest lurches.

Wordlessly, her lips tremble as I turn and head out the door.

Holy hell, how did I get this lucky?

Thirty-Eight

HADLEIGH

Sitting on the edge of the bed, on top of fresh sheets, I wonder what the heck is happening. One second, he's saying he doesn't know if he wants to try, and the next, he's here, talking dirty like the old Hudson used to.

I can't lie. I've missed it too much to question any of this. To question whether he truly wants this.

Will he move here? Will I have to move there? I guess I can maybe find a teaching job somewhere else, and Holden can go to school in town. It's a conversation we need to have. Not now, though. But soon.

Getting up, I head into the large walk-in closet, finding him something to wear. I'd sometimes lock myself in here and cry. That way Holden wouldn't hear me. I'd lie on the sofa in the corner and sob until tears crusted over my face, until I woke up the next day realizing I had fallen asleep in here, amongst his things. The ones I could never get rid of.

It's as though he never vanished. His essence was in everything. But that's because love, the kind we shared, doesn't get easily erased. So I held on.

I'll always be here holding on.

Rummaging through the rack of shirts on his side, I pull out one of his favorites. A silly one I got him one Valentine's Day that says, *You can't tell me what to do. You're not my wife.* He would wear it out. He would wear it to bed. He just loved it, mainly because I gave it to him.

I bunch it in a tight fist and bring it to my nose, as though some part of him still remained. But that's a fallacy. Every remnant of his scent has been wiped from my memory.

The door creaks, and I hear his footsteps thud across the room, nearing me.

I hold my breath, waiting to see what he'll do. Desire unfurls inside me like only he can bring out.

"You kept all my clothes."

It's not a question. He knows. And that voice—it's a rugged male baritone, setting me on fire.

"Yeah." I peer back at him, afraid I'll burst into tears and send him running. All of this just breaks my heart. "I never exactly moved on, Hudson. I never quite wanted to let you go."

I miss my husband. Miss the man he was.

In his place is someone I don't yet know, but someone I want to. Because no matter what, I'll always want Hudson, even if he never remembers me.

His eyes turn molten. Something in them shifts with heated appetite as he moves even closer.

With a hammering pulse, I turn toward the clothes, searching nervously, pretending I'm looking for something else for him to wear, when in fact I'm trying not to look at him for one more moment.

Because if I do, I'm bound to kiss him. Bound to beg him for things he may not want to give. A life he's not ready to share with me.

I register the heat of his body right before his palms clasp my elbows, and even through my floral blue robe, I can feel the burn of his touch coating up my arms, leaving a trail of goose bumps behind.

"I'm sorry," he whispers, hands riding up to my shoulders. His voice sounds so broken, and I want to make it whole again—make us both whole. "I'm so sorry I left you."

His warm breath coasts up my neck until it brushes against that spot below my ear. Until my nipples grow taut. Until the ache between my thighs turns poignant and insatiable once again.

It's maddening, how badly I want him. Whatever happened before was not nearly enough, not after all this time.

"Touch me," I pant. "Please…I need you, Hudson. I've missed you so much."

"I'm right here, butterfly."

Oh, God. That name…

His fingers sink around the belt fastened at my waist, and carefully, he undoes the knot and pulls the robe free of my body. It pools around my feet while his fingertips glide feathery soft up and down my hips.

I reach around to cup his hard-on, needing to feel it in my hands, in my mouth.

I stroke him while he growls in my ear so seductively my toes curl, and his palms come to cup my breasts, pinching both nipples just enough to send a jolt between my thighs.

"Fuck, Hadleigh. Keep touching me like that and I'll have you on your knees, mouth stuffed full of my cock."

"Mm… Do it, then," I coax him.

He mutters a curse while I squeeze the head of his rigid length, his teeth raking up my neck. One of his big, strong hands rides south while the other grasps my jaw in a rough cinch.

"Do you want me to fuck this mouth, baby?" His thumb strokes my lips.

Before I can even answer, he roughly spins me around and plants his large hand on the top of my head.

His eyes zero on mine. "Let's see how wide your mouth can open."

Then he's pushing me down onto my knees, hand twined in my hair as he yanks my head back.

"Take it out," he demands, and a shiver races up my spine from the way he sounds—so in control, so domineering.

I crave every inch of this man.

Hurriedly, I yank down his sweats, and his cock springs free—thick and rock hard.

When I reach to touch it, he shakes his head.

"Mouth only, wife. You don't get to touch it yet. Not until I let you."

Oh, God. The things he's doing to me…

My chest heaves from rapid breaths.

With his other hand, he grips the base of his hard-on and pushes my face onto it, until my lips mount every inch of his thickness.

He doesn't let the back of my head go, keeping me there, full of him as he promised, until tears form in my eyes.

"That's it. Gag on it. Show me how badly you want it," he practically roars, so deep in his chest.

The old Hudson has never said those words to me before.

I love it, though.

I ache so badly for him, my core clenching to be filled. So I let my fingers fall to where I want him desperately, and I work myself while sucking him with everything I have.

"Oh, fuck," he groans while controlling my movements, controlling what he wants and how he wants it. "You're so beautiful. Naked, sucking me like you were made to do this."

A fistful of my hair in his grip, he increases his tempo, his dick jerking against my tongue until I taste his precum.

"Hell, you're touching yourself?" he growls while I draw circles around my clit, whimpering for another release. "Don't you dare come." There's warning in his tone. "The next time you come is on my cock, and I won't be wearing a condom."

I cry out around his thick length while he bobs my head. And the more he does, the more I need that release. I don't think I can hold it.

"Was he this rough, Hadleigh? Did he force his cock down your pretty throat? Did he make you gag, or was he gentle? Shit…" He groans, flexing his hips when I roll my tongue around the head of his erection.

"Tell me." He forces my head back, freeing my mouth. "Tell me if he was different."

I can't tell him lies, because Hudson may have been dirty and rough, but he wasn't this rough. I want him to be.

"No." I shake my head. "He never had me like this, on my knees, forcing me to take him."

A smirk edges to the corner of his mouth. "Good."

Then he's feeding his cock back into my mouth so hard, new tears line my eyes, and I love it. I love this version of him—this possessive, jealous version of Hudson.

Was it hiding there all this time? Was he afraid of being that rough with me? Did he want to be? These are questions I'll never have answers to.

I cup his balls, squeezing them in my hands while he continues his unrelenting, delicious torment.

"Fuck this..." In one quick move, he pulls me up until I'm standing, kissing me hard while forcing my body backward against the ladder lying across one side of the closet.

His hands are everywhere at once, while mine are on his back, nails sinking into all that hard, well-defined muscle.

He wrenches away, clenching his jaw. "The first time I come, it'll be inside you."

"Please..." My teeth swallow my bottom lip.

"Turn around and bend over," he demands. "And make sure you hold on to that ladder, angel, because I'm not going to be gentle."

Angel...

He called me angel. Like he once did...

Was it a coincidence, or is that another sign?

I grasp on to the hope that he can come back to me.

But before I can analyze further what that means, he flips me around and pushes me down by the back of my neck, cheek planted against one of the ladder steps.

"So fucking perfect." He slaps my ass hard, continuing to imprison my head with his palm. "Now, I'm gonna see how perfectly you take my cock."

From behind my shoulders, I watch as he steps out of his pants and yanks his t-shirt off one-handed. His bicep jerks when my gaze takes in all of him, from his heavy length to the muscular torso of his body.

Hudson has always done it for me. From the moment we met, I could admit to myself how attractive he was, how much he turned me on. And through the years that has only electrified. Now, him this animalistic, this wanton? God, the things I want him to do to me.

He comes to stand behind me, his cock twitching against the

crook of my ass. "Did he ever take this hole?"

A single finger enters me with just the tip, and I instantly contract around it, not used to the intrusion.

"No." I tremble as two fingers of his other hand sink into my pussy and he pumps into me from both ends.

"I love knowing that I can give you things he didn't."

He's thrusting so deep that I feel full everywhere all at once. My walls clench around him, and the groan escaping his lips is every indication that he feels it. Feels the power he wields over my body, the tormenting way he has me under his grasp.

"I don't know what you ever saw in him or me," he growls. "But I promise, from now on, I'll be the kind of man you deserve."

From now on? Does that mean—

"Oh, God!" I scream as his tempo intensifies.

The responsive moans coming from me are far too shameful to ever make in public. He makes me feel everything—my body and heart blazing in unison.

He slips out of me and uses the same hand to grab me by my throat, whispering against my ear, "I can't wait to sink inside you, to feel your needy pussy hungrily tighten around me."

With his other palm, he positions his cock around my entrance and slams home.

"Yes!" I scream unabashed. "It's been so long."

My hips jut out, and it makes him groan. He yanks my head back and takes my lips in a rough kiss, not allowing me reprieve as he pounds into me like he's possessed. Like he's damned if he'd ever do anything but fuck me as hard and as deep as he can.

He dips his hand between my legs and works my clit at the same time, sending me so close to the edge, I'm about to free-fall headfirst into oblivion.

"Is this what you want?" His voice is a hoarse and raspy

concoction of sin.

And as our eyes connect, as the sound of skin on skin reverberates through the room, he pinches my clit between his fingers. I scream out his name as I let go, feeling the wave of ecstasy undo me.

"Hudson…" I gasp. "Yes!"

This feeling, it overtakes me until I'm floating, my toes curling as he continues to pump into me.

His growl is beastly as he releases himself inside me, yanking my hair until my skull hums with a burn.

"That's it," he rasps. "Take every drop of my cum inside that hot little pussy. Take it all."

The more he talks, the more turned on I get.

And just when I think we're done, he slips out of me, flips me around, and lifts me in the air by my hips.

"What the…" I gasp before I'm impaled on his cock, already hard. "How are you ready again this soon?"

My teeth sink into the corner of my bottom lip.

"One look at you, and that's all it takes." He thrusts me up against the wall, jutting out his hips until my eyes roll back. "Now, how about you show me what a good wife you are and squirt this time?"

And God, I do. I give him everything. Over and over until we're both spent and in each other's arms, where we belong.

HUDSON

She's tucked against my chest while the letter she wrote me burns in my hand. I'm afraid to read it, knowing it's going to break my heart all over again.

But I know I have to. I need to know everything.

Dear Hudson,

I can't believe how much you've missed out on. Years have flown by. Sometimes, I go back to that day you disappeared and relive that morning when you made us breakfast. When we sat together at the table for the very last time.

It makes me sad to think about it, but happy too. Because I can go back to that day whenever I want to, and it plays in my mind as though it's happening.

But then I open my eyes and realize you're not there. You may never be. And that only kills me.

Elowen and Leighton urge me to let the idea that you're alive go, but I can't do that. As long as that phone rings and your voicemail answers, I hold on and keep swimming through the rough seas. I know you're there, being swallowed by a dark, angry ocean. But I'll find you someday. I know I will.

Holden is three and looks more like you every day. He's such a good student and has already started to read. His favorite books are anything with dogs or dolphins. He's been begging me to get a dog for months now, but it wouldn't be fair to the dog. I don't have the time with work and everything. He even picked the breed and a name. He said he wants a Cavalier King Charles and wants to call him Gatorade. Yes, like the drink, because I told him that was your favorite.

He knows everything about you and asks about you all the time. Knows your face from all the photos we have around the house. You're everywhere, baby. In everything.

I talk about you to him. I tell him how amazing his father was, how much he loves us, how much he wishes he can come home.

The girls think I should tell him you died to make him process better, but I can't do that. Because you're not. You can't be gone. I don't accept that, Hudson. You hear me? I don't accept that.

I still wear my wedding ring. It'll be on my finger until my last day. Because I'll die as your wife, Hudson Bradley Mackay.

So you come back to me. I'll be here waiting.

Love,
Hadleigh

With my eyes blurring from my emotions, I flip the letter facedown on my chest and glance at her: my gorgeous wife. She held on longer than anyone else would. She deserves to have a man who'll hold on now. Hold on to everything.

Lifting my head, I kiss her softly against her temple, inhaling the hint of jasmine in her shampoo.

"I'm not going anywhere, butterfly," I whisper. "They won't be able to tear me away from you this time. Not if I can help it."

Thirty-Nine

HUDSON

The following morning, with my son and my wife around the kitchen table, I flip some chocolate chip pancakes in the pan while Holden gawks excitedly.

I made them look like hearts as he requested and even added extra chocolate. At this point, I'd do anything he asked. It's the guilt. The hole in my heart that reminds me I missed out on so much of his life. A pang hits my chest as I stare into his face, unable to pry my eyes away.

When did he take his first steps? When did he say his first word? Was it "Dada"? Did he grow up hurting when he'd see photos of me and none with him and I? There are so many pictures here of me in this house.

Staring at him is like staring into the face of a ghost. He's me, yet he isn't. It's the craziest thing.

I catch Hadleigh's attention, and her soft smile makes me want to kiss her, to take her in my arms and make love to her slow.

I was too rough last night. But fuck, it was this pent-up need in me. The crazed way I wanted her.

Next time, though, it'll be slow. I'll take my time. I'll kiss on every inch of her body until every single part of it feels worshiped.

"Daddy!" Holden giggles. "You're burning my pancake."

"Oh, shit," I chuckle, turning to get the damn thing on his plate.

"Oooh, Mommy, he said a bad word." He puts on a mischievous grin. "You have to put a dollar into the swear jar, Daddy."

"That's fair." I turn the stove off and grab two plates—one for her and one for him—and place it before them. Reaching for her, I kiss the top of her head.

"Yep, it's Mommy's rules!" he informs me.

"Well, your mother is not only beautiful, but smart, and according to my shirt…" I stare down at one she gave me to wear. "…she's the only one who's allowed to tell me what to do, so a dollar, it is."

She shakes her head with a laugh. "It's okay. You're new here. It's an adjustment. We'll let it slide this time. Right, buddy?" She gives him a little wink.

New here…

I let the words sink in. And fuck, did they just hurt.

I clear my throat and go back for my plate before pulling up a chair between them and settling into it.

Before I can get a bite in, the front door opens.

"Who's hungry?" A voice I despise carries toward us.

My eyes glare at hers. "What the *hell* is he doing here?"

"Swear jar," Holden whispers with a giggle.

I force a smile and ruffle his hair, but my insides are filling with venom.

"He has a key, and I—" she explains.

But my attention immediately jumps to my supposed brother, who's walking into her kitchen like he lives here. Like he's her fucking husband.

You're new here.

Yeah, I can fucking see that perfectly well.

His eyes snap to mine and his brow arches. "Oh…"

There's a paper bag in his grip. My jaw tics, and my fist curls on top of my thigh, not wanting my son to see how angry I am.

"Uncle Brooks!" Holden jumps out of his chair and runs to him.

Rage instantly fills my bloodstream at seeing my child with this man. I hate it. I hate knowing he watched my son grow up. A son who probably saw him as a father figure.

"Hey, little man!" He lifts him up and kisses his forehead. "Did you get taller since I saw you last?"

"You saw me like a few days ago." Holden rolls his eyes and laughs.

Brooks lowers him onto his feet and glances at the table. "Looks like you guys already have yourself a nice breakfast."

"Yeah, we do. You can go." I grind my molars. "We're good."

"Hudson…" Hadleigh gives me a look that says I'm being an asshole.

Ask me if I care.

He wants her. I don't give a shit what she believes. He wants my wife even now, the way he's glancing at her with that smile I want to wipe clean off his face.

I swear I don't even recognize myself right now. But this bastard brings out the savage in me. Maybe I have more in common with the old Hudson than I realize.

"Hey, Hadleigh," he says. "Think I could steal Hudson for a moment? I think we're overdue for a chat." His eyes bounce to me. "Don't you?"

"Let's go." I push the chair back a little too loud. But before I go, I drop my mouth close to her ear. "I'm sorry."

My lips land against her cheek, and before I walk away, she grabs my hand and kisses my palm. In her eyes, I find understanding.

My heart clenches painfully. Because looking at her the way I'm doing, it tears me up. To feel the way I feel for her while knowing I felt so much more before I vanished is destroying me.

"You're not leaving, right, Daddy?" Holdens zaps my attention toward him.

Letting go of her hand, I kneel before him and grab his. "Never. Never again will I leave you or your mom. I love you."

And fuck, I want to say those words to her. She deserves to hear them. But I'm afraid that it's not the right moment or that I don't even know what love is.

She deserves those words when I know in my heart that I mean them with no doubt.

"Come on," I tell the asshole, brushing past him as he follows me out of the kitchen and through a long corridor.

I enter the first open door, finding a game room with arcades and a pool table. He shuts the door behind him and leans against it, his arms crossed over his chest.

"So, you hate me." He smirks. "I get it."

"No," I snap. "You don't get anything. You've been here while I've been there, not knowing that I'm this whole other fucking person." I step up to him until merely an inch remains between us. "But I'm here now, and she's mine. Do we understand each other?"

He raises both palms in the air. "I got it, brother. She's yours." His arms fall to his side. "I won't lie to you and say I don't have any more feelings for her, because I still do, no matter what I made her believe."

And there we have it. I fucking knew it!

"But I'm still your brother and your best friend. I'd never cross that line now that you're back. And I *am* happy that you are, man." His jaw tenses. "I know you hate my guts, and if I were in your shoes, I probably would too. But you have to know that while you were gone, I made sure they were taken care of just like you asked me to on the day you disappeared."

"I must've been drugged that day."

His laughter echoes through the room. "I fucking missed you." He shakes his head. "But yeah, you did ask me. It's the only reason I stayed in their life the way I did. I wanted to make sure I kept that last promise to you. It meant a lot to me. Then you were gone, and I had this heavy baggage I was carrying. And yeah, sure, I'm sorry I fell for her in the process. But can you fucking blame me?"

I hate this guy. But it *is* Hadleigh. Who wouldn't want her?

"No, I can't."

"Well, great, then." He grins. "At least we agree on something."

"Don't push it." I glare.

He chuckles. "Wouldn't dream of it." Easing off the door, he says, "But look, you know, give it time. I think you'll like me again."

I stare coldly. "Doubt it."

"You know, you said the same thing when we met at ten years old. You hated me. Then we became the best of friends in every sense of the word. And when the world gave you a gift and the Quinns made you a king, you didn't forget about me. You made sure I had what I needed. I couldn't have been that bad, could I?" A smile plays on one side of his mouth.

"Maybe I was just an idiot."

"Well…" He shrugs. "Won't get an argument from me."

Am I wrong about him? Is this just maddening jealousy?

"Did you sleep with her?" I can't even get the question out without sounding like I'm about to tear him to pieces for even thinking it.

"Of course not. There was a kiss, but that was—"

"A what?" I snap, my pulse rattling like damn thunder in my ears.

My nostrils pop as I advance closer, until we're nose to nose.

"Look, man, I thought you were dead. I—" He peers down for a moment. "It's over. Nothing will happen again. She said your name as I kissed her, and she stopped before it got anywhere, so don't hate her for it."

"I could never hate her. But you…" My eyes widen. "What kind of person tries to take his brother's place? Hmm?"

"The kind that has a heart. I'm sorry, Hudson, but she's special. I couldn't stop what I felt for her. Watching her hurting the way she was for years…" He pinches his eyes closed. "I'm sorry, but all I wanted was to make her happy."

"If you expect a thank-you, you won't get it from me."

I don't care if I sound bitter. That's because I am.

"No." He shakes his head. "I don't expect that, not after everything you've been through. I'm a stranger to you. Just some asshole who tried to take your woman. You have every right to wanna knock my face in." He's smirking again. "Wish you wouldn't. Kinda like my face."

"Mm-hmm. Don't expect me to ask you to stay for breakfast, either."

"Seems like I've got a bag full of food, so I'll just go. Maybe you and I can get a drink sometime. I can fill you in on all the shit we got into as kids." He exhales a short breath of laughter, looking distantly before he sighs. "It was good having you there when things were bad."

"Bad?"

He nods. "Yeah, shit was bad. Our adoptive parents were not the nicest people, especially to me. But you…you always defended me."

Fuck. I don't want to know. Yet I do.

"Maybe we can get that drink sometime."

"I'm looking forward to it." He starts to head out. "So, you're really back permanently?"

"Yeah, though I'm still figuring out the logistics. I'm not leaving them. Not ever again."

He smiles tightly. "Good. They need you."

"I need them too."

HADLEIGH

"How's this detective?" he asks later that day as we drive off to the precinct.

When Detective Tompkins called after hearing Hudson was back, she wanted to meet him to discuss what he knows so she can help get to the bottom of it.

"Honestly?" I grimace. "She's kind of a bitch."

He chuckles. "I can handle her. Don't worry, baby."

He squeezes my hand, and my fingers wrap around his. Every chance I get, I want to touch him to make sure he's actually real.

I huff out a breath and lay my head against his shoulder. "So, you and Brooks managed not to kill each other. I'm proud of you."

"Uh-huh…keep talking, angel, and I'm gonna turn this car around and kill him just for kissing you."

Oh, God. He told him…

"I'm sorry." I clasp his cheek and peer at him even as his attention remains on the road. "It sounds worse than it is."

I swallow past the lump in my throat, feeling like I cheated on him all over again.

He doesn't say a word as I continue. The only thing I notice is the way a muscle in his neck pops.

"It was the night I got the call from Grant that he found you," I explain. "I was at a benefit honoring you and all these feelings of missing you came storming in, and when he asked me to dance, I just…" My voice goes out, like a flame that flickers out into darkness. "In my head, it was you, and I got lost for a moment. Please forgive me."

He finally returns my attention as we arrive at the police station and he parks the car.

"Of course I do. I don't like it, but I do." Heavy emotions thread through his gaze, and the back of his hand strokes down my cheek. "You have nothing to be sorry about, Hadleigh. I'm just mad at myself," he whispers, cupping my face in both hands.

"We're both a mess, aren't we?" My laughter is as sad as his smile.

"Yeah, we are. But we're in this together. You're not going to be alone anymore."

And I hope that's a promise.

Because I can't lose him again.

HUDSON

"Nice to see you alive and well, Mr. Mackay," Detective Tompkins says as we sit across from her.

And Hadleigh was right; she is a bitch. I didn't like her as soon as I stepped foot inside.

My gaze stabs her with contempt. "Nice to be alive."

"Can I get you two something to drink? Our coffee here tastes like piss water, but I can get you guys some sodas." Her gaze drifts between Hadleigh and me.

"We're fine." I grab my wife's fidgeting hand and hold it on my lap.

She doesn't want to be here. Her nerves are dripping out of her pores.

"We want to go home to our son, so if we can get on with this?"

"Alright." She gives me a half smile that never quite reaches her eyes. "I'd like to know everything you may recall from your life as Preston and Hudson. Your wife told me you have no recollection of your past? Not at all?"

I can tell she's not buying it.

"I don't remember being Hudson. I don't even know him. I can tell you don't believe me." I incline my chin. "But I don't care. Because I can't tell you what I don't know."

"So, you have no idea how you became Preston?"

In a perfect world, I'd trust her to help me figure out exactly that, but we have never been in that world. Iseult doesn't want anyone else involved, especially the law. If they catch wind of what happened with Peters and accidentally tip off the culprits before we get to them, I may lose my one chance at finding the truth.

"I don't know how I got a new name. The people in town will tell you I was in an accident and that caused me to lose my memory, but that they all knew me as this Preston."

She flips the pen in her hand, staring at me thoughtfully. "I believe you. I'll be interviewing those townies. Seems like someone lied to you, Mr. Mackay, and being in your line of work, I'm sure you have lots of enemies. Any suspicions?"

I snicker. "Like I told you, I don't remember anything."

"Okay, then." Her eyes narrow, mouth forming the barest smile.

"We're done here. Welcome home, counselor." Her eyes fill with a cloud of disdain. "Will you be practicing again?"

"No, Detective." My mouth curves. "Wouldn't be too good at something I don't ever remember doing, would I?"

"Right." She grins. "Of course. I keep forgetting."

Sure, she does.

"Were we on the same cases a lot?" I ask. "Is that why you don't like me?"

Her laugh falls cold. "You could say that, yeah. Two ring a bell, actually." Her jaw tenses. "Eighteen-year-old stripper, gang raped by your clients, then butchered until not even her parents recognized her."

Beside me, Hadleigh's shoulders rise up and down with heavy breaths, and I hold on to that hand, hoping she doesn't let go.

"Then there was a case of a cop who one of your clients cut up into pieces."

She grins with so much hatred, but I can't even blame her. Sure, I was doing my job, but to her, I was letting savages roam free.

"His wife and his young son couldn't even say goodbye."

"I'm sorry about that. But everyone deserves a defense, and everyone is innocent until proven guilty. It's how our country works."

"I don't need a civics lesson from the likes of you." She narrows her gaze.

"If it wasn't me, it'd be someone else." I get to my feet, and Hadleigh follows. "People need lawyers, Detective."

"It's a good thing you won't be one anymore." Delight spreads through her features.

"Enjoy your early Christmas present." I level her a playful stare. "But you should know by now, don't ever underestimate me."

Forty

HADLEIGH

When Elowen and Leighton both called earlier today, I told them all about how Hudson came back yesterday, but that we haven't figured out where exactly we fit in his new life. It's a conversation I keep postponing.

But why rush it? He's here. He's happy. We're happy. Why ruin that?

"How do I look, Mommy?" Holden grins in front of my full-length mirror, examining his fishing outfit: army-green baseball cap with jeans shorts and suspenders over a bright red t-shirt. He picked it out himself and is mighty proud.

Standing behind him, I say, "You look handsome, buddy. You did so good picking out your clothes."

His gaze snaps to mine through the mirror. "You look pretty too, Mommy."

My face brightens as I give myself a once-over. I must've gone through ten outfits before settling on skintight jeans and a simple white tank top.

"You two ready?"

At the sound of his deep tone, my heartbeats stutter in my chest, and slowly I wisp around to face him.

Our eyes connect from across the room, that instant connection sizzling between us. And my mind immediately goes to last night.

The way we made love, the way he kissed me. Not a simple kind of kiss, either. The kind that lasted. The kind that felt like it was more. A breath of what once was. The Hudson-and-Hadleigh kind of kiss that transcends time and space. The passion seeping through our marrow. It felt as though he was asking me for more. Hoping for it.

And me? I've been hoping for him for so long, holding on to this feeling I've been chasing that I will welcome anything he has to give.

In his arms, I slept better than I've slept in these last few years without him.

"You look beautiful," he rasps.

"Thank you." My cheeks warm.

It's as though we're dating again. That sensation in the pit of my gut is so familiar because I only had it for him. My gaze wanders down his green t-shirt, one that matches Holden's hat so perfectly, I know he did it on purpose.

"You look very handsome," I tell him.

His smirk suddenly appears, and it makes me shivery. Are my cheeks growing hot again?

As he struts closer, he gives Holden a high five. "I love the hat."

"Thanks, Daddy! Can we go now? I wanna touch the worms."

"Sure can. You ready, angel?"

I battle deep-seated emotions in my throat. There's no way to help them, not when he calls me these little names he once did.

"I am."

"Alright, guys. Time to catch some fish."

He grabs Holden in his arms and grips him on one side, throwing his free arm around me. And we walk out just like that.

Together.

A family.

Sort of.

HUDSON

I can't help catching her eye every second that I can. With every passing moment, I get it. I get why I fell in love with her. Why I chose her to be mine. She's soulful and beautiful and has this energy around her, etched with kindness.

If I was as bad as I seem to have been, wanting someone the opposite of me would make perfect sense. She balanced me.

Sometimes, I wish I could talk to my old self, to learn everything I can about her. To be right for her. It's like I'm in this competition with him, and I want to win. I want to deserve her the way he never did. Because that bastard should've done better. Instead, he lived a life of murder and madness.

I don't want that. I don't want that for Holden either.

If I get a second chance with them, things will be different. They have to be.

Holden yanks at the fishing line.

"Oh my God!" he yelps. "Do you think it's a big, giant one?"

"I think so." I really try to draw that sucker out, but he sure has a will to survive.

Don't we all?

"My goodness, you boys are so good at this." Hadleigh sits on the edge of a wooden dock, overlooking the lake she took us to.

Her eyes gleam as she watches us, and I see it there, in the speckle of her gaze, the joy radiating out of her.

"You should try it too, Mommy!"

"She will. Won't you, baby?" I smirk. "I'll help you."

Her cheeks grow with color, and fuck, the shit it does to me to know she's attracted to me. I mean, I know I'm her husband and all that, but it's just different for me.

"Sure, I'll give it a go," she says. "But only because Daddy will be helping. Knowing me, I'll fall right in the water."

She scowls, and Holden giggles.

"Then I'll jump right in and save you."

She clears her throat, face getting rosier, gaze skittering far out into the water.

With a knowing grin, I start pulling out the fish.

"Oh…" Holden sounds disappointed. "He isn't that big."

He's right. He's about the length of half my arm.

"He's strong, though," I tell him. "Size doesn't always matter, buddy. It's how much fight you have in you. Do you understand what that means?"

He looks up at me, brows bunched in thought. "I think so. It means even if I'm small, I'm still strong. Right?"

"That's right. You are strong. So is your mom."

I longingly glance at her, and in her eyes, I find emotions misting through. A smile stretches on her face, and it makes my heart catch.

"We're gonna let him go, right?" Holden asks.

His sweet, innocent voice puts a smile on my face. Good and kind, just like his mother. Thank God for that.

"Of course." I start to unhook it. "We'll let him swim back with his fish friends."

He releases a big sigh. "Good. I don't wanna kill him."

I toss it into the water, and it splatters, disappearing from view.

"Okay, Hadleigh, think it's your turn now."

"Ugh..." She frowns playfully, but starts toward me while Holden settles down, feet dangling happily from the dock.

Standing behind her, my body tight against hers, I bet she can feel my growing need for her. Her chest rises and falls with rapid breaths while my hand drops to the top of hers.

"You ready?"

She nods wordlessly, and I swear I'm about to take her home and get her naked. Making love to her is my new favorite thing.

"I'm ready," she breathes, and together we cast the fishing line into the water, feeling the rapid beats of her heart.

A minute later, the line jerks, and Holden gasps.

"Maybe it's the same fish again, Daddy."

"Never know," I chuckle while we both fight like hell to get that sucker out. She pulls hard, while I yank harder. "Damn, he's definitely a big one."

"You're not kidding," she groans, tugging with all her might. "I think we almost have it! Just a little more."

"Come on, Mommy! Daddy!" Holden claps, jumping to his feet. "This is fun!"

"Ton of fun," Hadleigh grits while the damn fish fights hard, dragging her to the edge. "Oh my God, I'm gonna fall!"

"I've got you, butterfly."

I curl one arm around her middle, but as I do, my foot somehow gets caught with hers, and we stumble backward. She falls hard on top of me, both of us laughing while our son giggles beside us.

I flip her around, pinning her under me as we keep laughing like two teenagers. And slowly, that laugh turns husky, until all that's left is silence, our eyes boring into one another. In this moment, I know she feels what I do. This undeniable chemistry. It's a shame Holden is here, because I would've taken her back to the car and ended this torture.

"Hudson," she whispers, a hand cupping my cheek.

"Right here, angel. I'm right here." My lips fall to hers, and I kiss her—slowly, deeply.

Nothing in this world can stop me.

We burn like the phoenix, and together we rise.

Because this woman was meant to be mine.

And whoever fought to tear us apart didn't succeed, because I think I'm falling in love with her all over again.

"So, I gather we knew each other well?" I grin at Hadleigh's friend, Elowen, while she's in the bedroom, getting ready for our dinner date.

Holden is with her, keeping her company. That boy sure loves his mother, not that I can blame him.

"Quite well." Elowen's pale gray eyes take me in with a cautious smile. "Please excuse my staring. It's crazy seeing you again. I just can't believe it." She shakes her head. "I mean, I'm beyond thrilled for all of you, but it's just nuts with you having a new identity and everything."

"I can imagine," I scoff. "It's crazy for me too, believe me."

"Yeah… I'm sorry." She glances at her feet before looking back at me.

"Don't be. Can't dwell on that. I have a whole new beginning with them now."

Her features pull with emotion, her fingers threading through her blonde hair. "I'm glad you asked her out to dinner tonight. You two need that time alone."

I nod in agreement. When we left the lake, I asked Hadleigh on a date, and she immediately agreed.

"Thanks for babysitting. I appreciate it."

"Always. I love you both very much." Her brows knit. "So anything you two need, I'm here."

I inhale a single long breath. "I'm glad she had you. I'm glad I didn't leave her all alone."

"Oh, Hudson..." Her head falls toward her shoulder. "She was alone." Her eyes glisten with moisture. "She had me and Leighton and Brooks, but..."

But fuck that guy? Yeah, let's pretend he never existed.

"But she was alone in all the ways that mattered," Elowen goes on, oblivious to my inner thoughts. "She was hurting, missing you, raising that amazing boy without you. We were never enough." Tears catch within her lower lashes. "But you? You always were."

What the hell do I say to that? I feel like I'm repeating my own inner thoughts, wishing I could recall every vivid memory, every instance of the love we shared. But what's the point of dwelling on something that may not ever happen.

Before I can get the lump out of my damn throat, *she* walks out, and I swear my heart stops beating.

"Wow..." I whisper, and I don't even realize I've gotten to my feet.

Unable to peel my eyes from her, I take in every breathtaking inch—that strappy red dress which flows out from her waist, hitting right below her knees, and the V-cut elegantly revealing ample cleavage.

"Doesn't she look like a magical princess?" Holden gawks at his mother.

"She sure as hell does."

"Swear jar, Daddy…"

Without taking my eyes off her, I reach into my wallet and hand him a bill.

"Here's twenty," I say, my voice hoarse. "I'm gonna be swearing a lot."

Her red lips curl, and my jaw tenses, my pulse firing off. And I just about have a talk with my dick because I've got to be a gentleman tonight, even while every single part of me wishes I didn't have to be.

Ripping that dress right off her while those black high heels remain on is exactly what I'd like to do.

There's always tonight, though…

Even her damn toes are turning me on, polished red to match her dress.

"Jesus Christ," I mutter, running a palm down my face, cupping my mouth. "You're the most beautiful thing I've ever seen."

Elowen sniffles behind me.

Hadleigh pops a shoulder, fingers flinging through her hair, slick and shiny, the ends slightly curled against her shoulders.

"You bought me this dress after our first date." Her growing smile warms my heart. "Somehow it still fits."

My feet advance, eating away at the distance between us, until she's right before me. I take both her hands in mine, gaze fastened to hers.

"Everything somehow still fits between us too, doesn't it?" I whisper, my own emotions grasping, taking root inside me.

"Yes." Tears start to fill her gaze as she takes my knuckles to her lips. "There's no me without you. There never was."

"Can I please stay up until you come home?" Holden pleads

through hopeful eyes, interrupting us.

Hadleigh tears her attention from me and kneels down to his level. "I know you want to be a big boy and stay up really late, but a growing boy needs his rest, so you have to go to bed when Elowen tells you, okay?"

"Okay, Mommy." He sulks.

"That's my boy." She clasps his face and kisses his forehead.

"Alright, you two," Elowen says. "Better get out of here. Holden and I have lots of fun planned, don't we?"

He grins then. "Yep! We're gonna order pizza and make some brownies while we wait, then we're gonna watch *Finding Nemo*."

"That sounds like fun, buddy," I tell him. "Think you can save a brownie for me and Mommy?"

"Of course, Daddy! I'm a good sharer."

"Must get it from your mom."

"No, Hudson," she says softly as our eyes connect. "I think he got that one from you."

Forty-One

HUDSON

As we arrive at an upscale steakhouse I found not too far from where she lives, what she said before we left still rings in my head.

I think he got that one from you.

Did he? I wonder.

Did I give our son a piece of who I was? Are there more parts of me within him? Has he been carrying me within his heart this entire time?

I know he's my blood. I don't need a test to prove it. He looks so much like me. But I thought that was where our similarities ended.

Could I have been wrong?

Did I have redeeming qualities? Was I more man than monster? Because that man, the one who wrote her those letters? I don't want to be him.

"Are you okay?" she asks as we take our seats in a quaint corner, a candle flickering between us, the small room dimly lit.

"Yeah…" I shake my head briskly, because it isn't the truth. "Fuck, Hadleigh. I don't want to lie to you."

She stretches her arm toward me and takes my hand, thumb rubbing circles over my skin. "It's okay not to be fine. No one would be in your situation. We just take it day by day." Her kindness shines through her eyes. "It's enough to be here with you. To have you. You don't have to worry about the rest."

"It's not right," I grit through clenched teeth. Leaning toward her, I stare deeply. "I want to *kill* whoever did this to me. Because they hurt *you*." My heart raps against my ribs, faster now. "They *hurt* Holden. They hurt our *family*."

She twists her mouth and releases a burdened breath.

"I've wanted them dead too," she admits on a whisper.

Someone so good admitting to something like that… It almost doesn't sound right coming out of her. But she deserves revenge for what was taken from her.

In a way, it's easier for me. I don't remember any of it, while she had to live years remembering everything she lost.

"I read your letter when you were asleep that day," I tell her, realizing we never discussed any of it.

"I kinda gathered that when I found them all on the dresser the next day." Her mouth twines softly. "I made you videos too."

"What?" I drag my hand away from hers, heartbeats quickening. "What kind of videos?"

"Little bits of our life." She shrugs with so much melancholy capturing her golden eyes, I almost break down. "I figured if you wrote me letters to tell me things, I could make you videos to show you so much more. And I thought…" She removes her cell phone from her black handbag. "…that when you returned, I could show you everything you missed."

"Hadleigh...fuck." I palm my mouth and roll my hand down.

My heart's heavy, fearing what I'll find in those videos. Fearing the pain of it. Fearing that maybe I won't connect to those moments that meant so much to her.

"You don't have to if you don't want to," she says, voice filled with understanding.

"No." I grab her wrist and stop her from placing her phone back. "I want to."

Letting go, I move to sit beside her, bringing my chair close.

"Okay." She glances at me. "Are you ready?"

"Not at all." I laugh dryly. "But play it anyway."

She opens up her videos. "This is the first time I brought him home."

And when she presses play and I see his tiny face yawning, tears slam into my eyes.

"Jesus," I whisper, blinking back these feelings weaved intrinsically through every facet of my being. "He's so fragile. How did you do this on your own?"

Her tears reflect in mine as she says, "I had no other choice except to keep going, and he was the reason I did."

My palm falls across the side of her nape. "I'm sorry, butterfly. I know I've said this more times than I can count, but it doesn't feel like enough."

"I know you are, but it's neither one of our faults." Her hand drops to the top of my free one.

"Show me more," I plead. "I want to see everything. Every single instance of your life that I missed."

And she does. For hours, I watch glimpses of the past that I was stolen from, ripped from the root by evil.

But with the help from the Quinns, I will find that person who did this, and I will give them hell.

Maybe I am like the old Hudson.

And maybe that should scare me.

But it doesn't.

HADLEIGH

"Any dessert for you two?" the waiter asks after we've finally eaten our meals.

They were generous enough to let us stay for almost four hours while we basked in conversation full of painful memories and happier times.

But it was freeing to talk to him, to show him all the videos I had been saving. I waited for this very moment for so long that I started to believe it would never happen. But it did. The hope I carried…it brought him back to me.

"We're okay," I tell the waiter, who nods, handing Hudson the check before he leaves.

"Are you sure you don't want anything?"

"Well…" My brows bow. "I was thinking we'd go somewhere else for that."

"Oh yeah?" He smirks. "Is it anywhere that would allow me to rip that dress right off of that gorgeous body?"

I gape, heart racing, before a small laugh escapes me. "If you play your cards right, Mr. Mackay, maybe you'll get lucky."

"Answer me one thing," he whispers, dropping his face nearer from across the table, blue eyes shimmering with lustful intentions. "Are you wearing panties?"

My face grows hot. I lift the cup of water before me, and with a knowing smile, I take a sip.

"Hadleigh Mackay..." His jaw clenches as he hurriedly grabs a bunch of cash from his wallet and leaves it on the table. "Better tell me where we're going next, 'cause I've just about had all the patience for tonight."

My heart pumps rapidly against my rib cage from the way he's staring at me, like a meal he wants to enjoy slowly. "Won't see me complaining."

Pushing his chair back, he grabs my hand. "Come on, we're leaving. Now."

My giggle races out of me as he swings his arm around my hips, rushing me out of there.

HUDSON

"There's this café that serves the softest pancakes ever, and they pair them with souffles. I've been dying to try it," she explains as we start out of the restaurant.

"Believe me, I don't care where we eat, because you're the only dessert that matters tonight."

"Is that so?" She quirks a brow as we walk out into the nearly empty parking lot.

As we advance toward my rental, someone in a black hoodie brushes past us.

"What the..." she whispers.

"Excuse me," the man mutters, dark eyes connecting with mine.

Eyes I don't recognize. But somehow, I feel like I should. He holds my stare for a few seconds too long before he struts off, hands in his pockets.

"Let's get out of here," she breathes. "That guy gave me the creeps."

Me too.

Something was off about him. I just can't put my finger on it.

"Mrs. Mackay?" a woman calls suddenly from my right.

At first, she's merely a shadow, and Hadleigh rushes even closer toward my side.

"Who's that?" she asks.

The woman approaches, black hair pinned up in a tight bun, large sunglasses covering her face.

"Adalyn?" Hadleigh gapes. "Is that you?"

"Yes…" Adalyn's attention jumps toward me. "Oh my God. Mr. Mackay? You're…you're alive?"

"What the hell are you doing here, Adalyn? Were you following us?" Hadleigh's tone grows irate. "Do I need to call the police?"

"N-n-no." She trembles with a cry. "Please don't. I came to warn you."

"Warn me about what?"

"Be careful and trust no one."

"What the hell are you talking about? Who are you?" I ask, my pulse speeding in my ears. "Are you trying to scare my wife?"

"No, sir. I—I would never do that." Her words are thick with obvious fear. "Don't you remember me? I worked for you, Mr. Mackay. I made mistakes, but I'd never hurt you."

Hadleigh grabs her forearm. "What mistakes, Adalyn? What have you done?"

The woman shakes her head. "I—I—I…have to go." She steps back. "I already said too much. Just forget I was here, okay?" Her lips quiver.

"We're leaving," Hadleigh informs her. "I don't want to see you ever again. You understand me? If I do, I will make you regret it."

Why does she hate this Adalyn so much?

"You'll never see me again."

I remove my keys from my pocket, but as I'm about to click the doors open, I find that same man in the hoodie staring at us from a few yards away.

"Come on, Hudson. We need to go." Hadleigh grabs the keys and—

"Hadleigh, NO!" I bellow, because as I looked at him, something in my gut stirred.

But it's too late.

She clicks the doors open, and just as she does, an explosion hits, fire erupting all around us.

And before I'm expelled into the air, I push her out of the way, hoping I did enough to save her.

Forty-Two

HUDSON

"Hadleigh? Where are you?" I bellow, my eyes seeing only darkness. "Hello? Anyone here? I need help! Hadleigh! Answer me!"

Where the hell is she? I have to find her. I have to make sure she's okay.

"Help. He-l-l-p-p," my voice echoes. "What the fuck?"

Panic races up my spine, rushing through the endless dusk.

"Hadleigh, please! Where are you, baby?"

If we were still in the parking lot, there would be cops and flames. Where is she?

Oh, God. If she's…

No. I can't think that way. She can't be gone. It can't all end like this. I won't let it.

A round of beeps starts in the distance, causing me to halt, listening for it.

"What's going on?" I tread closer and closer, but it's like I'm in an infinite room of blackness.

"He's in a coma," a woman's voice explains.

Yet I don't know who or what or how I'm hearing it.

"How long until he comes out?"

Brooks.

I instantly recognize his voice.

I don't understand what's happening. My chest tightens, hands gripping my shirt. My soaked shirt.

"What the fuck?"

I draw my hands away and stare down at my blood-soaked fingers. And somehow, even in the dark, I'm able to see them.

"Well…" the other voice explains. "I can't give you a timeline. Every case is different. We just wait and see."

"Jesus Christ," he sighs.

Who hit their head? Me? Are they talking about me?

No. I can't be in a damn coma! This must be a fucking nightmare.

"I'm right here! Anyone hear me?"

"Where is he? Where's my husband?!"

My heart instantly beats faster.

"Hadleigh?" I gasp. "Where are you?"

"Mrs. Mackay, you shouldn't be out of your hospital bed."

Hospital bed? She's hurt?

Fuck! I can't even see how bad.

"I'm fine!" Hadleigh bellows with a heavy pant. "Oh, Hudson," she cries.

And right then, I register the warmth against my cheek, like she's touching it, stroking it.

"Hadleigh…" I whisper, tears filling my eyes as I close them, because I know right here and now that she can't hear me.

I'm unconscious.

"You saved my life," she goes on. "You saved me. You've always done that."

Her sobs grow, and I can feel this heaviness in the center of my chest, as though she's lying against it.

My arms reach out toward her—or where I think she'd be right now—and I hold her. Through space and time, I hold her ghost. Or she holds mine.

God, I hate that she can't feel my arms.

"The doctors say you'll be okay," she murmurs. "But me? I'm scared, Hudson. I can't lose you again. Please get better. I need you, baby." She sniffles. "We can move to your town, or you can live here. I don't care where we go, as long as we're together. You hear me? You don't even have to love me. I understand if you can't just yet. But I love you and I hope you're okay with that, Hudson Mackay, because I never quite knew how to quit you."

"I don't know how to quit you either."

My face grows warm once more, and I close my eyes, tears filling them.

"I need you to wake up," she pleads.

"I want to," I whisper. "I just don't know how."

HADLEIGH

I can't get the explosion out of my head. Those flames erupting around his rental car. The beeping of the nearby vehicle alarms. There were at least ten cars there in the lot.

I haven't even processed any of it. It was so fast. One second, he's screaming no, and the next...

Boom.

If he hadn't shoved me out of the way, if he hadn't taken the brunt of it, I don't know where I'd be right now.

After I saw Hudson a bit ago, the doctors forced me back into my room. He looks like he's dead, and if not for the heart monitor, I'd think he was.

"Hadleigh, you need to rest," Brooks warns, concern bathing his eyes.

It's a good thing Holden wasn't with us.

Oh, God. Imagine if he was? If he…

Emotions scratch up the back of my throat. I can't think that way. Everyone is alive. We'll be okay.

But who could've done it? How is Adalyn connected? And for her to show up like that? It makes no sense. And who was that man in the hoodie? Were they working together?

A set of footfalls grows closer until I find Detective Tompkins strutting in. Same hair in a tight bun, same smug look.

"Trouble seems to follow you, doesn't it?" she quips.

"Get the hell out of here," Brooks snaps. "She doesn't need you upsetting her."

"Upsetting?" she scoffs. "I'm here to find out who almost killed your girlfriend. You should thank me."

"I'm not his girlfriend," I fire. "And you've never done shit for us, so how about you *leave*?!"

"Can't do that, Mrs. Mackay. I'm investigating the explosion that almost took you and your husband out. You could've ended up like poor Adalyn."

"W-w-what?" Goose bumps feather across both arms. "Are you saying…"

"That she's dead? Yeah, that's exactly what I'm saying."

"Oh my God." I slap a hand around my mouth.

Was someone trying to keep her quiet? Or was she an innocent bystander?

"Yeah, real shame." She shakes her head, mouth forming a thin line. "You know, I can't quite figure out what she was doing there in the middle of the night at the same place you two were at."

"She was probably following us."

"And why would she want to do that?"

"Because she hated me from the moment Brooks broke up with her." I quickly peer over at him, and from the way his jaw pops, I know he's pissed. "She blamed me for it."

"And were you at fault?"

"That's enough!" Brooks hollers. "None of this has anything to do with the damn car bomb!"

"Of course it does." She gives him an impatient stare. "If Adalyn had motive, she could've planted that bomb herself. You think she was capable of that?"

She waits for Brooks to answer.

"You did date her for a while." Her mouth spreads into a wicked grin.

"Sure," he replies coolly. "I think anyone is capable of anything if they're backed into a corner."

"Hmm," she considers. "I think you're right, Mr. Bardin. I think you're right."

The following day, after I'm released from the hospital and forced to go home, all I can think about is when visiting hours are again so I can return to him.

Only a couple of hours until then, but this time, I don't intend to go home. I'll be at that waiting area all damn night so I can be there the exact moment he opens his eyes.

The on-call doctor told me I needed rest instead of sitting in the hospital, waiting for news on Hudson. Though I didn't get hurt the way Hudson did, I'm still banged up with the cuts to my arms and forehead.

With Holden sobbing in my arms, I sit on the edge of my bed and let him get it out. He was so worried when he heard about our accident. That's all I told Elowen to tell him. That we got into an accident and that Daddy is resting, and once he's better, I can take him to see Hudson.

My poor boy. In one moment, he gets his father back, then has him ripped from his life again.

"Will Daddy die?" He snivels, swiping under his eyes as he peeks up at me.

"No." I shake my head, the words a punch to my gut. "He's gonna be just fine. The doctors just want his head to rest a little. That's all, buddy."

I try to keep my voice even, but it cracks a little, my true emotions seeping through—the fear, the unnerving feeling that something will happen. Something worse.

"Why can't I stay here with you?" he cries. "I don't want to go to Aunt Elowen's for a sleepover."

"I know you don't, sweetheart." I tuck his face in between my palms. "But Mommy has to go to get another checkup with the doctor, and then I wanna go see Daddy's doctors, and I can't take you with me."

"Why not?" he pouts. "I'm a big boy. I won't do anything bad."

"Of course not!" My heart aches to see him this way. "But the hospitals have rules, and they don't let kids there."

I don't want to tell him I'm going to see Hudson. He won't understand that I don't want him to see his father that way.

"Can I see Daddy tomorrow?" Hope springs in his tear-stricken gaze.

"I'll ask the doctors today, okay?" I drop my lips to his forehead, swallowing down the thundering ache in my throat.

When will this nightmare be over? When is it finally our turn to be happy?

An hour later, there's a knock on my door, and it's not Elowen. She came earlier to get Holden. And though he wasn't happy to go, he immediately perked up when he saw Cassidy. He managed to grin, all toothy and adorable. And I knew instantly he'd be okay.

Opening the door, I find Brooks there, his eyes full of exhaustion, bags under them. He's barely slept since the incident. He stayed all night in the hospital. He wanted to make sure the doctors were doing everything they could for Hudson. And he knew that I'd worry since I couldn't be there myself.

"Come in," I tell him. "Maybe you should rest here while I drive to the hospital myself."

He came to pick me up for visiting hours, and that's only because I was dizzy for a bit after the incident and the doctors didn't want me driving yesterday. But I'm more than capable of doing that today. Hopefully, when I see the doctor later, he can clear me to drive.

"No, absolutely not." He moves past me. "You aren't getting behind the wheel until that doc says you can."

"Fine." I roll my eyes playfully. "I'm ready to go."

Grabbing my handbag from the vanity in the foyer, I rush toward the closet to get my shoes.

"Actually…" He yawns. "Mind if I take a quick shower? I feel like shit, and that'll help."

"Oh! Yeah, of course!" I shake my head, feeling like a complete asshole for not offering him one. "I can get you some clean clothes. You and Hudson are about the same size, and you know where the towels are."

"You're a damn lifesaver, Hadleigh." He drops his canvas messenger bag down against the wall and removes his sneakers. "I'll be five minutes, tops."

"Take your time." I wave him off. "We're early anyway."

Together, we head up the stairs, and while he goes into the bathroom and starts the water, I go to get him a t-shirt and sweats.

"Here you go." I strut into the bathroom, and he turns toward me, a lopsided smile falling to his face.

"Thanks." He grabs the clothes. "Five minutes. I promise."

I nod and shut the door behind him, returning back down the stairs to get some water. My cell is there on top of the kitchen island, and of course I was gonna leave the house without it. What an idiot. What if Elowen called about Holden? Or the hospital?

Grabbing a bottle of water from the fridge, I drink a few sips, finding a text from Iseult.

ISEULT

> We're on the way to New York. I just got the call from Brooks this morning. But I only just listened to the damn voicemail, because I was out on a job. I'm so damn sorry. How is he?

HADLEIGH

> No news yet. Still in a coma.

ISEULT

> Unbelievable.

> Someone is really getting scared that Hudson is gonna remember something. That's why they tried to kill him.

Oh, God. She has to be right.

HADLEIGH

> I can't think about that right now. Let me know when you guys arrive. Heading back to the hospital to see him. Will be there all night.

ISEULT

> Okay, I'll see you soon.

As soon as I finish typing, my phone rings. It's a number I don't recognize, but with a local area code on the screen.

I answer immediately. "Hello?"

"Hi there, this is Nurse Lisa from Snyder Hospital."

"Yes?" My pulse turns erratic until I taste it in my throat. "Did something happen to my husband?"

"He's just fine. It's why I'm calling."

"What is it?" My gut tightens.

"He's starting to wake up and was asking for you."

"Oh my God!" I jump off the chair.

"He's still in and out and very disoriented, but I know you wanted to be here as soon as he fully wakes up."

"Thank you so much! I'm on my way. Please tell him I'm coming now!"

She doesn't even finish when I hang up, my body pumped with adrenaline as I find his number in my cell, needing to hear his voice to know he's really out of his coma.

The water runs upstairs, Brooks still taking a shower, giving me a few minutes to talk to Hudson.

He's okay. He's actually okay.

The phone starts to ring. And ring. And ring.

But the sound? It's coming from inside the house.

"What the…"

Goose bumps pebble across my body as the coldest shudder seeps into my skin because I know his phone isn't here. It's at the hospital with him.

It rings again and again as I head toward the foyer, until my feet are perched right in front of…

"No," I gasp in a breathy whisper.

I stare down at Brooks's messenger bag, where the phone continues to ring.

"It can't be…"

"This is Hudson Mackay. Leave your message after the tone."

I called the wrong phone. I called Hudson's old number…

"No…" My hands shake, my cell slipping from my grasp, clanking against the marble floor.

The water instantly shuts off upstairs while my heart races until nausea swirls in my gut.

I pick up my phone and stuff it in my pants before my hands jump to the bag. Eyes scattering up the stairs, I unzip it, needing to see it for myself.

And as soon as I do, tears blind my vision.

Because inside it is not only Hudson's cell phone, but…

I remove the black baseball hat. The same one I saw Tanner wear the night I was chased on the road.

But it wasn't Tanner, was it? It was him?

No. It can't be. How? Why?

"Oh my God…" I cry just as I register a creak behind me.

"Oh, babe," Brooks husks. "You weren't supposed to see that."

Forty-Three

BROOKS
TWENTY-THREE YEARS AGO
AGE TWELVE

"How was school today, Holden?" Marcella asks my adoptive brother.

I can't call her "Mom." She's a bitch. She'll never be my mother.

Holden picks at his green beans. "Fine."

Pietro, her husband, gets off his chair and helps himself to more pot roast.

My plate is empty, though. I'm not allowed to eat. I wet the bed last night, and she's starved me all day. If it wasn't for Kelsey in class, who noticed I had no lunch or money, I'd really starve.

My stomach growls. And their eyes go to mine.

"Shut up," she snarls. "Or I'll send you to the basement with the rats."

Not like I can keep my stomach quiet.

"Can I give him my vegetables?" Holden asks.

She tsks and smiles at him. She always does. That's 'cause he's the favorite. He gets more food, more attention. They hurt him less than me. And if something happens, they blame me. They always believe him. While I'm the bad one.

I'm not bad. I've never been bad.

Would I have had a better life with my real parents?

I don't know who they are, though. Probably some losers.

"He isn't eating today." She gives me a tight glare, her round cheeks all red like she put too much makeup on, but it's just how she looks. Like she's always pissed. "Maybe if someone learns how not to be a disgusting idiot, he'll be allowed to eat again."

"Fuck you!" I grin. "I should piss on you next."

"Ben..." Holden shakes his head, eyes cowering in fear. "Shut up."

But it's too late, and quite honestly, I don't even care.

Her blue topaz ring sparkles under all the bright lights in the large dining room. But the house is ugly. Old-looking furniture, dust floating in the air. Holden and I are the only ones who clean this place. We have to. We have to do everything they tell us.

Slowly, she gets up, shoving her chair back. Her wide frame towers over me.

"Wanna piss on me, huh? You ungrateful sack of garbage!" Her punch to my jaw comes hard and fast, the ring burning across my skin. "You were nothing before us. Just an unwanted, pathetic kid whose own parents didn't want him."

Holden glances down while Pietro laughs like she just told a joke. But me? My gut is churning with so much rage, I picture taking an ax to both their heads.

"Nothing to say now, Benny boy?" She punches me again as I snicker, wiping blood from my lip.

"Let me take a crack at him." Pietro gladly jumps to join in the punching parade.

They enjoy that. Seeing me suffer. Holden has it easy. They barely ever hit him. Sure, they're not the nicest, but at least he doesn't have to endure this. Because Holden is a good boy. He doesn't wet the bed.

She moves to make room for her husband, and he gives me a once-over full of malice.

His hand fists the collar of my white t-shirt. "Gonna make you wish you were dead, boy."

Then he's throwing me on the ground kicking me over and over, until every inch of my body aches. Until I hear a sob, realizing it's me.

"Come on, Holden. It's your turn now, son," Pietro adds.

From the corner of my eye, I see him: my so-called brother, the one who swore he'd have my back against these people. Yet he does nothing.

"I don't wanna," he cries like I give a shit.

If he wasn't a coward, he'd sit there and let them give him this kind of beating for once. Worst they ever did to him was punch him a bit and lock him in a room and starve him a few times. Not like that's a big deal. I'd take that any day. But the golden child is special.

"You don't got a choice if you wanna live here!" she bellows. "Now get your sorry ass off that chair, or I'm gonna whip you until you do."

Love to see that happen.

He whimpers as he obeys her. He always ends up obeying.

Climbing up, he advances toward me, panting as he comes to stand next to Pietro.

"Kick him!"

Holden shakes his head while I try to get my breathing to normalize. But that's pretty damn impossible. My whole body feels like it's dying. Maybe it would be better if I died. Would save me a lot of misery.

What life will I have with these people? I'll never be able to escape them. Where would I go anyway? Live on the street? Would Holden come with me? Or would he choose them?

Why do I even care? He doesn't love me. Not really.

"Kick him, I said!" Pietro looks a bit displeased.

I laugh, and that causes a vein in the old man's forehead to jolt.

"You've got until the count of three to kick him before I take my gun and shoot him in the foot."

"Right foot or left foot?" I quip. "I think that's a very important difference."

"You little!" The kick to the underside of my jaw hits hard until stars erupt behind my eyes.

"Leave him alone!" Holden cries. "I'll do it, okay?"

He kicks me, but it barely connects.

"Harder! Make it count!"

He does it again, just a bit more pressure.

"If you don't kick him like you know I'm asking of you…" He lowers and presses his face into Holden's. "I'm gonna use him for target practice."

Reaching into the holster around his waist, he removes one of his many pistols and points it at me.

"Okay!" Holden cries. "Here!"

He kicks me so hard I wince.

Pietro indicates with his hand that he wants him to continue. So he does, kicking me time after time until I've lost count. Until both of us are crying.

But only one of us is on the ground.

And I've always stayed that way.

In his shadow, waiting to come out into the light.

Except I never did.

I stole it. I took whatever I could. Every little bit of the light he never let me have.

He had everything.

Fame. Money. Power.

He even had *her*.

But see, I saw her first. Those beautiful honey-colored eyes smiled at me when she took that elevator up with me to see him the day she came to seek that divorce from Tanner.

I wanted her. And I was going to ask her out as soon as she was done. I figured she'd need a good rebound guy, and I wouldn't have minded helping her that way. Beautiful woman like that would have been scooped up real quick. I could have made her fall for me. I'd have done anything for her.

But of course, he claimed her first. After that meeting with him and his boss, they were instantly inseparable. I stood there watching them every day, pretending I didn't want to bash his head in the way I bashed Marcella's head in when we were sixteen.

That was the first time Hudson and I became killers. She was being her typical self, coming after me for spilling milk. Meanwhile, we both did it. But she always had tunnel vision.

Hudson was gonna have us run, but instead, Pietro came home early, and when he saw what happened and saw the baseball bat in my hands…well, he started after me. Shot off a few rounds of his gun while I ran, dropping the baseball bat.

But see, little did Pietro know Hudson took that moment to finally be a brother and bashed his head in.

Now we were both involved. And we swore that we'd take that day to our graves. But the thing with secrets is, they never quite stay buried.

"It's a real shame what I'll have to do to you," I tell Hadleigh, who's still beautiful, zip-tied to the chair, fat tears running down her rosy cheeks.

But fuck, I'm done waiting. I've waited years for her to be my wife, but all she wanted was Hudson.

Even after everything I did for her and that kid, she still chose a dead man over me. Still left him voicemails, begging him to come back. I hated hearing her cry for him. She should've loved *me*. But no. She wanted him instead.

Hudson, Hudson, Hudson.

It's always been Hudson. Everyone wants him.

Even when he went to juvie, he managed to get lucky. Found himself a real big fish: Patrick Quinn. And look what that did for him. Made him a fucking billionaire, while I got paid pocket change working under him.

Brooks, the paralegal.

I snicker.

The plan was supposed to work. We did everything right.

We made sure every T was crossed and every I was dotted.

I guess this is the final show. She must die. My beautiful Hadleigh. But it's all his fault.

She screams and cries to no avail, shaking herself in that chair.

"Come on, now. Stop that, sweetheart. You're gonna hurt yourself."

Shaking my head at her futile attempt, I remove my phone and dial a number I know in my sleep. Marching a short distance away so she doesn't hear my conversation, I wait for the voice to answer.

"Yeah?"

"We have a situation. You need to come to her house now. Gonna need you to make a body disappear."

"Fuck. She found out?"

"Yeah."

"Stall. Need time to get there."

"Hurry up, or I talk. I won't let you throw me under the bus."

My pulse roars savagely in my throat while I stare into the eyes of the woman I love. The one I will kill.

But she hasn't given me a choice, has she?

The laugh on the phone deepens. "I know you're not that stupid. You talk, and you're as good as dead."

"I already am."

Forty-Four

HUDSON

"Sir," a nurse softly murmurs. "Please lie down. You can't sit up so quickly."

"Wh-where is…my wife?" I croak, forcing myself up on my shoulders, my head spinning as I adjust to the blaring lights above. "Can you make the damn lights less bright? Please."

I sound like I'm going to cut her head off. But I can't think with these damn lights hovering over me.

"Of course." She scurries off toward the door and lowers the lights. "I actually called your wife earlier when you were in and out. She's on her way."

"She isn't hurt?"

"No, she's okay."

Relief washes over me.

She's okay. Hadleigh is okay.

"Let me go page the doctor. You just rest." She smiles tentatively, like she's not sure if I'm going to flip the bed or not.

Right now, even I'm not sure. "How long have I been in a coma?"

She jerks her head back. "How did you know you were..."

"Heard it. Guess the meds weren't that strong." I rub at my eyes and grab the cup of water beside me and drink the entire thing, but it does nothing to quench my thirst.

"I'll get you more water. Be right back."

While she disappears out of view, I grab my cell on the tray attached to the bed and go through some texts, returning some from work. When Iseult's name pops up, I open that next.

ISEULT

> You idiot. You go and lose your fucking memory, then get your head blown off? What's next? A bullet wound to the chest? I swear if you die and hurt Hadleigh, I'll kill you in hell.

> Also, wake up. Bye.

I grumble, returning her kind messages.

HUDSON

> I'm awake. Thanks for the concern.

ISEULT

> Oh, there you are. Glad you made it to the other side. I'm on my way to New York. Should be there soon.

But before I can reply, I find a message from Hadleigh come through. With the biggest grin on my face, I open it.

As I start to read the words, a cold rush pounces across my body and I'm hurrying to my feet, fighting the light-headedness, running on adrenaline.

I need to get to her. I need to get to my wife.

Ripping the IV off my arm, I grab my clothes and belongings and order a car. Quickly getting dressed, I make my way out of the room, looking both ways to make sure none of the nurses are around. When I think it's safe, I find the nearest elevator and head down.

I stare at the phone once more, panic gripping me.

HADLEIGH

911. Send help to the house.

HUDSON

I'm on the way. Calling the cops now.

As soon as I'm inside the car that's already waiting, I dial the police, hoping they get there before I do.

"911. What is your emergency?"

"My wife, something is happening at her house. She texted me an SOS." I sound like I'm half-dead.

"What's the address, sir?"

I give it to her.

"We'll send someone there now."

"Thanks."

I hang up and text Iseult.

HUDSON

Something is going on at Hadleigh's. She texted me for help. She wouldn't have unless something really bad was happening.

ISEULT

Fuck! Calling Gio. He's closer.

HUDSON

I'm ten minutes out.

ISEULT

Let me know. If I don't hear from you, I'll know it's bad.

But I already do.

HADLEIGH

Tears run down my face while my hands are tied behind my back by a man I trusted. A man I opened my home to. My family to. Because I thought *he* was family. I thought I could trust him.

I thought wrong.

Too many questions flounder through my mind, and I can't get answers with this damn gag in my mouth.

My heartbeats pound endlessly in my chest while his onyx eyes take me in as though deciding what to do with me. But I already know what he wants to do. He wants to kill me. I can see it there in the flicker of his gaze, that idea taking root until it sprouts so widely, he won't be able to see through it. That's what happens when someone discovers your secrets. Secrets that could destroy you.

And I discovered his.

Nausea hits me as I try to grasp to clues in the past years, anything to tell me he's been lying all along.

Did he watch me cry for Hudson, calling his phone, wondering who had it and he was the one all along? What does it even mean? Did he take Hudson's phone after he went missing? Did he *cause* his memory loss? How was he involved with his disappearance?

And the hat…

Is that just a coincidence? Or did he know about Tanner and pretend to be him to scare me?

My God, all these thoughts are doing is sending me over the edge all over again.

I cry for help, but all that comes out is a mumbled mess of words. Groaning, I scream, struggling to loosen the zip ties. The need to fight, to claw my way out to my son—my little boy who can't lose me—overwhelms me until my heart aches.

If I can just loosen the binds that hold me prisoner, I can find a way to get help.

Little does Brooks know, Iseult taught me a thing or two after I learned of her real identity. She showed me how to shoot and how to get out of a sticky situation like this one. She figured being in this life, I needed to learn how to survive. At the time, I thought she was ridiculous, but I listened and learned and hoped I never had to use anything she taught me.

But maybe all those lessons will finally pay off.

I continue to shriek, wail, anything for him to remove this gag and let me talk to him. I know I can get through to him. He cares about me. I know he does.

He approaches me, fingers slowly growing closer toward my face. "I'm sorry, Hadleigh." His chest rises faster with each second he stares. "I never meant for it to be this way."

His face twists into remorse, and his eyes shine bright with his tears.

If I can just use that. If I can make him think he has a chance, maybe I can save myself. My brow bends, and I nod and groan, hoping he takes this damn gag off.

"I'll take it off, but only if you promise not to scream. I'd hate to hurt you. I'm not that man."

I nod. I'll make him believe he's the hero if that's what he wants.

His hard stare cuts into me. "If you lie to me, Hadleigh, I'll have to kill you, and I'm not ready to end your life yet."

Yet...

My heart sinks into my stomach.

I nod again, and that's when he slowly lowers that thing from my mouth.

Closing my eyes, I take my first big breath. And my hands? They feel a little looser. Now if only I can get him out of this room somehow and use my phone to call for help.

"Please, Brooks," I beg. "Tell me what's going on. I don't understand why you're doing this. Did...did I do something?" My voice grows pained and trembles.

He laughs and shakes his head. "Come on, Hadleigh. You saw what you saw. We both know you aren't stupid, so how about you stop acting like it?"

"All I saw was Hudson's phone. I don't understand. Did you find it after he disappeared? Did you keep it because you cared?" My pulse pounds, fear enveloping me.

"I'm so tired." He shakes his head. "I'm fucking tired of pretending I gave a fuck about him. I *hated* him."

His teeth snap and his eyes grow cold until they turn icy, hard enough to hurt.

Oh, God...

Fresh tears coat my eyes as I force the next few words out. "I know you, Brooks. Holden and I, we love you. You're not whatever this is. Please just talk to me. Tell me how I can help you."

He sighs, shoulders dropping. "I love you too. It's why I had to do it, you know? It was the only way."

"Only way for what?"

Just keep him talking. The more he talks, the longer you're alive.

"To keep you all to myself." He smirks, his eyes languidly dipping down my curves.

I suddenly feel bare, and a creeping feeling passes over me until something ugly and cruel drops into my gut. I try not to grimace and succeed.

"Just tell me what happened. I know Hudson isn't perfect. Did he do something to you? Did you two have a fight? How did he become Preston?"

I could kill you, you son of a bitch!

He groans, scratching his head while pacing, as though he wants to tell me, but is wrestling with whether to spill the truth.

"Come on, Brooks. Please, I need to know," I cry. "I'm tired of the lies, and you were the one man I thought I could count on to tell me the truth, even above Hudson."

That causes him to stop and look at me. "You really wanna know what happened?"

"Yes," I whisper, my body shivering. "Tell me everything."

"Okay, Hadleigh." A slow-growing sneer pulls at his mouth. "Here goes."

Forty-Five

BROOKS
THE DAY HUDSON DISAPPEARED

"**Y**ou need to relax," I tell Hudson. "Perez will be fine once we give him Evan's name."

Except poor Evan is innocent. I just needed someone to take the fall.

"You don't know that!" he bellows in the basement of my home.

He does that. Freaks out a lot. Always worried Hadleigh will stop loving him.

It's too fucking bad she won't. But she never deserved someone like him. The shit he does. The people he's been involved in killing.

I don't care about them. It's her I care about.

It's why I did what I did. It's why we planned to have him killed. Each of us with our own purpose, but with one end.

His *end.*

He needs to go. It's the only way for me to get Hadleigh.

The plan was easy. Dig up the bodies of our piece-of-shit adoptive parents. Make him scared. Write some notes to make him think he had to run. Then when he did, my partner would send someone to take him out.

But of course, we were smarter than that. We had a plan B. Something else to guarantee his death.

I actually thought that would be the easiest of the two plans. But hell, I was wrong. I thought it'd be enough to forge his signature on some billing papers, get Perez to kill him, and that would be it. But fucking Perez had to make it harder on me.

Even that son of a bitch liked Hudson enough not to kill him.

"You've gotta tell Hadleigh what's going on," I tell him.

Maybe if she knows, she'll leave him. And I'll be there, picking up the pieces.

"Are you fucking insane?" he snaps. "I can't have her involved. If she knows, she'll divorce me."

He never saw it, did he? He never saw how much I really hated him. How much I wanted to destroy him. He had everything, *and he never deserved any of it! What made him so fucking special? Why did I end up with nothing, while he had everything I ever wanted?*

"Are you ever going to stop being such a fucking prick?" I ask him, rage settling in my chest until I can't control it anymore. "She deserves better than you."

"What did you just say to me?*" His jaw tightens dangerously, and he rushes toward me.*

Maybe this is it. Maybe I can kill him right here. Would be easier than all this planning that's gotten us nowhere.

"You heard me." I curl my fingers until a white-knuckled fist forms, and I push my face into his. "If you were half the man you

pretend to be, you'd have left her. You wouldn't involve her in the shit you do." I shake my head in disgust. "One day, they'll come after her, and when she's lying on the ground bleeding, I'll be there to remind you it was all your fault."

He roars right before the first punch lands on my cheek.

Then it's fucking war.

"You asshole!" I slam my fist into his nose, blood seeping through both nostrils. "I'm done!"

I kick him hard in the stomach, and he smashes his foot into my thigh. And somehow, we both end up on the ground.

"You're right! You're done!" he snaps.

"I'm gonna destroy you." I chuckle coldly, throwing punch after punch. "You'll have nothing!"

He rolls over and hits me back until there's so much blood, I don't even know who it belongs to anymore.

My knee lands on his balls, and while he groans, I rush for the chair by the bar. When it's in my hands, I stand over him, my teeth bared, and I stare into his eyes right before I smash it against his head. I do it again with so much force, a wooden leg breaks off.

He groans, thick crimson rolling down his forehead in rivers.

I drop the chair with a loud thud, my palms on my knees, breathing heavy until my lungs roar with a burn.

I get my phone out and dial my partner's number. "Yeah?"

"He's in my house. Take him out of here. We can dump the body tonight."

"What the hell have you done?"

"Shut the hell up and get here!" My pulse spikes.

While I'm slipping the phone back in my pocket, Hudson begins to get up.

"I'd stay down if I were you," I warn. "Wouldn't wanna do that again."

"Hmm?" he mutters. "Where...where am I? W-who a-are you?"

I snap my head back. "What?"

Does he think I'm an idiot?

"Shut the fuck up." A laugh escapes me.

"Please. I—I'm bleeding. Call the police."

"No shit." Pierced laughter rolls out of me.

"Please..." He attempts to get up, but doesn't get far, blood spilling down his forehead.

Did I hit him that hard?

Even if he isn't playing me, he could remember at any moment.

I pace back and forth, unsure what to do.

His head wobbles as he fights to get to a seated position.

"Jesus Christ. Don't move. I'll call for help."

"Tha-thank you." His breaths rush in and out as he lies back down.

"Do you know your name?" I ask him while I reach down and feel his pockets for his phone. I take it as soon as I find it, and he doesn't even notice.

His exhales rough out of him. "I? I don't. I—I don't know who I am."

I can hear it.

I can hear the truth shrouded between his breaths.

Holy shit. He may not need to die. What we can do to him can be far worse than that. Just have to make sure he forgets permanently.

I grin. "It's okay. We'll figure it out. Don't you worry."

"W-what's your...name?" he asks, and I don't even think he can see my face through all that blood.

"Brooks." I grin.

But as I stare down at him and jolt him, I realize he's passed out.

Damn, this is easier than I thought it'd be.

HADLEIGH

I attempt to keep my tears at bay, but they fall like the years of betrayal he's made me a part of.

He hurt Hudson, and somehow, he made him disappear. He didn't outright say it, but it was there on his face as he relived the events of that day.

That scar on Hudson's forehead. That was how he got it. Goose bumps prickle my skin, and I shudder. There was never an accident. The whole thing was a lie. He was spoon-fed, wasn't he? Every bit of it was a fabricated illusion to make him believe he was someone he wasn't.

But who else was involved? Who was Brooks's partner?

"Who did you call that day?" I whisper. "Who helped you?"

He laughs, a cruel laugh.

"Was it Adalyn?" I push. "Was she the one involved?"

His laughter dies, and in its place is a cold sneer.

"Adalyn?" He snickers. "No, she's too stupid to ever pull off what we did. She helped at first. Helped us scare Hudson into leaving by handing him notes we planted, but that asshole was too stubborn for his own good. But she did become a bit obsessed with you after she learned of my feelings for you." His mouth quirks. "She found out I was the one who sent you one of Hudson's letters and realized I wanted you and…well, that didn't go very well."

He chuckles, and my body turns ice cold.

"It's why you saw her at the store and why she confronted you at Hudson's gala. She was following you. And once she realized I had something to do with Hudson's disappearance, my partner and I warned her about what would happen if she told anyone. That we'd kill her." His jaw tics as the threat leaves his mouth.

I gulp down my tangible fear. How did I not see this? How did I not know how sick he was?

"Now, stop asking questions," he goes on. "And rest up. You're going to need your energy."

"F-for what?"

Instead of answering, he turns away.

"Please," I pant. "Just tell me. I deserve to know what you'll do to me!"

A crestfallen smile takes root on his features. "I love you, Hadleigh. I would've made you happy. I would've been a good husband and a good father to that boy."

A muscle in his neck jolts. He really believes in this fairy tale he's created. Anger gnaws; I want to tell him how twisted he is instead.

"I was the only real father he knew, and you took that away from *both* of us. I tried so fucking hard!" He bellows, taking in a deep exhale as his eyes close. When he opens them, he stares at me. "I did everything I could to make you forget him, to make you fall in love with me. But no matter how hard I tried, the things I've done, you never saw me, did you?"

"What kinds of things?" I ask, my temples throbbing with pain. Every inch of me hurts.

"What?" he questions.

"You tried to make me fall for you. What did you try?"

I have to know what else he's done. His cunning deeds have no end. I don't believe for one moment that he didn't try deceiving me in other ways.

"Does it have anything to do with that hat?"

He chuckles like the villain he is, before his face loses all sense of mirth, and that gaze falls prey to his evil. "So you saw it. You told me you only saw the phone."

"It's Tanner's, isn't it?"

"No." He shakes his head slowly. "Not at first…"

A creeping feeling rushes up my spine.

"It was actually Pietro's. My adoptive father's. He wore that thing everywhere." He gnaws his teeth. "Hudson gave it to me to throw out after he killed him. Instead, I gave it to some kid about my age. He was with some friends, told me he liked the hat, and I gave it to him."

My vision widens. "Tanner?"

He nods. "I only realized the connection after I met you. I mean, what are the fucking chances, right?"

"But…" I swallow past the lump in my throat. "How do you have it?"

He laughs slowly, deviously, but instead of answering, he pivots away, heading out.

"Wait! Please," I call. "Don't go!"

But that's exactly what I need him to do. It's the only way I can get help.

From behind his shoulder, his mouth tips up. "Don't worry, I won't be going far. Just need to make a call."

His feet pound across the floor until he's gone from view and the slam of my front door registers.

And as soon as it does, I quickly release one wrist out of the zip ties, fetch my cell from my pocket, and shoot off a text to Hudson, knowing he's my last chance. Once I finish, I start on one to Iseult.

Suddenly, the faint sound of footsteps echoes, and my breaths still like statues in my chest.

I fumble with quivering hands to stuff the phone into my pocket, to slip my hand back into the zip ties.

But I never get the chance.

Because he's there at the threshold, a predatory grin marking his face. So icy, I've never felt this kind of coldness whip across my flesh.

The phone stumbles out of my grasp and clanks against the floor.

"I'm disappointed," he says coolly, glancing at it. "I had a feeling you were up to something."

He takes a step forward, so many, until only a few feet remain. Just seconds before I die.

This is it, isn't it?

"I must say…" He reaches for the phone and picks it up. "I am impressed by your resilience. Didn't think you had it in you."

He presses a finger to the screen, clearly reading the message I sent.

"Oh, he's awake." He twists a brow. "Well, isn't that exciting." His smile may as well be sent from hell.

"I'm sorry, I—I had to. You're not thinking straight. Let us help you."

He sighs. "You really shouldn't have done that, Hadleigh."

"Please, Brooks," I snivel. "I'm begging you for Holden's sake, please don't kill me!"

My throat fastens closed, every breath a battle to pull.

He brings his face near mine. "Don't worry, I'll take care of Holden for you."

Laughter creeps out of him, full of malicious intent. Before I can wonder what he'll do next, he snatches my hair in his fist and yanks me off the chair.

As he drags me across the floor, I scream, clawing his arm. "You're no better than Tanner! You're a monster!"

He stops mid-stride, eyes haunted as they stare me down.

Then it hits me…

"Is that who has been helping you? Is it him? Is it Tanner?"

Forty-Six

HUDSON

I stop the car a few houses away, just to veer any suspicion that I may be here.

The sun blares above, but the street is fairly quiet, except for passing vehicles whizzing by.

I gently undo the latch to the back fence, and as I do, I hear her cry. It's faint, like it's somewhere deep in the house, but I heard it. Knowing where she leaves a spare key, I slowly open the door, not knowing what waits inside as I creep in.

"Please," she cries. "Please, Brooks…"

But that's all I register when I'm rushing closer, my heart pumping.

That asshole. I knew I didn't like him.

Grabbing a knife from the kitchen, I follow her voice—her broken voice that's begging him to stop hurting her. And when I enter the den, my lungs drown all the air from inside.

He's got her on the ground, his hand wrapped around her throat, her face red as she fights him off.

"You son of a bitch!" I roar as I rush for him, the blade glistening as he jumps to his height, realizing he's no longer alone.

"Look who's here. My long-lost brother. Welcome." He removes a gun from his waist. "It's fitting. I get to kill you both. Together. The way you always wanted to be."

He points the barrel of the gun toward my chest.

"Hudson! NO!" Hadleigh screams, blood across her lips.

Blood he put there. Her hands are tied in front of her, so tightly I fear she's losing circulation.

"It's okay, baby," I tell her, wanting to hold her in my arms, to tell her I'm sorry for everything.

It's all my fault. It has to be.

"Once this is over, we will have a life together. I promise you."

"I wouldn't get her hopes up like that," he scoffs. I glare at him as he adds, "Any last words?"

His smile is that of the serpent I knew he was.

"You're scared." A grin spreads across my face.

"Of you?" His eyes widen before he laughs. "Never."

"Then drop that gun and take me like a fucking man," I grit. "I bet even at half capacity I can take you."

He shakes his head, laughter heavier now. "We've been here once before, brother, and you fell at my sword. Do you really want to do that again?"

"What?" Confusion creeps in.

"It was so easy once I realized you didn't remember who you were. After our fight, when I knocked your head the fuck out, I told you how you never deserved her. Deserved any of it…"

He places his gun back into its holster as he goes on.

"You forgot who the hell you were, and that was my chance to take it all from you. But I wasn't alone. I met someone who hated you just as much. And together…" He chuckles. "Together, we gave you a whole new life. And you had no idea what was missing. *Who* was missing."

He glances at a sobbing Hadleigh.

My heart…it thuds like thunder across the sky.

He did this?

He took her from me?

Took my son from me?

He took years of a world I can't get back.

And now… He. Will. *Pay*.

With a roar, I drop the knife on the floor and rush for him, needing to end his life with my bare hands.

My fist lands first, followed by a kick that has him on the ground. We exchange blow after blow.

Is that what happened the first time?

"Tell me who else is involved! You fucking son of a bitch!"

I flip him onto his back, me under him, my forearm wrapped around his throat. He fights me, trying to get my arm off, but fails. Fuck, I want to choke him to death, but I need answers before I kill him.

"You should have seen your face when you got those notes," he chuckles with a croak. "The ones that said you had to disappear before the cops would find out that you killed our parents." His taunting grows bolder even as he chokes the words out. "I wish you had your memories back just so you could know how much this all means."

If we were as close as Hadleigh said we were, maybe it's best I don't remember. He betrayed me. Betrayed our friendship. Maybe it's why I hated him. Maybe it was more than just him wanting

Hadleigh. Maybe my heart was telling me what I didn't want to see before I lost who I was.

My distracting thoughts cause me to lose focus, and he takes that moment to slam the back of his head against my nose.

With a growl, my arms loosen, and he slips out, both of us on our feet again. I back away, needing to get to my weapon before he gets to his.

As I do, something gets caught between my feet and I stumble backward, the back of my head landing hard against an end table. Pain shoots out as I fall, eyes growing dizzy like they did at the hospital.

"Hudson!" Hadleigh's scream seems more distant now, as though it's growing in and out of focus.

I close my eyes, drifting off. But this time, there's no darkness. Images appear, blurred at first. Until they slip into focus, as though something clicks them into place.

Brooks.

Us fighting. But it's not from today.

My pulse hastens, my breaths laboring out of me.

"Hudson, let's play baseball. Bet I can strike you out."

"Yeah, right."

"No…" I whisper, but the images don't stop.

Children. We're mere kids now. I can see it. Feel it. I know them. I know *him*.

"Fuck."

More images appear as I fight to bring air into my throbbing lungs. We're older now, maybe teenagers. We're digging, sweat coating our foreheads. I can feel it as though I am that boy.

"Come on," I say to Brooks. "Let's grab her first."

"Do we take her ring?"

"Nah, let's bury the bitch with it."

More faces come, memories racing as though on a loop, but I'm younger in all of them. Juvie, the way Marcella and Pietro hurt us, the way they hated us, him more than me. Everything plays, speeding past my eyes.

Then I see *her*.

That day I met her. That fear in her eyes when she talked about Tanner.

"Butterfly…" I whisper, tears slipping from the corners of my eyes.

Our first date comes into focus now. The first time I kissed her—the image of us together, it's brazen and vivid. And this overwhelming feeling in my heart spreads across my limbs. She's there in my mind. But I want more. I beg for more.

"Please, give me all of them," I breathe. "Let me remember. Let me have that."

But just as quickly as they came, the images vanish, and I'm lost to the darkness.

"No!" I shout. "No!"

A vision flickers in and out, and then I see her: the woman who's been haunting my dreams. When her face clears up, it's Hadleigh smiling down at me. Her long fingers reach for my face, and I soak in their warmth.

"Wake up now," she says. "Wake up. Hudson."

"No, I—I need to remember. I need to remember everything. It can't end here."

"It's okay," she calmly murmurs. "This is enough. You're enough. So wake up now. I need you."

My eyes shoot open, my vision clouded, as I stare up at something bright.

"Get off of me!" a woman shouts.

No, not a woman.

Hadleigh.

I jump to my feet, shaking off everything except the need to kill.

Brooks places his hands around her throat, sucking the life from her.

He doesn't realize I'm on my feet yet, the gun in my hand as I prod closer, a few short feet between us.

"I remember you," I tell him.

He drops his hands from her, turning toward me.

A leery grin grips his mouth. "Which part?"

"Enough of it."

Pop.

Without hesitation, I shoot him in the calf, and with a scream, he falls, while Hadleigh cries, probably wondering if I remember her too. But I don't remember enough. And that's the worst thing of all.

"It's over now!" I pin him with a lethal stare, advancing closer, pointing the gun at his face. "You'll never hurt her again."

"You're the one who's been hurting her." He winces. "She deserves better than you."

Those words…I've heard them before…

"You're right. She does. But she doesn't deserve someone like you either."

Pointing my weapon at his other leg, I let another round into his thigh this time.

"Ahhh!" he screams. "You're gonna die! You just don't know it yet."

"Was it you who put in that car bomb?"

He chuckles, pain evident in his tone as he glares up at me. "No, that was all my partner. I'm not the only one who wanted you dead, brother. You have lots of enemies."

"None as big as you."

Another bullet enters his arm, and his pain splits through his voice. "Fuck you!"

I chuckle coldly, wanting to do this all day. To hurt him the way he hurt me.

"Please, Hudson, call for help!" Hadleigh pleads.

"I did. The cops should be here soon, but I need to do this before they get here." With a gun pointed to his temple, I say to him, "Tell me everything you've done, or I'll kill you now."

Before he can answer, a creak sounds off to my right, and when I look that way, my vision lands on...

What the hell?

"Oh, what a mess we have here." Detective Tompkins shakes her head with a huff.

"Took you long enough," Brooks mutters.

Shit. It can't be.

"You..." Hadleigh cries. "No..."

My gun remains pointed at him, while my mind tries to make sense of it all. She's been working with Brooks?

She whips out a weapon, and this time, she's pointing it at Hadleigh. "It seems like we're in quite the pickle, Mr. Mackay, aren't we?"

"Don't kill her," I plead. "Whatever you want, it's yours. Money? Whatever you want."

Fear and panic envelop me.

"I don't care about any of that." Bloodcurdling wrath snaps within her gaze.

"Then why?" I ask. "Why have you done this?"

"Why did I place you in that town? Make you Preston, Mr. Mayor?" She laughs, and the sound spreads like ice in my veins. "Well, for revenge, of course."

"Revenge?" My pulse pounds. "For what?"

"For a man you got killed. A man you gave up to the Russian

Mafia."

My gut lurches.

"See, you were so used to giving people up for the slaughter that he meant nothing to you, but he meant the world to *me*."

Hadleigh sobs as the detective goes on.

"His name was Jerry. Not only was he a cop, but he was my *brother*." Her teeth snap. "And you? You took him from me. And now, I'll take *her* from *you*."

Pop.

Forty-Seven

HUDSON

"NO!" I bellow, rushing to her side to take the bullet that should be meant for me.

But it's too late.

It rips into her shoulder, the raging agony burning through my heart as she screams in pain.

As I drop to my knees before her, tears soak my eyes while her blood soaks through her shirt.

"Do you feel that?" the detective asks with not a trace of sympathy. "Do you feel that heartache? That feeling inside you, as though you're dying?"

She snickers when all I do is let my tears fall, clasping Hadleigh's hand. My weapon's still in my grasp. But if I shoot her, she'll definitely kill Hadleigh. I can't risk it.

"I'm sorry, baby. I'm so sorry. Hang on for me."

"She's gonna die." Tompkins huffs out a laugh. "You're going to feel what I felt when I found my brother, knowing what those savages did to him all because of *you*!"

She jams the barrel hard into Hadleigh's temple.

"Don't!" My nostrils flare. "You still have time to save yourself. The cops will be here soon. Then it's over for you."

"How cute." She laughs, throwing her head back. "You think they're coming? Oh, counselor, they're not. Because I called them off. Told them I knew this house. Knew your wife well. They think I'm handling it. Think I'm doing quite well, don't you?"

My entire body shudders.

"Please…" I beg her, tears running down my face.

"Anything you wanna say to her before I kill her?"

My hands tremble and Hadleigh sobs.

"At least I'm nice enough to let you say goodbye. Never got that chance with my brother. Neither did his wife. My nephew still cries for his daddy." She drops her face to mine. "You did that. You destroyed my family, and I had a lot of fun destroying yours. But now it's really over. I'm gonna make you watch as I kill her, and then I'm gonna make your son an orphan."

"Please, kill me." I grab her forearm. "Don't take her! I know what I did was wrong. Nothing will ever take that back, but you can be better than I was. You can do the right thing. Please, Detective! I beg you!"

Her mouth curls. "I love hearing you beg. Been waiting so long for it. But it'll do you no good, I'm afraid. I've waited far too long for this moment." She shakes her head with a scoff. "You know, when I approached Adalyn to help me access your files, to build a case against you, hoping to ruin your life, she didn't believe you were a monster. She didn't believe all the things I said you'd done. Until I showed her the proof." Her upper lip curls. "You had everyone fooled, didn't you?"

She rights herself and flings my hand off her.

"But then she told Brooks about what I was up to, and he convinced her it was the right thing to do. Then he and I joined forces, and we figured killing you was the best option. Had Adalyn hand you those notes I wrote. Had I known your best friend hated you as much as I did, I would've done it sooner. Of course, then Adalyn realized what we were up to and threatened to expose us, but we made sure she knew that meant death."

Now it makes sense why Adalyn warned us before the car bomb went off. She was warning us about them.

"Brooks filled me in on your earlier life," she explains. "About those parents you two killed, the abuse... And he confessed he's wanted you dead for years."

She ignores Hadleigh's wails while Brooks lies there, breathing heavy. I snap my attention back to the detective.

Her eyes turn colder, angrier. "See, me? I wanted to kill you. But then you lost your memory during the fight with Brooks, and he thought what better way to ruin you than to take her away from you?"

She whips Hadleigh hard on the temple with the butt of the gun.

Hadleigh cries, cowering in a fetal position.

"Don't fucking touch her!" I jump to my feet, and as I try to slam her face with my gun, she jumps back, shooting a warning shot in the ceiling.

"You try that again, and I'll put a bullet in every part of her body."

Everything in me wants to kill her. But I can't. Not yet.

"L-let her t-talk," Hadleigh begs, tears running like two rivers down her cheeks, her eyes streaked red.

"Yeah, listen to your wife, Mr. Mackay. She was always smarter than you were."

"Just get this over with! Tell me everything."

"Gladly." She sighs as though with boredom. "It took a lot of planning to do what I did."

She appears proud of herself. But doesn't she realize she's become what she's hated? A monster?

"I agreed to go along with Brooks's plan of giving you a whole new identity. I had friends in that town. It was so small, no one would find you. So we put you there, gave you a job, and somehow you became the goddamn mayor. That wasn't exactly part of the plan, but you can't stop people from falling for that charm, can you?" She heckles, giving me a once-over filled with contempt.

"And Tanner?" I ask. "How did he fit into all of this?"

She chuckles. "You know, I almost forgot about him. But I'll tell you, seeing as Brooks is gonna die anyway. Loosing too much blood there, aren't ya?" She directs that question at him.

"H-h-help me, you bitch," he groans.

"Why the hell would I want to do that? You were just a means to an end. And you know too much to survive this anyway."

"You fucking cunt!" he snaps, trying to rise up on his shoulders, but the bullet to his arm stops him. He falls back down, his chest heaving.

"Brooks here…" she explains. "…called Tanner and told him where Hadleigh was."

"What?!" I rush up, my heart racing as I stand above him. "Is that true? Did you call him? I swear to God, if you did—"

His laughter swells in his voice, blood lining between his teeth. "What will you do? Nothing more can be done to me now."

"Why? Why would you do that? How could you hurt her this way? How could you bring that monster to her doorstep?"

He turns his head to the side, catching Hadleigh's eye. "I'm sorry, Hadleigh. I'd never have let him touch you. But I w-wanted you to believe he was back. I wanted you to need me to keep you safe."

"Where is he now?" She sniffles.

"He's dead. He'll never hurt you again. I promise. I saved you. *I* did that! Not Hudson!"

"What the hell do you mean, he's dead?" I grind the heel of my foot into the bullet in his thigh, ignoring his attempt at making himself out to be some goddamn hero.

"Fuuuck!" he grunts.

"Talk!"

"How about I tell you?" the detective intervenes. "Would probably be much faster."

I stare at her, wide-eyed and full of fury.

"Brooks did call him. And once Tanner made it to the city, he set a trap for him and locked him up in his basement. The same place he knocked the shit out of that head of yours."

Hadleigh gasps.

"He forced Tanner to write those notes to Hadleigh. That way she'd know without a doubt it was Tanner."

"Jesus Christ," I mutter.

"He even took Tanner's hat that he knew he wore all the time and pretended to be him. The guy at Hadleigh's school who gave that student a note wasn't Tanner." She grins. "It was Brooks. And when you got chased down…" she tells Hadleigh. "That was him too."

"Oh my God," Hadleigh cries, new tears filling her eyes.

I glare down at this man who ruined our lives, and the things I want to do to him…

My body shakes with pure rage.

"I told him that was a very stupid idea," the detective continues. "He could've gotten caught. But he was so obsessed with your wife that he wanted her to be completely dependent on him."

I let my foot off his wound.

"He wanted her to love him, but he was too stupid to see she'd never do that." Her brow rises. "She'd always stay true to you. I knew that. He didn't, though."

"The letter…" Hadleigh tries to control her breathing. "The third letter I got from Hudson, was—was that you?"

She pants, peering back at Brooks.

He shuts his eyes, and as he opens them, he says, "I had to make you believe he was out there, refusing to come back."

"You knew about them? The letters?" she whimpers.

He nods once. "He told me he was writing them, and I knew one was at the office, hidden in one of his law books."

"I hate you," she whispers. "I hate you with every fiber of my being."

He closes his eyes and doesn't say a word.

"This is all great," the detective mocks. "But it's time for all of you to die. Don't worry, it'll be easy."

She struts away from Hadleigh, and momentary relief washes over me.

"I'll just blame your murders…" She points the weapon at Brooks. "On him."

Pop.

Hadleigh screams while I stare at the eyes of the man who once swore to always have my back. And this is all we have now: lies and blood.

"Say goodbye, Mr. Mackay." She paces closer to Hadleigh with the weapon aiming at her, while I advance step by step, needing to shove that gun out of her grasp.

"Please…" I beg, placing my weapon in my waistband, hoping she takes it as a sign that I'm not going to use it.

Hadleigh can't die.

I'll never let that happen.

Her mouth twines, enjoying her defeat.

And as I rush toward her with a roar, hoping to distract her enough to drop her guard, the door jerks open just as the windows explode and glass shatters all around us.

That's all it takes for her to lower the gun off Hadleigh, and as she stares around the room, seeing all the new bodies enter, I kick her legs from under her.

The detective topples to the ground, and I bend her wrist and snatch the weapon out of her grasp. She fails to fight me off. And with a quick jerk, I pummel the barrel into her temple.

She groans, and I finally look around the room again, seeing a familiar face greeting me.

"Shit, man…" Gio grins with a nine-mil in each hand. "Looks like you owe me one."

"Hadleigh. Get Hadleigh."

"Already did," a man I don't recognize says.

"Who the hell are—"

"That's my much less attractive brother, Michael." Gio chuckles, and Michael grunts.

"It's okay, Hadleigh. You'll be alright," he tells her, ripping the shirt from his body and tying her wound tightly with it. "Taking her to our doc now."

He brings her into his arms.

"I'm coming with you." Letting go of the detective, I allow Gio to take over.

"What a fucking mess," he says, his foot pressed to her back while she stares up at me with a menacing curl of her mouth.

"Who in town was involved?" I snap at her, needing to know.

"You'll never get that info." Her bitter laugh makes me wish I shot her instead. "That's gonna die with me, and no amount of torture will make me talk."

"That's okay." Iseult suddenly walks through the door as though she owns the place, long red hair falling down her back. But she's not alone.

She's dragging a man in with his head down.

I don't have to look at him to know he's covered in blood and welts from the beating she gave him.

"I know exactly who was involved." Iseult grins at the detective. Tompkins's eyes grow in horror.

"Hey, bambina." Gio winks. "I've missed you."

He grabs a fistful of her hair and kisses her roughly. Right here amongst the chaos, he kisses her like the world is ending and all they have is each other.

And I want that. I want Hadleigh to feel that kind of love, and I want to be the one she feels it with.

Iseult rolls her eyes as he pulls away, but a smile flitters there in her expression. "May I finish what I was saying now? Our friend is gonna wanna hear this."

"My apologies, wife." He gestures with an open palm. "Do go on."

She forces the man's head up, and when our eyes connect, my chest lurches and disgust pools in my gut.

"Sheldon?" I make it a step closer, seeing his one good eye. "You? Fuck! No…"

My pulse slams in an uneven pace. He betrayed me? Of all people? All this time…

My fist comes swiftly, right into his nose.

He was never a friend, was he? Was everyone in town in on it?

"Yeah, he has been working with Tompkins," Iseult clarifies. "Apparently, he was her dead brother's partner. Isn't that right, bitch?"

"Don't say anything, Sam," she tells him.

Sam? Sheldon wasn't even his fucking name!

"How did you find out?" I ask Iseult.

"I started to get suspicious about the detective when Hadleigh told me how she thought she hated you. It was hard." She snickers. "The bitch knew how to hide the connection to you. But when one of our men broke into her house today—"

Tompkins grunts.

"Don't fucking look at me like that, bitch!"

She kicks her right in the face, blood spilling from the detective's mouth. Kneeling, Iseult picks something up.

"Oops, looks like you lost a tooth there." She throws it right on top of her back. "Anyway, as I was saying, my man found a photo of her and your Sheldon here."

She advances toward him and grabs him by the throat, staring ruthlessly at him.

"So, of course, I had to pay him a personal visit." She scoffs with a wicked grin. "And he was such a good little boy and told me everything. Isn't that right, Sammy? I can call you that, right?" She pats him on the face, but it's more like a slap. "I mean, you did try to kill me." She pouts.

"What?" My head buzzes as I attempt to take in all this deception. How much more of it is there?

"Oh, yeah. I forgot the best part," Iseult says to me. "Your buddy here? He was the sniper who took out Peters. That was his job. Killing us was just a bonus." She slams her glare back at him. "Isn't that right? And the asshole told me he had your house bugged. That's how he knew where we were."

No...

Fuck! I can't believe I was conned by so many people. How could I have been this stupid?!

"You fucking weak, pathetic excuse of a man!" the detective

roars. "How could you talk?! He would be ashamed of you!"

His breaths labor out of him. "And what do you think he would say about you?"

My footfalls grow nearer until I'm face-to-face with him, pressing the barrel in between his eyes.

"You stayed around all these years while hating me?" My other hand balls into a tight fist until my hand aches. "Tell me!"

My body buzzes with so much fury, I can't hold on any longer. I need to end this once and for all.

"I…I didn't hate you all the time," he whispers through a busted-up lip. "I kinda felt sorry for you after a while."

"You fucking asshole!" I snatch up his shirt at the collar, and my fist connects hard with his gut.

He groans, doubling over, but I don't let him off that easy. Grabbing his hair, I yank him upright while Iseult holds his arm.

"Who else?! Who else in town knew what you all did to me?"

"Just…" He swallows thickly. "Just Peters and the medical examiner. Th-that's it. I swear."

"Guess we're killing him too." Iseult grins.

I push off him, pinching the bridge of my nose and shaking my head. Everything has been a lie. The truth was out there, and I was too blind to see it.

But there's one other thing I have to know.

"You once told me I dated someone who cheated on me. Was that a lie too?"

He lifts his face to meet mine and doesn't say a word. And I know instantly. He made it up.

"You son of a bitch!" A hard blow lands on his cheek, and he winces.

"We…we couldn't let you go searching for your past." His chest rises higher with each inhale.

"You made me lie to her!" I slam my fist at him again with rage coursing through my veins. "You made me hurt her!"

Another hit connects to his jaw, and another and another, until he doesn't even make a sound.

"We've gotta go!" Michael calls. "Either you're going, or I'm leaving without you."

"Do whatever you want with them," I tell Iseult. "I'm done here. I need to be with her."

"We've got this." Gio slaps me on the shoulder. "Go." He nods once.

With a sigh, I rush out of there, just as two bullets ring in succession. And when I'm in the jeep with her in my arms, I know it's finally over.

Maybe we can start again.

The right way this time.

Forty-Eight

HUDSON

P acing around the underground hospital the Messinas have built, I keep going to the worst-case scenario.

What if she lost too much blood? What if she's already gone and the doctors haven't told us yet?

"Fuck!" I yank at my hair.

"It's worse when they're the ones who're hurt." Michael's voice rings from behind me, his dark eyes filled with understanding as I turn to look at them. "When Elsie was shot, all I could do was blame myself. I hated knowing it was my fault. That I put her in harm's way and let it happen."

He fastens his eyes, brushing a hand through his thick, black hair.

"I'm grateful every day that my wife and my children are okay. My family is everything to me. So hang in there." He clasps my shoulder, the long, angry scar on his right cheek jerking as he tenses his jaw. "We built this hospital with the best surgeons in the world. She's in great hands."

I nod. "How long have you had this place?"

I glance around, and from every appearance, it looks like a real hospital. Except it's not. There is no reception. No paperwork to fill out.

"For about four years. Started it shortly after you disappeared. We needed it." His expression grows thoughtful. "Too many questions when our people got shot, and we want the very best for our people. Having one doctor without the right tech wasn't gonna cut it anymore."

"Mr. Mackay," a man in a long white coat calls as he removes his blue cap.

I'm already rushing over, my pulse racing. "How is she?"

Please, let her be okay. I know I did a lot of awful things, but she's done nothing.

"They're doing great." He grins.

"I'm sorry." I weave my head back, puzzled at his choice of words. "They?"

"Yes…" His expression narrows. "Your wife and your baby."

"A baby?" Tears spring into my eyes. "Wh-what?" I manage to choke out.

"Oh…" His eyes widen. "You didn't know."

I shake my head, and Michael's palm falls to my back.

"Well, I'm sorry this old man has to be the one to tell ya," the doc chuckles. "But you and your wife are expecting. Well…she's expecting. You just have to do whatever she says for the next…well, forever."

"She's pregnant?" I can't even process this right now. "H-how?"

"I mean, I'd imagine you know how that part works." He laughs. "She's very early, so I doubt she even knows. Luckily, we tested her blood before the surgery and that picks up HCG, the pregnancy hormone, about a week after a woman ovulates. Bullet is out, by the way. She's going to be just fine."

With a heavy cry, I collapse to the floor, face in my hands, emotions overtaking me.

She's okay.

We're having a baby, and I'll be here for that this time.

Every memory. Every single moment will be ours.

No one will take that away from us.

Not anymore.

HADLEIGH

Something heavy pushes into my left shoulder, and I wince as I attempt to move, unsure why a shooting pain erupts as I do.

"Don't move, baby." His calming baritone lulls me, and I open my eyes to find Hudson sitting beside me.

"Where am I?" I choke out with a parched mouth, trying to process my surroundings.

"You're in the hospital. You were…you were shot, but you're okay." His eyes swim with emotions.

The memories return. Brooks. The fight. Tompkins…

Oh, God. Does it mean it's finally over?

"It's over," he assures me, as though hearing my thoughts. "God…I'm *so* glad you're okay."

Forcing a tiny smile, I lift my good hand in the air and hold his cheek in my palm. "*We're* okay. We're going to be okay."

He presses his eyes closed, and in the corners, I find his tears. I can tell there's something he's not saying.

"What is it?" Worry etches in my gut. I can't take any more bad news.

"I need to tell you something. Something good."

Exhaling deeply, I stroke the stubble of his jaw. "I could use some good news."

"The doctor, he…" His mouth winds up even as his voice overcomes with emotion. "Hadleigh…we're having a baby."

Suddenly, the cloudy feeling vanishes, and my mind is in complete focus.

"I'm sorry, what?" I huff out a laugh. "The doctor told me when I got pregnant with Holden that it probably wouldn't happen again. So I never even…"

He nods, large tears swimming in his eyes. His hands reach to tuck my face between them.

"It's true. We're gonna have a baby, angel. Holden is going to be a big brother."

A sob escapes me, and moisture leaks out of the edges of my eyes.

"I love you, Hadleigh." Fiery devotion ignites in his soulful gaze. "And I need you to know, baby… I never moved on either."

"W-what?" I tremble out the words, unable to stop my heart from racing.

"What I told you about the woman? They lied to me, Hadleigh." The words catch in his throat.

I pant, my heart beating frantically, unable to stop these tremendous feelings of joy. "You weren't with anyone?"

He shakes his head and smiles. "I waited for you while you waited for me, butterfly. If that's not love, I don't know what is."

Then he kisses me, lighting up a thousand little fires until I burn everywhere. For him. For us. For the future that's meant to be ours.

"I love you," he whispers in between kisses, and his eyes bore into mine. "I've loved you even before I knew you existed, Hadleigh Mackay. I've loved you in my heart and in my dreams. I've loved you through space and time and infinite moments." His gaze glistens as he goes on. "I may not ever remember our marriage, but I don't need to remember it all to know that I love you. And every single day, I'm going to love you more than he ever did. Because he may have loved you then, but I want to love you now. I want to love you forever, Hadleigh. If you'll let me."

His lips land against mine so softly, I cry even harder.

"Marry me. Again," he whispers, brushing his mouth with mine. "Be mine."

"I'm already yours." I sob silently against his beating heart as those strong, protective arms hold me gently.

And together, we find solace and peace in each other, morphing into something different. Something new.

But that's life sometimes, isn't it? Adjusting to changes. Making it work.

And I know Hudson and I will have the life we were meant to have, for however long we have to live it.

Because life isn't made from perfect moments. It's created from small fragments of imperfections.

That's love.

It's real.

It's raw.

And it's beautiful.

Forty-Nine

HUDSON
TWO WEEKS LATER

It took us a while to process the news about our baby. After all the infertility we had gone through, Hadleigh thought it was a mistake. But there was no mistake. We're having a child, and I can't fucking wait.

We haven't told anyone yet. Hadleigh's nervous, wanting to be sure everything is okay before we do. And of course, I'll go along with anything she wants. A damn billboard in Times Square announcing that we're going to be parents? No problem.

I'm just glad she's alright. That the bullet wound has been healing great. The thought that I could've lost her still haunts me.

"You okay?" She takes my hand in her lap and lets it rest there while I use my other to get us to an appointment with the top neurosurgeon in the city.

We saw him last week for some testing, and today he's giving us his opinion.

"It's okay if you're nervous."

"I'm not. Because, Hadleigh, I don't care what that doctor says. Sitting here with you..." I glance down at her stomach. "With our baby... I'm lucky." A grin emerges on my face. "So, if I never remember everything, I hope that's something you can live with, because I can."

Her mouth splits into a big, beautiful smile. "Eh, I like you more than I did him, anyway."

I chuckle. "You're such a liar, but I love you for it."

She sighs and plops her head against my shoulder, holding on to my arm. "I love you both, Hudson. I'd love you in any form. In any universe. It's how our love works."

"I'm so lucky you're mine." I kiss the top of her head.

"I know you are." She giggles just as we pull up into the parking lot. "Are you ready to face the town tomorrow?"

I release a heavy sigh. "I'll have to be."

After I left, I decided to not return to my made-up life and moved in with Hadleigh. But I spoke with the council and chose a new mayor: Dolly. I haven't had a moment to call her, but I hear she's already doing a fine job.

The people in town heard about what happened to me. About Sheldon—or Sam. Whatever his name was. And news like that spreads in a small town. I'm sure Dolly especially will have lots of questions.

Opening her door, Hadleigh gets out, and I follow. With our hands clasped tight, we enter the two-story clinic and check in.

We're put into a room for a few minutes before the doctor steps in.

"Nice to see you two again," he says, pale green eyes brighter through his glasses.

"Thanks, Doc." My pulse suddenly spikes. "What do you have for me?"

Hadleigh squeezes my hand and leans into my arm.

He opens the folder that holds my fate. With a deep inhale, he closes it and looks me square in the eyes. "The problem with a TBI—a traumatic brain injury—is we can't always tell if memories will come back. Post-traumatic amnesia is a tricky thing." His attention jumps between us. "Memories are the slowest to recover after an injury. And your case is a bit rare, as most patients do recover their memories in months' time."

"Lucky me," I snicker.

He nods with compassion. "I wish I had better news. But with some severe head injuries, the blow to the head can lead to damage of the memory-storing area of the brain, which sadly, in some cases, can lead to permanent, irreversible damage."

Hadleigh sucks in a breath, and I'm the one squeezing her hand now. But I think I need her more right now than she needs me. I thought I'd be okay hearing that I may never get all of my memories back, but now that he's said it…fuck, it hurts. I wanted to remember more. I wanted to remember our marriage.

"I can't guarantee that your life before the accident will return, Mr. Mackay. But I will say that it's possible, especially since you got some memories back. You may just have to give it time."

"Time," I scoff. "Yeah, I'm not banking on that." I start to rise. "Thank you for giving us your opinion. I think I needed to hear this so I can give up on the hope of ever remembering."

"Hope is a complicated thing…" He purses his mouth. "But sometimes, it's worth holding on to. So live your life, make new memories, and maybe you'll get the old ones back one day. But if you don't, you have to make peace with that too."

"Yeah, I will have to."

"Well, if you two have any questions, you call me at any time."

"Thank you, Doctor," Hadleigh whispers.

As soon as he walks out of the door, she turns to me and cries against my chest. And I hold her, not knowing what else I can do to make it better.

Returning to this town I called home for so many years is a bit bittersweet. I know why I ended up here, but there were good people here too. Kind people.

But I have to let that all go and return to the life that was actually mine.

Dolly sighs, sitting across from me and Hadleigh. "I don't know what you were thinking picking me as the mayor." She rolls her eyes. "The only thing I ever ran was this diner. What do I know about running things?"

"Mrs. Baker?" A waiter approaches her. "Table six doesn't remember the name of the item he usually orders. Says you always did it for him. Says it was some meat dish."

She glances back. "That's Mickey. Get him the sirloin sliced thin, medium rare, and instead of mashed potatoes, make it hashbrowns with gravy."

I pop a brow. "Pretty sure you know how to run things just fine."

She lets out a chortle. "If you say so, Mr. Mayor."

"Not the mayor anymore." I take Hadleigh's hand and kiss the top of it.

Dolly's face lights up. "I'm sorry, you know. I'm sorry for what those awful people did to you both. We all understand why you can't stay."

Suddenly, the townspeople start to come out from the back of the diner.

"What is this?" I ask, looking around at the happy faces all staring back at us.

"We all just wanted to say thank you." Her eyes shine, and she sniffles back her tears. "You were good to us, and we want you to know we will always be there for you two." She leans in and swipes under her eye. "You're family."

Everyone else murmurs the same. It fills me with a sense of warmth to know that after all the awful things I may have done, I managed to do something good too.

"I'll miss you." Dolly takes in a long breath and sighs. "This town will miss you. But you go and be with your beautiful family, because that's where you're needed most."

Hadleigh gets off her feet and embraces her tightly, while I greet each person who came to see us off.

Because they matter to me.

A part of me will always be here with them, and that's okay too.

HADLEIGH
THREE DAYS LATER

Holden plays in the den while Hudson and I are in each other's arms on the sofa. He flips through the channels, finding something family-friendly to watch.

"I can't believe our wedding is in a week," I say, my heart burning with complete adoration, wanting to marry him again so badly I ache.

"I don't know how Gio's mother can plan something like a wedding in such a short period of time."

A laugh bubbles out of me. "Well, Gio did say his mother has a knack for these things. Plus, she seemed so happy to do it."

I grin, remembering how excited Fernanda was to plan our wedding here on our estate. We have acres of land and a beautiful pool, where we will be hosting the cocktail hour. And between all the people from town and all the friends we have, it will be about one hundred guests. Plenty of space for that.

"I can't wait to be the ring boy!" Holden announces from the floor as he races three cars at once.

"You know, buddy…" Hudson says. "It's a huge responsibility to carry the rings. You sure you're up for it?"

Holden jumps to his feet and salutes him. "Aye aye, Captain Daddy! I'm ready."

"Show me how we practiced." Hudson hands him one of the throw pillows from the sofa and puts the remote on it.

I can't help but laugh, my eyes practically watering over as Holden holds that pillow with a serious face and walks in a perfectly straight line until he reaches the other side of the room.

Once he's done, he turns to us, hopping over. "How did I do?"

His eyes sparkle wide, and the remote topples to the floor. I bite back another bout of laughter.

"Wow!" Hudson claps, and I join in. "That was impressive. I have never seen any ringbearer walk that perfectly. Right, baby?"

"Yes, sweetheart, that was amazing!"

Holden appears satisfied and rushes back to playing.

But as soon as Hudson gazes at me with a heavy-lidded gaze, butterflies erupt in my stomach. Because all I can think about right now is the orgasm he just gave me, bent over the bathroom sink.

"Don't look at me like that," he whispers against the shell of my ear, and goose bumps spring to life across my delicate skin.

"Like what?" My gut tightens when he clenches his jaw, the hollows beneath accentuating deliciously.

His mouth brushes against my earlobe, hand clasping my upper thigh, thick fingers pressing into my flesh, so close to where I crave him. All he has to do is slide his fingertips a little more north…

"Like you want me to take you back in that bathroom, spread that pussy wide with my cock, and see how loud I can make you scream my name."

"Jesus, Hudson," I pant. "Holden is right here."

"Didn't stop you from soaking up the floor earlier."

My core throbs at the way he talks to me, knowing just how to set me off.

"Come on," he grunts. "Let me make you feel good again while he's distracted."

"Okay," I breathe, starting to get up when something on TV catches my attention.

I freeze in place, and Hudson does too.

"Turn it up," I say, staring at a photo of Brooks on the television.

"The cold case of the two dead bodies discovered in Windy Pine years ago has finally been solved," a newscaster announces as the words *BREAKING NEWS* light up the screen. "The police have connected this man, Brooks Bardin, to the two murders."

Brooks's photo moves to the right of the screen as she continues.

"Mr. Bardin's fingerprints were found on the bodies. Police believe he killed Pietro and Marcella Gentile. They have been identified as Mr. Bardin's adoptive parents. He was adopted by them when he was just a young boy."

I squeeze Hudson's hand.

"The police don't know why they were killed, and they may

never get the answer because Mr. Bardin has recently passed away in a car accident out of state. His blood alcohol level was above the limit, and his vehicle was found wrapped around a tree. Mr. Bardin also worked as a paralegal for Hudson Mackay, the lawyer who disappeared and has now returned unharmed. Mr. Mackay has been cleared of any connection to these murders, and his whereabouts in the time he was gone have not been revealed. Back to you at the studio."

Hudson's eyes flick to meet mine.

"It's really over," he whispers.

"I can't believe Iseult and Gio pulled all this off."

He grins. "Yeah, I knew they would."

When Iseult told us her plan to make Brooks's death seem like an accident, then pay their cop friends to ignore the bullet wounds and set him up for the murders of Hudson's adoptive parents, I was scared it was going to blow up in our faces. But they did it. I should've had more faith in her. I bet she's going to tell me "I told you so" as soon as I see her.

Staring over at Holden, I watch as he continues to play. I'm glad he doesn't know anything that happened.

He asks about Brooks, but we told him he got a new job and had to move. That he left him a note to say goodbye. I wrote the note, of course. My boy doesn't have to know that a man he looked up to betrayed us. Let him keep his innocence as long as he can.

Hudson swings his arm around the small of my back and brings me closer to his side, then presses a kiss to the top of my head. "I love you, butterfly. I promise, I'll do everything I can to keep you both safe."

"I know you will." I close my eyes and smile, happy for the first time in a long time.

There's a sense of peace now. I haven't felt it in so long.

"I love you too, Hudson."

Cupping my lower belly, I cradle my baby, grateful that Hudson and I can watch this child grow together.

My soul beams that after everything, I have him back.

And maybe he is a little different. But when you love someone, does it even matter?

Fifty

HUDSON
ONE WEEK LATER

I wait at the altar for her to walk down to me in all her breathtaking glory. Beside me, Holden grins and waves to the guests, all of them seated in an elegant ceremony with countless white lilies hanging over an intricate canopy.

On the other side of the estate, a large tent is decorated with long tables, lit up with candles adorning the center of it.

Gio and Iseult spared no expense, and though I wanted to pay for the wedding, it was their gift to us. Iseult is kind of growing on me. I can see why I liked the Quinns.

Criminals? Sure. But a close-knit family who would literally die for each other? Definitely. And I'm a part of that family.

Patrick stands to my right, and beside him are Gio, Michael, and their oldest brother, Raph. It felt right having them as my best men.

Raph and his wife, Nicolette, stopped by to check on Hadleigh after she came home, and though I don't know them, I instantly liked them both. Raph is reserved and quiet, and Nicolette is kind-natured. They have an almost twenty-year age difference between them, but they make it work well. You can just tell how much they love each other. Even now, he's got his dark eyes on hers, and she's got her pale green gaze locked on his.

Iseult, Leighton, Elowen, and Dolly talk amongst themselves on their side of the altar, waiting for my wife to arrive.

"You nervous?" Patrick asks, slapping my back with a heavy palm. "Not like you haven't done this before."

He chuckles, and I'm laughing too. Because if you can't poke fun at your own fucked-up life, what can you laugh at?

"I'm lucky, you know?" I glance at him. "In all these years, she never moved on. She could've. Many would've. But she never did."

He nods, thick gray brows scrunched in thought. "Love is a funny thing. You don't truly know if someone really loves you until they prove it. And that woman? She loves you. So you make sure you treat her right. Though I don't think I have to tell you that, now, do I?"

The music changes, and everyone rises.

"No, you don't," I whisper as soon as she makes an appearance.

Tynan, Iseult's oldest brother, walks Hadleigh down the aisle.

Her strapless ivory lace gown sparkles around her waist, but nothing is as bright as that smile meant just for me.

As soon as she's before me, Tynan kisses the top of her hand and stares hard at me. "You break her, I break you."

I think he's joking. But then again, this son of a bitch doesn't smile, so no one knows what the hell goes on in his head. Figured that part out in the days I've spent with the Quinns and the Marinos.

Hadleigh laughs and gushes. "You're like the brother I never had."

She gives him a quick hug while he continues to glare as he takes a seat in the front row beside his much nicer brothers, Fionn and Cillian.

They're both chuckling at him as the minister begins the service. Holden rushes to her other side and stares up at his mother in awe.

"You look like a princess, Mommy!" he whispers.

"Thank you, buddy." She grins.

Dropping my lips to her ear, I say, "He's right. I can't keep my eyes off you, wife. There's never been anyone in this world more beautiful than you."

"Oh, Hudson," she breathes as the minister clears his throat.

"The groom has written his own vows that he'd like to share," he says.

Hadleigh's eyes widen. "That's not fair. I didn't prepare anything."

The guests break with laughter.

"You already proved your love for me, Hadleigh. It's my turn now."

Tears fill her eyes, and her chin trembles as I start.

"I don't know much about the world. I don't know its secrets. I don't know how or why things happen the way they do. And I don't know why I had to go and leave you. But I'm here now." I take her hand in mine, my gaze fastened to hers, ignoring everything else but this woman I love so much. "I'm here to be your husband, your partner, the one you come to when you need your feet rubbed."

Everyone laughs, and she sniffles with her own giggle.

"You *are* pretty good at those foot massages," she muses.

"Not the only thing I'm good at," I mutter playfully, and the crowd cheers. "But on a serious note, I just wanna be there, Hadleigh.

I wanna be there when you go to sleep. When you wake up in the morning. I want to be there for every single moment of your life and Holden's life, and…"

She nods, tears growing in her eyes.

"And for our new baby's life."

The crowd gasps for seconds before the whole room erupts with well-wishes, and whistles and clapping.

She throws her arms around me and silently cries.

"I hope that was okay to share," I say.

"More than okay." She pitches back, and Holden is there, yanking on the jacket of my tux.

"What baby?" he asks.

The room suddenly goes quiet.

Hadleigh kneels to his level and clasps her palms around his cheeks. "Well, I have some important news, buddy."

His awestruck eyes and open mouth are all the answer she needs to go on.

"You're going to be a big brother."

"Really?" He gasps.

"Yeah." I nod. "Mommy has a baby in her belly."

"Oh my God," he whispers, mouth popping wider, and everyone tries to stifle their laughs.

"Think you're up for the challenge?" I lift a brow. "Because that baby is gonna need some stinky diapers changed."

He grimaces, his blue eyes capturing mine.

"Can I feed the baby instead? Will it like chocolate?" He grins, all toothy.

"Umm…" Hadleigh twists her face. "Pretty sure the baby can't have chocolate."

"Not even with broccoli?"

"Not even with broccoli." Her smile lights up the entire room.

"Well, that's boring," he huffs in a horrified expression. "I'm so glad I'm not a baby."

"You're not, are you?" My voice grows tight, remembering the video of him when he was just born. All the other ones I've seen since.

My heart is heavy with loss. I'll never get those days back.

"It's okay, Daddy," he says, "you don't have to be sad. I'll always be your baby."

I crouch and grab him in my arms, emotions pounding in my chest. And when Hadleigh curls herself around me and lays her head against my shoulder, I feel complete, like the world has granted me a gift after taking so much away.

"Oh, bloody hell," Patrick mutters. "Someone got a tissue? My allergies are out of control."

Fernanda shakes her head and hands him one.

With the people we love all around, we stand together as one while the minister finishes the ceremony and reaffirms our vows, the ones we promised to one another so long ago.

The ones I hope to remember for always.

HADLEIGH

We're finally alone. The whirlwind of the wedding is now behind us. Fingers in my hair, he lathers me up, growling when I moan from how good it feels to have his hands there, massaging my scalp.

I drop my head against his strong chest, and his eyes drink me in hungrily from above.

"Are you sure about this?" I ask, referencing the conversation we had earlier about him wanting to stay as a silent partner at his firm while teaching law.

One of his colleagues offered him the position at a prestigious law school, and he decided to accept yesterday. When picking up some of his law books, it called to him, and he thought with some studying, he'd be able to teach. To give back in some way.

"I don't care if you want to practice again," I tell him while his hands glide down my shoulders, then veering to cup my breasts.

His thumbs stroke my nipples while his thick, hard cock thrusts between my ass cheeks. "I don't want it to be like it was, baby. I don't want to spend long hours at the office. I want to be home with you and our son."

With my eyes shut, I smile. "I like the sound of that."

"Good." His voice turns sultry, and he suddenly flips me around and pins me to the wall, capturing my mouth with his in hungered passion.

His tongue sinks into my mouth while his fingers roll ever so slowly down my hip, tracing down my slit. He teases me there without touching my clit, while his hand fists my hair, grunting when I bite his bottom lip.

Slowly, he slides two fingers up and down, stroking my clit between them. The thrill overtakes me, and I cry out.

"Fuck," he groans, wrenching back.

His gaze burns hot, and without looking away, he thrusts his fingers inside me, so deep, my eyes roll back.

"That's it, baby. Take it."

He moves in a maddening rhythm, and the fierceness with which he owns me causes my body to tremble with electrifying need.

"About to add another finger," he warns right before he does, his thumb playing my clit like an instrument he knows well. "Don't you dare close your eyes." He hisses the words through his teeth.

I didn't even realize I was, the sensations spilling into my limbs until I'm practically floating.

He slams so roughly into my G-spot, I whimper and moan for more.

"Yes…please don't stop. I'm gonna come…"

"That's right, you are," he snarls, and it's the most primal thing. The way he takes me, the way he looks at me, like a beast unleashing.

He pinches my clit, and stars erupt, my body quivering as warmth spreads through my blood. And he's there, holding me upright, keeping me steady. The way he always has.

"You're incredible." His teeth graze my jaw while his fingers continue to pump every ounce from me. "I love watching you come."

I don't know if I'm actually talking, or if I'm mumbling.

He chuckles with raw sensuality. "Turn around. Hands on the wall, angel, and bend that pretty ass over nice and wide."

When I can barely move, he spins me around by my hips and folds my body over. He grabs a fistful of my behind before he slaps it hard, the sound of skin on skin making me wanton.

"Please fuck me," I beg, glancing at him from behind my shoulder.

His body is sleek and drenched from the showerhead. When he runs his hand through his hair and his large bicep curls, I squeeze my legs.

"I love you, Hudson," I whisper, my heart exploding with my emotions.

I've loved this man for as long as I can remember. From the moment we met, if I really admit it. I may have not known it at the time, but now I know for certain. He was my destiny.

He clamps his jaw and winds his arm around my front, bending his body to mine.

"Say that again," he growls while positioning his cock at my entrance. "Tell me you love me."

In his voice, there's a tendril of vulnerability I'll always come to cherish.

"I love you, Hudson Mackay. I'll always love you."

He wraps his hand around my throat and uses his thumb to push up my jaw to his mouth. "I love you, butterfly. More than he ever will."

But I don't have time to argue when he slams his cock, balls deep, until I'm crazed for everything he offers. This man who's my whole world.

Hudson may think that the man he is loves me more than the man he was, but none of that is true. They both love me. Maybe in different ways, but with the same passion and the same heart.

I'm grateful for what we have. I'm grateful I never gave up on us, even when every day was a struggle.

Sometimes it's hard to see it at first. But hidden there in the future are pockets of happiness. You just have to find them.

And I found mine.

Epilogue

HUDSON
ONE YEAR LATER

A yla sleeps in my arms, her tiny little body peacefully curled around my chest. "Daddy loves you, my beautiful girl."

She coos as though she's heard me, but her eyes remain fastened, and a grin spreads on my face. There was nothing more magical than watching her fight to make it into the light. Her cry as bold as her bright blue eyes.

My one-month-old daughter gave me something I've been missing: being a part of her life from the moment she entered mine. I don't take a single moment for granted. Diaper changes, bottle feedings, sleepless nights…I do it all. I want to. I missed out on everything with Holden. I'll never miss out on her life.

"I can take her so you can have a break if you want." Hadleigh softly plods across our bedroom after putting Holden to bed.

"Just a few more minutes." I inhale that baby scent.

Hadleigh lies beside me and kisses my temple. "You're so good with her. A complete natural."

"She makes it easy." Tenderly, I kiss my wife. "I love that I get to be here for every little moment. I don't want to miss a single thing."

She sighs deeply. "You never will."

Hadleigh has been my rock through it all, and I have been hers. Though it's still hard on her knowing I haven't remembered anything new, we have come to accept it.

It's who we are now. This new version of us.

And I could be angry. I could live in that world until it consumes me. But what good would that do?

Because in the end, our enemies didn't win.

We did.

HADLEIGH

The following morning, Hudson's the first one up, making breakfast in the kitchen.

I don't know how, considering he was up with Ayla more than I was. He's been the best husband. There for every moment, never complaining about any of it. But I think even if he was the old Hudson, he'd still be the same. He'd be up with our baby, changing diapers and feeding her. He'd make sure I was rested while he was the one who didn't sleep a wink.

It's who my Hudson always was: a lover, a giver, a man who was devoted to me selflessly.

"What are you making, Daddy?" Holden jumps on the swivel chair set around the island, while I settle Ayla into a portable bassinet.

She coos, clucking her heart-shaped lips before she closes her eyes and drifts off.

"Well, for you..." He glances back from behind his shoulder, turning off the stove. "I've made chocolate chip pancakes. But for Mommy, I've made sausage and eggs." His eyes go to me—warmly, tenderly.

My smile tugs at my lips, my heart heavy as I remember the last time he made me that before the accident.

I told him all about our last day as the old Hudson and Hadleigh. And when he makes me the same breakfast, I know he's trying to give me some of it back. But it's never going to be like it was, and I'm okay with that. I made peace with it a while ago.

I'm grateful he remembered me at all. Remembered the first time we met at his job, remembered how I made him feel. That's something. We can hold on to that.

Hudson places the food before me and Holden, then makes his own plate.

"So yummy." Holden practically stuffs the entire pancake in his mouth.

"Daddy's happy you love it."

But Holden doesn't even notice the way his father looks at him—with so much love, it pours out of him. He may not talk about it, but he's still hurting with how much he missed out on. It's not something a parent can just get over.

So I let him be the fun one. The one who gives Holden the extra cupcake. The one who lets him stay up a little past his bedtime. Whatever he needs to compensate for what he lost. I can't imagine it.

Hudson pours us both a cup of coffee when the doorbell rings.

His eyes connect with mine, and his mouth thins with a smile. Because we both know exactly who that is.

"I wonder who that could be," Hudson muses.

The bell goes off again.

"Are you gonna get it, Daddy?"

"Maybe we can get the door together."

"Okay!" He jumps off his seat and rushes over to Hudson, grabbing his hand.

And watching my two men together like this… My heart swells.

Following them, I stand back as the door opens and a man hands Hudson a large box.

"Thanks," he says before shutting the door with his foot.

"What's inside?" Holden's eyes pop excitedly while Hudson carries the box to the kitchen.

We've planned this for a few months now and couldn't wait until this day came.

"Well, how about you help me open it?" he tells our son, lifting him up onto his lap.

With both hands, Holden lifts up the top and…

"A puppy? Oh my God!" He gasps, his little hands already digging inside to pick up the new member of the Mackay family.

"Not just any puppy," I say. "A Cavalier King Charles, just like you wanted."

His face splits with a grin and he closes his eyes, holding the white and brown pup close to his chest.

"I'm gonna call him Gatorade." Holden sighs. "Thank you, Mommy and Daddy. I'm gonna take care of him every day."

"We know you will." Hudson locks eyes with me then. "Because you're just like your mom."

I pick up my husband's hand and squeeze. "No, Hudson. I think he got that one from you."

Epilogue Two

GIO
ALMOST SIX YEARS AGO

"Tell me your name," I ask this beautiful stranger, my lips brushing against hers.

"Not gonna happen," she sighs, her fingers rolling up and down my back.

I drop my face lower, kissing her jaw, teeth grazing down her throat.

My hand returns between her silky thighs, and with a jerk of a finger, I push her panties all the way to the side, exposing her perfect little pussy. A single digit slides into her slit once more, feathering over her wet clit while I keep our eyes connected.

Her brows furrow, her back bowing while she gasps with uneven breaths. I tease and flick until she grows every bit turned on, making those sexy sounds, her body getting wetter and softer for me.

"I'm gonna spend my time tasting you," I promise, the words slipping past her ear. "And after that, you will tell me that name of yours."

"I'll never tell you," she pants.

"Oh, Red, you will." I chuckle, looking back at her. "You're gonna tell me everything."

I sink down her body, kissing along her throat and in between her breasts, leading a path downward until I'm right where I want to be.

Picking up the back of her knee, I spread her open, kissing the soft, velvety skin of her inner thigh, leading an upward trail.

Her hands ball around the comforter, her spine curved, her eyes shut tight.

Two fingers hook into each side of her panties, rolling them down her long legs until they catch in her high heels before hitting the floor.

She returns her attention to me when I palm her pussy, riding it slow while she writhes and moans.

"You look good on that bed, being obedient, letting me do whatever the hell I want."

Her eyes fill with quiet disdain while she grinds herself harder on me.

I knew exactly what I was doing. She likes it when I talk to her that way.

"I suggest you stop talking and get to eating me out," she demands, and my chest warms with a small laugh.

"I hope I get to satisfy Her Highness." I drag her dress toward her hips, her ass fully exposed.

"The dress stays just like that," she cautions, and I once again wonder why.

"You're one demanding hellcat," I whisper, my hands sliding

under her ass, my mouth descending lower until I cup her pussy.

My tongue gives her a leisurely swipe from entrance to that throbbing clit.

"Oh my God…" Her eyes roll back, fingers splicing through my hair, yanking so hard she's about to rip off some strands.

My tongue snakes up and around that spot that has her thrashing wildly. I sink two fingers inside her, wanting my cock there, stretching her to fit me like a glove.

The erotic sounds escaping from her throat echo through the room while her hips roll like she's trying to both escape the way I'm making her feel and get more of it.

"Mmm," I groan when I feel her clutching my fingers like a vise, her release getting closer.

"Don't stop," she quickly whispers.

I don't have any plans to. If watching her fall apart is the last thing I see before hell calls to me, then I'll gladly meet the devil with a smile on my face.

"Yes, yes, yes!" she cries when I thrust deeper, hitting her G-spot, sucking her clit into my mouth.

Her body shudders like she's about to let go, her whimpers of pleasure climbing higher. And with another swipe of my tongue, she screams out a curse.

"Oh, fuck!" Two fists pull on my hair as she comes all over my tongue, tasting like poison and honey twined into one.

Before she can realize what I'm doing, I gradually climb up her body while reaching into my pocket.

My body drops over hers, fitting just right, my cock rocking between her thighs as I lift her hand in the air. Silver cuffs dangle from my grasp, and within seconds, I have her wrist in one of them.

"Wha—what the fuck?" She looks up, trying to push me off just as I fasten the other end to one of the poles of her headboard.

She yanks her arm, eyes laced with rage, just as I start to rise off the bed. She stares up at her restrained hand before her gaze darts to mine, daggers shooting out of it.

"You have *two* seconds to let me go," she hisses, grinding her teeth.

I fold my arms across my chest, popping a brow. "Don't think I will."

The flush on her cheeks is all kinds of sexy, and so is that glare.

I stare with a satisfied expression. "You look too good lying there, all flushed and spread open like my personal offering."

She groans, balling her hands. "I'm going to kill you for this, whoever you are, whatever the fuck your name is. And nothing and no one will save you."

"I'd like to see you try, bambina." My eyes take a lazy stroll down her body, her pink pussy still completely bare and glistening. "Seems like whenever you pretend to hate me, we end up with you coming like my personal little whore."

"You bastard!" Her cheeks turn crimson and her eyes narrow. "This is *not* funny. You'd better let me go. Now!"

"Nah." A proud smile plays on my face. "I think instead, I'm going to teach you a lesson that lying to someone will get you into lots of trouble."

"What kind of trouble?" Her chest rattles with forceful breaths, her wrathful gaze hungry to make me her next kill.

"This kind." I settle on the edge of the bed, taking the right side, my hands cupping her hips, fingers delving deeper while she watches me, making no attempts to push me away.

She clasps the comforter with her free hand, her gaze hard, yet slinking with her unsurmountable desire.

When will she realize fighting me will get her nowhere? Though I do enjoy it when she fights.

Before she has a chance to protest, I flip her over, her hips on my lap, her ass mine for the taking. And what a beautiful ass it is.

"W-what the hell are you doing?" she stammers, peering over at me from behind her shoulder.

But the way her voice swells with an erotic current lets me know she has no qualms about what my palm plans to do to that ass.

I fist her hair, yanking her head back, keeping her head prisoner, while my heavy hand lands hard and loud against her round and curvy behind.

"Does that answer your question, Red?"

"You are *not* spanking me." Indignation settles on her features as she fights my hold, staring at me with a twist of her neck.

Yet…her hips grind against me like she's enjoying this a little too much.

So I do it again, spanking her ass harder with a grin on my motherfuckin' face. "Who's gonna stop me?"

"Shit," she cries when I let my palm slide under her, working her clit on it, forcing her to ride my hand as she groans.

She's fighting it, fighting the sensation drifting through her limbs.

She's slick and sensitive, throwing her head back, her low moan of satisfaction trembling throughout her body.

"Look at me." I slap her roughly. "Look at me, Red, or I stop and leave you here begging for it."

"Fuck you," she seethes.

My finger sinks inside her real slow, my eyes locked on hers as I curl it inside her, twisting and thrusting.

"Oh, shit," she whimpers with parted lips.

"You like that?"

She clenches her jaw.

"Stubborn girl." I add another finger. "I asked you a question."

I slam inside with a single thrust up to my last knuckle, pushing deeper with every stroke.

She tightens her thighs around me, not wanting to come. But her eyes roll and her features grow tense.

"Since you're really not enjoying yourself, bambina, maybe I should stop." I slip my fingers out of her and grab a handful of her ass, taking a little bite before I throw her back on the mattress.

As soon as I rise, she attempts to grab my forearm.

"Wait," she calls.

But I'm already walking away.

"Don't you *dare* leave me like this!" She flips to her front and roughly pulls down her dress, but that short thing barely covers her.

And I'm back to wondering why she didn't want to take it off for me in the first place.

"I'm not leaving." I stare at her pussy for a moment, flicking my eyes back to hers. "But I'm hoping in the meantime that the ache between those gorgeous thighs tortures you into obedience when I return."

"Where the hell are you going?" Her eyes narrow.

"Going to take a shower, then order some takeout. And if you're a good little girl, maybe I'll feed you." I give her a once-over, a smirk overtaking my face. "You look so good handcuffed to the bed."

She huffs with rage, her cheeks growing crimson as she stares at me like she's going to rip my head right off. It only eggs me on.

"Where are your clean towels?"

A vein practically explodes from her neck.

"Fine, don't tell me." I shrug. "I'll find them myself."

"Folded in the *fucking* bathroom," she hisses, ready to stake me. "Don't you dare go rummaging through my things."

"Why? Hiding a vibrator in your panty drawer?"

I start for the dresser, and she instantly sits up against the headboard, her shoulders rocking with such force, I wonder why there's no steam coming out of her head.

"Maybe I can use it on you when I'm nice and clean. Would you like that, bambina?"

She stares heatedly at me while I chuckle, heading for the top drawer, and as soon as I open it, my grin widens.

"Look what we have here…" My fingers skim across all those lace panties and bras neatly folded.

And just as predicted, there's a bright pink vibrator tucked in the corner, one end with a suction cup and a tongue-looking thing.

Wow.

"My, my. Little Red likes to play, huh? Well…" I grab the toy and stride back to her. "Lucky for you, I have all night to see how many times I can make you come with this thing." I lean into her ear. "Then if you're lucky, I'll let you come on my cock."

She stares at me with ire, scoffing as she glances at my dick. "Please. I bet you're five inches."

I extend a hand and grab her jaw, tilting up her face. "How about we double that number? Will that do, Your Highness?"

Her chest trembles as she pants like she's about to come. I watch her toes contort, her thighs tightening into themselves.

I drop her toy beside her and let my fingers skate down her torso, my eyes on hers as my fingers flick her clit.

She gasps right before I force three fingers inside her hard.

"Oh, God!" she screams, gaze perched to mine while I clutch her throat, thrusting so deeply and roughly that her walls clench, her sounds of pleasure loud and shameless.

She couldn't control this if she tried.

"Yeah, that's it. Spread those legs wider, let me finger-fuck that perfect pink pussy. And when I finally give you my name, that's all you'll be screaming for the rest of your life."

"I'll never say your name," she groans. "Unless it's to curse you to the pits of hell."

"Will you come with me, baby?" I decrease my tempo until I stop completely and slide out.

She grunts in frustration, fighting to get me back inside her.

"Greedy girl." I slap her wet cunt.

"Oh, f-f-fuck…" Her body heaves as she attempts to control her breathing.

Picking up the vibrator, I straighten to my full height and roll it up and down her thigh, purposely avoiding her core.

My smirk only pisses her off, blistering contempt snagging her features.

"Uncuff me and get the fuck out of here."

I place the toy on her nightstand. "I know you're used to telling people what to do, expecting them to listen."

I drop my face close to hers a second time, my lips fledging across her ear. Her breath hitches.

"But I'm not your boy-toy, Red. So I'm going to go take my hot shower, and when I'm done, I expect you to be on your best behavior."

I right myself, starting to undo the buttons of my suit jacket, shrugging it off before placing it on the edge of her bed. My fingers lower to my belt and I begin to remove it, the clinking reverberating through the room as she watches me, unable to take her eyes off my movements.

The shirt comes next, the pants and boxers following, until I'm completely bare. My cock is thick and heavy, and her eyes definitely don't miss that.

"Like what you see, bambina?"

"No," she snarls.

"I think you do." I fist myself, stroking nice and slow. "I think you like it a little too much."

"I bet you don't even last long." Her tongue swipes across her lips, her eyes bouncing between me and my dick.

"Oh, baby, you didn't just say that." In one quick step, I'm right beside her, my hand snapping around her nape, tugging her hair back and forcing her to look up. "Just for that, I'm gonna fuck you for hours until your body can't physically come anymore."

"That's not even possible," she challenges with a glint in her eyes.

"I'll make it possible."

Her exhales ravage faster, her chest climbing higher and higher, and goddamn, I have every urge to rip that dress to shreds and fuck every inch of her.

"Now…" I drop my hand to my side. "I'm going to go get clean, and I expect you to stay here and not cause trouble. Think you can manage that?"

"Go fuck yourself," she grates.

"I think I will, thinking about you." I take a lazy stroll down her figure. "At least in my fantasies, you're looking at me like you like me and not like I'm Satan."

She flips me off while I chuckle, turning to head out into the living room and finding the door to the bathroom. Stepping inside, I turn on the water, letting steam fill the room. The scorching drops run down my body when I walk in, washing away the invisible grime on me from someone I killed tonight.

Minutes later, the sound of a bang and then another loud crack swells through the room.

What the hell?

I quickly shut off the water and grab a towel from the stand beside me. Drying myself with one, I take another to wrap around my hips. I'm out in seconds, marching back to the bedroom, wanting to make sure she's okay.

But when I return, I don't see her at all, and that pole she was attached to? It's missing.

"Shit."

Want more Gio and Iseult? Read *Twisted Promises* and dive into this twisty, steamy reverse grumpy sunshine mafia story.

Playlist

- "You're Gonna Get What's Coming" by Klergy feat. VG LUCAS
- "The End" by Klergy
- "Lips on You" by Maroon 5
- "Honey and Milk" by Andrew Belle
- "Innocence and Sadness" by Dermot Kennedy
- "Where Your Secrets Hide" by Klergy feat. Katie Garfield
- "To Run" by Luca Fogale
- "One Last Goodbye" by Klergy
- "For Island Fires and Family" by Dermot Kennedy
- "Nothing Is Lost" by Luca Fogale
- "Yesterday" by Jamie Grey
- "After Rain" by Dermot Kennedy
- "Hurts Like Hell" by Wrabel feat. Sadie Jean
- "Used to It" by Michal Leah
- "Feel It" by Luca Fogale
- "Where Do We Go From Here" by Claire Guerreso
- "Face in the Crowd" by Freya Ridings
- "Nothing Left to Say" by Katie Garfield
- "Down" by Simon feat. Trella
- "Evergreen – Piano" by Luca Fogale
- "Without You With Me" by Matt Hansen
- "Dancing With Your Ghost" by Sasha Alex Sloan
- "Moments Passed" by Dermot Kennedy
- "Unraveling" by Aron Wright feat. Klergy
- "Electric" by Alina Baraz feat. Khalid

- "Lost" by Dermot Kennedy
- "Endgame" by Klergy
- "At the End" by Valerie Broussard
- "Dancing Under Red Skies" by Dermot Kennedy
- "Proof" by Luca Fogale
- "Here" by Tom Grennan
- "I Don't Want to Lose You" by Luca Fogale
- "Don't Forget Me" by Dermot Kennedy
- "Six Feet Under" by Billie Eilish

LISTEN ON SPOTIFY

Also By Lilian Harris

Fragile Hearts Series

1. *Fragile Scars* (Damian & Lilah)
2. *Fragile Lies* (Jax & Lexi Part 1)
3. *Fragile Truths* (Jax & Lexi Part 2)
4. *Fragile Pieces* (Gabe & Mia)

Cavaleri Brothers Series

1. *The Devil's Deal* (Dominic & Chiara)
2. *The Devil's Pawn* (Dante & Raquel)
3. *The Devil's Secret* (Enzo & Jade)
4. *The Devil's Den* (Matteo & Aida)
5. *The Devil's Demise* (Extended Epilogue)

Messina Crime Family Series

1. *Sinful Vows* (Michael & Elsie)
2. *Cruel Lies* (Raph & Nicolette)
3. *Twisted Promises* (Gio & Iseult)
4. *Savage Wounds* (Adriel & Kayla)

Savage Kings Series

1. *Ruthless Savage* (Devlin & Eriu)

2. *Brutal Savage* (Tynan & Elara)
3. *Filthy Savage* (Fionn & Amara)
4. *Wicked Savage* (Cillian & Dinara - May 8th, 2025)

Marinov Bratva Series

1. *Konstantin* (September 8th, 2025)
2. *Aleksei* (Winter 2025)
3. *Kirill* (Spring 2026)
4. *Anton* (Winter 2026)

Standalone

1. *Shattered Secrets* (Husdon & Hadleigh)

Lilian HARRIS

WITHIN EVERY HEARTBEAT,
THERE'S A STORY.

For Lilian, a love of writing began with a love of books. From Goosebumps to romance novels with sexy men on the cover, she loved them all. It's no surprise that at the age of eight she started writing poetry and lyrics and hasn't stopped writing since.

She was born in Azerbaijan, and currently resides on Long Island, N.Y. with her husband, three kids, and lots of animals. Even though she has a law degree, she isn't currently practicing. When she isn't writing or reading, Lilian is baking or cooking up a storm. And once the kids are in bed, there's usually a glass of red in her hand. Can't just survive on coffee alone!

FIND LILIAN ONLINE

Made in the USA
Columbia, SC
04 April 2025